D1153898

COBWEB BRIDE
(Cobweb Bride Trilogy: Book One)

Vera Nazarian

Cover Art Details:
"Perdita" by Anthony Frederick Sandys (1829-1904); "Street in Venice" by John Singer Sargent, 1882; "Swinton Park Tree by Night" by Andy Beecroft (geograph.org.uk), January 14, 2007; "Tree silhouetted in radiation fog" by Andy Waddington (geograph.org.uk), November 22, 2005; "Star-Forming Region LH 95 in the Large Magellanic Cloud," Credit: NASA, ESA, and the Hubble Heritage Team (STScI/AURA)-ESA/Hubble Collaboration, Acknowledgment: D. Gouliermis (Max Planck Institute for Astronomy, Heidelberg).

Interior Illustration:
"Map of the Realm and the Domain," Copyright © 2013 by Vera Nazarian.

Cover Design Copyright © 2013 by Vera Nazarian

ISBN-13: 978-1-60762-113-3
ISBN-10: 1-60762-113-4

Trade Paperback Edition

July 15, 2013

A Publication of
Norilana Books
P. O. Box 209
Highgate Center, VT 05459-0209
www.norilana.com

Printed in the United States of America

Cobweb Bride

Cobweb Bride Trilogy: Book One

Leda

an imprint of

Norilana Books

www.norilana.com

Acknowledgements

There are so many of you whose unwavering,
loving support made this book happen—
My gratitude is boundless, and I thank you
with all my heart.

First, my dear friends and fantastic first readers:
Susan Franzblau and Anastasia Rudman.

Kickstarter Acknowledgements

And all the generous and wonderful **Kickstarter backers**, you
who are amazing friends, colleagues, supporters, readers, fans,
and one-time strangers who are now friends:

Alan Levi
Alexander the Drake
Alfred D. Byrd
Allison Lonsdale
Anastasia Rudman
Andrea Brokaw
Andrew Hatchell
Ann Walker
Anne Landaker
Anne W. Brown
Anonymous

Anonymous
April Steenburgh
Auntie M
B. Ross Ashley
Belle Shalom
Berry Kercheval
Brian Springer
Bridget McKenna
Brittany Warman
Brook and Julia West
Carl's London Blog

Caro Soles
Carrie
Catherine Lundoff
Cheryl L Martin
Chris Hansen
Christine Verstraete
Craig Smith
Cynthia Ward
Dave Bloom
Dawn Albright
Dayle Dermatis

Deanna Hoak
Deborah J. Brannon
Dino Mascolo
Deborah Koren
Donna Boswell
Eben Brooks
Elinor Pravda
Elisa Hategan
Elizabeth Davis
Estara Swanberg
Francesca Myman
F.R.R. Mallory
Gavran
Geoffrey Jacoby
Gregory S. Close
Harriet Culver
Helen E Davis
Hervey Allen
Hetty Lacey
Ilana Kats
Jess Haley
JB Murphy
Jamie K. Schmidt
Jane Tanfei
Janice Y.
Jay Denebeim
Jean Mornard
Jean Tatro
Jenn Reese
Jennifer Chun
Jill Gewirtz
Joan
Joan Marie Verba
Joanne Renaud
Jodi Davis
Joseph Hoopman

Judith Ditzler
Julia Dickinson
Kaila Yee
Kari
Kathryn Huxtable
Kathryn Llewe
Kelly E.
K. M. Fields
Keslynn
Klaus Kluge
Kristen Bell
Kristine Smith
kyle cassidy
Larissa Brown
Lilly Ibelo
Linda
Lisa Bouchard
Leslie R. Lee
Lydia Ondrusek
M Reid
M.K. Hobson
Maggie Brinkley
Maria Vagner
Marian Allen
Mark Galpin
Max Kaehn
Megan Korchinski
Melanie Fletcher
Mia Nutick
Mike Garrett
Michelle
Michelle
Nathan Blumenfeld
Neile Graham
Nin Harris
Pam Adams

Penn Davies
Peter David
Raechel Henderson
Rebecca Newman
Rene Arnush
Richard G. Molpus
Richard Suitor
R-Laurraine Tutihasi
Robert Brandt
R W Glover
Robin Burzan
Ron Collins
Rosie
Rudi Dornemann
Samantha Henderson
Sarah M. Heile
Sarah Liberman
Shannon
S
Simo Muinonen
Stella Bloom
Susan Franzblau
Swapna Kishore
Sylvia Fragner
Thomas Krech
Tammy DeGray
Terry McGarry
The Creature From
Dell Pond
Trent Walters
W. Scott Meeks
West McDonough
William J Bowles
Wtaylor

My deepest thanks to all for your support!

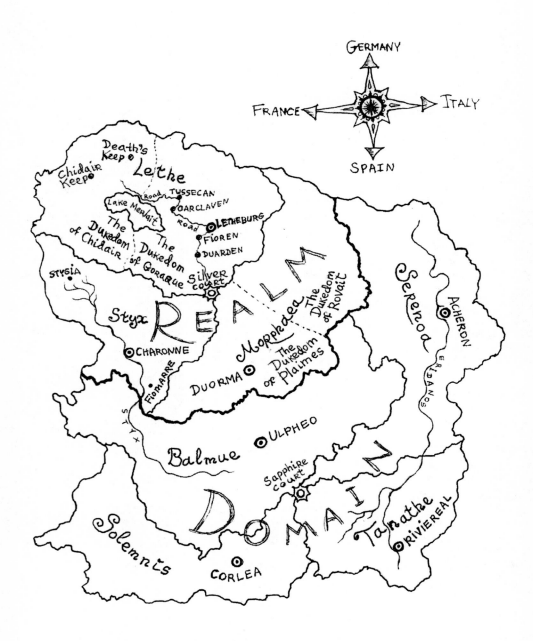

Map of the Realm and the Domain

For all those who have gone before . . .

In the absence of Death,
In the presence of Death,
Only one thing remains,
It is Love.

Cobweb
BRIDE

Cobweb Bride Trilogy
Book One

vera nazarian

Chapter 1

He came to them in the heart of winter, asking for his Cobweb Bride.

He arrived everywhere, all at once. In one singular moment, he was seen, heard, felt, remembered. Some inhaled his decaying scent. Others bitterly tasted him.

And everyone recognized Death in one way or another, just before the world was *suspended*.

But Death's human story began in Lethe, one of the three kingdoms of the Imperial Realm.

It was evening, and the city of Letheburg reposed in amber lantern lights and thickening blue shadows. At some point there had been a silence, a break in the howling of the wind, as the snow started to fall.

The silence preceded him.

Flakes of white glimmered through the frost-blurred glass of the myriad windows of the Winter Palace of Lethe. In moments the snowflakes turned into armies. They piled and compounded, stretched and distended into geometric symmetry. Folding into garlands of impossible gauze veils, they appeared at last to be the faint and vaporous spinnings of a sky-sized ice spider casting its web upon the world.

While the pallor and the darkness grew outside, Death was arriving within—inside a bedchamber permeated with illness, the boudoir of the old Queen.

In silence *he* formed out of the cobwebs of the gilded crown molding near the ceiling, the dust motes of desolation, and the fallen shadows in the corner. All these tiny bits and pieces of the mortal world rushed together to shape him.

He began as grey smoke. Then, darkness deeper than soot. His form solidified into a man, gaunt and tall, clad in black velvet like a grim Spaniard. He wore no cape, but somehow his face was hooded, as though a veil rippled between him and anyone who might look.

The first to notice him was the woman sitting in a chair at the foot of the great bed, farthest away from the fireplace—a regal middle-aged woman in a heavy brocade dress of deep green. She saw him and gasped, forgetting her stoic demeanor.

At the woman's reaction, the distinguished man with silver at his temples, standing next to her—leaning as he had been, for hours it seemed, over the bed and its decrepit occupant—turned to look. And he was taken with paralysis, able only to stare.

Finally, the fading old creature who lay in the bed— ethereal as a desiccated fairy, sunken in layers of soft winter mahogany fleece and cream silk—turned her clouded gaze in the direction of the presence.

"Who are you?" the seated woman in the green brocade asked at the same time as the man leaning over the bed exclaimed, "Guards!"

But the old woman lying in bed merely rattled the air in her throat and lifted a gnarled trembling finger, pointing.

There was profound relief in that gesture, a final offering of the self.

But the one who stood before her—before them all—did not respond. Moments gathered around him like the fluttering yet unfailing pulse-beat in the old woman's throat.

And then, at long last, he spoke.

"No."

With a clanging of metal, guards came running into the chamber. But they too seemed to lose urgency, and lined up at the doors watching with transfixed faces.

"No," he repeated, in a voice as distant as the falling snow outside the window. "I may not have you. . . . Instead, I must have my Cobweb Bride."

"Who are you?" the woman in green tried again. Underneath her formally coiffed hair, the color of dark tea, bright drops of faceted yellow topaz sparkled in her earlobes, reflecting the flames. Tiny pearls sat in the intricacy of her collar lace. But her voice was dull, without inflection, for she knew very well who it was.

"Death stands before you," he replied with a softness of the final breath.

"Have you come to take from us Her Majesty, my Mother and our Queen?" whispered the man who had summoned the guards. He wore expensive velvet garments of deep mourning and had a stern face framed by dark hair with its beginnings of grizzle, undisguised by a powdered wig. There was no need for ceremonial formalities in this bedchamber—at least not today.

"No, Prince," Death replied. "I have come for my Cobweb Bride and none other. No one else will I take unto me until I have her at my side."

"What does that mean?" said Roland Osenni—he who was indeed a Prince of Lethe, and who would have been King in the next three breaths had they been the old Queen's last.

"A Cobweb Bride?" echoed Lucia Osenni, the woman in the chair, who was the Prince's wife and consort, and would have been the new Queen. "Who is this Cobweb Bride, and where might she be found, to be delivered unto you?"

Meanwhile, the old Queen, Andrelise Osenni of Lethe, let her hand drop on the coverlet. Skeletal fingers twitching, she lay gurgling, drowning in her own spittle, the death rattle in her throat an unrelenting rhythmic sound.

"Oh God, have mercy!" Princess Lucia stood up in reflex at the awful new sound, and came forward to stare at the dying Queen, wringing her own hands clad with heavy gold rings. She clenched her fingers so hard that the metal and jewels cut into her flesh. Pain shot through her, clean and sharp. Pain, cleansing the mind.

But there was to be no clarity and no death that night.

"Bring to me my Cobweb Bride. Bring her to the gates of Death's Keep that stands in the Northern Forest. Only then will I grant relief and resume taking your kind unto me. Until then, none shall die."

And as the voice faded into echoes of cold stone, so did the form of shadows and black soot, until only mortals were left in the room.

Did they imagine it? Had it been a flicker of the mind, a waking dream?

The crackling flame in the fireplace cast a golden-red glow upon them all.

And the old Queen's death rattle continued.

Death's second stop was simultaneous, yet many leagues away, to the north.

Evening twilight encroached with blue and indigo upon the whiteness of the frozen Lake Merlait. It was a scene of slowing battle between the forces of Duke Ian Chidair, known as Hoarfrost, and the armies of his neighbor, the Duke Vitalio Goraque. Neither side as yet had the upper hand.

Winter wind howled in fury while heavy cavalrymen and horses struggled in a slow melee, immense metal-clad knights bringing broadswords and maces down upon each other, to cleave and bludgeon. Joined with the screaming wind in a discord were the clangor of iron and shouts and groans of agony as the wounded and the slain soldiers piled upon the whiteness. Footmen slipped and moved between the feet of the great warhorses, and long pikes pierced chain mail and mail plate, butting up against the ice.

There were places where the ice had cracked. Here, men and beasts had fallen through into the gaping blackness, the sludge water thick and slow underneath the ice. The dead and the living had intermingled, and common blood stained the top layer of the ice with dark red; pale rose in places, deep as burgundy in others.

Then, all of a sudden, the wind died.

Except for the ringing metal and human cries, there had come silence.

With it came horror.

One beheaded soldier continued to move. His severed head together with its helmet, eyes still blinking, mouth distended into a cry, rolled into the gaping hole in the ice, sinking into the breach. But the headless torso, now blind and staggering, continued to wield the sword, and to swing it wildly.

Behind him, another soldier, wearing red and gold, Duke Vitalio Goraque's colors, was pierced through the heart with a long pike. Instead of collapsing, he froze in place for several long shuddering moments. Then, as the one who struck him down stared in disbelief, the soldier took hold of the shaft and pulled it out of his own chest, shouting in agony. And he continued to fight, while blood darker than his tunic poured out of his wound in a spurting fountain.

A few feet away, a knight in an over-tunic surcoat of palest frost-blue—its color blurring into the surrounding ice in the intensifying twilight—decorated with the ornate crest of Duke Hoarfrost, fell from his warhorse from the impact of a great broadsword blow. He fell upon the ice and *through* it, for the burden of his plate armor weighted him down as though he were an anvil.

The knight sank, screaming, while the sludge blackwater closed over his head, seeping into his under-tunic and all the crevices with a shock of excruciating cold. And he continued screaming silently with all the force of his lungs that collapsed and then filled with the ice water while he was being consumed by universal agony of cold fire and impossible stifling pressure. All his muscles spasmed, and yet his heart did not shut down instantly from the shock.

His heart went on beating, slow and stately like an ice drum, then slowing down gradually, as though unwinding mechanical gears. While his blood—now as cold as the water in the lake—crawled through him sluggishly. And still the knight descended, flailing his limbs in the absolute darkness and cold while his mind chanted a prayer to God for an end that would not come.

Eventually he hit the bottom of the lake, thick with mud. He lay there, unable to move from the weight of his armor and from the constricted and frozen muscles of his body; unable to breathe and suffocating without end, yet not losing consciousness. His face, now invisible to any other living being, was clenched in a rictus of horror, and prayers were replaced with madness.

Directly above him—no more than fifty feet through the freezing waters, upon the ice crust surrounding the breach through which he had fallen—the battle went on. But it had taken a turn of unreality.

Men on both sides continued to strike mortal blows, but their opponents faltered only briefly. Many of the slain picked themselves back up from the ice and continued fighting, even though they were soon drained of all blood. Others stood or lay howling in unrelieved pain from deadly wounds and mutilations, neither losing consciousness nor life.

"Sorcery! By God, this is dark witching sorcery! Fall back! Fall back!" Duke Vitalio Goraque cried, thrown into sudden mindless terror by the realization of what was happening around him. It did not matter that he was surrounded by a solid circle of his best knights and henchmen, while behind him rode the loyal pennant bearer, holding aloft the red-and-gold banner with the

Goraque crest. It did not matter that they had advanced such a significant distance across the frozen lake, and were more than halfway to the western shore that marked the outer boundary of the lands held by his enemy, Hoarfrost.

None of it mattered. The red Duke attempted to fight his way back from the middle of the frozen lake to the eastern shore where his reserve detachments waited.

On the other end of the lake, a mere ten or twenty feet from the western shore, flew the pennant of the palest blue, now obscured by evening murk, with the crest of Chidair. Duke Hoarfrost himself, Ian Chidair, sat on his tall grey charger like a rock, while continuing to swing his broadsword at the enemy knights.

Next to him fought his son, Lord Beltain Chidair, protecting his father's formidable back. He moved, deep in a berserker fury, demonic and terrifying. No matter how tired he had to be at this point, few dared to approach the young knight who had never been defeated in combat.

The few remaining Chidair knights at their side were dull with exhaustion. None had yet noticed the peculiar consequences of what should have been mortal strikes, attributing it to the enemy's tenacity—after all, Chidair had been pushed back into retreating to their own shores of the lake. And the cessation of the ice wind against their numb faces was merely perceived as a blessed minor relief.

But then they saw in the distance near the heart of the lake that Duke Goraque's forces seemed to be regrouping and then retreating east.

It made no sense. Why was Goraque retreating? He had the upper hand!

Though evenly matched in general, the battle had been hardest upon Duke Hoarfrost's army, especially in these last minutes. The only explanation for the uncalled-for retreat of Duke Goraque's men was that they must have been deceived by something in the growing dusk. Or maybe they were unwilling to continue the battle at night.

"Accursed cowards!" Duke Hoarfrost exclaimed, panting hard. With a great backhanded blow he delivered a killing strike to the neck of the last Goraque knight within sword range before him—a strike that should have severed collarbone and ribs and cleared the immediate area of any remaining opponents.

The knight did not fall but slumped forward in the saddle to lie against the neck of his warhorse from the impact of the received blow. Blood spurted down the front of his already ruddy surcoat as his heart pumped the life-liquid out of the damaged body. Within moments he will have drawn his last breath.

Himself near collapse, breathing in shuddering gasps of exhaustion, Duke Hoarfrost turned his back to the defeated enemy and addressed the pennant bearer of his House.

"Laurent . . ." he spoke between breaths. "Raise the banner to its fullest. . . . We will now rally to strike them and drive them—"

He never finished. Because in that moment a long dagger was lodged and twisted with surprising force in his lower back near the kidneys, deep to the hilt, in that vulnerable spot right between the mail plates. And a moment later a broadsword point struck him higher, between the ribs, running in through the heart and out the front of his chest cavity. The point of the sword was stopped only by the hard inner surface of the chest plate.

Then the blade was withdrawn.

Searing agony.

An instant of vertigo, that should have been followed by instant oblivion.

But Duke Hoarfrost, Ian Chidair, mortally pierced twice, remained alive. And alive, he screamed in impossible pain.

He screamed, while blood came spurting out of him, from his back and his chest, from the hole near his kidneys, and past the clenched jaws and into his mouth so that he tasted his own serum and bile, choked on it, while his lungs were filling rapidly so that he was now drowning.

And yet, slowly Duke Hoarfrost turned around. Staggering in the saddle, he faced the slain knight who once again sat upright in his own saddle, and who held a broadsword covered with Hoarfrost's blood. The dagger remained lodged in Chidair's back.

"No!" Beltain, his son, cried. "No! *Father!* Oh, in the Name of God, no!"

Duke Hoarfrost gurgled, unable to breathe. And then, with a supreme effort he threw himself at the enemy knight.

The two of them went down from the impact. Neither one cared any longer that to be unseated meant they would likely be unable to rise up and mount again—that it meant sure death.

What difference would it make when they were dead already?

Or, *undead.*

For neither of them could possibly be alive.

The impact of two bodies collapsing against the ice resulted in a slow fissure, then a growing crack. Their warhorses stumbled, yet managed to regain footing and scrambled away to a safe distance, while all around, the Chidair knights backed away, leaving a perimeter around the collapsing ice.

Down the incline and into the churning sludge the two fallen men slipped, weighed down by the immense poundage of their armor, still grappling with each other as the thick waters closed overhead, bubbling.

Within moments there was only stillness. The ice pieces gently bobbed on top of the sludge.

"Holy Mother of God . . . have mercy upon your loyal servant Ian Chidair and receive him unto your bosom," Beltain whispered, crossing himself. He removed his helmet in grief and in final honor of his fallen Lord father. In the dark, his eyes were without an end, places leading only into hell; his hair, like filaments of the night.

Some distance away there were various sounds of retreat. Goraque soldiers returned to their own side of the lake, while straggling figures of Hoarfrost's men started to fall back to the place where the Duke himself had just sunk in the waters so near the shore.

In the darkness it was not clearly visible that some of these men should not have been walking upright. Indeed, many did not realize their own condition, feeling only numbness and winter closing in, and attributing it to the circumstances of battle. From the shores came the reserve troops, soldiers carrying torches to illuminate the scene of battle, for at last it was true night.

"Soldiers of Chidair! All of you now my men—good, brave men," Beltain continued, his face illuminated with the angry red flickering of torches. "I promise to you, his death will not go unavenged. I now count on your loyalty to—"

But his words tapered off into silence. Because in that moment the ice at the shore of the lake began to shudder, and then was shattered violently from the inside . . . out.

It was broken by the blow of a metal-clad fist emerging from the lake itself.

The fist was followed by an arm, and then another. The two hands tore and pounded at the ice, until it cracked and shattered, and the hole widened, became the girth of a man's body, then wider yet. At last a human shape burst forth, sputtering and gasping, then throwing up water mixed with blood upon the shore.

He stood up, the waters coming up to his waist. Then, bracing himself with his arms he crawled out and lay upon the surface at the edge of the hole, clad in mail and a soaked darkened surcoat that should have been faint blue, the color of frost.

He had lost his crested helmet underneath the ice of the lake. But the hair plastered to the skull with ice water was unmistakably that of the Duke Hoarfrost, Ian Chidair, Lord of the west lands of Chidair within the Kingdom of Lethe.

He lay twitching upon the ice, while lake water and the last vestiges of his own blood came pouring out of the fissures in his body. And then he slowly raised his head.

Illuminated by the torches of his own soldiers, a pale bloodless face of the man they knew and served looked at them impassively.

He was like a god of Winter, white with a bluish tint. The water was freezing into true ice upon the planes of his face, rimming his brows and hair with dead crystalline whiteness.

Duke Hoarfrost stood up, while many, including his own son, reined in their mounts to move away, and foot soldiers took an involuntary step back and unto the shore, away from the ice.

"Father?" Beltain Chidair whispered, his voice cracking. "Are you my father? Are you . . . *dead?*"

And the man before him parted his frozen lips, and then spewed forth more brackish water and the last taint of living blood. He then moved one awkward hand behind him to pull out the dagger from his back.

"My . . . son," he croaked. "I . . . don't know."

Death's third stop was intimate, and once again no time had elapsed.

In a poor house with a badly thatched roof, no attic and a drafty ceiling of old wooden rafters—one of the most decrepit dwellings in the village of Oarclaven, in the Dukedom of Goraque, which in turn lay within the Kingdom of Lethe—an old peasant woman lay dying.

She was Bethesia Ayren, possibly older than the elm tree growing in the back yard. She was a widow, the mother of two sons one of whom owned this house, and the grandmother of one grandson and three granddaughters. It was a rather small family, as peasant families went.

Bethesia had been beautiful in her day, with cream skin and

bright auburn hair that was long and soft as goose down, and shimmered as apricot silk in sunlight. She wore it loose once or twice when a maiden, and it had caught the eye of a passing lordling's handsome son. As a result, Bethesia was made to braid her hair tightly, cover her head with discreet cotton, and was married soon after to Johuan Ayren, a solid young man of a respectable village family.

Very quickly after that she gave birth to a handsome boy. Bethesia's husband was a kind and fair man, and he took the boy and treated him as his own. Eventually a second son was born, and this one resembled the father in his plainness and kindness.

By the time Bethesia and Johuan grew old but not quite decrepit, the older son, handsome Guel, had prospered and married an apple orchard owner's daughter who bore him a healthy son, and the three of them had gone to live in the large town Fioren, just south of Letheburg. It was the second son, Alann, who had remained with Bethesia and his father, to care for his aging parents. Johuan died shortly after, and there was no one but Bethesia and Alann to tend to the crumbling house and the small plot of land with the field and the vegetable garden.

Alann took a wife then, and she resembled his mother in many ways. Niobea was a beautiful woman from Fioren who had the mixed fortune to work as a lady's fine seamstress. She married poor Alann Ayren because no one else would have her after she too had caught the roving eye of her lady's son and could not avoid his even more roving hands.

In the lady's household Niobea had been taught how to read in order to entertain the mistress at her sewing, and thus acquired a fine taste. Niobea gave long and elegant names to her peasant daughters as they were born almost one right after the other, with not a son in sight.

The eldest daughter, whose father may or may not have been Alann, was called Parabelle. She was fair like a field of flax, and delicate like imported porcelain in the fancy town shops. Her hair was rich and bountiful, a sea of dawning pallor with a hint of amber and gold—several shades lighter than her grandmother's had been, but of the same glorious texture, falling like a cloak around her when unbound. Her body was slim and well proportioned, and as she approached womanhood she stood nearly as tall as her father. Even when she worked in the field at Alann's side, the sun was kind to her. It ripened her apple-golden, and her skin did not lose its fresh elasticity, or its delicate sheen. Belle was beautiful indeed, and they came to call her thus. Additionally she was obedient, humble, intelligent and soft-spoken—a perfect daughter and granddaughter, loved dearly by all.

The second daughter came two springs and a half later, plain and dull, and was given the name Persephone. It was as though all beauty, all the life juices have been wrung out of Niobea in the birthing of Parabelle, so that none of it was left over to imbue Persephone with energy.

Percy was a sickly child, somewhat dull-witted and slow, likely to stop her work and stare at shadows, at nothings. She was darker, her hair of an indeterminate color somewhere between brown, black, and ash. Her skin and face were anemic pale—not frail in a lovely way, but unhealthy. She burned readily in the sun, unlike her older sister, and soon enough would be peeling and covered with red welts. Eventually they made her wear an additional cotton scarf in the field, to cover most of her face and her neck, not to mention shirts with extra-thick long sleeves.

Percy was also stocky, with a straight waist that would never be willowy, leaning to fat, and clumsy like a dog let loose in the house. She broke crockery every other day it seemed, so that her mother Niobea sometimes cried just looking at her, for she knew that to get her a husband might be an impossible task. Worst of all, Percy was a willful child, and would ignore tasks she had no heart for. "Good for nothing," Niobea called her, "a clod, a stubborn idiot girl." And Niobea prayed for a more graceful child next time.

Indeed, because nature always seeks a balance, beauty returned to the family. The third daughter came three summers later during the autumn harvest, and she was an angelic child who promised to be as beautiful as the eldest. Niobea spoke a prayer of thanks and named her Patriciana.

Patty was not as exquisitely beautiful as Belle, but she made up for it in vivacity and energy. A child with ruddy cheeks and curly chestnut locks, before she was old enough to work she ran around the house singing and wailing and laughing. And she tormented old Bethesia with stories and questions, until Belle would gently scold her while her mother would hide a smile and give her an apple and tell her to run and play outside.

Often, as little Patty came outside after the mild scolding, Percy would be working in the vegetable patch, and she would wave and beckon. And as soon as Patty settled down next to her ungainly dirt-covered older sister, Percy would resume pulling the carrots and pruning the spinach leaves, appearing so intent on her task. But eventually, without fail, Percy would launch on a strange tale, usually filled with frightful creatures and mysterious happenings, all of it told in an oddly compelling voice, and using root vegetables like puppets, for colorful props.

They grew together thus, until Belle was eighteen, Percy sixteen, and Patty an energetic thirteen year old.

It was then that their grandmother's time drew to a close, and Bethesia lay dying.

Evenings came early in winter, and ailing Bethesia was laid out in a corner bed, as far away from the drafts as possible, and wrapped in several old woolen blankets. The fireplace had been lit early, a mixture of dry and sodden logs and twigs crackling and sputtering angrily with smoke, as the wind outside howled and gusts of it came tearing down the filthy chimney. The windows were shuttered tight but it was not enough to keep out the winter cold, so Belle—now a willowy maiden, beautiful despite the grey homespun dress and work-calloused fingers—

went around the house and stuffed additional bunches of folded rags in all the crevices and along the windowsills.

"Why is it so dark, child?" suddenly came from the bed in the corner, as Bethesia spoke in a faint rasping voice. "And why is it so quiet?"

Belle stopped her task and came quickly to her grandmother's side.

Lying against the lumpy pillow covered with faded cotton that was worn thin from endless washings, Bethesia's wrinkled face had turned white-grey. Eyes the color of coals reposed deep in sockets of bone and skin, and her withered hands had been bent into gnarled claws by arthritis. Belle held them now, feeling the cold fingers. They were like branches of the old snow-covered elm outside.

"It is dark because a storm is rising," Belle said gently in a melodic voice. "I've lined the shutters tight and lit the fireplace."

"Gran, can you not see the fire?" a younger voice sounded, as Patty came forward from her place at the wooden table where she was mixing buckwheat flour batter and peeling stale turnips for their evening meal. Patty's bright eyes and cheeks were warmed by the light of the flames, and her nose had a smear of dirt from the tubers she'd been cleaning.

Their mother, Niobea, a gaunt, middle-aged woman, sat in another chair in the corner, holding a long piece of homespun that she was quilting with precise deft movements of a seasoned seamstress. "Might as well light us a candle, Patty," she said. "It *is* too dark."

Niobea's greying hair was concealed by a simple woolen scarf, where it would once have been decorated with a lace bonnet. There was no more lace to be had, and the last of it, left from her younger days, yellowing and tattered, was stored in an old treasure trunk underneath their bed.

The front door opened with a blast of ice-cold, just as Patty went to rummage in the cupboard for another precious tallow candle that they used only for special occasions. A man's tall broad-shouldered figure came inside, followed by a smaller figure. Both were carrying loads of kindling and both were dressed in tattered straw-stuffed coats, and had their heads wrapped in homespun scarves underneath his hat and her shawl.

Gusts of frozen wind and swirling flakes came after them, and the fireplace crackled loudly in protest as the wind from the chimney found a sudden new outlet.

"Argh! Brr!" Alann exclaimed, slapping his mittened hands together and stamping his burlap and cotton-wrapped feet to shake the snow off him. Then, turning to the figure behind him, he said: "Quickly, shut the door now, Percy!"

Niobea frowned. "Stop making a mess, Alann. Wipe your feet before you take another step. And you too, girl."

Percy, swaddled in the only woolen shawl that the sisters shared between them when taking turns going outside, clumsily shifted the bundle of kindling from both hands to one. She then used her shoulder to slam the old wooden door behind them, lifted the bolt and drew it in place.

"Ah, that's better!" Alann said as he put down his bundle on the beaten earth floor near the door and started to scrape the snow off his wrapped feet. "There's an early blizzard gathering, you know, wife. Good thing I stocked up on the hay and the flour. Put the extra blanket on the horse too, just in case, in that drafty barn."

"Good," Niobea said. "We can't afford to lose that horse."

Percy meanwhile dumped her bundle of kindling on top of the rest. She untied the woolen shawl, and underneath it was another cotton one that she kept on, since the inside of the house was chilly despite the lit fireplace. She hung up her coat and shawl and the mittens on the rack in the corner, received her father's hat and coat and hung them up, then crouched down on the floor and started to wipe her own feet and the snow-sodden bottom of her burlap skirt.

"Why is it so dark?"

From her narrow bed in the corner, Bethesia spoke. Her voice was louder this time, tremulous and somehow frightening.

"What is it, mother?" Alann said. "What's wrong?"

"So dark!" repeated the old woman, and then moaned.

"Oh, blessed saints . . . Patty, the candle, now!" Niobea said anxiously.

"Oh," said Patty, who'd gotten distracted by the new arrivals and now hurriedly resumed rummaging through the cupboard.

Percy stood staring at her youngest sister's quick panicked movements. And then she wiped her forehead tiredly and said, "I thought we used the last candle for All Hallow's Eve."

Patty stopped, turned around, her mouth falling open.

Niobea frowned. "You're sure, child?"

In that moment the wind outside rose with a banshee scream, rattling the shutters, and then all of a sudden there was absolute silence.

Not a gust. As though someone had torn all the noise from the universe. It was so silent that everyone paused involuntarily, listening.

And in the silence, old Bethesia's breath came rasping.

"Mother!" Alann said, feeling a sudden ill premonition. Forgetting his sludge-covered feet he took the steps to cross the small room to his old mother's bedside.

"Oh, Gran!" Belle said, the same premonition bringing terror to her eyes.

Niobea stood up, dropping her needlework, and she crossed herself.

"Granny!" Patty exclaimed.

Percy remained standing near the door. She had grown absolutely still. And while the others had all their attention focused on the grandmother, Percy was looking to the shadow in the corner, the thickening of darkness at the head of the old woman's bed.

Percy blinked, while cold filled her, a cold beyond all colds, beyond Winter itself.

The cold of recognition.

Because she *knew* that shadow. She had seen it before, in the indigo twilight, lurking beneath the trunks of the thickest oldest trees in the forest, at the edges of the lake where the shore sloped into nothing just before it touched the water.

The edges of things contained traces of it. The endings.

Most recently it had slithered in her grandmother's dark irises and then sank away into the pupils, appearing then dissolving, as though not wanting to be caught just yet.

And now here it was, fully formed in the thickness of shadows.

Percy was not surprised at all. She looked at it blankly, and wondered why no one else in the room had bothered to glance in that shadowed corner at the head of Bethesia's bed, why no one else seemed to notice this thing for which she had no name.

"So . . . dark and . . . quiet," Bethesia whispered, her breathing coming laboriously.

"Oh, God!" Niobea said, trembling, coming to stand before the bed, while Alann put his hand on his mother's cold and clammy forehead.

"Ah . . . Alann . . ." Bethesia breathed, each intake of air a great harsh shudder. Her shallow chest rose and fell.

It was interminable.

"She is going . . ." whispered Niobea. "No time to get the priest. He wouldn't come in this storm anyway, not for us."

"Silent, woman," Alann said in carefully controlled anger, not wanting to raise his voice so near the old woman, and yet wanting to yell, to scream. "Don't speak this way, Niobea, don't speak a word, if you must. Belle, Percy, someone get water!"

"Yes, I . . . I'll heat some water in the kettle," Belle said. And she turned hurriedly to refill the kettle from the clay water jar.

"Look in the back there on the second shelf," Niobea

whispered. "I've saved a small box with dry tea. Make it, now."

"Yes, Ma."

"Aaaah. . . ." Bethesia moaned.

"Oh, God in Heaven, have mercy!" Alann held the skeletal hands of his mother, stroked her forehead. His strong rough-hewn face was contorted, and he was biting his lips.

They stood thus, long moments filled only with the regular sound of harsh breath issuing out of the old woman, while Patty and Belle searched for the box of tea, and the kettle water boiled.

Niobea pulled up a bench to the bedside, and made Alann sit down, while she sat next to him.

The fire crackled, and Percy took several steps forward, ignored by all, until she stood near the head of the bed and faced the shadow.

Up close, it had no face. There was neither shape nor texture to it, only a sense of *non-being* so pronounced that it stood out.

"Who are you?" whispered Percy—so softly that her mother barely raised her head, then looked away again. Niobea had taken a tiny holy icon of the Mother of God from its nook altar in the corner, and now she held it gingerly in her hands, reciting a voiceless prayer with her lips only.

The shadow remained silent.

The kettle had boiled and Belle poured the water over a small sprinkle of precious dry tea leaves in a large wooden bowl. She stirred it with a wooden spoon until the water turned the color of amber, then even darker, and a faint barely pungent vapor curled from the surface.

Long moments passed while the tea cooled somewhat. Belle poured it into a mug over straining cloth and passed it to Alann who attempted to lift Bethesia's head up just enough so that he could tip the mug at her lips.

The old woman lay passive, a doll. She did not make any attempt to part her lips or swallow, so that the warm tea dribbled down the withered skin of her cheeks, ran down her chin and throat and soaked her thin cotton nightshirt.

"No . . ." she gurgled eventually, her voice faint as a feather. "Let me be, son. . . . See, it stands here waiting for me . . . My time . . . at hand. How quiet. . . ."

Patty frowned, looking around then, glancing at the silent shutters on the windows, and the barely crackling fireplace.

"It really is odd," she whispered. "Why has it gotten so quiet?"

"What, mother?" Niobea said gently, "What do you see?"

At which point Alann began to weep. He hid his face against the old woman's chest and his form shook silently.

"I see it," Percy said, responding in her grandmother's stead. "There's a thing of shadow that is standing right here in the corner, near Gran's head. I'm not sure what it is, and it does not seem to be frightening or even moving. It's like a strange sentinel."

"Hush!" Niobea exclaimed, turning to her middle daughter with anguish and outrage. "How dare you say such things, horrible child, and at a time like this! Have respect for your poor grandmother!"

Percy looked directly in her mother's eyes. "But," she said. "But I can see it!"

"Get out!" Niobea screamed. She was trembling, clutching the icon of the Lord's Mother wrapped in their best cotton towel, so that it nearly dropped to the floor.

Percy's eyes were great and dark and liquid.

While Belle and Patty stared at their sister in silence, she turned away slowly. And then Percy walked to the corner rack where their coats and shawls hung. Moving as though in a dream, she took the only woolen shawl down from the peg, wrapped it around herself, then took her ragged coat and put it on.

What are you doing, child?

But no, she had only imagined it. The words seemed to ring

in her mind, soft, kind, even though no one had spoken. They were the words she wanted with all her heart to hear, from someone, anyone. Words that would have given her a reason to pause.

Had it been another time, maybe her father would have spoken them. He was always the kindest, and he seemed to notice things a bit more than the others.

But now Alann was made insensitive by grief, his face hidden in his dying mother's chest, oblivious to all around them.

And thus the words were not spoken at all.

And Percy did not pause but pulled up the bolt and then parted the door a bit, feeling the evening twilight and the icy cold rush in all at once.

She stepped outside in the quiet, closed the door securely behind her, and made sure it was sealed tight. Knowing that no one would bother to look back to watch her passing, she did not want them to grow chill—not from her own carelessness.

Then Percy stood on the porch of their house, bathed by an impossible silence. There was no wind, only peculiar gentle snowfall. In the twilight the snowflakes came in delicate clumps or individually, crystals from the sky. They dusted the white ground with a fresh crisp layer, and they sparkled on the branches of the old elm tree in the backyard and the thatched roof of the barn beyond which lay their tiny field, and across the street, the neighbors' houses. They landed on her eyelashes and swept her cheeks.

The world was suspended.

Percy stood there like a dolt, having nowhere really to go, and indeed no will to do anything. She then slowly lowered herself on the ground and sat down in a lump right in front of her father's house, feet tucked underneath her, wrapping the burlap skirt tightly to keep out the ice and tucking her hands in her sleeves since she had forgotten her mittens.

She froze gently and watched the snow.

Something strange was happening, and it had to do with the shadow in the corner, the one that had stood sentinel over Gran's head.

Persephone, strange girl, knew somehow that, although tonight had been her grandmother's time, yet at the same time it *had not*—would not be. For she knew with a certainty that death was not going to claim her, or anyone else for that matter.

Neither this night, nor the next.

Chapter 2

Death's fourth stop was magnificent and most distant of all, to the south, in the heart of the Realm. And, as with all the others, not a heartbeat elapsed.

The Silver Court was the Imperial Seat of power of the Realm—the capital and the center of all things. Neither a full-fledged city nor a proper citadel, it retained elements of both, incorporating splendid structures of the grand Imperial Palace, three immense cathedrals, including the Basilica Dei Coello, numerous galleries, lyceums, ornamental gardens, and outlying estates.

Situated at the exact meeting point of the three kingdoms—Lethe, Styx, and Morphaea—the Silver Court was officially its own entity, and the three kingdoms surrounding it sprawled outward like subservient petals from its neutral core. In theory this ensured that the Emperor could never play favorites among the vassal kingdoms. In practice, the kingdoms of the Realm eternally vied for imperial privilege and attention, and could only be united against a common threat to the south, beyond the foreign borders—a chronic threat issuing from the Realm's grand neighbor, the Domain.

The Silver Court of the Realm took its name from the grandiose silver-trimmed Hall of the Imperial Palace where the

Emperor Josephuste Liguon II and the Emperors before him held the most splendid balls in the world. The Hall's lofty ceiling was painted by the great Fiorello into a scene of Heaven where each cloud had not merely a silver lining but was coated completely with a paper-thin sheet of pressed silver, and where the Figure of God shone with the purity of this metal while the beatific Angels wore silver halos.

Gold had been deemed too much of a worldly metal by the ancient Emperor whose conceit this Hall had been. And unfortunately, since silver tarnished so easily, the whole of the grand Hall had to be polished and restored every season by a cadre of Imperial Silversmiths.

From the ceiling were suspended a hundred chandeliers of transparent crystal, while more crystal hung in garlands on the walls that were the color of deep burgundy.

The Emperor Josephuste and the Empress Justinia held court while seated upon silver thrones trimmed with burgundy velvet, and the light of a thousand candles shone upon the mirror-polished wooden mosaic of the lacquered parquet floor.

It was the depth of winter now and the roof and overhangs of the Palace were covered with the ermine coat of snow. Within the walls the myriad corridors were a hive of mayhem as servants of every rank sped about on their tasks. For, tonight was the great Birthday Feast of the Infanta, only beloved daughter of the Emperor, and all of the nobility were invited, including select foreign royalty.

Outside the Palace the wind howled, swirling snowflakes into a haze of whiteness, and the darkening sky was the color of faint mauve twilight and milk. Aristocratic carriages arrived one after another at the gates, met by liveried servants who seemed permanently fixed in bowed stances from their non-stop genuflecting and from the relentless cold.

Today the Infanta turned sixteen, and would make her social debut as a grown Princess of the Realm and no longer a child.

The Infanta, Claere Liguon, was a slight and sickly creature, and her ailments were so plentiful and frequent that she was almost never seen in public at all. Tonight she was to put in a brief appearance as the clock struck eight, and then, after a dutiful hour of hearing out the Court's congratulations and receiving gifts, she would once again retire to her living quarters and immediately to bed where she spent most of her time.

The Silver Hall was filling with noble guests as Peers of the Realm arrived in elegant haste yet with a proper semblance of nonchalance—dukes and baronets and marquises and counts and minor lordlings accompanied by their bedecked spouses, all having surrendered their winter furs and capes at the Palace foyer into the accommodating hands of imperial liveried lackeys.

The Chamberlains had grown hoarse from announcing His Lordship so-and-so and Her Ladyship this-and-that with every breath. The great long gift table on the side of the hall was overflowing with garishly sparkling wrapped boxes, containers of all shapes and sizes, chests, baskets, trinkets, trifles, and curiosities. There were numerous clockwork toys, for none could rival the clockmakers of the Realm for their skill with the delicate timepiece mechanisms—armies of windup miniature horses of lacquered wood and ivory bore upon their backs tiny metallic knights, and reposed on platforms in military lineups; delicate copper and gold birds with jewel eyes perched within filigree cages; porcelain courtier dolls wearing full crinolines or jackets of lace and crimson silk stood in various poses of suspended half-life.

Meanwhile, gossip bounced like champagne bubbles around the hall.

"Can you imagine the poor sickly dear finally venturing forth into *le haute monde* on her sixteenth birthday?" the distinguished and well-preserved Duchess Christiana Rovait of Morphaea uttered in a stage whisper, fanning herself and inclining her grand-wigged and powdered head closer to the equally grandiose head of the Countess Jain Lirabeau whose northern estate lay within the same kingdom.

"Oh, tonight is going to be very interesting," the sultry Countess Lirabeau replied in a softer voice. She was young and beautiful and yet powdered so that her skin was fashionably wan and matte as porcelain, while her lips were a shock of delicately outlined crimson. Her wig stood up a foot and a half over her head, its ringlets meticulously arranged and strings of pearls winding through the silver locks. "I dare say the Infanta will be coddled as always by her Imperial Papa, and then rushed off out of sight. That's when the real excitement will begin. His Imperial Majesty has more pressing matters in the form of Balmue-flavored politics. The envoys of the King of Balmue are here. Look, there, toward the back near the Duke of Plaimes and his gawky son—see those four men clad in silver and sienna brown? Those colors they wear are shades of Balmue. And if I am not mistaken, there are enough secret sympathizers in the Silver Court to make things very interesting indeed."

"Interesting and quite tense—goodness, is that the wind I hear outside? Interminable blizzard. Now, what of the outcome of the confrontation between the Red and Blue Dukes tonight? Any news on that? Oh, how I do adore Lethe's chronic military antics—or what passes for such, directly under the nose of their poor Prince Osenni. He is not here, is he? No, I dare say not—not with the old dear Queen Andrelise so very indisposed."

"I am certain all of Lethe stayed home. We are stuck with our own, and most of Styx. They even brought His youthful Majesty King Augustus Ixion. There he stands, the poor boy, surrounded by grave old men. Most depressing, I dare say, if he is hoping to get more than a moment with the Infanta. But then, one is never too young to start planning royal connections."

But the Duchess Rovait barely deigned to glance in the direction of the very young and newly orphaned King of Styx, a thin, anxious-faced youth of no more than fourteen, overdressed in pearl-embroidered crimson and black velvet, bewigged like a gilded doll, and surrounded indeed by distinguished "advisors." Royal children did not interest her, and neither did political puppets, and she was apparently more interested in discussing Lethe.

"Goraque's retinue is noticeably absent," the Duchess Rovait continued. "And as for Chidair, Lord knows he is a strange fellow, and is not to be expected to be present, not even with all of Balmue knocking at our gates."

"Yes, Duke Hoarfrost would much rather pummel his neighbor than an actual adversary," remarked Jain Lirabeau mockingly. Her eyes glittered remarkably tonight, with belladonna-enhanced dark pupils, under the thousand candles of the Hall. And, oh, how well her cornflower blue crinoline dress offset her porcelain pallor. . . .

"Now, Vitalio Goraque, on the other hand, he would have been here no doubt—"

"Fie! That is absurd! How could he manage to be here on the same night as the battle? Were he to ride breakneck and put three horses to lather, he'd still make it to Court only by morning, at the earliest."

"Oh, no you misunderstand, my dear," said the Duchess Rovait, laughing. "The very notion would be ludicrous, just taking into account the distance between here and there. And indeed, no man is expected to forgo the military pleasures for any other enterprise. What I meant was, Goraque is a true man of Court—even if the rest of Lethe leaves much to be desired in that respect—and he would have been here, if such a thing were achievable."

"In that case, I do see what you mean, Your Grace. Though, indeed, a man of one court does not equal a man of another. They cannot hope to rival the refinement of Morphaea with its urban splendors of Duorma—Letheburg's Palace is nothing to Duorma's Palazzio. We breed nobility, lofty and true, I always recall, when I am back at home up north, or when I visit your own idyllic estate, or when I attend the gracious court of His Majesty Orphe Geroard. Nothing but the Silver Court itself will ever exceed the courtly pleasure of sweet Morphaea."

"Yes, and now you flatter and tease, my charming dear girl—but, do go on in this precise manner, with such delightful exaggerating!"

"Well, only a little!"

In that moment of their rapturous native reminiscence, a slim, dark nobleman approached the Duchess and Countess. He bowed deeply before them, interrupting the splendid stream of gossip with his sudden presence.

"Ah, my dear Vlau! I am perfectly flabbergasted to see you here after all!" exclaimed the Countess Lirabeau, and even the white sheen of powder could not conceal a sudden blooming of rose color in her cheeks. "For some reason I didn't imagine for a moment that you were seriously planning to attend. But you are here, and I am . . . gratified!" With a flutter she turned to her more matronly companion, saying, "Your Grace, may I introduce the Marquis Vlau Fiomarre?"

The Marquis bowed again, his impeccable elegance of movement so pleasing that the Duchess Rovait could not help but allow her gaze to linger on the young man's willowy frame clad in somber black. His serviceable, but badly fitting wig was almost carelessly under-powdered, revealing at the edges his real hair with much of its natural darkness showing, gathered behind him in a queue. But none of it mattered, for his shoulders were wide and his eyes black, disturbing with their intensity. His eyes affected her with a thrill, for despite her maturity, the Duchess was not immune to male charms.

"It is a pleasure, Your Grace. And well met again, My Lady Lirabeau. My deepest thanks for your most kind references in my admittance to this Imperial Assembly."

The Duchess Rovait dropped her fan so that it dangled on a satin tassel at her wrist, and then picked up her lorgnette and trained it at the young man. "Fiomarre," she mused. "Why do I know this name? Is that one of the south-east provinces?"

"Almost correct, Your Grace," he replied in a somber voice, focusing a gaze of his beautiful, disturbing eyes at her. "It is a small Styx principality to the south and west of here, bordering with Balmue. We grow grapes and olives, Your Grace. That is, my father's lands grow these crops—"

"Aha!" Christiana Rovait said, as her brows swept upward and her lorgnette dropped back on its golden chain. "Now I recall, young man, Fiomarre cognac! I knew it sounded familiar. Wonderfully virile, dare one say it—erotic stuff."

For the first time the Marquis Fiomarre's serious face allowed a faint trace of a smile to soften his expression—but only for a moment. And he bowed once again, acknowledging the Duchess's blatant compliment.

There was a lull in the chatter as noteworthy new arrivals appeared at the grand entrance of the Silver Hall.

"The Right Honorable Lady Amaryllis Roulle of Morphaea, the Right Honorable Lady Ignacia Chitain of Styx, and the Right Honorable Lord Nathan Woult of Morphaea!" a Chamberlain announced.

And the Silver Court turned to ogle the newcomers, for these were three of the most dashing and popular of the younger set, and together they called themselves the League of Folly.

Lady Amaryllis was a slim tall beauty with black hair and pale delicate skin—a dark antique pagan goddess. Tonight she wore a brilliant scarlet gown trimmed with black velvet and braid of the exact deep ebony shade as her hair that, unfortunately, in all its resplendent glory, was fashionably concealed by the powdered pallor of a tall wig. Lady Amaryllis had the tongue of a wasp and the sharpness of an angry fae, but also knew how to be so charming that she was everyone's darling, and ruled the Silver Court like the Faerie Queen herself.

At her side, Lady Ignacia Chitain wearing jade green, paled into insignificance, despite her equally marvelous wig and powder concealing what was known to be radiant auburn hair, and a fair flawless complexion.

Finally, came the young Lord Nathan Woult dressed in silver velvet. His own disdainful elegance, a pristine metallic wig over midnight hair, and pale bloodless features, made him a fitting consort to the unspoken Faerie Queen of the League of Folly and the Silver Court.

"Trouble is here," said the Countess Lirabeau, glancing at the newcomers.

"Ah, poppycock," the Duchess Rovait retorted, once more lifting her lorgnette to examine the elegant newcomers, and Lord Woult in particular. "These are lovely children, my dear, and you must learn to observe them as such. They are a fair source of entertainment."

"They are wicked!" Jain Lirabeau said in a loud whisper. Somehow it coincided with a general lull in conversation and was thus heard all the way down the Hall. Realizing her own blunder, the Countess bit her lower lip and sighed.

"Wicked? Who is wicked?" Lady Ignacia exclaimed with a giggle, while Lady Amaryllis said, "It must be us, my dear." And, without changing the expression of her haughty blank face, she headed straight for the Countess Lirabeau's group.

"Now see what you've done," the Duchess Rovait said in affectionate frustration. "We must now deal with *les infants terribles*."

"Your Grace!" Lady Amaryllis curtsied deeply before the Duchess. She then repeated the curtsey, but lingered mockingly, before the Countess. And then she paused before Marquis Fiomarre, seeing him for the first time. Dark capricious eyes observed another pair of dark eyes of unusual intensity.

"My sweet girl," the Duchess Rovait said with fondness, nodding in acknowledgement. "You are wicked indeed, as Jain informs us, and none of it is news. But here's a lovely young man straight from the country of wines and cognac, and you must be kind to him. May I present the Lady Amaryllis Roulle—

the Marquis Vlau Fiomarre."

Fiomarre barely touched the delicate gloved hand of Lady Amaryllis and, bowing, brought it near his lips without making contact, in a semblance of a courtly kiss.

Lady Amaryllis lifted one dark perfect brow but said nothing, for his vacant nonchalance struck her somehow. So very few—indeed, close to none—would forgo the opportunity to press their lips firmly upon her gloved hand. She had never seen this young man at court before, and his manner was more aloof and distracted than she was accustomed to observing in the male sex, especially where it concerned their attentions to her.

Other general introductions followed. Lady Ignacia chattered about the contents of the overladen gift table of the Infanta and fanned herself with a pretty contraption of sandalwood and satin and feathers. Minutes slid away while the grand Silver Hall continued to fill to bursting with the *crème de la crème* of *le haute monde*.

At last the Chamberlains cried for silence and announced the full roster of names, pedigrees, and titles of the Emperor and Empress. And then trumpeters stood forth clad in crimson and silver livery, and they played the processional that announced the arrival of the Imperial Pair.

The morass of nobility parted, making a wide pathway through the middle of the Silver Hall, and the double doors on the opposite side opened wide, revealing two life-size doll-figures of regal splendor.

His Imperial Majesty the Emperor Josephuste Liguon II, frozen in a dramatic pose at the entrance, wore a heavy gold brocade jacket and trousers, Imperial Epaulets and red sash, and the Medal of the Crown and Cross that covered his small chest like an ornate buckler of spun metallic lace. His greying head and bald spot were concealed underneath an impeccable powdered wig of spun silver, and his white-gloved fingers rested like perched doves against the pommel of the ceremonial Sword of State and his wide gilded belt.

Standing next to the Emperor in an equally poised manner was Her Imperial Majesty the Empress Justinia, a similarly petite creature in a gown of many layers of satin and brocade, of a color that was warm golden like a blazing fireplace, and yet silvered through and through with fine metallic thread. The silver wig of the Empress was piled nearly two feet high and topped with a golden coronet from which hung garlands of pearls and topaz. Around her pale throat rested a choker necklace of emeralds, diamonds, and rubies clustered thickly like a colorful bouquet of impossible value. A matching ring of similar stones sat on her gloved index finer, and similar heavy earrings hung from her lobes.

The Emperor had a washed out face and pale brows enhanced by powder and rouge and kohl, while the Empress was likewise wan underneath her layers of Imperial makeup. They stood posed like dolls while the court gazed upon them in awed silence, and then after an appropriate time they stepped forth into the Silver Hall and walked like dancers across the aisle vacated by the court toward their thrones, flanked by two rows of bedecked Guards of the Chamber.

The Emperor sat down first, with a slow awkward movement, and then froze in that position, while the Empress took a moment longer to unfurl her bulging crinoline skirts while two Ladies-in-Attendance came forward to fold and rearrange them at her feet.

Finally the trumpets blared again and then Josephuste Liguon II uttered in a high-pitched voice, "We declare the Festivities Open!"

Immediately the trumpets went mad with fanfare and the musicians placed all around the Silver Hall joined in with lutes and violas, with cymbals and drums.

They were signaling the entrance of the Infanta.

"Oh, here she comes, the poor dear," the Countess Lirabeau whispered, while the Duchess Rovait trained the full power of her attention and her lorgnette upon the grand doors.

Next to them, Vlau Fiomarre stood and watched the doors intensely, his dark soulful eyes unreadable, while Lady Amaryllis threw several irritated and ignored glances in his direction as she exchanged barbs of wit with the sarcastic Lord Woult.

As the fanfare died away into silence, the Chamberlain announced: "Presenting Her Imperial Highness, the Infanta Claere Liguon, making her Debut as the Grand Princess and Heir of the Realm!"

The Infanta, all in winter white, entered the Silver Hall. She was thin and shallow-chested, with arms like twigs, and her small pinched face nearly drowned under the elaborate monstrosity that was her powdered silver wig sprinkled with diamonds and pearls that created the illusion of a sparkling snowdrift from a distance. Delicate curled ringlets of hair rested sadly against her bony sagging shoulders. Her smoke-grey eyes appeared great and luminous in the hollowed sockets, encircled by darkness of exhaustion or disease, and were her only feature of beauty.

The Infanta moved slowly, taking uncertain steps that lacked grace but disguised her shortcoming by the care taken in each placement of small tiny-heeled slippered feet, one before the other, as though she were counting the paces in her head. Indeed, maybe she was. Maybe she measured and timed each pace and each shallow breath, and each flutter of her weakling heart and lungs.

The Infanta walked the length of the Hall and paused before her Imperial parents. Clutching her crinoline skirts, slowly she curtsied—first before her Emperor Father who gazed at her enchanted with an adoring smile, then before the Empress her Mother, who smiled and nodded.

Then, the Infanta walked several steps forward and a silver chair was brought for her, which she took almost with gratitude, folding her skirts around her feet and placing her impossibly thin white-gloved hands in her lap. The pre-arranged placement of her chair had assured that she was thus seated in the center of the Hall, half-turned to face her Imperial parents and also turned to face the crowds of the nobility.

The Gift Ceremony was about to commence.

"Happy sixteenth birthday, my dear child!" said the Emperor. "May this be the beginning of greatest joy! We love you dearly and we all wish you well in your youthful entry into the ranks of the world. Now, the Silver Court would like to express their great adoration for you and to honor you with Gifts on this Great Occasion."

The musicians around the hall struck up a gentle stringed melody while from the grand entrance of the hallway entered a line of beautiful child pages dressed as fanciful fae in wispy delicate silk and gauze, and carrying the edges of a long white carpet that they unrolled as they moved. Behind them came more children holding filigree gilded baskets filled with cut hothouse blossoms of various pale hues which they scattered along the white carpet and threw into the crowd of courtiers lining the aisle on both sides.

Soft gasps of pleasure, female giggles and exclamations were heard as the blossoms and petals rained upon the Silver Court.

"Ah!" Lady Ignacia squealed and moved back a step, nearly falling into the arms of the Marquis Fiomarre. A great white carnation struck her in the face, followed by the cream petals of pale winter roses that rained upon her wig and stuck to her exposed décolleté, then slipped down the layers of her crinoline skirt.

The Marquis obliged her by reaching out a somewhat stiff hand to hold up her elbow, while Lady Amaryllis gave a charming peal of laughter and exchanged a superior look with Lord Woult.

"Careful, Marquis," Amaryllis Roulle said. "For you will

only have the flowers to blame for an untoward caress."

The Marquis Fiomarre had not been paying her the least bit of attention all this time, and now he turned the soulful dark gaze of his eyes to Lady Amaryllis. Then he glanced back to Lady Ignacia whose gloved elbow he continued to hold absentmindedly and now released with abruptness as though realizing the impropriety. He said in a somewhat stumbling manner, "I beg pardon of Your Ladyship, I meant no offense. . . ."

Lady Ignacia continued her breathless giggling, while Lord Woult turned his handsome head closer to the dainty beauty of Lady Amaryllis and whispered, "I see we have a country buffoon."

Lady Amaryllis's lips trembled in sarcastic rapture. "Yes, apparently there won't be much sport. It is too easy."

Fiomarre did not show any indication that he'd heard the exchange. He now stood stiffly at a polite distance and watched the procession.

The child pages swept the length of the hall and emptied their baskets at the feet of the seated Infanta, strewing the most fragrant and delicate petals directly closest the hem of her resplendent white dress. Then, like fae creatures they ran back and disappeared, while in their place came a lovely solitary boy, no older than seven. He was dressed all in white and silver, his face and hands and long platinum-flax hair dusted in silver powder, and his lashes and brows silvered to highlight his pale grey eyes. The Snow Child walked the length of the white carpet, stepping like a dancer upon the strewn flowers, and carrying before him a white silk cushion upon which rested a coronet encrusted with so many diamonds that they eclipsed the metal and it was impossible to determine if the crown was silver or gold.

Pausing before the Infanta he kneeled delicately and waited, his head inclined before her.

"My dear," the Emperor Josephuste said. "Behold Our Gift of the Imperial Crown. May you take it and wear it at all Court occasions until it is your time to succeed me and wear my Medal of the Crown and Cross, at which point you will be free to wear any other headdress as is befitting an Empress of the Realm."

The Infanta paused for an instant while the Silver Court made a collective "ah" of admiration.

In that moment, outside the Palace came a sudden strong gust of gale-force wind which rattled all the windows, and then just as suddenly there was perfect silence. The wind died away into oblivion, yet no one inside paid the least bit of attention to it. For they all watched the Infanta as she reached out and took the Imperial Crown with slightly shaking hands, and then she placed it on top of her wig. Immediately the Snow Child stood up and readjusted the Crown so that it sat just right, and the Court "ah"ed once again, for now that the Crown was elevated nearer the chandeliers it shone like a cluster of stars.

"I thank You dearly, Your Imperial Majesties, my Father and my Mother," said the Infanta, speaking for the first time, and her voice was hollow and faint, that of a child, in the new silence. She rose and curtsied deeply before the Imperial Thrones, then lowered herself down once again with barely perceptible difficulty. She would stay in the seat for the remainder of the evening, for the other gifts and well wishes would be from the rest of the nobility, and would not warrant more than a polite nod of acknowledgement.

"Line up for the Presentation of Birthday Wishes!" cried the Chamberlain. At this point the Snow Child disappeared along the length of the white carpet and at the far end of the carpet nearest the entrance a line of nobility formed. All present came to stand in the queue to have a chance to express their well wishes and congratulations to the Infanta. At the head of the line stood the young King of Styx—the only non-Imperial Royal present—then the highest-ranking aristocrats, dukes and marquises of the three kingdoms, followed by counts and viscounts and baronets.

"Time to speak a pretty word or two to the dear child," the Duchess Rovait said as she moved with a grand rustling of skirts into the line of well-wishers. The Countess Jain Lirabeau tapped the elbow of the Marquis Fiomarre with her fan, and he blinked, then nodded shyly, and with a peculiar expression that may have been confusion, he followed her into the greeting line.

Lady Amaryllis stepped forward just behind Fiomarre, and stared at his tall back and well-proportioned shoulders. She also noted his slightly trembling hands.

"How wildly provincial," she turned around and whispered to her accomplice Lady Ignacia.

"A wager?" retorted Lord Woult who stood just in back of them. "Fifty standings on the Marquis stumbling when he bows before her."

"No, I do believe he will remain upright, but I insist he will stutter," hissed Lady Ignacia.

"I say his voice will crack, and he will start to cough," Lady Amaryllis snickered. "Fifty standings, and you are on, my dear Nathan."

"This is wicked precious, and he will do at least one of these things or otherwise make a fool of himself!" Lady Ignacia whispered. "I can't wait! Now the tedium of this night will surely be alleviated. Oh, how I adore wagers as a cure for everything!"

"Thank heaven for such prime fodder for our wicked fun," Lady Amaryllis replied, stealing another glance at the pleasing form of the young man before her.

The line advanced quickly. Each noble lord and lady bowed or curtsied before the Infanta and whispered a word or two of greeting accompanied by a range of smiles—from the sincere, to the formal courtly, to the ingratiating. Claere Liguon's small pale face was also frozen into a courtly smile that evolved more and more into a rictus of tension and eventually became a poor grimace of exhaustion.

"Happy Birthday, Your Imperial Highness!" they all said.

"May your future be filled with pleasure and delight!"

"This day is a glorious holiday for the Realm!"

"Your beauty and kindness grow every year!"

"No words can express our fondness of Your Imperial Highness!"

"You are the dearest most lovely Grand Princess in the history of our proud nation!"

The Infanta listened to them, nodding gently, repeating the words "thank you" in a faint whisper. At some point she was taken with a fit of coughing, and the old grand dame who was congratulating her in that moment went into a sympathetic fit of flutters, wringing her own hands and offering a silk handkerchief which the Infanta took with gratitude and placed against her lips momentarily, then lowered it to her lap.

She then continued to nod and smile faintly, but her facial expression now resembled the emptiness of a corpse.

"Oh, the poor dear is not holding up very well," Jain Lirabeau whispered to the Duchess ahead of her, as the greeting line moved rather quickly and they neared the Infanta. One or two more lords and a lady in front of them, and it was now the Duchess Rovait who curtsied elegantly and stood before the seated Infanta, speaking something warm and genuinely kind to the Grand Princess.

The Marquis Fiomarre took yet another wooden step forward as the woman before him, Jain Lirabeau, now swept a deep curtsy and her voice carried as she spoke her greetings. His heart had grown cold as ice, and his extremities too were cold, like the winter outside, despite the pleasantly maintained warmth of the Silver Hall.

He should turn back. He could do it, simply fall back out of line, and walk away—but no, he should simply walk forward and proceed to speak the greeting, as everyone else, and nothing would happen. Such an easy thing he could do, just keep walking forward and go through the motions as everyone else. . . .

Like everyone.

Another instant, and the Countess Lirabeau was done, and the moment was at hand. His moment.

Vlau Fiomarre stood before the Infanta.

The world had stilled around him, around them, and he heard a distant rush of something in his temples. He looked at her, seeing only great silver-grey eyes looking up at him tiredly, barely registering him as a passing shadow before her field of vision.

He looked and saw the true pallor, the greyness of her skin up-close, barely concealed by powder. He saw the weight of the glittering whiteness that was her wig and Crown. And it was that last thing, a cluster of diamond snow stars, that he focused on, that reminded him of his purpose as he stood, his lips parting not with words but upon a silence, while his right hand reached to the folds of his black velvet jacket, and with a long-practiced movement drew out a small sharp thing of steel.

That dagger had been in the family Fiomarre for generations, and it was the same one that had been used more than once for acts of ultimate honor.

And now, Fiomarre felt its grip, ice-cold and sure. And in silence he plunged it forward, taking an additional step, closing the distance between them, taking hold of her pale exposed shoulder and thrusting the blade into her. It was at that touch on her shoulder that she started, made a sound of surprise, awakening, and then, the next instant the steel was inside her like a lover, striking her directly underneath her shallow left breast as she gasped.

The rest of the moments elongated and became dreams.

The Infanta's faint cry; a second gasp coming in unison from all throats in the Silver Hall.

Then, long and short distorted screams all around, a clatter of armor from the Imperial guards as they moved in too late; the feel of merciless hands upon him as he was taken in a vise of iron and then dragged backward, beginning to cry out, on top of his lungs, "Death to the Liguon! Death to the Deceiver and his filthy Line!"

Clamor and madness and again terrible silence—for as Fiomarre cried out, he was dealt blows on his face, blows on his chest which took his breath and silenced him momentarily, while he panted in fury, in exultation, knowing now that he had accomplished what he had dared only in his dreams, and that Fiomarre was revenged at last and he could die with honor. . . .

But the silence had come because the Infanta stood up now, slowly, trembling.

She stood, hands upraised in a gesture that was a question and surprise, while the dagger of Fiomarre was lodged up to the hilt in her chest, and a crimson stain bloomed from its centerpoint like a winter rose. The stain increased, blood running down her chest in rivulets, making patterns of red icicles on her dress, her crinoline skirt, while she looked down on it, eyes great and filled with strange new life, a sharp awareness, as though in death she had come to be fully *alive* for one acute final moment.

The Infanta's lips were parted, and they mouthed a silent "why?" while a tiny trickle of red came at the side of her lips, to slide gently down her white cheek.

And then because she yet did not crumple, did not fall as expected, the physicians who had been summoned and who had come running in seconds, stood a few steps away from her in odd expectancy, while the Emperor and Empress stood also, having gotten up from their Thrones like broken gilded puppets.

There was a circle of emptiness around her.

The Infanta stood while her blood continued to empty out of her chest. Her gaze was clouded with pain yet did not lose its impossible intensity as she searched the crowd and then found him and stopped to look at him. She looked at the one who had struck her this blow, who now stood restrained by many guards, stricken in his own way. He was watching her in return, in horrible wonder, as everyone else in the Silver Hall.

The Infanta took a step toward him, stepping in a puddle of deep red—her own blood. "Why?" she said softly. "What have I done to you?"

"Die, Liguon!" he whispered hoarsely. But when the guards on both sides of him threw him to his knees, she raised her hand in a stopping gesture.

"No," she said in a loud strong voice the like of which had never before issued out of her. "Do not yet kill this man as he had tried to kill me. I must know why he did this thing, why he hates me so. He must live until I know."

And then her upright position faltered, at which point the physicians rushed to support her, to check the wound in her chest.

One doctor wanted to pull forth the dagger, while another prevented him in terrified silence, knowing that the dagger was also a precarious safety plug over a hole that contained unknown internal damage, and that its dislodging could cause a final bleeding.

And yet, thought that same doctor, how was it possible that this was not a fatal wound? For it was right at her heart, and yet the Infanta lived. "We must take her to her quarters, tend to her, quickly now!" he and the others muttered.

But in that moment the Infanta's small hand reached down—while they fussed over her, holding her up, trying to make her lie down, trying to carry her, or feeling her brow, her pulse, her throat—and she pulled out the dagger from her own chest.

Blood came gushing out, the last vestiges of it; rich like wine. And in unexpected terror they attempted to stop it, putting up ripped pieces of her skirt, holding bunches of fabric at her chest against the flood, against the inevitability.

And yet she lived, and her breath seemed to have stilled,

but she watched them. One of the doctors listening to her chest exclaimed suddenly, in horrified awe, "Her heart! It has stopped!"

"But no, it cannot be!" the others said.

There was absolute quiet in the Hall, and the winter wind had long been silenced outside, as though swallowed by a void.

And she shook them off then—shook off their useless touches and ministrations, and threw down the bloodied crumpled rags, and got up.

The Infanta stood in the Silver Hall, covered with her own life blood, red upon white, while her heart had stopped many moments ago, and her lungs did not fill with breath unless she consciously willed it.

There was no need for heartbeat, or for breath, now.

The Infanta stood before them, dead and yet living, and their hands shook while they crossed themselves, in terror.

"I will see the Birthday Gifts now," she whispered.

The man came riding like the wind. He swept through the darkness of the village Oarclaven, waking Percy from her freezing sleep as she sat on her father's porch.

He wore red and gold, muted by the night, and yet the design of his livery and the pennant he bore was recognizable as the Duke Vitalio Goraque's own colors.

"Neither side wins!" he cried. "It's a riot, but neither side wins! Witchcraft and unholy abomination is upon us!"

And as people started to come out of their houses, the messenger's hoarse voice continued railing and dissolving into echoes as he receded along the streets, on his way to the heart of the Dukedom, the Castle Goraque.

Percy got up, stomping her wooden feet, not feeling anything in her frozen extremities—were these *her* toes, *her* fingers, or some other's?—just as the door behind her opened and her sister Patty's face peered from the inside, silhouetted against the fireplace glow.

At the same time the neighbors from two houses down opened their door, in turn causing old uncle Roald from directly across the street to step out into the cold in nothing but his long nightgown and sleeping cap. "Heh? What was that about?" he bellowed, sending the dogs to barking and thus waking up the rest of the neighborhood as surely as the messenger had managed to disturb only a portion of their slumber.

Percy's father was now standing behind her, his face shadowed, and his large palm on Patty's tiny shoulder, moving her gently out of the way and stepping onto the porch.

He saw his middle daughter and came awake, it seemed. "What's this? Go inside, girl, you'll freeze . . ." he whispered hoarsely, his voice leached of all strength by tears.

Percy obeyed, gratitude welling within her—despite a wall of winter-ice atrophy that seemed to have grown solid, taken hold of her flesh (death had latched onto her but did not consume). She had dreamed as she sat in the cold, it seemed, dreamed of unresolved moving shadows and delicate white cobwebs. And now she slipped past her father and sister into their dwelling, into the firelight and the stilled death and air only slightly warmer than the winter outside.

Out in the street the neighbors continued conversing. She heard their familiar voices talk of Ducal armies and battles fought on ice in the dark. But all she could see was her mother Niobea's stonelike form, sitting at the bedside of Gran, holding the icon of the Mother of God at her breast, while the same shadow stood in the corner.

That and her grandmother's rhythmic death rattle.

It would not stop.

Hours later came dawn, but no respite for old Bethesia. Only the winter sun had risen, turning the sky milk-grey.

Belle and Patty had fallen asleep in their chairs, and Niobea seemed not to breathe as she sat with her eyes closed, as the dawn seeped in through the slits in the poorly shuttered windows.

The fire in the hearth had burned down sometime in the middle of the night, soon after Alann had gone to fetch the priest after all. The priest's residence was on the other end of the village and he would probably show up only after it was light.

Percy sat at the table, watching them all, hearing Bethesia's regular dying breath, until her thoughts clouded with weariness and she was hallucinating.

Or so she thought. Because the shadow of darkness seemed at times to move like vapor and then again be frozen in repose as a human figure, never looking at her or anyone else but the old woman, watching and waiting.

As the light outside deepened, there were harsh sounds of metal and many horses—heavy cavalry. The Duke's knights were returning.

Niobea looked up once, slowly, her gaze drawn to the windows, but she did not go to open the shutters. This was an ongoing wake and death was in the house. Or so she thought.

Belle came awake with a start. Her first look was toward the old woman in the bed, but no need to ask—the labored breathing could be heard from across the room, dissonant solemn music. And so she moved and stood up, shivering, and then gently came to stand at Niobea's side.

"Should I start the fire?" she whispered.

Niobea wordlessly nodded.

Outside in the street, under a silent dusting of snow, Duke Vitalio Goraque's army continued their clanging march home.

Alann came back with the priest just before noon. Father Dibue was a large man with a craggy face, coarse ruddy skin, and a jutting chin. He wore his hood tight over his face and underneath there were many layers of grey shawl. His mittens were thick and barely worn, and his woven belt held a number of key rings and pouches.

"Ah, blessed Mother of God!" Niobea exclaimed at the sight of him. She quickly stood up, losing balance for a moment from having sat still all night long.

"Bless you, my daughter," the priest replied in an automatic and habitual monotone. "Make room now," he added, stepping forward to lean over the bed.

He stared in silence, punctuated only by the old woman's breathing, then straightened and said, "Rejoice, Alann. Your good mother is not of this world much longer, and a finer place awaits her clean soul. She is fading even as we look upon her."

Alann cleared his throat.

But it was Niobea who again spoke. "She's been fading thus since last nightfall, Father, and it does not look like she will be taken into the Arms of the Lord any time soon."

Father Dibue cleared his throat, wiped his forehead with the back of his hand, then began removing his coat and shawls and mittens. Underneath he wore the dark wool robes of the parish. Belle stepped up to receive his articles of clothing and hung them up carefully on pegs near their own.

"Sometimes," Father Dibue said, "though everything is in the Lord's Hands, undoubtedly, there's the urgent need to administer the Holy Sacrament of the Last Rites. Otherwise, the humble servant of the Lord lingers, such as now, waiting for grace, for absolution."

"Then proceed, Father, I beg you," Alann said.

The priest nodded and reached for his bag.

Chapter 3

He was numb and cold as winter.

Ian Chidair, Duke Hoarfrost, had no blood inside of him. It had drained completely from his body by the time he walked up the sloping incline of the shore and stopped before his men.

The soldiers stood holding torches against the heavy blue twilight, some mounted, many on foot. His son, Beltain, sat on his warhorse.

They had grown silent, all of them. It was peculiar to observe the stricken expressions on those nearest, and the hastily concealed signs of the cross that swept across the ranks in pure animal reflex.

"Father? Are you my father? Are you . . . *dead?*" his son had asked him.

And Hoarfrost had to pause and think, his mind sluggish and devoid of emotion as though he resided in a waking dream.

"My . . . son. I don't . . . know." The words came with uncustomary difficulty, forced and hissing, because his chest was constricted somehow—indeed, frozen like a side of meat.

Ian Chidair realized that he was not breathing and made a conscious effort to inhale, so that he could form words, so that he could speak. But as his chest expanded that first time, his lungs were burning, seemingly on fire, endlessly so, with . . . ice; they had stiffened in rigor mortis.

Or maybe it was the simple action of cold upon water. Each intake of air caused him to fight against a new crust of ice that filmed over the insides of his lungs, and each ballooning of the membranes was breaking that ice, over and over, so that there were permanent razor-shards inside him. . . .

Along with the everpresent ice there was pain. At first it was raging mortal agony, foremost in his mind. But then it too had grown numb in the cold—in particular when he was first submerged in the icy waters of the lake. He didn't know cold could burn so. Cold burned with an inferno without end, and then it . . . receded. And thus pain became secondary, a constant sensation of remote horror that simply slipped in the back of his mind and lurked—for now.

Or, maybe pain was just a memory, and was not there at all.

Duke Hoarfrost pumped his chest in and out, or did something that caused a movement inside of him. Something; he was not sure what. He could hear the cold air swishing through the holes in his flesh, a soft hiss. It was almost curious to consider it, to listen. . . . Too bad he was so stiff, so cumbersome—he had never remembered being so peculiarly solid and heavy before, as though he was not made of meat but granite.

Am I dead? he thought, for the first time voluntarily, directly. But it was a lazy thought, a dreamlike passing thought with no emotion attached to it. And so he did not give it more than cursory attention, let it pass on into the void with other insignificant filaments of images and dream-fragments.

As though he had mused out-loud, Beltain, his son, spoke.

"What has happened, father?" he whispered. It was unclear whether he was afraid to speak up in a full voice or if he was unable to do so from the shock.

"What has happened to me?" the Duke echoed. He listened

not to Beltain but to his own words. Somehow he found it now easier to speak once again, to form words on the exhalation of breath, as though the practice of pumping his own lungs was merely an old rhythm he could reclaim so that it was again becoming a habit. Inhale, exhale, his mechanism was working like clockwork.

And then he shook himself like a dog with great sudden strength that was not inhuman but merely impossible, considering the condition of his body. And he sent bits of water and ice flying around him. He flexed his arms, stomped his feet, his torso covered in iron plate and wet tunic.

"Am . . . I . . . dead?" he said out-loud, practicing, as the air hissed out of his chest.

And suddenly there was an unexpected answer.

A man stepped forward stiffly, from among the ranks of his foot soldiers, and he said in an equally wooden, stone-cold voice. "My . . . Lord. You're not the only one. I fear me, I'm dead too."

He pulled off his damaged helmet and showed a head wound that could not belong to a man walking upright. Hair clotted with blood at the left side of his temple showed broken bits of skull and brains pouring out of him in rivulets, freezing against his bluish-white face.

There were groans and exclamations in the crowd.

Beltain pulled his warhorse up tight, for it started to snort and roll its eyes in terror.

And then, one after another, more men stepped forward. They removed hauberks and shirts, parted chest-plates, raised sleeves and lifted helmets. What was revealed could not be called a proper nightmare. For no human history had the words in any language to describe the carnage done to a body that is dead and ravaged and void of living fluids, missing limbs, with stilled organs and lack of movement, yet which continues supporting the living soul.

There were old legends, tales told to scare the young, of the blood-drinking vurdulak and vampir, the God-forsaken undead who rested in their coffins during day but rose at night to walk the darkness in order to appease an unholy hunger. Other legends spoke of incorporeal ghosts, skeletal creatures that would not rest, of ghouls and shades and bodies possessed by demonic forces, of drowned maidens that devoured men, of hoary forest spirits that lurked below the roots of ancient trees and swallowed the living beneath ground.

Yet there was no mention of men who simply would not die, would not leave their mauled and broken bodies, no matter how terrible the damage was. Men who could not leave the trappings of flesh, meanwhile imbued with the ability to feel every bit of pain and think the same fallible thoughts—neither good nor evil, merely ordinary human.

And now, the scene on the bank of the lake was that of military disaster. Soldiers had all broken ranks at this point, the living shying away in terrified suspicion from those around them they deemed dead, when sometimes it were themselves. Men looked closely at those nearest them, at themselves, at their noble Lord and his son.

Some wept and embraced like brothers, forgetting mortal shame. For, in the torch-lit winter night, next to a field of recent battle, this was a time of intimacy. Tears came from what remaining fluids their poor broken bodies still held in reserve. Tears flowed and froze against cold dead skin—for some, their last tears, for when their internal water was depleted the dead body would process no more. And they did not know it yet; if they did, would they save their tears?

Suddenly, in a loud rasping voice, Hoarfrost said, "Enough!" His timbre was different from the first attempts moments ago; it was now fixed in that new mode, as though the peculiar voice came as a result of turning machinery, hand-cranked gears. And it was once again strong and sure, as it had been when he was alive and cantankerous with passion.

In a steady inevitable motion, like ice transforming water, the tall, heavy-set man raised his massive hands above his head to signal for attention.

And then, turning his body still awkwardly to face his dazed son, he said: "My horse, Beltain. Bring me my horse. Now!"

There was a moment of pause, during which decisions were made that would change everything—or not.

"My . . . Lord," Beltain replied, after a deep shuddering breath of winter air. "I know not what has come to pass here, with you, with all of them. But I am yours, and . . . I obey."

With those words, Beltain turned to the knights at his side and gave the command. In moments the Duke's great charger was brought forward. The noble war-beast had escaped the cracked fissure of ice earlier while its master had not been so lucky. And now the horse snorted in confusion, for it could smell nothing but fresh blood and brackish lake water from the man-shape of his former master that now stood before it. And when Duke Hoarfrost neared the horse and mounted, it neighed in sheer terror, but stood its ground. Even the weight of this rider was different, heavy as an anvil.

"Listen to me, my men!" exclaimed Hoarfrost, sitting in the saddle like a boulder. "Something terrible has come to pass this day, this night, to you, to myself, to all of us! If it's Goraque sorcery, as I suspect, then—as God is my witness—I will find this sorcery and uproot it! Vitalio Goraque will pay for what he did this night!"

The soldiers cheered weakly, most still staggering barely on their feet.

"What's this? Are you men or drunken wenches?" Hoarfrost roared in his usual command. "Dead or living be damned! Form rank, all of you! And we march home!"

And they complied, coming to attention, lining up in their proper order the best they could. Beltain took his cue, and so did the other captain knights. Under their orders the army started to come back together, despite everything. In fact this normalcy helped.

Yet while they picked themselves up, and cavalry then foot soldiers started to advance back inland away from the shore, torches flickering orange, there were still moans and hushed whispers. Quite a few men had to carry each other, due to severed body parts, torn off limbs, for there were no crutches for so many. Some of the most seriously dismembered had to be carried alongside their own heads; the heads looked on sadly, eyes unblinking, mute—for they were separated from the throat and larynx and the nerves severed—and yet, somehow, they were aware.

It was the stuff of nightmares.

Hoarfrost took his usual place at the lead of the cavalry vanguard, with Laurent his standard bearer at his left side, and Beltain on the other. There was uncustomary silence between them, indeed among all the ranks, punctuated only by creaking metal armor and footsteps crunching over the fresh powder of snow. They started to turn onto the road leading deeper into Chidair territory, heading North.

Just before they turned onto the deeply rutted stretch of roadway leading away from Lake Merlait, sounds of a mild commotion carried from the rear of the marching columns. Apparently a messenger was heading their way from the enemy's side.

Within seconds, the messenger appeared, dressed in the red and gold colors of Goraque, galloping with a white banner aloft in one hand.

Hoarfrost signaled to stop their march and half-turned in the saddle to watch the new arrival. The Duke was without a helmet and his wet hair was completely frozen to his scalp in a wild bramble-tangle, with a light dusting of snow, while his skin was matte with a crystallized sheen. His eyes, gradually freezing in their sockets, had difficulty turning, so he simply turned his neck.

Beltain appeared not to look at his father directly, but threw occasional glances sideways at him.

The messenger was a young slip of a boy. Yellow-corn hair, a frost-bitten face and pale eyes in the torchlight stared in wild desperation as he brought his horse up short, then bowed his head in greeting and delivered his message.

"The Duke Vitalio Goraque honorably requests a truce of the Duke Ian Chidair," the boy said breathlessly. "Due to unknown circumstances and unknown terrible forces, a strange curse has come upon his men. This may be very hard to believe but no one on the Goraque side is able to die, not even the mortally wounded. My master the Lord Duke Goraque suspects sorcery or a curse, and swears upon his honor that he is willing to continue this conflict at some future date."

"Harumph!" Duke Hoarfrost said, watching the messenger with unblinking dark eyes.

The boy blinked but that was the only indication he made of being terrified.

"So, tell me, young soldier, is it true, this crazy thing your Duke claims?" Hoarfrost continued.

The messenger gathered himself up proudly, and then said, "Yes, my Lord, it is all true!"

"And why should I believe you?"

"Because, my Lord, I see now that this curse has fallen not only upon Goraque, but upon your own men!" the messenger exclaimed. "As I rode here just now, past the army of Chidair, I saw it, my Lord. I saw everything. The dead march alongside the living. It is the exact same thing in our own ranks."

"Hah!" Hoarfrost said. And then he turned his head fully and trained the intense look of his fixed dark eyes upon the boy.

"Look at me, soldier . . ." the Duke said. "What do you think? How do I look to you? Think you I can dance a cotillion or a gig? Well?"

Placed in a difficult situation that was getting worse by the minute, the young boy apparently decided, to hell with it. "I beg pardon, my Lord," he said. "But—but I think you're dead, M'Lord. You look blue and white with cold, like no living man but a corpse. And yet, dead though you might be, begging pardon and all, I think you could dance a fair swell gig, I would bet my shirt on it!"

In reply Duke Hoarfrost roared. At the first sound of his deep thunderous voice the messenger started, shifting in his saddle involuntarily. But the roar was laughter.

The Duke laughed and shook, like a Winter avalanche, ice clinking against armor plate. Finally he quieted, and nodded to the messenger. A difficult crooked smile remained on his face, but it was grim and edged with sorrow. "Well said, soldier boy, well said. Your honesty does you honor. I appear indeed to be a walking corpse, run through by another man who should've been dead—for I had killed him first, and had I not turned my back on him, my heart would be beating now. Maybe the Lord has decided to punish me in my moment of arrogance. But—never mind." He paused. "And yet I am oddly glad to hear from you—all of this. Because I see now that this is not Goraque's doing, none of it, but something greater than either of us. So, I agree to his offer. Tell him—we are under truce. Until we come to the bottom of this, all of it, the dark sorcery or curse of hell, we will set down our arms and return to our lands. Now, go, tell him my words. Oh, and be sure to tell him that I am dead. The Chidair corpse sends his greetings and his regards! What a wonder, eh? Now, go!"

And the Duke again began to laugh, starting out soft then harshly, his perforated body whistling with air.

The messenger nodded his head in a crisp salute, and turned his horse and galloped away to relay the message, quickly disappearing into the bluish-shadows and the sweeping line of the Chidair army in the direction of the lake.

Hoarfrost raised his gauntleted hand, stiff and creaking as a frozen haunch of meat, and the stalled army once more resumed movement.

They were heading North, home.

The Winter Palace of Lethe echoed with the death rattle of the old Queen Andrelise. All night it resounded, into the dawn hours and the following day. It filled the mind of Prince Roland Osenni and—he had no doubt—the mind of his wife Lucia.

No matter what room he entered, Prince Roland could just hear it at the edge of his auditory sense, the endless breathing, in and out, as though an anvil lay upon his mother's chest. The weight was pressing down, down, choking her, and yet she breathed. . . .

He could no longer be in that chamber of unending death.

Being *there* made him want to scream and do violence to her, to himself. Nor could he concentrate upon any other daily routine.

Instead he walked around the halls and corridors aimlessly, startling the Palace serving staff. Or else, after locking himself in his personal quarters for most of the waking hours, he paced like a caged beast back and forth along a narrow long stretch of room.

Princess Lucia shared two of his meals this day and they ate in grim silence, served by a cadre of impeccable servants who moved in such a funereal hush so that not even their trays clanked; nor silverware or bone china.

Finally, during supper, Roland could not stand it. He opened his mouth, but his wife preceded him.

"What—does Your Highness think?" Princess Lucia said, raising her gaze from the contemplation of a plate of sawdust-tasting soufflé before her. "Was that creature, that man-apparition in her chambers, really . . . Death?"

"Hell be damned if I know," the Prince replied, watching his own plate of beautifully presented delicacy that tasted like dried straw. Was it soul-sickness and a trick of the senses, or had food indeed become unpalatable?

Her Highness might have dropped her patrician jaw at such language in the dining room at any other occasion. Today she merely observed him.

"I don't know," he repeated. "I only know this is interminable. And it sounds callous for a son to say such a thing, but I wish Her Majesty would pass along already. She is in agony, my mother is."

"I agree."

The Prince looked up. His wife was looking at him, and her eyes glistened, were full and dark with moisture, reflecting the bright candlelight.

"There must be . . . something that can be done," she continued.

The Prince frowned. "What do you suggest?"

"Oh no, God in Heaven, no!" Princess Lucia hurried to negate any notion of acts of a dark nature that her words might have planted. "I would never imply such a horror as you might *think* I mean, no. Indeed, how could Your Highness think I ever could? I love her as much as you, with all my heart—"

"Then what?"

The Princess took a deep breath so that her lace quivered around her décolletage. "Your Highness will not like it, I expect. But—I must say it. You must send for Grial. She is the only one who can help, give us guidance."

Prince Roland put down his silverware with a clank. "I will not tolerate the endless chattering and malodorous concoctions of that witch! Not here, not ever again!"

"She's not a witch! She saved your son, Your Highness. He would not have been born living, and you know it."

"The priests at Holy Mass and my physicians saved my son!"

"No. Without Grial, he would never have passed out of my

body safely. I would have been dead too." The Princess's expression began to take on a feverish intensity.

"Lucia . . ." he said at last, this time softly. "I do not want her here. I know you and everyone in this blessed world likes her, and it may be uncharitable of me, but—what she is, everything about her disturbs me. It is unnatural—unholy."

"My beloved, it is merely very old. Please, I beg you. She is harmless, a truly good woman. Let her come and speak to us. You already have your priests reading the Mass, and surely the Lord in Heaven is magnanimous enough to allow a genuinely kind woman's folk ministrations down here on earth alongside the holy prayers of his priests."

There was a long pause of silence, during which Prince Roland could surely hear his mother's agony-rattle twelve rooms away, drilling at his mind, his sanity. He could hear it resounding in the china and the polished stone of the floor.

"Well, then. Let her come tonight," he said while ice settled in the back of his throat. "Only this once."

Grial was shown into a small room of the Palace. She was a middle-aged townswoman with very lively dark eyes, dressed in what could easily be described as unwashed rags, with unruly and brittle witch-hair—ash and silver and black all intermingled into an uncombed mess barely contained by a knotted multicolored kerchief—so it was no wonder the Prince considered her an unholy sorceress from the forests. However Grial was merely from the depths of another sort—the narrow refuse-alleys and cobblestone streets and grimy filth of poverty.

Grial had prospered somewhat in the recent years from her unusual midwifery and healing skills, and not less from her even more uncanny ability to foretell events and interpret signs of things to come. But to admit need for such extreme services was not easy—most came to her in clandestine supplication, and she assisted with matters that were deemed beyond hopeless by the doctors and clergymen. Healing warts and easing women's bleeding was rote; healing the mind and easing sorrow, now *that* was a real feat. They paid her well enough so that she could first open her own stall in the markets of Letheburg and then buy a storefront and put up a shingle—though she never seemed to manage a new dress or pair of clog shoes.

Anyone else in her position would have been driven out of town. But Grial was not the typical fortuneteller or herb-and-sorcery woman who spoke in cryptic omens, scowled, and kept to herself. Indeed, Grial was an oddity because, except for her dandelion mess of hair and infernally grimy clothes, she was so *normal*—a cheerful and sociable personality, a gossip, and seeming to be in all places at once over town, friendly to everyone and with an impossible memory for human detail. Wherever you turned in Letheburg, there was Grial, in the markets, sticking her nose into bake and tobacco shops and taverns and arguing with the old and young men who lined up around alehouses, chatting up priests and merchants, waving in good cheer to whores and fine matrons alike whether they knew her or not, and acting in general as if all of the city was a tiny village of no more than ten folk and she knew them all as good neighbors.

Such was Grial. So, why then did the Crown Prince of Lethe find her so unpalatable, nay, terrifying?

The answer lay in himself. Roland Osenni did not trust things or people that seemed too good to be true. When Grial saved the life of his newborn son, he was grateful as any man would be and paid her handsomely as only a prince could. And yet, he had never forgotten the intense look of her dark eyes as she watched the mother and the child lying abed after the difficult birth. He remembered it because he did not understand it, was unsure what was underlying her expression. In that moment her eyes were so dark, so *other*, it seemed to him, despite her warm true smile. They roiled with deep shadows of the forest and old things lurking just underneath the surface.

Later, when he considered what it was that he saw, he realized it was *power*, surging, barely contained.

Power that should not have been.

That was so many years ago. And now. . . .

When Prince Roland and Princess Lucia entered the room, Grial rose hastily enough to be respectful, yet Roland thought he saw a shadow of mockery in her movements, in the very slant of her back as she bowed before them and the posture of her wiry tall frame as she stood up.

Grial was not an old woman. Or, at least she appeared not to be. Despite having been around for as long as he could remember, she was ageless or stuck in the ripe middle years, with a rather supple figure and smooth albeit dirt-mottled skin of her face and throat. Her face could be called attractive (if he could forget the power surging behind the surface of those eyes). Her hair—he simply could not understand how it could be so frizzy, so unkempt, as though she knew nothing of a comb. Thank goodness she kept it covered, more or less.

"Grial!" Princess Lucia exclaimed, jolting the Prince out of his unsavory ruminations. The Princess approached the townswoman with sincere joy and took her grimy thin hands in her bejeweled own. "My heart is gladdened to see you, Grial!"

"And mine leaps in my chest, much like a wee baby deer, Your Highness," Grial replied. Her voice was deep and sonorous. "And speaking of wee babies, how is the young Prince John-Meryl doing? What is he, seven years and ten months and four days now, Highness?"

"Oh, he is a fine and sturdy young fellow, yes, but how did you remember?" Lucia smiled fondly and in amazement.

"Indeed . . ." Prince Roland spoke for the first time.

Grial turned to face him. "Now, how could I forget that child?"

True enough, the Prince thought, slightly mollified. She would not forget assisting a royal birth.

"A child with such squinty but fine pale blue eyes when

you could see them open and with silvery specks, and cheeks with four dimples no less, and that ruddy newborn skin with just a smidgen of jaundice around the neck and forehead which cleared up fast, all things be praised!"

Prince Roland felt a wave of cold fear wash over him, returning. . . .

"But I carry on so, forgive me, a doddering magpie, Your Highnesses," Grial said with a faint smile. "Your son's a precious angel to dwell upon, but I know you have something else to discuss here, and that's why you called me over, not to hear my pretty voice, eh? So, out with it!"

No one else but Grial would have the crazed cheerful audacity to speak so to the liege Lord and Heir of the Kingdom. And no one else would get away with it.

Princess Lucia looked at her husband, and joy once more slid off her face, replaced by chronic anxiety. It was as though she was wondering which one of them should begin.

"It is Her Majesty, the Queen Andrelise," he said, beginning to pace. "She is . . . my mother is dying."

"Ah . . ." said Grial.

"The point of the matter is," Princess Lucia said, taking a few anxious steps also, "she has been the same for more than a day now, the same unchanging state of severe near-death. I've never in my life seen anyone like that—someone who was so ill, so far gone, and yet who is still . . . here, in the world of the living."

"Last night," the Prince said, "there was a man here. No— not a man. A being. He was dark, all dark. Empty, like a void. And he appeared out of nowhere in Her Majesty's bedchamber, just at the moment when she appeared to be going at last. But there was no sense of wickedness emanating from him, no deviltry. It seemed he was merely—*not there*."

"He spoke . . ." said Lucia.

"Yes, yes," Grial interrupted suddenly. "Death was asking

for his Cobweb Bride. I know all about that."

"How did you—" began the Prince.

"Oh, it's all over the markets and the streets," Grial said with a chuckle. For some reason such an ordinary thing as a chuckle seemed to lighten considerably the psychic thundercloud that had come to press upon them at the memory of the dark being of the night before.

"It seems, some guard or servant talked to their cousin or sister or two . . . or three. And now everybody's talking about what happened in the Palace, Your Highnesses. Everyone's wondering whether it's really Death that he was, or merely a bad scary dream that somehow happened to a crowd of tired people gathered 'round a deathbed."

"It wasn't a dream," the Prince said coldly.

"Oh, there's no doubt it was real," Grial said.

"So then . . . you think he really was there? Death was there in the mortal flesh?" Lucia said.

"Who else? Not the Headless Horseman, that's for sure." Grial snorted. She rubbed her nose with the back of one hand, then rubbed her palms together, and finished the gesture by wiping them on the apron front of her dirt-covered dress.

"Then what do you suggest we do?" the Prince said, watching her movements with distaste and irritation. "We have no understanding of his demands. I've asked my advisors, consulted with the archbishop himself. Who or what is this Cobweb Bride? Where is she? How do we satisfy him? And is it indeed true that he, Death, has somehow suspended the natural act of dying of Her Majesty?"

Grial arched one dark brow and craned her head to the side so that her mane of frizzy hair spilled forward along one shoulder. Still craning her head she raised a hand and suddenly pointed a finger at the ceiling. "What's that?" she said.

The Prince and Princess followed her finger and craned their necks to stare up at some gilded frieze work and ornate crown molding near the ceiling. "Where? What?" they both asked.

"That's what I mean," Grial said with a satisfied smile and dropped her hand.

The Prince and his royal consort stared at her in complete confusion.

"I know as much as all that," replied Grial. "My point is, Your Highnesses, you can only comply with what Death seems to be demanding from you—indeed, from the whole world—in plain speech. He says he wants a Cobweb Bride. So, you must do all within your power to give him one."

She paused, watching them meaningfully. "Think, what is within your power? Why, the ability to command your subjects. So, command away. Tell them all that Death wants a Cobweb Bride. Tell them that, since obviously a Bride is a woman, and as a common rule rather young, then all the young women of the Kingdom need to pay heed. Now, Death mentioned something about a Keep in the Northern Forests, didn't he?"

"Why, yes, I believe he did!" Princess Lucia exclaimed.

"Well then, so we have at least that much. Death's a gentleman, and indeed, since he takes all of us and all of what is ours in the end, he must have amassed quite a fortune—enough to buy a Keep or ten, not to mention a castle or a city or a whole realm, or all of them. Thus, we know where the Cobweb Bride must end up, after all is said and done. To the Keep she goes, lucky girl—well, not so much lucky, but you know what I mean," Grial said.

"Yes, I follow you . . ." said the Prince pensively.

"Don't follow me, follow this track of thought, Your Highness," Grial said. "And so, the next thing you must command of your people is that the young women—the ones who are *willing*, that is, for you are not one of those foreign despot beasts to insist things be done against the better will of their loyal subjects—those willing young women must all congregate to the Northern Forests and search for the Keep, so as to present themselves before the Deathly Gentleman as potential Brides."

Grial smiled brightly and again started rubbing palms against the apron and the front of her dress, which probably explained why it was indeed so dirty and grease-stained.

"A fair solution, Grial," Princess Lucia said softly. "But I am a little confused as to how any woman might be willing to do such a thing. . . . To go and face Death! For, whatever else could it entail, this being a Cobweb Bride, but being dead? Whoever would be convinced to willingly go to her death?"

"And a fair question you raise, Your Highness," responded Grial. "The solution seems to be already at hand, and it's Death's own doing. No one can die. Neither Her Majesty the old dear, nor any soldier, nor beggar, nor anyone. And some desperately need to be dead, as you can see. Because to be dead is not such a bad thing when it is your time to be dead, to be relieved of pain and suffering. And so, there must be plenty of loving and kind-hearted young women in the Realm, who are willing to do this thing to help out those who are in need, those whom they dearly love."

"But that's not being willing!" Princess Lucia said. "How can you call that willing? It is a sacrifice of oneself."

"And indeed it is. But it does require a will and a choice and a decision to proceed . . . does it not, Highness?"

"Enough," said the Prince suddenly. "I have decided. I know what must be done, and no, I am not a despot, but I do command my subjects."

He looked at the humble yet not so humble woman before him. "I didn't expect you to be of any use to me in this, but of all the others you alone gave me the reasoning I needed."

"I am so glad!" Princess Lucia said, looking at her husband, then clasping her hands together in an odd combination of chronic neurosis and relief. "We must of course reward this good woman, do you not think, my dear—"

But Prince Roland Osenni was looking at the strange one,

the wild witch with brittle hair and intense dark eyes that saw through him and to the other side. She, unlike everything else in this Realm, it seemed to him, looked in that moment so much *alive.*

P ercy watched in silence, huddled in a corner of the room farthest from her grandmother's bedside, as the Last Rites were administered, prayers spoken, and the priest packed up and left in a hurry, carrying in his purse the added weight of Alann Ayren's few coins in payment.

Father Dibue had been called away and his services were now required by several others in the village. It had always been thus, it seemed; the priest never lingered overlong in their poor household.

"She shouldn't be long now, my son," Father Dibue had said to Alann gently, as he headed out the door. "I will pray for her soul and for this house, you may be sure, tonight, and on the morrow. Now, be sure to let me know when her time comes. . . ."

"Yes," Alann had replied in a wooden voice. He knew it was futile to point out to Father Dibue that nothing seemed to have changed. The priest was gone soon enough, and at least they've had the Last Rites for Bethesia—as though that merely involved packing a reticule for a long trip, and she was all ready to embark.

It was late afternoon, and after a brief meal of bread and onion barley pottage—the usual winter swill that no one seemed to properly taste, today in particular—the vigil continued.

Niobea rose in silence from her seat at the table and immediately returned to the old woman's bedside, while Patty and Belle proceeded to clear the dishes and Percy carried the blackened pot with the remaining pottage back over to the fire.

Occasionally, past the grating sound of Bethesia's harsh breathing, they could hear their neighbors outside. And now and then Alann, sitting in his chair, raised his head to stare at the closed shutters when their voices carried too loudly.

At one point, there were particularly loud squeals and then female screams coming from about three or four houses down. The squeals and screams continued for long moments, piercing to the ear and bizarre, until other noises came to the fore—those of closer neighbors opening their doors—and of course there was the deep bass of old uncle Roald from across the street as he roared "Blessed Saints in Heaven! What's going on?"

Alann got up, his expression troubled. "That's Mistress Marie Doneil's daughter, I think? She's got a squeaky voice. She must be hurt."

Sitting near the stove Belle furrowed her brow and said, "Pa, I don't think that's Jenna Doneil. May the Lord forgive me, but it sounds like a real pig squealing. They've got two as of last month."

"That's right," said Patty. "I'm sure that's a pig voice, Pa. Though, Jenna could be a pig too, when she's in a fierce mean mood—"

"Hush!" Niobea interrupted. "Don't be rude, child, not now, not before your grandmother."

But the screams, squeals, and general mayhem outside on the street continued.

"I'd best go look," Alann said. "Maybe someone really is hurt and they need help."

"I'll go with you, Pa?" Percy said softly. Her tone of voice was tentative, as though she were afraid of her father's reaction. What if he said no, rebuffed her now?

But Alann looked at her and nodded.

And so Percy and her father dressed in overcoats and wrapped themselves against the cold and went outside into the grey-white daylight of early evening.

The sky was slate, slowly going dark blue. There was no rough wind, only light snowfall, and yet, a peculiar menacing chill filled the cold air. Their footsteps crunched on the frozen ground over freshly fallen powder that managed to obscure the deep ruts made by army carts and heavy footprints of soldiers and hooves of cavalry horses that had passed here early in the morning.

Alann, with Percy in tow, joined a couple of neighbors as they were heading around the street bend.

"Good evening, Mister Ayren!" said a tall bundled man.

"Same to you, Mister Jaquard. Any notion what's happening over at the Doneil house?"

"No idea, but it sounds bad."

As they walked, the screams came stronger. Percy shuddered from the strange rending sensation she got every time the high-pitched squeal sounded. Someone was in agony. . . .

The Doneil house was a narrow two-story, with the bottom being the livestock room, while the family lived upstairs. They were a somewhat odd lot, the Doneils. There were always underfed chickens running around in their low-enclosed front yard, and often a sheep or goat pair or other livestock boarded inside, for lack of a barn. The Doneils sold eggs and tanned leather and sometimes, when there was a cow, they were the local dairy shop.

A small crowd of neighbors had gathered in front of the house, and there was animated talk, much gesticulation and several people making sings of the cross, while the screaming inside continued.

As Alann approached the closest one to ask, young Faith Groaden, who stood near her father began to cry, sobbing uncontrollably. "Poor pig!" she managed to get out, in-between shuddering sobs.

"Butchering didn't go too well," the neighbor from the crowd said to Alann. "Really strange, if you ask me, but that's the pig squealing. Been squealing like that for a long time. Wouldn't stop! We got here, and the Doneil girl came out, and she was all a mess, crying and stuttering. I say she's daft, but she says the pig's been cut, but it's refusing to die. Her old man did the butchering and supposedly he's still in there. Doing God knows what to that pig. Taking a horrible long time, if you ask me."

In that moment a girl in a kerchief and woolen house-dress came running out of the front door of the Doneil house—the daughter, of no more than twelve years. Her face was contorted and red from weeping, covered with tears and snot and a general mess, and her sleeves were pulled up to her elbows, heedless of the cold, while she clutched her hands and wrung them, then beat her fists against her sides and periodically bent and straightened her knees as though straining to jump out of her own skin. Her apron was red and blood-splattered since she usually assisted her father. As she came out, Jenna Doneil started screaming again, shrill and insane, at the top of her voice.

"It ain't dying! It ain't! Oh God, Our Father, it ain't!"

"Argh! Dammit! Get back in here, girl!" From the inside a male voice roared. Nicholas Doneil could be heard banging inside, heavy dull thuds against wood and metal, the sound of crashing, while the infernal squealing continued.

"Are you all right in there, Nick?" a neighbor yelled. "Need some help?"

"Damned pig! Cursed beast! Won't shut up!" Nick replied. His voice was gruff and it was obvious that something was wrong indeed. Nick Doneil was usually a quiet solid man, did his butchering cleanly—if such a thing could be said—and yet never had he sounded so out of control as he did now.

Jenna Doneil wailed in reply, getting down on her knees and pounding her fists against the ground. There were smudges of pink where her blood-stained fingers touched the snow. "No, Pa! Please, no! No more, Pa! It ain't dying, no! Don't hurt it no more!"

"Shut up, idiot girl!" her father roared again. "Stay out and let me finish this!"

"I'm coming in, Nick," again said the neighbor. But those

standing closest put a hand on his sleeve to stop him, making silent "no" gestures.

Inside the house there was a heavy thud sound, as though a huge object was thrown.

The squealing suddenly stopped. "There!" Nick yelled triumphantly. "Bashed its head in, that should do it. Got no face now, pig. No face, no mouth to squeal, you stubborn damned beast."

Jenna was still whimpering, panting and wiping snot from her cheeks. Shuddering, she turned her head to stare at the doorway of their house.

And then from the inside came another grunt and a loud stream of curses from Nick. "What the devil? Why are you still standing?" he was screaming. "What in all the unholy hell? Die, you goddamned—"

"Someone get the priest," a woman neighbor muttered. She leaned forward to raise Jenna up and embrace her, leading her away from the front door. "Where's your mother, child?" the woman asked. "Is Marie hiding as usual, upstairs when the butchering's happening?"

"Yes, Ma'am . . ." Jenna sniffled.

"Well, I don't blame her," the woman said. "Don't blame her one whit. And you should be up there with her. Your Pa shouldn't force you to do the bloody work with him."

"I don't like it, Ma'am . . ." Jenna whispered.

In that moment there was a shadow at the doorway and Nicholas Doneil slowly came out of his house and just stopped. He seemed to stagger once, and his hands hung limp at his sides, powerless like rag-stuffed sleeves of a scarecrow. He was covered in blood up to his elbows, and all of his apron was red. His face, in contrast, except for the splattered droplets, was pale and drawn.

Everyone froze in silence and turned to stare.

"It won't die . . ." he whispered. Then, louder, "Pig . . . It won't die!"

Signs of the cross travelled the crowd in waves.

Alann's strong hand reached to clasp Percy's small frozen one. It was shaking.

Things got worse as the evening wore on. Father Dibue was having a particularly hard time of it. By the time he got to the front yard of the Doneils' place, he was hunched over, and he'd seemed to have lost or forgotten his shawls somewhere, so that his woolen hood slipped down constantly, revealing his scraggly head. He carried his bag with him as an afterthought.

It turns out he'd just come from the bedside of a boy who'd been stabbed in multiple places on his body, in a brawl. They were mortal wounds, and there was nothing the holy priest could do but speak his prayers and watch the blood pour out despite the bandages set by the old local doctor.

Except that, when the blood was all out of him, and the heart fluttered and stopped, the boy still lived. He lay, pale and cold, watching the priest and the doctor and his family gathered all around him—watching them with frightened, occasionally blinking eyes.

So now, Father Dibue, having said the Last Rites, and then having said all the prayers in his arsenal, with the family kneeling at his side, had to admit there was nothing more that he or anyone could do. It was in the Lord's hands now.

When he got to the Doneil's house, he was tired. Soul-sick and weary and, possibly for the first time in his life, frightened. The face of that boy just wouldn't leave him—those pain-darkened eyes, the anemic skin, completely bloodless, the silence of a stopped heart! The boy lay there, surrounded by sobbing kinfolk, and when he'd turned to go, the boy was getting ready to sit up. . . .

This had to be deviltry. Something terrible was in the air.

Father Dibue stared at the sizeable crowd of village folk that had gathered in front of the Doneils' place in the thickening twilight, and it did not bode well, not at all. The muttering and the hushed talk, and the signing of the cross going on, and several women and children crying.

Just as he approached the small picket gate, there was a loud commotion sound from behind him. And as Father Dibue turned to stare, there were torches and riders in the distance, coming down the bend of the road from the east and south.

"Father Dibue! May the Lord be praised, you are here! There's unholy goings-on!" someone cried from the crowd in front of the house, noticing him, but then everyone was staring at the approaching lights and sound.

Down the road came five riders. Four of them carried torches, and by their flickering orange illumination that dispelled the twilight, it could be seen they were wearing the Royal livery of Lethe. The fifth one wore the livery and the additional cape of a Royal Herald.

What in the world was a Herald doing, riding out in the cold dark, so late in the evening? Usually the Royal Proclamations were made on the morrow, and hardly ever past noon, so that the Heralds had time to make the rounds of the countryside and return before dark. This must have been something urgent indeed.

And why so many guards for one Herald? These were difficult times, true, with the ever-present threat of a major foreign war and many smaller internal skirmishes going on, such as the Goraque and Chidair matter, all of which made the roads generally unsafe—but four guards?

The riders came to a hard stop seeing the smallish crowd in front of the Doneils' place. Both horses and men were panting from exertion. "What village or town? Is this Oarclaven?" the Herald cried in a ringing voice, gathering his powerful breath.

"Aye, it is," the crowd answered with many voices.

"Hear Ye, O People of Oarclaven in the Kingdom of Lethe!" he began reciting the usual preamble to the news. "It is a

Matter most Serious and Grave, directly from His Royal
Highness, Roland Osenni, the Crown Prince of Lethe, speaking
on behalf of Her Majesty the Queen Andrelise Osenni of Lethe.

"A Royal Order and Decree is as follows." He unrolled a
parchment scroll and the Royal Guards closest to him drew their
torches nearer for better illumination. The Herald cleared his
throat and began to read. "Death has stopped! There is no more
death! No more dying! No relief from pain for us mortals—woe
to us! Death refuses to do his work until he is given his Cobweb
Bride. If you know of such a Bride, or if you are She in the
Flesh, you are ordered to comply immediately with Death's
wishes and attend him in his Keep in the Northern Forests—do
so for your Queen and Country!

"As for you, People of Lethe, if you have daughters of
marriageable age, you have the chance to be greatly rewarded
and honored. At least one of your daughters must choose, on
behalf of Queen and Country to give herself up as a possible
Cobweb Bride of Death, and must travel immediately to the
Northern Forests in search of Death's Keep. Daughters of Lethe,
heed this Decree! If you are chosen by Death, your family will
be honored and rewarded with a thousand Lirae, a Noble Title,
and a fair parcel of land. You, Cobweb Bride, will be
remembered as a Heroine of Lethe! This is effective
immediately, bearing the Royal Seal of the Kingdom of Lethe in
the Greater Imperial Realm."

The Herald went silent and began rolling the parchment
back together.

As he completed his task, the gathered crowd murmured
and whispered in half-voices. The Decree was insane. It raised
more questions than provided answers. But before any of their
voices became louder and more belligerent, the Herald signaled
to his guard, and two men drove on forward, then his own horse,
followed by the two guards to bring up the rear. Without another
word they thundered north and then again eastward along the
curving road, on their way to the next nearest town of Tussecan,

still in Goraque lands.

For one long moment Father Dibue stood petrified. He then pulled at the heavy chain hanging on his chest and the great cross, straightening it. And then he lowered himself, kneeling in the snow. Head inclined, he recited the Lord's Prayer out-loud, and one by one those of the villagers who noticed him, also knelt, until the street was filled with folk in prayer.

A few feet away, Alann came down on the cold snow, on his knees, making a grunt of pain, because his right foot and knee were bothering him as they had been since last year when he took a hard fall in the slippery muck of their barn. The thickly bundled smaller shape of Percy huddled at his side.

Percy shivered as she knelt next to her father. She appeared to be in prayer as everyone else, head lowered, arms folded, but inside there was silence and strange glimmerings of thoughts. . . .

Father Dibue finished leading the prayer, then rose heavily, everyone else following.

"What is to be done, Father? What does this mean?" everyone was asking, crowding around the priest.

"Who is this Cobweb Bride?"

"What does it mean that Death has *stopped?*"

"Well, it's just as that Doneil pig wouldn't die!" a man exclaimed suddenly. "Well, that explains it!"

"But what is it? Is it a curse?" several women asked.

Father Dibue raised his arms for silence. "The Lord only knows what is happening, in truth, my children," he said. "But in my great sorrow I must admit I'm not surprised by the Royal Decree of Lethe. What I've seen today with my own eyes was impossible. As I walked here, I was even then unsure how to think of it, how to explain it to myself. But now things are somewhat clearer. Take my word that I have seen men who *should* be dead and are *not*. Men with deadly wounds and broken bodies. It is unholy and terrifying and we must do all that we can to obey the Order.

"Do not try to spare your daughters, or to conceal them, for in doing so you will only be prolonging this hell on earth for all of us, indeed, for our immortal souls! If Death will not take us, then neither will the Lord! Our souls are doomed to remain here instead of finding solace in the Heavenly Realm in His bosom and under His wing!"

There was much commotion in response. Several women and not a few men began to weep, and children were sniffling.

"No!" one young girl suddenly cried out—almost a woman, and obviously of an age to marry. "Oh, father, mother, I beg you, I cannot go, no, I cannot! I don't want to die, oh, I beg you!"

"No! Oh, please, no!" another young woman exclaimed, and Percy recognized Bettie, a pretty girl from several houses down, only a year older than her, as she was consoled and held back by her two burly brothers.

The street erupted into chaos. In the twilight, screaming young women were seen scattering around the street, some held or pulled along by their mothers, and others being embraced.

A torch or two came to life, and in the flickering light the terrified faces of all were revealed, familiar faces blue with cold, smeared by weeping—men, women and children.

"Percy!" her father exclaimed, pulling her by the hand. In the flash of torchlight, Percy noticed, from what could be seen of his bundled face, his expression was grim and tragic, his eyes dark and bottomless, and she did not know what it meant.

In silence they quickly ran down the street toward home.

Chapter 4

The Infanta, Claere Liguon, sat motionless before a great window in her Imperial bedchamber. She was straight-backed and her shallow chest did not rise with breath. She still wore the magnificent birthday crinoline dress of white and the crowned wig of silver thread and pearl and diamond, though the front of her dress was stained deep crimson that was slowly drying and turning black—she would not allow them to remove it—and her skin was the color of the grey sky outside.

Indeed, after the initial mad scuffle by the doctors to get her to a bedchamber, she resisted all help. She had allowed no one to touch her and instead stayed for several interminable horrifying hours in the Silver Hall, pacing before the table laden with Gifts from the Court. As she moved back and forth, occasionally putting her cold sticky fingers—what was it that made them so sticky?—on the shining objects, a slick trail of her own coagulating blood formed on the shining parquet floor, and her delicate slippers were soaked. She had trailed the blood here from the place near the center of the hall where the silver chair still stood, the spot where she had been stabbed. In that spot on the floor was a large thickening crimson-black puddle that no one dared to clean up.

After about an hour of watching her, watching the

impossible spectacle before them, the petrified courtiers slowly regained a measure of something, if not sanity, and started to slip away one by one. The Emperor and Empress sat on their Thrones like two sacks—boneless, powerless, devoid of will and ability to think—from the shock. As the Hall emptied, except for the most essential attendants, they continued to sit, long past midnight, while the candles in the hall smoked, sputtered, and burned down. In only an hour or two, it was to be dawn. . . .

Eventually, as the nature of the dark in the windows started to change and the Silver Hall took on a hue befitting its name, the Infanta stopped pacing and pronounced that she wanted to be taken back to her quarters.

As she passed the Imperial Thrones, she curtsied before her devastated parents and then continued, as though this was but another ordinary audience. The grand doors were opened before her; she was gone. And yet they sat, Emperor and Empress, as the sky outside bloomed and the light filled the windows. They could not move—not yet, not ever. . . .

And now, here she was, in her bedchamber. Despite the early hour, an army of Ladies-in-Attendance, surgeons, priests, and other Imperial serving staff hovered around her in futility.

The Infanta's great smoky eyes were trained outside the window, looking somewhere beyond the delicate curtain of snowflakes that obscured the morning world with winter lace. Her hands were folded delicately in her lap, and for the first time ever she looked at peace, like a subject of a grand painting, stilled in an evocative pose for the ages, to be viewed and admired by future generations.

Now, of course, there would be no future generations stemming directly from her. In the unlikely event that the Emperor and Empress produced more children, there might be cousins who would one day in the distant future find a yellowing portrait of the Infanta dressed in splendid white, with a crown upon a silver powdered wig, archaic in its splendor, and eyes of dark receptivity in a pinched grey face. She would be frozen thus for eternity, for as things were now, Claere Liguon was never again to grow or age, or indeed *change. . . .*

It is possible that these and other thoughts tumbled through everyone's mind in those long excruciating hours of early dawn and morning. Lady Milagra Rinon, bearing the honor of First Lady-in-Attendance to the Grand Princess, stood trembling in her fulfillment of the task of Attendance, only a few steps away from the chair in which the Infanta now sat.

Lady Milagra's long-fingered hands were clutched together in a bloodless grip of terror, so as not to fidget upon the front of her plum-colored brocade dress or, God forbid, to call any attention upon herself now. And yet, oh, how she needed to be called upon to do something! Soft-spoken, with lovely unblemished skin of a deep olive hue and rich black hair underneath the platinum wig, Lady Milagra was a daughter of a fine noble house from the southern regions of the Realm, in Morphaea, where her family held lands very close to the border with Balmue. When the Emperor decided to honor her father the Marquis Rinon, one of the privileges granted was the acceptance of Lady Milagra into Attendance at the Silver Court. It might have seemed an odd choice considering how exquisitely beautiful and stately she was, and how much of a chance existed for her to outshine the bland Infanta. But Lady Milagra proved herself to be very loyal, self-effacing, and the perfect companion for her Imperial charge.

When the Infanta was attacked by the villain the night before, Lady Milagra was in the crowd of guests, and she had seen it all, screamed and wept along with most of those present and recognized the reality of the mortal blow. That her Princess walked and lived now, was a terrifying and incomprehensible thing. Lady Milagra had not been to bed that night, and the slow cold and shaking and shivering had overtaken her long before dawn when she finally followed the Infanta and her retinue into her chambers. And now, still wearing her ball dress, having had not a drop of food or drink or a moment to relieve herself, her face smudged and exhausted, she stood on her last reserves. Nothing was to be done while she was in Attendance—she could neither be excused nor ask to be excused, nor be noticed without the Infanta's initiative.

And the Infanta was *dead*. Though she occupied a chair and looked out the window, it appeared more and more that she would never make another request of her again. Thus, Lady Milagra prayed in silence for strength, for something, anything to happen, to deliver her and the rest of the Ladies-in-Attendance.

The other four Ladies Attending were also present—the red-headed and tiny Lady Floricca Grati of Styx, the blonde Lady Selene Jenevais of Lethe, the voluptuous and dark Lady Liana Crusait of Morphaea, and the youngest, Lady Alis Denear, also of Lethe. They all huddled together as a group, agonized and more frightened than they had ever been in their lives, only making desperate eye contact with each other and the others present in the chamber. Their usual tasks and duty would have been completed for the night many hours ago, and they would all have been in their beds asleep.

"Your Royal Highness," Doctor Belquar, the Imperial head physician was saying to the Infanta. "If I might only inquire as to how Your Highness is feeling? Is there . . . pain, by any chance?"

The balding middle-aged physician's voice was pitched in a peculiar high register, deferential and far softer than it had been with any of his other fine patients, even the Emperor himself. Indeed, how did one speak to a patient who was not supposed to be alive? A patient who was drained of the blood humour and stabbed in the heart—which was now stilled and probably as cold as the air in room. . . .

The Infanta's head did not turn, and she continued to stare out the window, unblinking. However, she replied politely, first making a peculiar effort to expand her chest, so as to inflate her motionless lungs in order to exhale air upon which words would be formed.

"No pain."

The doctor watched in horror coupled with professional curiosity the physics, nay, mechanics of her speech-making. For it was as though a mechanism was engaged, like that of an artfully created doll, for her to recreate the living act of breathing and speaking.

She had been thus for hours. All questions were answered in short easy phrases after some noticeable delay. And she never looked away from the window.

"It is wonderful that your Highness is not in discomfort, but maybe a glass of water or some hot tea would be helpful for the physique—"

Again that mechanical ballooning of the chest, the intake of breath, and she replied, "No, thank you. I am not thirsty."

Doctor Belquar looked behind him with frustration and made eye contact with a colleague, Doctor Hartel, a young brown-haired assistant and, in a manner of speaking, his professional rival.

"A hot bath with salts . . ." whispered Doctor Hartel.

But Doctor Belquar shook his head negatively.

"Perhaps, a light application of leeches. . . ."

"Are you out of your mind?" Doctor Belquar hissed. "The royal patient . . . has *no blood*, would you bleed her more. . . ?"

A few steps away, a breakfast service had been brought in, and it lay untouched upon the small table. The servants stood at attention, most of them looking directly ahead of themselves, so as not to be found staring at Her Royal Highness.

The great canopied bed of the Infanta was also untouched. The feather pillows had been plumped and stacked, and velvet coverlets had been turned down for the night. But when she was offered a chance to lie down, the Infanta refused, most vehemently of all—if shaking her head back and forth and saying "no" over and over in a monotone could be considered passion.

In the opposite far corner of the grand bedchamber stood two bishops and a host of priestly attendants. There was a non-stop soft hum of spoken prayer and wafting incense, but because the physicians had been given supreme authority in the matter, the on-going Mass was relegated to the back, so as not to disturb the unpredictable and precarious condition of the Infanta.

At about eleven o'clock in the morning, the Empress Justinia was announced, at the same time as she unceremoniously walked into the room, forgetting or discounting all Imperial protocol. The Empress had changed out of her eye-blinding splendor of the night before and wore a simpler gown of warm cream and pearl, and a plain powdered platinum wig. Her face was drawn with exhaustion and, lacking the usual artifice of makeup, revealed wrinkles and an unhealthy color, while her dark brown eyes were sunken and reddened around the lids.

Empress Justinia walked past the priests and the breakfast service and the Ladies-in-Attendance and the doctors. She stopped in silence before her seated daughter.

"Claere . . ." the Empress said. "Claere, my child, can you hear me? It is your mother. Look at me."

A pause. Even the whispering of prayers ceased.

The Infanta made that familiar-by-now effort of breathing. And then, slowly and stiffly she turned her head away from the window and toward the Empress.

"Your Majesty," she said. Her face was serene and blank.

The Empress suddenly burst into weeping. Her face contorted and she immediately covered it with her hands in a last vestige of protocol, for it was said nowhere that the Empress can be seen to weep in public.

"Mother . . ." Claere said. And she reached forward with her right hand, just barely touching the arm of the Empress with her fingertips.

Her touch was cold as the winter outside.

The Empress could not suppress a shudder and then was immediately horrified at her own reaction. She exclaimed hoarsely, "Leave us, all of you! Begone from this chamber and give us privacy."

The servants and attendants did not need to be told twice. The Ladies-in-Attendance fled in gratitude. Even the priests shuffled out in a measure of relief, and the two attendant doctors bowed their way out, casting pointed glances at their patient before the doors were shut behind them all.

Mother and daughter alone remained in the room.

The Empress still felt the aftereffects of that shudder of continued terror and revulsion, mixed with tenderness and anguish. But now at least she could allow herself normal human emotion without a facade of decorum. Justinia Liguon forced herself at first, forced her body to make that initial motion, and then her loving instinct broke through and she took the steps and closed the distance between her child, taking the frail Infanta in her arms, holding her with a force that she may never have allowed herself before, but now—none of it mattered, did it? Nothing could hurt her daughter again—now she squeezed and rocked and held on tight to the cold wooden thing in her arms. . . . And there was no more doubt.

She embraced a corpse.

And as the full realization came to her in that instant, the Empress broke down completely, became a thing of liquid pain without bone and muscle, and sobbed and sobbed, her face red and contorted, her tears and imperial snot running down and staining her cheeks and the cheeks and hair of the dead thing in her arms. At the same time, the drying red stain on the front of the Infanta's gown, crushed against her chest, was now smeared all over the Empress's cream dress, and it did not matter. . . .

None of it mattered.

"Mother. . . ."

The corpse was speaking to her. *No, no, her daughter was speaking to her!* In the same instant her fury at herself broke through the tumble of horror that was the dislocated contents of her mind. The Empress felt a strange expansion of the wooden chest against her own, and an intake of air, and then, the words came again, rattling softly against her own chest, like a sympathetic drum, flesh to flesh, living to dead.

"Please don't cry on my behalf, mother."

"Oh God in Heaven and Blessed Mother of God! You're all right, child, yes you are, you are!" the Empress said, her own breath coming in gasps, lips against her daughter's cold forehead and soft hair—her hair at least was still the same, soft, delicate, sweet cobwebs. . . .

"What has happened to me, mother? I don't know." Claere said. "I don't think I am the same. No. I *know* I am not. I should be . . . dead."

"Oh God, no, hush!"

But the Infanta was indeed no longer the same submissive creature, for she put her cold stiff hands against her mother's shuddering warm chest and she pushed her away, gently but firmly.

"No, mother. I am sorry, but I am—not alive. There is no pain, no . . . anything. I no longer *feel the world*. My fingers—numb—all of me. Not sure how else to describe—but I am . . . As though I am locked in a room with thick walls and thick glass windows, and I am looking out at you and everything through those impenetrable windows. Nothing touches me from . . . your side."

"Oh God! Claere, my little dearest, dearest one, but how could that be? How, oh how? You are here, you are here with me and you are alive, and—"

"When the knife entered me, it hurt. But only for a moment. Terrible pain, then it dissolved into nothing. Something—I felt something recede and it was like a blink of the eye. I was *not*, and I was pulled inside out and then. . . . And then, I was back.

Like this. Locked inside that thick room, feeling nothing."

"What he did to you. . . . He will pay, oh how he will pay!" the Empress exclaimed in a sudden fury. "The damned hellspawn of Fiomarre who . . . hurt you. He will be tortured and his family will be brought down at last, and even their memory will be rendered into dust—"

In that instant the door of the chamber opened, and even as the Chamberlain hurried to announce His Imperial Majesty, the Emperor himself walked in, followed by a tall dark bearded man of advanced middle years, with a steady willful gaze who was the Duke Claude Rovait of Morphaea, dressed in travel clothes that showed signs of his having travelled in haste.

The Emperor had also changed from his blinding formal splendor of court to an everyday coat and jacket of deep velvet. His face, scrubbed of makeup, was of an unhealthy color, and wrinkles showed readily. His wig sat almost crookedly over his balding pate, as though donned in a hurry, and his cravat was hastily tied.

"My child . . . There you are," Josephuste Liguon II said in a weary tremulous voice. "How . . . How do you feel?"

At his clumsy words, the Empress once again broke out into desolate weeping.

But the Infanta turned her blank face toward her father and she said, "Your Majesty, I am . . . fine."

The Duke Rovait took the moment to bow. "Your Imperial Majesties, Your Imperial Highness," he said in a deep voice, speaking with greater gentleness than might have been expected from his thick frame. "Most profound pardons for interrupting. I am newly arrived from my Letheburg visit—having attended the Prince and Princess and Her Majesty's bedside—with news of some great import, but first I offer my sincerest condolences at your . . . pain."

"There is no pain," the Infanta said again. And her mother, who had in the last several moments gone from silence to crying to silence again, burst into a new fit of weeping.

"Claere, child . . ." the Emperor said. "It is—well, the news the Duke has delivered to me, is something that must be told to you."

"It pertains to Your Imperial Highness's present . . . *condition*," added the Duke.

The Empress stopped crying and froze, staring at the Duke and then her consort. The Infanta merely turned her face slightly from one to the other, as though she were swiveling a doll's head along a neck that was nothing more than a wooden dowel.

"Well, go on, repeat what you told me," said the Emperor with a grim expression.

The Duke inclined his head and proceeded to tell a strange unbelievable story of what had come to pass in the Kingdom of Lethe the night before. He spoke of the apparition of Death, of the demand for the Cobweb Bride, of the old Queen who would not die, and of the armies of the marching living and dead that had returned, all to a man, from a near-slaughter to their respective Dukedoms of Goraque and Chidair. He spoke of the Royal Decree that had been proclaimed, compelling all eligible maidens of the Kingdom and beyond to go forth and present themselves to Death as potential brides. He had ridden hard upon the request of the Prince of Lethe, having put at least four horses into lather, and had arrived to personally warn the Emperor of what was happening.

"There is no more dying, anywhere," he concluded. "As of last night, the moment of the Apparition and the Demand."

"It must've happened just before the attack upon our child . . ." the Emperor mused.

"Then . . . I am dead indeed," Claere Liguon said softly.

"No!" the Empress exclaimed.

But the Emperor shook his head, his eyes dark and so very old. "She is but at the mercy of Death now. Suspended between life and the . . . other."

The Duke cleared his throat. "Indeed. Not only Her

Imperial Highness—hundreds, nay thousands of others are also suspended thus. Until this infernal Cobweb Bride is found and brought to the Northern Forest and presented before Death."

"What can be done?" whispered the Empress. "This is unbelievable and I just don't know if—"

"Your Imperial Majesty realizes, of course, that the world must be returned to its natural course. The dead must be allowed to proceed on to the next world."

"But—" the Empress said. "If—if so, then, Claere will really die! She will leave us! No, it cannot be!"

"Indeed. But—" the Emperor said, his brow twisted with a frown.

The Duke watched them both, and observed the blank face of the Infanta.

"Then I must be allowed to die," she said suddenly. "It is not natural that I am . . . like this. I am dead."

"Oh, but Claere, sweet child, no! You don't know what you are saying, this is just impossible—" the Empress began.

But the Infanta ignored her. "What—what can be done to find this Cobweb Bride? She must be found. I—I must find her."

And then, for the first time, an almost living expression came to her grey wan face. "What if I am the Cobweb Bride?" said the Infanta. "If I am she, then I must present myself before Death and allow him to choose me. Indeed, it makes good sense—since I am no longer one of the living, then it must be that I belong to him."

"Oh God, child, what are you saying?" the Empress exclaimed, putting her hands to the sides of her face, as though to frame the horror of her expression.

The Emperor meanwhile started to pace the chamber. His face was grim, while conflicting thoughts labored for dominance inside him.

The Duke Rovait continued to observe with some concern. Then, clearing his throat once more, he said, "I suggest that a similar Imperial Decree be proclaimed by Your Imperial Majesty, in regard to the Cobweb Bride. An edict that would bind not merely Lethe but all three Kingdoms of the Realm. I will personally convey your ultimate decision to my own King in Morphaea, and His Majesty King Orphe Geroard will comply immediately."

"Argh!" exclaimed the Emperor, putting a hand against his temples, squeezing hard, as though he could tear the weight of the decision out of himself. "If we do this, then we condemn my child to certain death. If we don't, then the world is—the world is not right, is—is—"

He roared in anguish and continued his pacing.

"I do not envy Your Imperial Majesty's grave decision," Claude Rovait said. "But—think of the greater balance, the greater good—"

"Greater good?" the Emperor roared once more, his voice no longer thin and wavering. "What greater good can there be when my child—my *life*—when she is gone? How can the world remain, the sun shine? Indeed, will it shine? How can the world go on? How?"

"Father, please . . ." The Infanta's soft measured words came like a balm of reason.

Slowly, and stiffly she took several steps forward and reached out to the Emperor her father. A cold wooden limb moved and it was her own. Her hand. With it she touched him on the cheek, an act that would have broken all protocol—but now she was no longer the same retiring and sickly Claere, and she could do such things with impunity, she could dare to do such things and more.

"Proclaim the Edict, Your Imperial Majesty, My Father. It is the only thing to do. And I am going to do the only thing also. I will find Death and he can have me. One way or another. As a Cobweb Bride or as a mortal woman."

"Claere! No, child, there must be another way!" The Empress began to wring her hands.

But Claere, dead and cold like the grave, like the winter outside, wore the most living expression in her eyes.

And at last the Emperor conceded. Nodding, he said to the Duke, "It will be done then. My beloved child will be taken from us in one way or another, but at least I will not go against her final will. So few get the chance in this life to know the true final will of the ones they cherish."

"My final will . . ." Claere said softly. "Yes, it is. And there is one other thing. The man who struck me this mortal blow . . . I must see him now."

"He will be executed tomorrow," said the Emperor fiercely. "The Fiomarre son will die as his father had before him, a traitor. Their family ends with him. His mother shall be stripped of their rank and the lands will be confiscated and absorbed into the Imperial Crown."

"No."

They looked at her.

"No," the Infanta repeated. "It is a portion of my final will that this man first come and speak with me, so that I can understand why he did this deed. Besides, you know he literally cannot die now. You can only ruin his body, with him still inhabiting it, a macabre horror that I beg you not to enact. Thus, instead, I must take the chance to understand him."

"What is there to understand, dear child? A horrible wicked traitor! He is an abomination and will be punished as befitting his crime. How can you even endure to look at him, the beast?" her mother said.

"And yet I must see him, if I am to have eternal peace," the Infanta repeated. "Please. . . . Now."

And with those words she turned around, turned her back on them all without being dismissed, heedless of Imperial protocol, and returned to her chair near the window.

Protocol did not apply to the dead.

Niobea stood at the bedside of old Bethesia, listening to her death rattle that had become the heartbeat of their home. A large basket filled with food and covered with a kerchief was sitting on the tabletop, next to a folded shawl.

It was the early dawning morning of the second day. The night before, Alann and Percy had come home in a rush with the news of the Royal Decree, and suddenly it all made sense. At least now Niobea knew why Bethesia was like this, why she was on the verge of going and yet would not leave the world.

Niobea also knew with a sickness that ate at her soul that she had to part with at least one of her daughters. The Decree left no doubt that someone of marriageable age had to go, and she would not be able to face the village if she withheld her daughters. All night they could hear the voices of their different neighbors and the sounds of weeping outside, as mothers grieved.

Alann had been of no help. After telling her what he learned, he gave Niobea one dark look of sorrow, then went to his mother's bedside and stayed there for several moments, then surprisingly went directly to bed.

Percy had stayed back in the room. After putting a kettle of water to boil she huddled in silence near the stove, watching Belle peel tubers for the next day's meal, and Patty sift old flour. They were all inordinately quiet after having heard the news.

"Well?" Niobea said suddenly addressing them all. "What is to be done with you, children?"

Silence.

And then, "I suppose I must go . . ." Belle said in a faint voice. Putting down the knife and the vegetables, she sat looking at her mother. "I am . . . the eldest and most marriageable."

Niobea stared at her fair oldest child and then her lips began to tremble, while liquid pooled in the corners of her eyes, blurring her vision.

"Ma?" said Patty. "Maybe—maybe I ought to go? I am young but, well, I think I am old enough to be a bride. . . ."

"No, what are you saying, idiot child? You are a little baby still, no! And may the Lord be praised for that!" Niobea exclaimed.

Percy looked at them all. She then threw a glance at her grandmother dying without end. And she glanced at the everpresent shadow in the corner.

And then she got up, and steeled her heart and her facial muscles. "It's all right. I'll go," she said in a dull voice. "Tomorrow morning."

There was silence.

And then Niobea looked at her middle daughter, and though tears still brimmed in her eyes, the pressure at the back of her throat lessened considerably. "Well, it's settled then," she said curtly.

And that was that.

Percy paused for a moment, because there might have been something else any one of them could have said to her at this point. But they did not. Neither Niobea nor Belle. Not even Patty. And Alann was in bed in the other room.

And so Percy muttered, "I'm going to bed now. So that I can get an early start."

Niobea had nodded then, and finally, as the girl was about to head to her corner, she said, "I'll pack you a basket."

It was the most she was going to get from Niobea. And the most that Niobea was able to give.

This morning however, Niobea, who had spent a sleepless night, got up in the pre-dawn dark and, tormented by pangs of guilt, put together a basket of their best, including all that was to be their dinner that coming day, two fresh loaves of oat bread, a jar of raspberry preserves, and a small bag of dried raisins that had been a precious gift from a distant relation earlier that autumn. She did not know what it was, why the guilt ate at her so much—but no, she did know very well. It was guilt at the relief that Percy had granted her, relief that she was not about to lose either one of her two favorites.

And then Niobea thought about something else and returned to her bedroom where Alann was sleeping like a dead man—or possibly pretending to be asleep—and she pulled out the trunk under their bed that contained her ancient yellowing lace, a few books, and all her treasures from the better days of her youth. There was a shawl there, woolen and fine-spun, yet thick and folded over, then sewn together in a double layer for warmth, one that she never used, considering it too fine for their present life.

But now, she knew exactly how it was to be used. Niobea sniffed the shawl one last time, drawing in the memories of the past with one moldy whiff of mothballs and violets and then folded it on her bed and replaced the chest underneath.

In the dark she took the shawl to the kitchen and left it lying next to the food basket. All the while, a few feet away Bethesia continued to breathe, making the horrible death rattle, as though to reassure Niobea that everything was indeed proceeding as it should.

When the milky grey dawn light started to seep in through the cracks in the drawn shutters, Percy rose from her narrow bed alongside the wall, near her sisters' beds. She had thought she would not sleep that night from the cold terror and emptiness that had gripped her as soon as she had announced her decision to go. But at some point in the darkness she had fallen into a deep bout of unconsciousness, so at least there was something.

But now she was fully awake; worms of worry and fear crawling through her empty stomach.

What had she volunteered for? This was insane! The realization struck her full-force in the morning, and she considered waking up Alann and Niobea and then falling down on the floor before them like a baby and just weeping and begging to be released from this. But the next instant she thought, then Belle would have to go in her stead, and how fair would that be? Nothing about any of this was fair. But because Percy was going to be missed least of all, for that alone it was her duty to go.

And so Percy steeled herself against the fear and instead took a deep breath, drawing in courage together with the morning chill. Then she went to use the chamberpot, washed her face from the bowl in the corner, and got dressed.

As she put on her usual clothing she thought of what she was about to *do*—go outside into the snow and just . . . keep walking. She had no idea where she was to go. She was certain that very soon she would tire and then freeze to death, probably this very night. Maybe that's what it meant to be a Cobweb Bride? Whatever it entailed, death was the key factor there, the one inevitable factor. Even if she was not the one eventually chosen, she would still very likely be subjected to the winter cold and the eventual death from exposure to the elements. . . .

Bethesia's death rattle breath intruded upon Percy's grim thoughts as she quietly moved about in the corner getting her socks and thick underpants and all her warmest clothing. As she listened to the breath, it occurred to her that she was doing it for grandma. She was going to relieve her of this unending agony, by God! And for Belle! She was doing it for Belle so that Belle could have a life and get married and have a family of her own. And she was doing it for her mother Niobea, so that she would not lose the two daughters she truly loved. And she was doing it for Alann, her father who would be proud of her in the end, proud that she did not live in vain, and that at least she *tried*. . . .

And then a sudden realization of crystalline clarity came to her—she could go through the motions and "die" out there in the cold, but she could not *die*, because death had stopped! No matter what was to happen, cold, starvation, hardship, she couldn't even die now! None of them could!

And for some reason this one insane thought made Percy

feel much better. She was, like the rest of the world, suspended in a bubble of life and thus *immortal*, at least for the moment.

What a strange dizzying thought. . . .

In the kitchen, Niobea was bustling with her back turned to her, the kettle had boiled, and a warm mug of apple cider-flavored bark tea sat on the table, waiting for her. Right next to it was a huge basket and a wonderful folded woolen shawl that Percy recognized vaguely as one of her mother's heirloom treasures.

"Good morning, child," Niobea said, with her back still turned. "There, it's all for your journey. The food should last for at least a week if you ration it out properly, and then, Lord knows if you might come upon an . . . inn or an eatery, or some kind soul with food to share."

"Ma!" Percy said in amazement, "I can't take your best shawl!"

Niobea turned to look at her. There was a look of intensity in her moist glistening eyes. "No daughter of mine is going out in public looking like a beggar," she said coldly. "The shawl's very warm, and you'll need it out there."

"Thank you, Ma . . ." Percy's voice became a whisper.

"Now, eat well, and be sure to drink that warm tea, child. Then we'll see you on your way . . ."

And so it was that Percy sat down to eat one of the heartiest breakfasts of her life, which included a whole egg scrambled with onions, potatoes crisp-fried with sunflower oil, a large crunchy pickle, and a warmed thick slice of bread slathered with butter and jam.

While Percy was eating, Belle had risen from her bed, followed by Patty and finally Alann. The two sisters stood with backs propped against the walls, as though trying to disappear into them outright, watching their third sister, while Alann stopped in the middle of the room, frowning.

Suddenly Belle began to cry. She then muttered, "I'm so sorry, Percy!" and ran off into her parents' room.

Patty too stood with quivering lips, watching Percy.

Percy swallowed another bite of eggs then said, "Stop it, Pat. Nothing to weep about, you just watch, I'll be back. There'll be a fancy noble maiden chosen as the Cobweb Bride, I'm sure, and the rest of us ordinary girls will get to go home."

At those words Patty broke down completely, became a mess of uncontrollable sobbing, and rushed out of the room after Belle.

"Daughter," said Alann suddenly. "You don't have to go. When was this decided, last night? Why wasn't I told?"

"You were abed," Niobea said. She had a peculiar expression on her face as she turned to her husband.

"It's all right, Pa," Percy said. It was getting to be easier and easier for her to insist on going, now that they were actually giving her reasons not to.

"I mean it, child!" Alann continued. "You are not obligated to do the duty that should fall, by all that's fair, to an older daughter."

"Alann!" Niobea exclaimed. Suddenly she looked agitated, and had dropped the cover of the pot she was handling. "It's already settled, say no more, I beg you!"

But Alann's frown only deepened and for once he stared directly back at his wife with intensity. "How was this settled, wife? Did you make her feel obligated to volunteer? Is that what you call settled?"

"How dare you!" Niobea's voice rose a notch.

"Ma, Pa, please!" Percy suddenly cut in. She then looked back and forth between her glaring parents. "Everything is fine, and I am going."

"Decree be damned, girl, you can stay here and let them all go to hell around us!" Alann said, his eyes reflecting the angry licking flames of the hearth fire.

How I love you, if only you knew, Pa, how much I love you. Now, of all times, your words give me joy. . . .

With a burst of hope and pride, Percy set down her spoon, emptied the dregs of her mug, and got up. And suddenly a smile broke out on her lips.

Alann and Niobea watched her, both stilled in a strange combination of horrified anticipation and remorse.

Percy went to get her overcoat and put it on in the quiet of the crackling firelight and the death-rattle music coming from her grandmother. She bent down, wrapped her feet in a second layer of socks and slipped her feet into the bulky woven snowshoes. Last of all she approached the table and took the shawl. With care and awe she unwrapped it, was assailed with a faint musty smell and the scent of flowers; and then she drew it over her head and wrapped it tight around her throat and tied the ends together.

The shawl draped itself with immediate luxurious warmth around her shoulders and reached all the way down her lower back and hips. It would serve her more than well as an extra protective layer against the cold wind.

Percy stood up straight, pulled her old mittens out of the coat pocket, drew them on, and then took hold of the heavy basket filled with food.

"I am ready," she said.

There was a pause.

Alann came up to her and took hold of her in a bear hug. He kissed her forehead and she felt the power and love in his arms and it gave her an extra resolve, added to her strength.

"May the Lord watch over you, child . . . my Persephone," her father said softly into her hair.

When Percy was finally released from the embrace, Niobea was holding the icon of the Mother of God. She took a step toward her middle daughter, and she raised the icon and held it near Percy's forehead.

"Bless you, child . . . Go with the Lord."

"Thank you, mother, father," said Percy. Suddenly there was the beginning familiar pressure at the back of her throat, a storm roiling to burst. And so, instead she turned her back on them quickly and went to the front door. She did not look back as she drew the bolt, opened the door and slipped outside into the world of cold grey dawn.

"Take this away. I am dead and have no more need of food," Duke Hoarfrost said to the servant who had brought in the morning tray up to his bedchamber. Usually he'd reach eagerly for the mug of strong tea and down it for the invigorating heat, the warmth, then begin on the toast and pungent herbed bacon. But now—

"Yes, M'Lord."

"When you are done, have my son attend me."

"Yes, M'Lord."

He barely turned his head to watch out of the corner of his stiff eye the movements of the man who bowed and began removing the service with an unreadable expression.

Hoarfrost was standing before the great window overlooking a vista of Northern forestland and just a slice of the Western hills in the distance that marked the edges of the Chidair holdings. The winter morning sky was grizzled and dull. Occasional black streaks of hunting hawks moved in silhouette against the vapid sky.

The night before they had returned to the Chidair Keep, a strange nightmarish army comprised of soldiers both humanly alive and no longer so—an army of men and living body parts. The cheers of the townswomen and children and the old men who greeted them soon turned to sobbing and cries of terror as they saw their loved ones returning in pieces or as walking corpses. As the day faded into twilight the wailing resounded non-stop, hushed only by the coming of the cold night and the snowfall.

But Hoarfrost continued hearing it, the music of winter and grief and passing. It filled his mind with dislocated pain and a confused jumble of thoughts. Even as he rode into the courtyard of his ancient family holding, followed by his subdued son and the remaining men of his retinue, the ghostly weeping echoed in the stones of the Keep, in the crowns of the evergreens growing alongside the road.

Later that night, he refused supper. And he did not sleep, of course. Bodily functions had ceased together with bodily needs; there was only the tedious sensation of imprisonment in this physical shape that no longer fully served him, no longer connected him via the senses to the world.

As the fire burned low in the fireplace of his bedchamber, he forced himself to bend, forced his stiff muscles to assume the proper shape, and then he sat down in the deep padded chair and watched the fading of the flames until the room was thrown into complete dark. He was not tired. It was merely simpler to sit than maintain the subtle balance to remain standing, for with the cessation of life in his tissues the interesting notion of physical balance became more relevant. Living bodies balanced naturally, automatically, while he had to make a specific effort, as though maintaining a juggling act with several separate weights—head, arms, legs, torso.

His bed remained untouched. His clothing, except for the outer armor, was still the same as the day before, decorated with drying bloodstains and torn in many places where the steel had entered his flesh. . . . Why bother removing it?

And he merely waited.

He waited, not sure for what, sitting there, knowing no drowsiness, no weariness—nothing, in fact, for his body had become a distant and thick layer of something between him and everything *else* around him. When dawn began to seep in past the shutters and the thick brocade curtain, he again made the supreme effort of straightening himself in order to rise. With measured steps he moved to the window, drew the curtains apart, opened the shutters, and just watched. . . .

He watched the coming of the light.

Beltain was awakened out of an abysmal deep sleep by the touch of a wide palm against his shoulder—gentle yet firm, and familiar. His old valet, Rivour, was shaking him lightly, whispering, "My Lord, very sorry to wake you, but your father wants to see you."

Beltain groaned, taking a deep waking breath, immediately feeling the post-battle soreness, the numerous bruises around his ribs, and the fierce sting of minor gashes and scratches that covered most of his body and face. Then, slowly he turned on his back in his warm large bed, moving carefully to stretch his muscled hands up past the coverlet. He flexed his battered swollen fingers with difficulty and pushed his dark brown hair out of his face.

"Damn . . . it's too early," he said hoarsely, yawning wide until something painful tugged at his jaw—another cut ending in a bruise. His brow gathered into a frown. And then, as the realization of everything came to him, "Oh, God . . ." he said.

Although he'd been weary to the bone, all sleep fled as his mind engaged, filled with clarity, and with it came terror. . . .

His father. His father was dead.

The battle. They were all dead, yet they were *not*.

He remembered everything—the fighting drawing to a close, the strange silence and then the ending of all that was ever normal with the world. He saw his father fall and *die* and then come back, a frozen creature of ice, breaking out of the lake, then coming to resume his command and riding home in the torch-light, their homecoming, the sounds of weeping all through town. . . .

Oh, God. . . .

Beltain sat up in bed, ignoring his injuries, swept his longish hair out of his face once more, then rested his face, its well-formed planes and lean angles, in his large hands and took in a shuddering breath, then smoothed his brow.

Rivour observed him with concern on his wrinkled face.

Another breath and Beltain pulled himself together. He turned the focused gaze of his slate-blue eyes to his friend and confidante of many years. There was enough resolve on his earnest face to push back the shadow of uncertainty that lurked in the background of his mind.

"How is . . . my father?" Beltain asked.

Rivour shook his head. "Hard to say, my Lord. He . . . speaks, moves. But—"

"But he is not exactly himself. I know."

"Is he . . . ?" The unfinished question hung in the air between them.

"I don't know," Beltain responded. "I don't understand any of this—deviltry or God's curse or whatever it is. But while he is able to command, it is my duty to obey him as a son."

"I understand, M'Lord." Rivour nodded, then proceeded to lay out fresh clothing.

"Ah, by Heaven, I wish there was time for a bath . . ." Beltain muttered as he rose from the bed, still wearing the same tattered and stained tunic and longjohns that had gone under his knight's armor the day before.

Rivour observed his condition and the fouled bed with distaste, and again shook his head. "A bath would indeed be appropriate. Why did you not call me last night to help you out of this?"

"I don't remember. . . . I think I came here and passed out. After all that happened."

"Ah. . . ."

Beltain used the chamberpot, then poured cold water from a pitcher and leaned over the basin in the corner to wash his face. As ice water came in contact with his sensitive skin, he grimaced and cursed.

"I'll call up a bath, you are in no condition to go anywhere," said Rivour.

"But if he expects me—"

"No matter. I'll come up with something to relay to His Grace, to stall him for an hour. For the moment you need a physician's attention and that bath."

And with those words Rivour exited the bedchamber in a hurry.

An hour later, after a brief soak in a tub of scalding-hot water, followed by the application of salve and bandages in many places over his body, Beltain was cleaned up, dressed in a comfortable shirt, jacket, and trousers worthy of a duke's son, and then made his way through the Keep to see his father.

"Where have you been, whelp?" Hoarfrost greeted him, the cheerful nature of his words marred by the wheezing measured sound they made and the accompanying strange mechanical rumble of his chest. Duke Ian Chidair stood before the window of his chamber, silhouetted against the bleak daylight. The air in the room was thick and heavy, and Beltain recognized a faint sweet scent of putrefaction.

"Forgive me, my Lord Father," Beltain replied as he took several controlled steps to approach him. "I came as fast as I could. My wounds—they needed to be cleaned—"

"Your wounds!" Hoarfrost roared.

And Beltain realized what he'd said and how it sounded . . . here and now. And so he bit his lip and remained quiet, while the Duke neared him, smelling of brackish lake water and old blood.

Hoarfrost slowly circled his son who stood looking straight ahead of himself, stiff as a post and taller than his bulky father by only half a head.

"Wounds, eh?" muttered the Duke, craning his neck only, while his face remained motionless and grey-white, and his eyeballs sat still in his eye-sockets like glass marbles.

"I am . . . sorry," whispered Beltain.

The dead face drew very close.

"Look at me, boy . . ." he hissed. "You see a dead man,

don't you?"

Silence.

And then, "I . . . don't know, my Lord."

"You lie!" exclaimed the animated corpse. "You always did lie poorly, which is a credit to you, my boy. But come now, don't be afraid of your own father now. . . . Am I dead to you?"

Beltain inhaled a shallow draft of the putrid air. "Yes . . . I believe you are dead. I saw you fall, Father, I was there. Yet somehow you are still here, just as all those other men who were struck mortal blows yesterday."

"Ah, yes. . . . What a riot it was. Ugly and treacherous. A true day of death, and yet. . . ." Hoarfrost slowly turned away from his son and again approached the window. "You know I cut him down first," he mused. "That knight of Goraque who then struck me in the back when I turned, thinking him done. He struck me. He should have been dead. The bloody whoreson killed me after he was killed already, killed and dead and—"

"I know," Beltain said. "I watched it happen. Forgive, my Lord, that I was only a span of a horselength too far from you to stop him. Forgive me. . . ."

"So, what am I then? What am I? A specter or a skeleton?"

Beltain lowered his gaze down to the level of his father's chest and waist, but now his eyes were taking in the grisly torn tunic and blood-clot stains and—he had to look away again, anywhere else, safe, anywhere.

"Well, whatever I am, I might be full of holes but at least I have all my limbs. Did you see some of those other poor bastards, coming home in pieces? Eh, did you see? Now, that's a real hell of a way to go, or should I say, *not* go."

"Is there something I can do for you now, Father, some way I can alleviate your . . . pain?"

Hoarfrost made a sound like a grunt, and more air escaping his chest added a polyphonic hiss. "There's no pain, boy. At least that's a blessing. No, nothing you can do for me anymore. I feel—if you can call it that—like a barrel filled with piss-flat beer. Just a weight of stone. Can't smell or taste anything, though I'm sure this body of mine's beginning to reek."

And then Hoarfrost expanded his chest and let out the air in a deep bass roar. Beltain almost jumped at the sound of it.

"Argh!" the Duke bellowed, then raised his hands squeezed in two fists to shoulder level and higher, moving stiffly until they were at the level of his head. And then he started to chuckle softly.

The chuckles became guffaws. Whistling with air, Hoarfrost laughed, while his son watched him in silent horror.

"I feel damned nothing!" Hoarfrost cried. "And now that I think about it, it's not a bad thing, to feel nothing! I like it! No gout, no back or gut ache, no battle bruises, no hunger, no thirst! Not even the smallest desire to rut with a wench!"

He turned to Beltain with a crooked broken attempt at a smile. His dark eyes burned with a strange stilled intensity in their sockets that somehow managed to be more frightening than anything else about him previously. "Well, boy, look at me, and tell me I don't cut a fine figure! Oh, and don't for a moment think that since I'm a reeking corpse you are the new Duke around here. Not so fast, whelp! For as long as I still move and can open my mouth to speak my will, you still owe me fealty."

Beltain raised an earnest gaze of wounded pride. "You are my Lord and Liege, Father! Have I ever not obeyed you? How can you doubt me! I swear I am yours now and always. I don't understand this, whatever has happened to you, to our men, but I know that when you speak, I will obey—for as long as you are able to command. I can have no claim while you are in this world."

"Ah . . . Good, boy, very good. In that case you and I have an excellent understanding. Indeed, you and I, yes—we're going to have a real time ahead of us, the time of our life, you might say. Because whatever this is, it makes us invincible. And you know what that means?"

Hoarfrost suddenly brought his fisted right hand forward and through the old glass of the window.

As the glass shattered, letting in the freezing cold winter air from the outside, Hoarfrost laughed, and then continued smashing his fist like a hammer against the razor shards.

Beltain watched his father with an unreadable expression.

Even without the outside air, the world had grown very cold.

Chapter 5

In the first bluish glimmer of dawn, Percy walked slowly down the narrow rutted street of Oarclaven, past neighbor houses. Her bulky well-wrapped feet crunched against the fresh powder of snow that covered the road with a deceptive blanket of smoothness. The basket of food made an uncomfortable weight in her mittened hand.

There were a number of neighbors who were also up and about at this early hour. She could hear voices coming from the shuttered windows and see thin slivers of light between the wood planks from breakfast hearth fires being lit. Smoking chimneys filled the cold air with pungency.

And then, as she turned the corner and approached the Doneil house where the worst of yesterday's excitement had taken place, there was Jenna Doneil. She was coming down their porch, wrapped up in many layers against the cold, carrying a small travel sack.

Percy paused momentarily, then raised her hand to wave at the girl.

Jenna looked up, froze for an instant, then hurried down their snow-covered front walkway to meet her on the road.

"Morning," Percy said, pausing to stand before the Doneil house. "You heading where I think you're heading?"

"Yeah . . ." Jenna nodded. "Pa and Ma say I have to go and be a Cobweb Bride, if he takes me. . . ."

"Yes, same here."

"I don't want to."

"Neither do I," said Percy. And then, added. "But, are you sure you're of an age to be a bride? How come you have to go? I thought you're a whole year younger than my little sis Patty."

Jenna raised her swaddled white face and there was a fierce expression in her eyes. "I am old enough," she said in a defiant twelve-year-old whisper, as though anyone from the house could hear her. "I got breasts already. Well, some. . . . And anyway, my parents think I'm old enough, cause Pa was gonna have me be promised to Jack Rosten's second son by spring so that they could get the bull and the two sheep."

"Oh, now that's a shame." Percy started walking again, and Jenna trailed after her, matching her strides. "The Rosten boys are trouble, aren't they? And the second son, what's his name?"

"Jules."

"Right, Jules. He's not that much older than you."

"He's gross. . . . And he has crooked buckteeth and he pulls my skirt and always pinches me here an' there. I'd rather die than go with him. But Pa says I have to. . . . And besides, I am afraid to stay in our house now, after yesterday—you know."

"I see," Percy said, thinking of the poor squealing pig from the night before and whatever happened to it, and indeed not daring to take that path of imagination any further. As they passed the main street there seemed to be a number of other girls and young women headed variously up the roads.

"Do you think they are all going to be Cobweb Brides?" Jenna said.

"I don't know. It's possible many of them are."

"Are you . . . I mean, do you know where . . ." Jenna began, then grew silent momentarily. "Do you know where you're supposed to, well . . . *go?*"

Percy turned her head to look at the girl at her side. She

pursed her winter-chapped lips, licked them to warm against the unrelenting dryness of the ice air. "We're supposed to head north, is what we're told. Into the Northern Forests. And then we look around for Death's Keep."

"How are we supposed to do that? What's it look like?"

Percy moved her basket over from one hand to the other to free up her hand closest to Jenna. She then took the younger girl's smaller mittened hand and gave it a squeeze. "I have no blasted idea," she said. "But how about you and I go looking together? You can walk along with me all the way, and we won't get lost."

Jenna's face beamed, and she turned to look up at Percy. "Oh, can I? Because I don't know if I can figure out this north any farther than the next town. Pa says it's right if I go east on the big road toward Tussecan. But after Tussecan there's just the one fork in the road and then I don't know. . . . And I don't even know Tussecan all that well, I only been there twice."

"After Tussecan we can ask the locals. We'll figure it out," Percy replied.

"Thanks for being nice to me, Percy . . ." Jenna whispered. "Everyone always says I am daft or feeble or skittish-crazy and jump around too much. I am no good, except to help Pa when he butchers. . . . But—"

"Well, now you can help me," said Percy with a smile. "I wasn't looking forward to walking alone, and this way neither of us will be scared. Right?"

"Right!"

"And probably neither one of us will get picked as a Cobweb Bride, so we can walk back home together too."

Jenna nodded and her posture relaxed visibly.

They continued walking, following the turns of the road heading east through town. As the day grew lighter, Oarclaven came alive, and Percy waved to familiar people who waved back. The mood was somber however, and smiles came uneasy or not at all. Seemed peculiar to think about it now, in the light of day, but only last night there had been the weeping and the panic as the young women ran and hid or else entreated their families to be spared the grim fate. . . .

"Percy?" Jenna said as they passed the Murel bakery where the strong warm aroma of fresh bread poured forth like fairy joy on the blistering wind. "What if we just ran away? Instead of going to the Northern Forests, I mean. Who's to know?"

"Hmm . . ." Percy replied, as they paused momentarily to watch the baker's daughters set out fresh golden crusty loaves on the display at the windowsill. She noticed that Flor, the eldest, was moving about with red-rimmed eyes and not even bothering to wipe her flour-dusted face or hands on the apron as she laid out the flaky pastries on the lacy doilies. For a moment she looked up and a desolate face met Percy's. She nodded in greeting, then cast her gaze down and resumed her work.

"I think Flor Murel's been told to go too," Percy said quietly. "Probably has to finish up her morning chores first, then, if she walks fast, she might even catch up to us on the road."

"Percy!" Jenna was tugging her arm.

"What?"

"Let's not go north, Percy, please!" Jenna started whispering. "We can just turn around and go roundabout but the other way! We can go down to Letheburg instead! I never been to Letheburg, and they say the Royal Palace there is so grand, like a whole ten houses! We can stay there, and maybe find a place to live? And we can eat pastries and never have to worry about anything, and we don't have to go looking for any old stupid Death—"

"Hmm . . ." said Percy again. "That does sound like a fine idea, especially in your case. You're a young one and shouldn't be involved in this mess. Maybe you really ought to head to Letheburg. But for me—let me think here for a moment. . . ."

She walked about ten paces, looking very much deep in thought, while Jenna threw anxious glances at her and occasionally rubbed her frosted pink nose with her mittens.

"Here's the thing," Percy said. "You know how Death has made it that nobody dies until he gets his Cobweb Bride, right? And my Gran Bethesia's been on the verge of going for a long time now, but she cannot. And she's suffering. And then there are all those other people who should be dead but aren't. And the animals too, I bet. . . . So, unless I at least *try* to do something to help them, all these people—and animals—may never get their blessed rest. Who knows what's a person's fate in this world? Maybe one is meant to try. Or—I can only speak for myself. It would sure be nice to just run away and hide out while all this is happening. But I know I can't just abandon Gran and let some other people do the hard work to put things right with the world."

Percy glanced at Jenna at that point, to gauge her reaction.

Jenna was frowning, as though she hadn't properly thought about it. "The animals too . . ." she muttered.

"Yes. The ones that got hurt and now cannot pass on."

"Then . . ." Jenna whispered, her face intense, "we probably better not run away."

Percy nodded. "That's what I'm thinking too. It's just something that has to be done. And—I don't know about you, but when the time comes for my soul to face the final reckoning, whatever it is, I'd go with a lighter conscience, knowing I haven't run away from something that was mine to do."

"We'll go on to Tussecan," Jenna said.

"Now . . . you're sure? You could turn around and head back right now. I probably ought to insist you do. It's not right for a little girl—"

"I am *not* a little girl!" Jenna sputtered.

And she did not say anything else for the rest of the hour, as they made it to the outskirts of town and began walking on the wide mostly empty road that became a thoroughfare.

The world was white and grey, with occasional spots of

black that were tree trunks or dots of hunter birds crossing
overhead. At times the shadow-flitter that was a red robin or a
crested cardinal burned fiercely in the branches. The shoulders
of the road were fringed with large snowdrifts over pasture and
occasional fields, with sparse evergreens on either side. Now and
then a cart clattered past them from either direction and they
would stand aside to let it pass. But it was not a good idea to
stop for too long, else the cold got to them.

In the winter you had to keep moving, Percy knew. Even
though they were bundled well and still reasonably warm, and
the sun was still rising out there somewhere in the dull morning
sky, the wind continued being sharp.

And as the hours passed and the day advanced, she knew it
would only get worse.

Vlau Fiomarre stood in the royal bedchamber before Her
Imperial Highness, the Infanta Claere Liguon. He had been
brought in rusted shackles from the dark and winter-cold holding
cell down in the bowels of the Palace. There he had spent the
night in absolute darkness chained by the wrists to the freezing
stone wall, his face swollen with the beating, his elegant court
clothing befouled and his jacket torn by the handling of the
guards.

And now even the faded daylight seemed too glaring for his
sensitized eyes.

Or maybe it was merely the sight of her. . . .

He had *killed* her.

And yet, here she sat, the accursed Liguon whelp, before a
window in this chamber. She was still wearing her court dress
from the night before, stained deep red-black with the blood
from the mortal injury he had inflicted upon her shallow breast.
On her head, the elaborate silver-platinum wig, and on top, the
bejewelled Crown. Her chest, waist, that of a wooden doll, a
mere twig. Her neck—

A surge of cold familiar hatred washed over him as he

remembered the intense focused moment of no return—pulling out his concealed dagger and striking her underneath her tiny rudimentary bud of a breast on the left side, directly in the heart.

In that instant the two of them became a single point, the center of all—swept inward into one thing by the centripetal nature of the connection, in the middle of the glittering Silver Hall, surrounded by the grandest court in history of the Realm. He remembered the feel of his knife going in. Just a slight resistance. . . . Saw the precise moment of the emergence of the deep crimson stain, at the same time as he glanced up momentarily and was fixed, branded, with a look of her suddenly dilated eyes—two great, deep, smoky things.

It touched him, just for that one instant, her dark strange innocent purity of pain.

And then the world twisted, narrowed in a funnel, drew in even closer, until he could see the dust motes in the air and there was a roar they made, swirling . . . everything coming at him, filling his ears.

It was then he felt a fierce triumph, and a culmination of himself—his life, his next breath, nothing mattered now; he was done. A life for a life; his tragedy-consumed family at last avenged.

The screams in the Hall, the sudden tumult and chaos of rushing figures converging upon the Infanta as she must have collapsed—though he could never quite see, nor did he care—pounding agony of blows upon his face, his chest, his ribs, his back, guards grappling him down onto the floor as he struggled in fierce exultation, not because he had any hopes or notion of escape but because struggle he must; it was the only thing left to him, to go out like a firecracker, a comet of fury, an angel of final judgment.

And then, through it all, her heard her voice.

"Why?" she had asked him, as she stood upright somehow.

And he, maddened by the intensity of the moment,

screamed insanities and his fury upon her, screamed things he could not recall now, something about death to the Liguon, Death to the Deceiver and his filthy line. The words came forth from him as gushing blood had come from her to stain the mirror-polished parquet floor.

"Why?" she had said. "What have I done to you?"

What had she done? What had the Imperial Crown done to his tortured blameless father who had remained loyal to the last? To his destroyed mother, to him and his brothers and sister? The stupefying horror of the things he could say now; they would pour out of him like black blood, in anguish. . . .

But no—his only reply again was a raving epithet devoid of substance. "Die, Liguon!"

And then, as the guards moved in to execute him on the spot, she stopped them with a sudden strange pronouncement. "No."

Do not yet kill this man as he had tried to kill me. I must know why he did this thing, why he hates me so. He must live until I know, she had said. And then she had faltered.

And she still *lived*.

Had his blow missed its sure and easy target, her heart, somehow? Or was she merely on her last breath, and was about to expire on the next?

And yet, others heard the enduring quality of her voice too. And the reaction of the court followed. He could no longer see any of it, forced down on his knees, then flat on the floor, cruelly pressed against the parquet by several booted feet, with his arms nearly wrenched out of their sockets from the back. But he could hear. And what he heard was a gradual terrible silence coming to the Hall, as waves and murmurs of voices faded, even the sobbing and moans of grief.

There was another moment of sudden activity, as physicians had come in full force, and through it all, yes, she still *lived*.

Then he heard a splatter of liquid hitting the floor.

A lot of liquid.

There was more sound, more silence, barely hushed exclamations of unrepressed shock.

And then he heard her voice again, living, clear, resonant in grand echoes through the Silver Hall—if such a thing were possible, a voice stronger now, more confident than it had been before—even though it was no louder than a stage whisper.

"I will see the Birthday Gifts now."

And after that he remembered nothing more, only the smooth impersonal chill of the floor, ringing footsteps of Palace guards, the vertigo of being dragged for a long time, and then cold darkness.

That was last night. . . .

And now, here he was, wrenched out of the non-life of the prison, and brought before her, facing her once more.

And she was still alive.

Impossibly unbelievably *alive*.

Or was she?

There was something undefinable, peculiar about the way the Infanta sat, half in shadow, half-silhouetted by the dim light of the winter day outside. Like a collapsed puppet. A doll propped up by an invisible something from the back.

And then she slowly turned her face to him.

"Leave him," she said to the two guards on both sides of him. Her intonation had the strange manner of rusty machinery.

And when the guards hesitated, she repeated, "Leave him here, with me. There is nothing more he can do to me now. No more . . . harm. Now, leave us."

The guards bowed, then retreated in grim silence, closing the chamber doors behind them. There was no one else indeed in the room with them. Only the killer and his victim.

Fiomarre stared at her. He stood, swaying slightly, lightheaded from his injuries, from the hunger and the cold. And he felt stupid somehow. Insane thoughts slipped in, taunted him.

What impossible luck was his once again! The fools left him alone with the Liguon! He should make another attempt at her life, he should do something, something. . . .

Instead he asked in a hoarse voice, "What does that mean, 'no more harm?'"

"I am dead," she replied simply. "You killed me."

He continued to stare, stupidly, but now he was also freezing ice-cold. His head—it was cold, and the cold rose in him, squeezing at his temples.

"I . . . don't understand," he said.

"Neither do I."

"My dagger struck you in the heart!"

Her smoky sorrowful eyes watched him. "Yes. And my heart no longer beats. Your aim was true."

The look of horror on his face was unspeakable. If his hands had been free, he would have made a sign of the cross to ward himself.

After a long pause, he muttered, "Then it's true, the Liguon are indeed unholy spawn of the devil. . . . What are you? If you cannot die, what abomination makes you linger?"

But the Infanta continued to look at him. Her gaze, so glassy, yet intensely focused. As though she could use her will only to control one aspect of her body at a time.

"Why?" she said suddenly, repeating the same question that he had never answered. "Why do you hate us so? What has the Imperial Crown done to you . . . and yours? Tell me . . . please."

Her words were gentle.

And it was the gentleness that suddenly touched him as nothing else had. A horrible impossible moment of remorse flickered on the surface of his thoughts. Here was the only daughter of his enemy—he had rid the world of the Imperial line, he was sure—and she was no different from her father whose hatred had destroyed Fiomarre. . . .

And yet. . . .

And for a moment only, watching her, seeing an undeniable

shadow of innocence, his own chest constricted with a sensation of grave error, an error of judgment.

But he willed himself past it, past the pathetic weakness of remorse—for he knew he was merely a man, not a murderer, and it was but the natural revulsion at the act of killing in cold blood, no matter how well justified, that now haunted him.

Something haunted him.

And so, to deny this weakness, he snarled at her, his words like a multitude of daggers hurled to riddle her chest with more intangible wounds. "Why not ask your Imperial Father, *Your Imperial Highness?*" His sarcastic emphasis on her title was deliberate, venomous.

But she did not react to his tone. "Why not tell me yourself?" she said mildly. "After what you did to me, do you not owe me at least a reason why?"

"I owe you nothing, Liguon bitch!"

For the first time her eyelids flickered in almost living reflex, as though attempting to blink away his epithet as something tangible that struck her.

"If you are—or had been until your traitorous act of last night—a Peer of the Realm, then you owe me the allegiance of loyalty, *Marquis* Fiomarre." As she spoke, her peculiar stilted breathing—akin to furnace bellows, it occurred to him in that moment—managed to enhance her voice so that it rose and echoed in the chamber. "And if I or the Imperial Crown have done something to no longer warrant your loyalty, then it is your duty to speak the truth, to explain yourself—if not before man then before God!"

Her words ended as abruptly as they began, and her chest and lungs stopped moving, returning into their neutral suspended state. But their shocking power still resounded in silent waves through him.

"You know my name?" he said. A stupid thing to say, stupid. . . .

"I know it now. Would you not make the effort to find out the name of someone who hates you to the point of death?"

He frowned, his mind in a tumult.

"Well, then," she continued. "Marquis, you will speak now. Enough righteous posturing. Tell me what has brought you to this hatred. For you and I are both in a situation of impossibility, and yet we may consider it an act of providence, an impossible fortunate opportunity to go beyond the limits of life and death."

Despite the Infanta's stilled face the expression of her eyes was *alive*, was burning.

And prompted by the nature of her expression, by the impossibility indeed of their situation, Fiomarre told her.

"My Lord, Father!" Beltain said in a loud voice that was at the same time carefully controlled and devoid of emotion.

He entered the Duke's chambers in a brisk walk, holding himself well and with an upright military bearing. He had no doubt he had successfully concealed the severe pain and the pulling stiffness of his muscles, still sore and aching all over. Yet the effort cost him, for his face remained a fixed mask, with hollows that sank deeper than usual between his elegant cheekbones and angular jaw.

"Forgive me for entering unannounced, Father, but I have news. Important news and an explanation at last—an explanation of what is happening!"

"And what is happening, boy?" said Hoarfrost. He was seated at a large mahogany table with a well-worn polished surface on which were spread out armies of miniature painted soldiers in formation. With one hand he was arranging several tiny figures in a double marching line, two abreast. His face was averted, so that Beltain could only see the back of his head, the terrifying matted tangle of hair, bits of lake weed, and clotted old blood. . . . He was never going to change out of that filthy torn blue surcoat, damaged hauberk, and undershirt of his, nor clean himself up. . . . What was the point?

The reek in the room had not increased, because of the one partially broken window, the missing glass of which allowed wintry air to enter and vent the worst of the stench. It also allowed small flurries of snow to pile near the windowpane and swirl in eddies deeper into the room.

It was infernally cold here. Not a living man's proper quarters.

Yet Beltain preferred this biting late afternoon cold to the stench of death.

Taking a deep breath of cold, he related the news of the Royal Decree that the King's Herald had proclaimed in town. A copy of the same Decree was now in his hand, crisp rolled parchment, with the seal of the Kingdom of Lethe, meant for the Duke's own eyes.

Beltain offered the parchment to his father.

Hoarfrost had listened to the explanation with a blank face, and an occasional shifting of his stance in the chair, moving his upright back for better balance. He did not blink, hearing of Death halting all acts of dying in the world until a Cobweb Bride is found. But when he heard of the Royal urging—nay, order and command—to all maidens of marriageable age, at least one per family, to make way to the Northern Forests in search of Death's Keep, then Hoarfrost reacted.

"So! A missing Cobweb Bride is the reason I'm still here in this mortal coil, eh?" he said, with a whistling hiss-intake and exhalation of air in his pierced chest.

And as Beltain watched him, the parchment still held in a proffered hand, Hoarfrost began to laugh.

Duke Ian Chidair shook like a great hollowed log, gasping spurts of air in chuckles, then followed up with a deep roar.

"A Cobweb Bride!" he bellowed. "He wants his Cobweb Bride! Well, damn him to hell and back again, but he will not have her!"

Beltain stilled to the point of holding his breath.

"And who's this Cobweb Bride anyway?" Hoarfrost continued, wheezing with chuckles. "Is she a fine bit of skirt, a young lusty woman of flesh and blood, with a solid pair of tits a man can hold on to, and a healthy rump to fondle? Or is she a monstrosity like myself, dead but not quite? And in either case, what does Death, that cold bastard, intend to do with her? Wed and bed her? Beget little dead whelps, eh? What kind of bloody idiocy is this?"

"She . . . could be anyone," Beltain said, holding back his facial muscles from moving into a frown. "The Royal Decree urges all marriageable women who might possibly fit the position to—"

"Enough! I got the gist the first time you said it. I might be dead but I'm not deaf, boy! Now, let me see that." And Hoarfrost grabbed the parchment out of his son's hand.

Beltain watched as his father's large, bloodless-grey hands with stiff thick fingers, torn fingernails and clotted dirt worked slowly to unroll the Decree. Another time he would have offered to assist, since Ian Chidair was ever clumsy with implements of the scribe's art, loath to hold quill-pen and paper. But now he stayed back, letting the Duke do it himself.

Hoarfrost perused the Decree, then made a spitting noise, and crumpled the parchment with one great meaty fist. "What does Lethe think I will do, comply with this idiocy, this drivel? Osenni is daft if he thinks I'll give up this miracle of immortality and invincibility, this divine grace that has befallen me! Or, he's a cow himself if he believes that I'd order my women and their girls to go to their deaths or on some wild goose chase, just so that the rest of the poor murdered fools and myself would get to croak. Hah!" And he banged the table so that some of the miniature soldiers scattered like colorful chips of wood.

"But—" said Beltain. "I don't think I understand, Father. Wouldn't it be the right thing to do, to humor Death's request?"

Hoarfrost's dark eyes seemed to move into a sharp focus,

and he trained the heavy gaze of them on his son. "What? You want me to *die*, boy? Are you, my own son, my flesh and blood, telling me you want me dead and gone?"

"Not gone, never that! But I want—whatever is right. This is not natural, my Lord. It should be the way things had been . . . before."

"Natural be damned!" Hoarfrost's petrified face was full of unrelieved anger like a rattle filled with sand that would not look any different on the surface no matter how much you shook it. "What's natural for a man in his prime to be sent to kingdom come from a cowardly strike in the back? I should've lived! I killed him first, in fair combat facing him squarely, and he was down. And then he came at me! What's right about that, eh? If Death hadn't decided suddenly he had an itch in his damned cold prick for a Bride, I'd still be alive now, a real man with warm blood in me! So then, I demand my time given back to me! And I will not give up what is mine, not ever again!"

Duke Ian Chidair paused, growing momentarily silent, while from the outside a strong gust of winter wind entered the icy chamber, pulling at his face, his hair, moving frozen filaments. . . .

"Cold . . ." he said then, turning his neck with an audible creak in order to turn his face to the window, speaking in a soft voice. Now that he spoke at a low volume, his chest's whistling came more pronounced in the quiet. "I am cold, yes . . . and I don't know it, don't feel. It's like I am already on the other side, seeing this world through a thick barrier. White as snow and thick as cotton. But . . . at least I am still here, even in part. Because what awaits me over *there* could be even colder. Death's cold. I cannot . . . cannot bear to know. Not yet. . . . Not ever."

"My father . . ." Beltain said. "If only I could give myself up in your stead. I am so sorry."

Hoarfrost looked around, back at his son. "Nonsense, boy,"

he said in a once more loud voice. "Your life is yours, and you should hold on to it as well as you can—while you can. And, don't be sorry for me. Because, my loyal whelp, I am not going anywhere! You hear that? And you, you hear, Death, you old ugly whoreson? You will not have me!"

"What will happen?" Beltain said.

There was a very terrible pause as something, like mechanical gears, went into play; it pulled at the Duke's frozen mask of a face, molded it into a perverse semblance of something that a living man would do naturally.

Hoarfrost smiled.

"I'll tell you what. We're going to have us a little war, a bit of military fun on Lethe's behalf. Why, we'll go patrolling the Northern Forests and catch us some pretty girls! That's what we'll do! Not a single one will get through, or I'm a lying sonofabitch!"

And as Beltain stared, knowing on some level that his father did not mean it, was only verbally baiting him, Hoarfrost roared, "By God and the Devil, It's hunting time! The season to snag me a ripe and willing Cobweb Bride!"

Chapter 6

There were few things more unbearable, Percy thought, than having to trudge in the winter snow along a rutted road between towns, in the middle of nowhere, holding a heavy basket, headed to one's certain freezing death—and having to listen to Jenna Doneil's teeny, slightly flat voice singing the same damn verse of a "song" she made up, over and over, for the last several miles.

"Cobweb Bride, Cobweb Bride!
Come and lie by my side!"

And again:

"Cobweb Bride, Cobweb Bride!
Come and lie by my side!"

And then, repeat this every two beats per measure, taking a step per beat, and occasionally skipping and hopping like a bunny rabbit, in-between the verses.

Lord, if you hear me, take me now.

And failing that, Death, if you hear me, and I am your Cobweb Bride, now would be a good time.

The road stretched and curved occasionally, around bends and up small hillocks, so that they had to make the extra effort to walk on an incline, their breaths coming in curls of white vapor in the cold air. At such times Jenna would forget her song and trudge uphill, but still with a sprightly bounce in her walk. Percy meanwhile followed her less exuberantly and in secret relief at the temporary silence.

She didn't have the heart to tell the child to hush—it was a good thing Jenna was in such high spirits, early in the journey. Very likely she had no true understanding of what potential difficulties lay ahead of them.

The first of such difficulties was looming fast. They would have to stop and rest at some point. Have a bite to eat. Answer the call of nature. But where, and how? It was not a good time or place to stop and sit around in the snow. And as the day advanced, there would be a further decrease in temperature and a hardening in the wind, even a possible blizzard. Already the sky looked angry grey up around the edges where darker monochromatic clouds moved in. By the time it got dark, there would be some ugly winter weather. And they were still more than halfway from the nearest town of Tussecan.

Percy considered how to gently suggest to Jenna that they should walk faster without alarming the girl.

Another possibility was to hitch a ride to town with some kind stranger. Only, for the last hour of walking they had seen almost no one else on the road—a very occasional bundled figure of a shabby homeless straggler, or a clattering donkey cart often rigged on sleds, whose driver did not look altogether friendly. In fact, being wary of possible dangers of another kind, Percy made sure they stayed well away from the road or even concealed themselves behind trees for most of the passerby traffic.

"Percy!" said Jenna all of a sudden, as they carefully came down an icy incline. "I'm cold . . . and I kind of need to pee."

Percy stopped.

"All right . . ." she said. "Let's see, hmm . . . All right, let's walk a little bit more until we see a thicker roadside hedge."

"All right," Jenna said, echoing her. And they continued for about a quarter of a mile until there was sufficient growth alongside the road that could properly conceal a person.

"Go on behind that one. And I'll stand here and watch the road," Percy said.

"You promise you won't go away and leave me here, Percy? Promise!" said the girl in a sudden intense voice. The expression of her eyes was startling in its vulnerability.

Percy pretended not to notice and shook her head with a teasing half-smile. "What kind of ninny do you take me for? We need to stick together. I'd be very afraid to go off on my own, to be all alone, especially now, so of course I won't go away. I need you, silly."

"Oh . . ." said Jenna, and apparently reassured, clambered behind a snowed-over hedge.

Percy stood in place, stomping her feet to keep moving, glancing around at the overbearing whiteness of the snowscape around them. She considered if maybe now was a good time to open the basket and see what was there to munch on. Except, she was really loath to remove her relatively warm mittens and dig around in there with fingers that would become icy in no time.

On the other hand, her stomach was rumbling, it was past midday mealtime, and eating would be something that can warm a person up—she remembered hearing this somewhere.

"Oh, confound it . . . *fire* is something that can warm you up," she muttered to herself out-loud. "Fire, we need warmth and fire. . . ."

"Huh?" came Jenna's voice from the hedge. "Did you say something? You're not leaving, are you? I'm almost done, please, I'm coming out!"

"Take your time," replied Percy.

At that point she heard the rumbling clatter of yet another

cart coming on the road from behind them, and the sound of several boisterous voices. It was coming from back where they had come from, Oarclaven.

Percy considered dashing behind the hedge, but in that moment Jenna appeared, straightening her skirts and patting down her kerchief. "All done," she said brightly, then skipped and hopped in place, thumping down the snow with her thick wrapped shoes.

The cart was slow-moving. Percy watched it come rolling from the distance, driven by a single large draft horse, and there were figures walking on either sides. They were all heavily bundled, and from the looks of it, all were wearing skirts.

As they approached, Percy and Jenna heard laughter and many female voices, chattering. What in the world? The cart was filled with young women. At least six were piled inside, their kerchiefs and hats clustered together from the distance and blending in like a bunch of brightly colored mushroom caps. Two more walked next to the cart.

When the cart was close enough to distinguish faces, the women suddenly started to wave and scream at Percy and Jenna in a sort of hysterical giggly chorus that only a bunch of barely pubescent girls could manage when they gathered together and things got too rowdy and fun.

"Oh, look!" Jenna said, perking up. "There's Flor!"

And indeed, there was Flor Murel, Oarclaven's best baker's eldest daughter, a bright red shawl over her blond hair and dark coat, her bundled feet dangling from the cart, waving at them.

"Hey, Percy! Look, everyone, that's Pur-seh-pho-neee Ayren! And Jenna! Jenna Doneil! Hellooooh there, Percy!" she exclaimed, her fine-featured, pretty face flushed and rosy, and not a sign of the redness of tears around her eyes that they had seen on her earlier this morning through the bakery window.

The rest of the young women picked up the yelling and there were even whistling and catcalls. As Percy and Jenna stared in amazement, the cart slowed down, and the driver—a slightly older woman bundled in a very dirty-looking, ragged, brightly multi-colored woolen kerchief—pulled up at the reins, saying "Whoa, Betsy!"

The great wheat-and-cream colored horse obeyed, and the cart came to a full stop only a couple of feet away from Percy and Jenna.

"Hello there, girls!" the woman driver said in a deep sonorous voice that immediately made Percy feel right at home. "Where are the two of you headed on such a cold day?"

Percy opened her mouth to reply, but once again Jenna was there first.

"We're looking for Death in his Keep! And we're gonna be Cobweb Brides!" Jenna exclaimed with the same level of cheer that someone would use to announce an outing to a fair to buy caramel apples.

"Oh, you are, are you?" said the woman, and her very dark eyes held a twinkle of amusement. "Well isn't that a lucky coincidence, girls, because so are we! Cobweb Brides, the whole lot of us—myself excluded, of course, I'm just an old bag, here along for the ride. I'm Grial, by the way, from Letheburg. This here is my cart and my horse Betsy—never mind, yes, I know the name's a bit odd and not very horsey at all—not Grial but Betsy I'm talking about—but she thinks she's a cow and that's her name, she tells me, so what can you do?—and so anyway, I'm just giving a ride to a couple of nice young ladies, and picking up some stragglers on the way. Do you realize that the road from Letheburg to here is practically crawling with all of you Cobweb Brides? Honest to goodness, you appear to be more plentiful than roaches. Much prettier than roaches, too, in most cases, I dare say—though it being winter and darn chilly, there aren't that many roaches running out in the snow, so a person cannot properly compare. Now, if you ask me, those little pests are far smarter than you'n me. When it gets cold they naturally scamper off into warm hidey holes near chimneys and—"

Percy listened to the rolling flow of the woman's words and felt a blooming of some kind of warm, comfortable feeling rise in her, so that for a moment she forgot the biting cold.

"But you know, I do tend to carry on a tad too much, till the cows come home and roost, or would that be chickens?" Grial said. "And so, let me ask you this, girls. Are you by any chance interested in traveling the rest of the way with us? The cart's got room enough for most of you, and the rest can take turns walking beside it. We have plenty of food between all of us, and what better way to keep warm than huddle together in a nice pile of hay? So, what do you say?"

"Thank you, Ma'am, for your very kind offer," Percy said. "I think it would be very nice, and I think we'd like that very much. Isn't that right, Jenna?"

"Yes, Ma'am!" the girl exclaimed.

"Ah, wonderful!" Grial said, then turned around and motioned to the women in the cart. "All right, ladies, how about two of you hop on out and let these two poor dears have a chance to rest their feet for a couple of miles? We're on rotation here, all proper and regimental. . . ."

And as two of the women started to scramble from their places in the cart, Grial turned again and said to Percy, "So, how long have you been walking now? Don't tell me you've made it on foot all the way from that last town—what was its name, Oarclaven?"

"Yes, Ma'am, we have," Percy replied, as she pushed Jenna up into the cart right next to Flor and then got in beside a thick-set girl with thoughtful grey eyes, in a plain brown wool coat and black shawl, whom she recognized also as a local from their parts. Her name was Gloria Libbin and she was the daughter of the town blacksmith.

"Hi, Percy . . ." Gloria said shyly. She was always a quiet one, and Percy didn't know her all that well. However she smiled in reply.

"Hi, and very nice to meet you, I'm Lizabette Crowlé," said

another young woman from behind them, with a pretty, slightly sharp-nosed oval face, sitting deeper inside the cart, dressed in a nice burgundy coat with proper buttons, and an almost stylish mauve hat. "That's Crowlé with an accented 'e.'" At which point the other remaining girl in the cart giggled and rolled her eyes. This last one appeared younger than all of them—indeed, not too much older than Jenna—with a round face, a blunt up-turned nose, and tufts of brown hair visible underneath her multi-colored woolen kerchief that she wore over a dirty-yellow coat.

"Hi, Percy, I'm Emilie, 'an there's no accented 'e' or nuthin' in my name, and my surname is Bordon. Pleased to meet you, my Pa is a swine breeder'n'herd down south, we're not fancy folk. Oh, and hi, Jenna!"

The four girls walking beside the cart introduced themselves one by one. One of the two who had given up their seats to Jenna and Percy was Regata, a tall younger daughter of a Letheburg merchant, with a friendly unpresuming face, dressed in a warm-looking coat of forest green, with dark brown fur trim along the collar, and a cape-hoodlet on top, also fur-trimmed, with a fine linen kerchief underneath. The other one to vacate her seat on their behalf was Sibyl, the kind-faced daughter of a tailor also from Letheburg, with lively eyes, the pale freckled skin and ginger brows of a redhead, and wearing a well-cut royal blue coat and hood, and a woolen mulberry scarf.

The remaining two girls who had been walking all along were Niosta and Catrine, two sisters from somewhere even farther down south than Letheburg; they didn't say where and really weren't all that sure. They were both heavily freckled and gawky-thin, their faces smudged, with weather-beaten tanned skin, and their expressions snide and street-smart. Their clothing consisted of worn flimsy footwear, drab wool coats with many tears, revealing in places the underneath-layers of homespun of indeterminate swamp-brown hues, and faded shawls that had seen better days and had holes worn to prove it. They frequently exchanged knowing glances, and gave Percy and Jenna some no-nonsense hard stares.

"All right, ladies, are we all ready to move on?" Grial said loudly. "Then we advance onward, I say! All men to the deck, starboard and portside! That is, all ye flaming cabinboys to the poop! Or is it legionnaires right foot forward and hold on to yer kilts? Oh, never mind! Whoa, Betsy!"

The Infanta watched with unblinking attention the strange hate-filled man who was the Marquis Vlau Fiomarre tell a peculiar story of grievances that made no sense to her, for they did not match any known history of this Realm.

"Fiomarre," he said, turning his scalding dark gaze upon her. "We are—or, have been—if not the most ancient, loyal, true, then surely one of the five such fundamentally noble families in the Kingdom of Styx, and rivaling any other in the Realm. And yet, through the cruel impossible whim of the Liguon Emperor, your illustrious damned father, we are destroyed. . . ."

This Fiomarre was a striking sight to behold, tall and proud of bearing despite his prison-mauled clothing, the bruises on his serious, once-handsome face lending an enhanced air of nobility to his deep fierce tone of voice. He might have been misguided but appeared earnest and somehow wild.

And his eyes—they were dark and horrible.

Although the Infanta felt nothing in actuality—saw the world as though the light and all things contained in it came to her from a hazy distance of thick layers of cotton—she could still experience a twinge of *something*, a last vestige of living curiosity that surfaced past the thick dullness of apathy.

He had killed her.

As she watched his eyes, she remembered over and over that terrible focused moment of sensory awakening, for there could be no other words for it, an awakening before oblivion.

That night, as she had sat on her silver chair in the center of the great Hall, trembling with her usual anemic malaise and exhaustion, listening in all effort of politeness to the endless drone of congratulations, growing dizzy with the visual and auditory assault, she felt herself beginning to disappear. . . . There had been snatches of color, bejeweled fabric, powder glittering on wigs, the stifling weight of her own wig and the Crown, voices raised, smiling faces of nobility as they bowed before her, knelt, leaned, nodded, lips moving like flapping marionettes. . . . And suddenly, there *he* was. He stood out from the rest of the carousel in her vision by the nature of his stillness. For he was motionless, next in the greeting line after some fluttering satin figure of a retreating countess.

He just stood there. He never bowed. Even before he had taken out the knife, she remembered a strangely invigorating second of sight—the sight of his intense, impossible dark eyes.

And then he moved forward, and there was an elongated shape of steel in his graceful hands—which for a moment she thought would turn out to be some kind of impromptu gift, which in a sense, it had—and he neared her closer than anyone had ever done, any stranger, and there was fast movement, then a shock of sharp indescribable pain. . . .

Then, silence.

A silence during which the winter wind outside stopped, and the Silver Hall and all in it winked out of existence into *nothing*.

She was *nothing*.

And then, strangely, everything came back. The turmoil, the tumult, brilliant candlelight in the chandeliers, his screaming contorted face, the guards, the madness.

Only—it was all different. For, she no longer *felt* it. The thickness of distance was upon her.

No more pain. The knife in her heart sat as though it was in its proper sheath. Her heart itself was silent. Her blood gushing forth, leaving her, was like someone else's rain beating upon an indifferent shuttered window. She was now an observer of her own self, not a participant.

And amid the thickness, the apathy, the suspension of being and non-being, there was one thing left to her.

The need to *know* why.

Why this stranger did what he did. Why-what-who was he?

For, his act of intensity had forged a strange bond.

Whatever happened in the several long hours following, in the endless-seeming bowels of hell that was that night, the ministrations and the shock, the frightened weeping and condolences, the interminable weight of time itself—she thought of this need for *why*.

She had to know. While she was still here, while she still could. . . .

And so, she said to him who stood now before her, "Proceed. Tell me how your family was wronged by mine."

For several long moments he stared at her as though uncomprehending, his loosely shackled hands lowered powerlessly, hanging before him in their chains. And then suddenly, with a guttural cry, he raised his arms, his face contorted, and he made a futile effort to pull the chains apart—all the while staring at her with pure black hatred.

"Filthy Liguon . . ." he whispered through gritted teeth.

"Yes, I've heard this already," she said. "You're becoming repetitious, Marquis. Have you nothing else to tell me but this feeble outpouring of black bile?"

His expression then was not bile but black fire.

"Oh, I have so much to tell, so much . . . where to begin? Well then, if it amuses you—or rather, *despite* your pleasure. Ten years ago is when it started. One summer day when my father, the honorable and generous, the faultless Marquis Micul Fiomarre was sitting in his green garden in our sprawling estate, enjoying the sun-drenched afternoon, with his wife, my mother, the Marquise Eloise, and his children. I remember it now like yesterday, branded in my mind, even though I was but a green youth—the dappled spots of sun and shade on the grass, the perfect breeze stirring soft leaves, the cool juice of sweet peaches and cherries in an iced glass. I remember my father laughing at something, his olive skin, his whiteness of teeth, the funny thick black mustache we used to tease him about, his white shirt stained with garden dirt. My mother was laughing too, and myself and my brothers and my one sister, rolling on the grass. It was a moment of heaven.

"And then the men came. They were a company of armed guards dressed in the Imperial uniform. They marched past the protesting household servants, past the steward and our own house guards, filling the garden. Suddenly everything went cold. My father—I can see his face now, it changed from friendly, open, warm, to a perfect blank. Expression locked down into nothing. My father was already gone before they even took him away.

"They took him away?" the Infanta said softly. "Why? What was said? What reason given?"

"Nothing! The hell began in that moment when my father questioned them and their captain announced a charge of Grand Treason against the Crown, and that he was commanded to come with them and obey without any other recourse. My father asked what did they mean, what had he done? His face was in shock, his eyes confused, completely innocent—anyone could see. My mother had stood up also, and questioned them, in tears. My brothers and I—there were no words, we froze, became stone. Our little sister Oleandre, who was half my age, began to bawl.

"But they did not give an answer. Instead, they threw my father down on the ground, and there was a table upturned, I remember, and all our glasses went crashing, and the juices spilled orange-red on the grass. Then they bound him, and they half-dragged, half-carried him away, even though he did not even struggle and would have walked. That was the last time I ever saw my father. I remember the back of his dark head, his wavy locks of hair that would often stick out funny. . . .”

Fiomarre began to pace, back and forth a few steps, for his feet also bore chains and he could not walk properly.

The Infanta listened.

“Soon after my father had been taken,” he continued, “we received an Imperial Sealed Letter of Condolence to the family, and within it we learned of his . . . execution. We still did not know why. What had he done? What, in the name of God? At least the Fiomarre were not stripped of noble rank for whatever it is my father had ‘done.’ The Letter of Condolence to my mother was a small useless Imperial gesture of recompense for the death of her beloved husband and our cherished father. We inquired formally, first in Charonne, at the Royal court of Styx, but the Ixion King—the elder, since back then it was King Claudeis and his sickly Queen Rea, while their son Augustus was only a tiny babe—the Ixion King did not know, or did not care to know, and we were referred higher up, to the Emperor.

“A month had passed during which my mother had become very ill. She remained thus, weak and ailing for nearly a year. We were also shunned by the neighbors, for rumor of the Fiomarre disgrace had spread like wild creeping ivy though the countryside, and indeed, all of Styx. No one wanted to have anything to do with us, the noble Peers in the city of Charonne had closed their doors, and even in our own neighborhood there were no longer any friendly visits, none from our distant cousins, and not even from the most solicitous kindly old widows who had been friends with my mother.

“As for my brothers and sister and myself, we were also shunned and mocked in the village—our own village that we owned! Even our tenants, those whose landlord my father had been, they too looked askance at us. The priest would not come to perform Mass in the traitor’s family chapel, and my mother took us to the back of the village church every Sunday where we sat alone in the pew. Even some of the servants left our employ.”

"I am sorry . . . for you, the children, and your mother, and yes, for him, your father . . ." the Infanta said.

But he glared at her.

"Your belated remorse doesn't bring back the lives. Not only my father. Let me continue, and you listen, Liguon! This went on for almost five years. We grew, and my eldest brother, Ebrai, who was now the new Marquis, was of an age to be received at Court. Ebrai was passionate, the most passionate of us all, and he had carried the burden of half a decade of loss and pain and humiliation. When he left for your accursed Silver Court, it was with the intent to confront the Emperor and ask for justice and recompense, and an explanation for his father's fate. Even though my mother wept and begged him on her knees not to do anything rash that would put him into peril or offense of the Crown, Ebrai was not to be moved.

"He departed for Court, and was gone. And we heard nothing, for a very long, nigh interminable two months. And then, an Imperial messenger came—a baron whose name I don't recall, for I only recall his careful pitying expression as he talked very quietly with my mother. He explained that my brother—my foolish passionate Ebrai—had spoken out against the Crown, fought a duel with another high ranking nobleman, killed him, and had been detained. He was imprisoned in the Palace, waiting for Imperial judgment for both treason and murder."

"I had not known any of this at all," the Infanta said. "I do not recall ever hearing of your brother or your father's names and their crimes. . . ."

"Ah, the ignominy of the despised few. . . . It doesn't surprise me," he replied with a twisted smirk. "The Emperor's only pampered whelp would not be informed of the dark things that take place in reality, under your nose, in the bowels of this accursed Palace."

"But—" the Infanta said. "This is very strange and I simply do not see why my father—who is a very mild-mannered man if you only get to know him, despite the layers of rank that he must always wear—why he would order a death and an imprisonment where there was no just underlying cause. The late Marquis, your father and then your brother must have done *something* to provoke such treatment. There is the murder, as you say—"

"No!" His voice was again a fierce, mad, snarling thing. "Nothing! Nothing! They had done nothing! Listen to me, I am not done! Listen, you damned. . . ."

Fiomarre started to pace once again, periodically striking himself in the chest with his fists as he spoke, like a denizen of a mental asylum.

"My brother, who had supposedly fought and killed a Duke's son or some other damned popinjay of fine blood, did *nothing* of the sort. The name of this supposed victim has been withheld from us. And when my mother arrived in grief and madness to see the Emperor the following month, to beg for her son's life, she was received very coldly and briefly, and told by the Liguon to return home, with an absolute refusal to explain what actually happened. Furthermore, as my mother spent a few days in the Palace, she heard some gossip that the victim of my brother was in fact alive, merely wounded, and recuperating nicely at his own ancestral estate. So, there had been no murder committed, and none to be punished for!"

"Isn't dueling illegal under the Crown?"

"Illegal, but not a mortal offense!"

A pause.

And then he continued. "My mother suffered a relapse of her illness, and at first could not even find it in herself to move from her Palace guest bed, much less travel. She attempted one more time to have an Imperial Audience, to see the Empress this time, to crawl on her knees and beg for mercy for her foolish son. But the Empress, your Imperial mother, was too busy apparently and would not see her. And so, my own poor mother had to return home to the Fiomarre estate, with nothing, and even less than nothing—no news of my brother's fate."

"What . . . happened then?" Claere Liguon said very softly. In the act of sympathetic listening she had grown even more still, if such a thing were possible for a dead woman.

"What happened was another death. Another Imperial Letter had come to us, hand-delivered by a different noble flunky of the Emperor—this one's face—I don't even have a memory of him at all. And this time there was no Condolence, not even the semblance of sympathy from the Crown. Only a cold announcement of my brother's execution, coupled with a warning that Fiomarre will be stripped of their rank and lands if they transgressed against the Crown ever again.

"My mother was confined to bed. She remained there for the next two years, slowly fading. Meanwhile I was the new Marquis. I had suddenly become an Heir where I had no interest or expectation of this dubious honor, ever. My brother's death was an unthinkable. No, not Ebrai. He was going to live forever. . . ."

"How she must have suffered, your mother . . ." the Infanta said. Her voice was labored as always—even and almost monotone, as her forced breath came like clockwork. And yet there was a hint of something new in it, while her blank gaze never stopped observing his face.

"Fortunately, her suffering is over. She was found lying in her bed, cold, one morning in the autumn of the third year since the loss of my brother. I was away on some meaningless estate business and it was my younger brother, Celen, who found her thus. My sister ran for the priest. . . . In death, I am told, Eloise Fiomarre was like the holy Icon of the Mother of God. It's the only thing I can say in consolation. And in her fingers she held an old letter from my father. . . . We buried her in the family crypt with that letter, and with all of my father's old things we could find—since she would never again lie next to his body. I don't doubt it was her wish."

The Infanta's breath came in a strange shuddering

exhalation, as though she was going to say something, but held the words back.

"Meanwhile," he continued, his face growing weary suddenly, "my sister, Oleandre, had grown to be a lovely maiden, of an age to marry. But because of our present state of disgrace, Oleandre remained alone and unclaimed by any neighbor nobility. No one wanted to align themselves in marriage with the despised Fiomarre orphans. The one family that had once expressed to my father an interest in betrothing their son to Oleandre, went back on their word. Their strapping son married another young damsel of a Styx family with far less worth . . . but also far less blemish. Indeed, it's not a difficult thing to find any family with less blemish than ourselves, these days. . . . Oleandre plans to take the vows soon, and I haven't the heart to dissuade her from the nunnery.

"My youngest brother, Celen, is all that's left. And the youth expects to—God only knows what he can do now. To enlist, maybe, somewhere, anywhere, for he has a death wish—but he certainly would die first before joining the Imperial military. He told me, when I was about to make this final trip, that he would go in my place, or we go together . . . And I didn't let him. At least one of us must remain in this world."

"What a truly tragic story, Marquis."

He looked at her in a sudden flaring of disdain. "You call me Marquis? I thought, daughter of Liguon, that I am a dead man without rank. Or is it that you make sport of me now, before I go to my execution?"

The Infanta slowly moved forward in her seat. "If you are a dead man, then what am I?"

"That, I still don't know," he said. "But I know that what I am now is *nothing*. Fiomarre is nothing. And thus, nothing matters anymore."

"Nothing . . ." the Infanta echoed quietly. "It is what I am also. We are suddenly much alike."

And then, unexpectedly, she rose from her seat. She stood

before Vlau Fiomarre who towered over her, despite the added height of her tall wig. The grey daylight came in to illuminate half of her face, leaving the rest in shadowed silhouette. He could see her pale bloodless lips, her great smoke-hued eyes.

Fiomarre involuntarily took a step back, his chains clanging.

"Are you afraid of me?" she said softly.

"I . . . don't know." His answer came softly also, after a delay.

"Your story is tragic and for that reason impossible. I want to believe you but it simply cannot be, such horrible injustice."

"Believe what you will!" he exclaimed. "I am done speaking, Liguon. You've had your amusement. Now, take my life or have me tortured first, and be done with it."

"But you are not done hating me," she replied. "And—I must have the truth."

Fiomarre looked down at her with black fire in his eyes. "I will be done hating you when the stars fall and the world ends, and no sooner!"

"You are unaware, I see," she replied. "For, the world as we know it *has* ended. Death and all dying has been stopped. I cannot take your life even if I wanted to, for none of us can die now, only malinger. . . ."

And as he watched her in slowly dawning horror, she called out loudly, "Guards!"

Immediately two armed guards, who had been standing ready outside her chamber's door, entered, coming to attention.

"There will be no execution," the Infanta told them. "Take this man to apartments appropriate to a guest of the Crown, and do not mistreat him ever again. Remove his chains. Have proper clothing and food brought to him. I will have need of him shortly."

The expression on Fiomarre's face was one of incredulity. And then it was replaced by suspicion, and again the hatred flared.

"Do what you will, daughter of the devil! Play your devious game, but you cannot touch me, not ever again, none of you, Liguon!" He spat the words out angrily, as the guards came to stand on both sides of him uncertainly, with suspicious looks.

"Unchain him," the Infanta repeated.

"Your—Imperial Highness, the keys—I haven't the keys here, Your Imperial Highness, they are in the prison below," one of the men said. "It wasn't expected that they be required, and it's always a precaution to not have the keys, so as not to give the dangerous prisoner an additional chance to escape. . . ."

"Enough. Go get the keys," she said.

The guard started, but immediately complied, hastening out, while the other remained in place, sheepish.

"Am I no longer a prisoner, then?"

"No."

Fiomarre was staring at her with a locked-down, no longer readable expression. Yet at the faintest edges of it, there was that same incredulity and just possibly, mockery.

But the Infanta had already turned away. Moving slowly like a puppet, she returned to her chair, sank down like a weight of stone. From there her voice came, toneless and yet empty now of the last vestiges of curiosity, or even that parody-shadow of life that somehow animated her.

"You are free . . ." she said. "If you have any honor, you will stay here in the Imperial guest apartments, and wait for the results of my investigation. That is—if there is that much honor left in you, of the ancient noble Fiomarre, as you claim to be. . . . And if not, you may simply go. You are . . . free."

And she went silent.

Fiomarre stood, stricken by something.

"Liguon . . ." he said. "Upon my word of honor, I will stay."

Josephuste Liguon II, Emperor of the Realm, could not sleep. It was the second night since the killing of his daughter. And although the first one was spent sleepless, in a kind of powerless torpor of psychological devastation, seated on the Throne in the Silver Hall next to the equally broken Empress, and the day that followed was such that no words were adequate to express anything, nor truly to comprehend—despite the weariness, and the compounding overload of insane events, there was no way to release the mind to sleep's oblivion. . . .

Everything was impossible, and suddenly hardly anything mattered. Human reactions no longer had a place.

Had there been a clear-cut death of the Infanta, the Emperor would have known how to act. He would have gone mad with anguish as would any father in his place. He would have grieved. He would have immediately punished the offender.

But there was no death here. There was murder, yes. Loss, yes, terribly so, for Claere his child was no longer; she was gone, and *something else* was now inhabiting her damaged shell of a body, something else was in her place.

And yet there was no ending. No completion, not even a way to complete the course of grief. And no way to properly punish the murderer, except for the application of prolonged and endless pain without actually damaging his body to the extent of death, at which point he too would become *someone else* and in that manner escape his punishment. Besides, Claere herself had requested, in a strange act of mercy, clemency for the murderer.

None of it made any sense, the Emperor thought.

For, in this suspended state, the world seemed to have taken a breath and was holding it. Nothing was ended, nothing could be over.

No rest . . . no peace.

And so, tormented by the bizarreness of it all, looking back on what had come to pass, and imagining impossible variations of what was yet to come, Josephuste Liguon II lay awake in his luxurious bed. At his side was his Imperial spouse who also seemed merely to lie motionless in empty silence. He knew the Empress was awake like himself, for her breath came in occasional shudders, and he sensed she was holding back sobs.

Eventually, toward dawn, sleep must have come after all, for the next thing the Emperor knew was a very gentle and polite touch on his shoulder by his Valet of the Chamber. The Valet had the singular Honor and Privilege of being permitted to touch Their Imperial Majesties, once per day only, if it were absolutely necessary to interrupt Imperial slumber.

Today the Valet of the Chamber used his Privilege just after dawn. His Imperial Majesty had an urgent demand for a formal Audience from the emissaries of Balmue, of all things. This was not to be put off, for all of a sudden they were leaving.

The Emperor groaned, squinting at the faint light of dawn coming through the slit in the window drapery and the newly lit roaring fire in the ornately framed fireplace. He rose, sat up in the grandiose bed, throwing one glance at the distant and motionless figure of the Empress at his far left, then nodded his permission. And immediately a cadre of silent and skillful servants went to work on getting him presentable for the day.

He had managed to avoid seeing the Balmue diplomats all of the last day, being naturally preoccupied as he was, but obviously politics could not take a break. Besides, the Balmue had been scheduled for an Audience with him a morning ago.

The Emperor drank a hot cup of breakfast tea, tasting nothing of the usually fragrant tea leaves, and refused his favorite crumpets and pastry.

Within a half hour he was in his Private Audience Chamber, dressed in a coat and pants of pale saffron silk and a platinum powdered wig, seated upon red cushions on a carved wooden throne of dark cherry wood. Just steps behind him, in a velvet draperied secret alcove were hidden the Duke Claude Rovait and the Duke Andre Eldon, of Plaimes. Both were clandestine Imperial advisors, here upon the Emperor's command, installed in secret in order to listen in on the upcoming Audience and later to interpret.

As soon as his men were in place and the drapery fell to the parquet floor to conceal them, the Emperor made a hand motion and the Chamberlain on the other side of the doors announced the Balmue diplomats—the Marquis Nuor Alfre and the Viscount Halronne Deupris, Peers of the Domain.

Two men entered.

They were clad formally for an audience, in the colors of Balmue, silver and sienna brown. The older, a ruddy-brown haired and bearded lord with weathered skin and a tall, lean built, was the Marquis Alfre, ambassador of Balmue. At his side stood his aide, a shorter, youthful man with a rounded, fair face and blond hair, the Viscount Deupris.

Both came forward and stopped the proper ten steps short of the Throne, then bowed with precision and remained thus until the Emperor indicated in a drained, powerless voice, "Rise, gentlemen."

They straightened, and the ambassador spoke: "Your Imperial Majesty, we thank you for the Audience, on behalf of our liege Lord, His Royal Majesty, King Clavian Sestial of Balmue, Vassal of the Sovereign Rumanar Avalais of the Domain and its Territories."

Marquis Alfre was an old-school diplomat, with many years of polish imbedded in him. But even he obviously found it difficult to follow a protocol under the current circumstances. He paused, cleared his throat and then said, "First, our sincere and profound condolences on Your Imperial Majesty's familial . . . loss—that is, on the situation with the . . . *assault* on Her Imperial Highness."

The Emperor did not blink, but his posture took on a particular stillness, in which he was a statue of frozen winter stone. And for a long moment he said nothing. He remembered, as an aside, that yes, the Balmue men had been present, had seen it all happen before their eyes. . . .

"Yes," he said in a wooden voice, after a very long pause. "Your condolences are . . . appreciated."

The Marquis exhaled his held breath, and so did the younger Viscount at his side. And then at last they got down to business.

"Our apologies, but the reason for disturbing Your Imperial Majesty at such an early hour," said Marquis Alfre, "is that we have been summoned to return immediately to our homeland. Unfortunately, we cannot extend our imposition upon your Imperial Hospitality for even an hour longer, and therefore this conversation must be brief while a more in-depth discussion needs be postponed for a future visit."

The Emperor nodded.

"Your Imperial Majesty," the Viscount Deupris spoke for the first time. "I was asked to convey on behalf of His Royal Majesty King Clavian Sestial that Balmue is extremely interested in furthering our positive relations, in discussing the border access protocols, the expansion of trade treaty, and the exchange of resources. However, as a vassal member of the Domain, Balmue is constrained by any limits placed upon it by the Sovereign, as you are well aware. And one of such limits has just been enforced, according to the correspondence we received today from the court of Balmue, as forwarded from the Sapphire Court."

"What is it? Speak clearly." The Emperor was exhausted and therefore blunt.

"In short, we cannot agree to the trade expansion treaty as written," Marquis Alfre said.

"Ah . . ." the Emperor sighed. "So, what did the Sovereign demand of your King now?"

"With deepest apologies, I was not informed of the details." Marquis Alfre bowed again, lowering his gaze.

"Or you're not at liberty to disclose, I know, I know. . . ."

"One thing I can reliably offer your Imperial Majesty at this point," Viscount Deupris added, "is that because of the situation pertaining to the so-called cessation of death, many things are changed, and plans are . . . reconsidered."

The Marquis threw the younger man a subtle look, as though he'd somehow said too much.

He then said, "Begging apologies once more for disturbing Your Imperial Majesty, but we must beg your leave to depart in haste. Is there anything—any words that Your Imperial Majesty would like to convey to our King?"

It hurt to think. The Emperor knew the beginnings of a headache encroaching, but he also knew he had to convey an effective parting tone.

"Tell your liege that Balmue remains our welcome neighbor. There is no reason the Realm and the Domain border access must be modified in the foreseeable future. I look forward to the continuation of our talks . . . despite these difficult times."

The diplomats bowed once more, their expressions taking on a blank polite facade, underneath which was a hint of relief. And then they gracefully backed out of the chamber.

When the doors were shut behind them, the Emperor eased, resting the back of his bewigged head against the carved wood of the throne.

"Rovait, Plaimes, come forth. . . ."

The Imperial advisors moved the drapery aside and entered the chamber. Andre Eldon, the Duke of Plaimes was an elegant dandified lord at first glance, a man in his prime dressed at the height of fashion. However, few knew that he was an accomplished spy in the service of the Crown.

At his side, the bearded Claude Rovait, Duke of Rovait, was a more sedate elder figure, with more of a sharp military bearing. He too was deeply embroiled in the workings of the spy network that extended into the criminal underworld.

"So, what are your impressions?" the Emperor asked.

The Duke of Plaimes cleared his throat. "A lot of usual

vacuous politeness, but the underlying tone is urgency. Obviously they were in haste to depart. Our contacts tell us that as of last night the Sovereign is suddenly in the process of repositioning her military forces all around the Domain. My suspicion is, within her structural framework Balmue is suddenly a pivotal point, since they share a border with us."

"It has to be the direct result of death's cessation," said the Duke Rovait. "There is no other overt catalyst, we are told. Spain and France are a very remote possibility from beyond the Domain's southern and western borders respectively, but there have been no particular exchanges between them recently to warrant such a movement of troops. Besides we share more western borders with France, our kinder neighbor, than does the Domain, and I do not think Louis XIV, *le Roi Soleil*, is interested in anything but decorating his beloved Palace at Versailles."

"So, it is death, then . . ." the Emperor mused.

"Incidentally," Rovait said, "I suspect the Balmue received their summons not from an express messenger but from someone local, working for their side. A plant. I think we are getting close to narrowing the short list of spy candidates that could be Domain plants, here in the Silver Court."

"Excellent, continue working on that."

"Majesty," the Duke of Plaimes said, taking a step forward, then starting to pace. "I regret to bring this up, but . . . Fiomarre. What should he be told of—"

"What?" The Emperor interrupted harshly. And then he sat forward in the throne. "Oh God, not that name—I cannot bear to hear it, not now, not . . . yet. It is intolerable that we must discuss this now. . . ."

Saying this the Emperor rubbed his forehead with his hand, where the headache was now drilling deep into the bowl of his skull.

"Unfortunately I must send a message to him tonight. Micul Fiomarre will expect the regular carrier bird promptly," said Andre Eldon of Plaimes.

"He does not know," Duke Rovait added gently. "None of it. He and his eldest son, both of them. Ebrai has not been in contact with me for a fortnight, in fact."

"Oh God!" The Emperor exclaimed, then groaned and put his head down in his hands. "Oh God, oh Lord of Heaven . . . Have mercy on your servant. Have mercy, mercy. . . . Fiomarre."

And then Josephuste Liguon II, Emperor of the Realm, stood up on shaky feet, slowly came down the three stairs of the dais and paused before his two closest advisors.

"I cannot . . ." he began. "I don't know how to deal with Fiomarre now—with any of them. Indeed, I cannot abide the sound of that name. It rings with madness inside my head!"

"A truly singular tragedy, indeed," whispered the Duke of Plaimes, looking at his liege with sympathetic eyes.

"Your Imperial Majesty," Rovait said, "I know how difficult it is for you, how intolerable, but Micul Fiomarre is our best man there, and my recommendation—for now, at least—is that he not be told at all. He is planted in such a sensitive position at the Sapphire Court that any jarring news of whatever nature might throw him off and blow his cover. As far as Ebrai, I will take care of letting him know, the next time he contacts me, and I will request that he holds off communicating any of it to his father."

"I will not be able to look him in the face," the Emperor said, beginning to pace slowly in a broken aimless circle. "Never again. Nor would I be able to bear seeing his face in turn. His son killed my daughter. Fiomarre the middle son, a madman, killed my beloved child!"

The two lords watched him carefully.

"Is there any precedent for this kind of thing in all of history of the Realm?" the Emperor whispered. "Is there a precedent on how to treat a decorated hero father when his son commits the act of a traitor?"

Silence.

"The tragedy is in the not knowing—on all sides," Duke Rovait said.

"They are so deep undercover that the family could not be told without compromising them," the Duke of Plaimes said. "Perverse circumstances, confound it! No one could account for the middle son reacting in such an extreme to the false story of his father's so-called death, and then Ebrai's fabricated death also. Who could have expected him to go so far overboard? Didn't the lady mother receive a partially encrypted letter from Fiomarre the elder, explaining his situation? Confound it, indeed."

"I cannot look at him when he comes home . . ." the Emperor continued to whisper. "Fiomarre. . . . How do I deal with him? How, oh God?"

"Who is to say what might happen, Majesty, by the time they do come home?" Duke Rovait spoke soothingly, watching the Emperor. "For the moment, all we can do is pray. And— avoid giving them any provocations and compromising them in the Domain."

"Then . . . pray," the Emperor whispered. "Pray with me, my lords. For strength, for justice. And . . . oblivion."

Chapter 7

It was dawn, and pale twilight in the family chapel of the Chidair Keep. A solitary knight outfitted in full battle armor knelt before the altar, his dark brown-haired head bared, helmet under one arm, his gaze directed to the icons of the Child and the Mother of God and the Saints, bathed in soft candle-glow. They watched him back with mystery in their ancient faces, a choir of dark vulnerable eyes rendered in pigment, all trained on him.

"What must I do? Tell me . . ." he whispered to the images.

The answer came from the doorway of the chapel. "Beltain, my son, you must do what you always do—what is true to your gut and your spirit," said the old priest, approaching the kneeling figure.

The son of Duke Ian Chidair turned his head slowly, revealing a drawn exhausted face, the effect of a probably sleepless night. And then he rose, armor creaking, made a sign of obeisance before the altar, and approached the priest.

"Good morning, Father Orweil. I am . . . about to be on my way."

"I know," the priest replied. "You are on *his* orders. And those unholy orders directly counter the Royal Decree."

Beltain sighed. "You know about that too?"

"Everyone knows, my son. We are praying on your behalf

and on behalf of the poor girls who are sacrificing their lives—their everything—as even now they make their way here and then onward to the Northern Forest in search of Death's Keep. The same girls whom you go to hunt."

Father Orweil was a stooped old man, small and frail, his frame a desiccated bundle of twigs wrapped in monastic burlap, his eyes filmed over in the wrinkled face. Beltain Chidair towered over him. And when the priest reached out to take the knight's large gauntlet-clad hands, it was like an oddly shrunken child holding the palms and fingers of a giant.

"I've made my decision, Father. Would you have me be forsworn?" Beltain said softly. In the soft twilight of the chapel his dark eyes had lost their slate-blue coloration and appeared nearly black, glittering with moisture.

"You have sworn to your father, the Lord and Duke of Chidair," the priest said, still holding the younger man's large hands in his frail own. "This one—he is not the same one to whom you pledged your loyalty, and you know it. Listen to your instincts, your heart!"

"I no longer know anything," Beltain retorted, his expression hardening. "I—I have made a promise to him, and he is *different*, yes, but he is still my father. I will not be forsworn! And now, I must hasten to do my Lord's bidding—the bidding of Duke Hoarfrost, who is still Lord Chidair, Lord of this Keep and of these lands, until Heaven takes him!"

And with those words, Beltain extricated himself from Father Orweil's grasp and turned away, walking briskly out of the chapel. His metal boots and spurs rang loudly on the floor and the echoes arose against stone.

"But . . ." the old priest whispered in his wake. "But Heaven *has* already taken him."

He was not heeded.

The forest was winter white. Silence, except for the occasional soft fluttering of tree branches as the weight of settling snow overcame them until they sprang back in rebellion, freeing themselves from the icy burden.

The young woman bundled in poor woolens made her way through the snowdrifts. She had lost the road and the smaller north-western path nearly an hour ago, and her small bag of belongings weighed heavily in her arms.

She was lost. North was somewhere ahead, and the forest not particularly thick. All she need do was keep going, she had been told. For the sake of your family, keep going. For the sake of those you love. Just don't think and keep going; don't think about freezing, about food, or a warm fire, or even a moment's rest. Somewhere out there, he waited, Death, in his cold dark Keep.

Somewhere. . . .

It was getting colder and the morning had advanced well into the afternoon. Wading through the pristine blanket of snow, nearly up to her knees, she listened to the overwhelming winter silence, and occasionally in the distance she thought there came the howling of wolves.

A lump of alarm formed in her throat.

A sudden bird fluttered noisy wings and burst upwards. The woman gave a scream, gulping lungfuls of freezing air, then laughed out-loud at her own skittishness. She was a bit simple, but not too dense to recognize a harmless robin taking flight.

Then, there was another sound. She could not identify it immediately, and cried out "Hello? Who's there?"

Her voice left a brief echo.

And then they descended upon her. A tall black warhorse burst from the shrubbery up ahead, bearing a knight, and from all sides came dark menacing figures clad in dull armor, carrying pikes, lances, and occasional swords. Blue surcoats fluttered against metal plate, and although the woman was not learned in such things, she thought she had seen this sky-color somewhere and it had a significance.

But it was all afterthought, because foremost she felt terror.

"Halt!" the knight cried—even though there was no need and she had frozen already of her own volition, bending her shawl-wrapped head downward and simultaneously raising one hand up, as though to avoid a blow.

He was wearing a full suit of war mail, and his helmet visor was lowered so that she could see no face and thus could not judge his intent.

There was only the voice. And it was harsh, virile. Not particularly angry or threatening, but a man's strong voice was plenty enough for her to cower.

"Please . . ." she managed to mumble. "Please don't hurt me, M'Lord, I'm just passin' on through, that's all."

"What have we got here, eh?" said one of the men on foot closest to her, and neared her, grabbing her firmly by the arm until she went limp with terror. "Who are you, girl? Well, speak up, so the Lord can hear."

"I'm . . . I'm Annie."

"What are you doing here, Annie?" another man said, not ungently, coming from behind her. Neither one of them were leering nor acting like the drunken louts she was used to avoiding in her town, but the woman did not see, because she was staring in agony of terror at the ground, at the beaten-down white snow, no longer pristine. . . .

"I. . . ." She could not answer, for her breath was caught in her throat, and her lungs suddenly refused to expand and take in the next breath.

"Are you on your way to be a Cobweb Bride?" The same male voice sounded suddenly from above, and she knew it was the dark mounted knight speaking.

"Yes, sir . . . M'Lord . . ." she managed. "I suppose I'm that, if Death think 'e might want me, that is."

"In that case, Annie, you'll have to come with me."

And before she could whimper in protest, the two men closest to her took hold of her, and then she was pulled along and eventually lifted with ease to lie across the saddle. She was held tightly.

Then there was movement underneath, and crashing sounds of tree branches all around, so that echoes seemed to fill the forest. Annie began to struggle against the solid rock, the metal-clad body behind her, feeling herself like a sack of potatoes, but it was too late.

"Please, no!" she cried, "I gotta be going, please let me go, I ain't done nuthin' wrong, please—"

But the grip of powerful hands around her only tightened, and the forest rushed by.

By mid-morning, the Emperor's splitting headache had turned into a raging beast of a migraine. Less than an hour after the Balmue envoys had left the Silver Court, Josephuste Liguon II received another urgent request for an Audience—this one from his daughter.

He attended her immediately of course, in her own quarters. Squinting from the agony in his head coupled with sleeplessness, he entered with slow paces so as not to collapse, then sat down heavily in a chair. Two servants offered a footstool to prop up his feet, and pillows for his back, while Doctor Belquar brought a foul-tasting but effective elixir to imbibe, and a hot and palate-cleansing cup of tea to follow.

The Infanta had been seated upright as a post in her usual chair near the window. As soon as she saw her father, however, she stood up and approached, then paused, dissolving into her customary stillness several feet away, waiting for the fussing servants to be done.

The Emperor rubbed his forehead while the room seemed to spin around him. He watched his daughter's once-pristine court dress stained with old blood and her mechanical movements with the same cold horror that had been eating at him all this time, and had only temporarily shifted to the background of his other sensations.

At last he waved for the servants to be gone and the room emptied. The bitter elixir he'd drank still burned the back of his throat and so he sipped the scalding tea once to wash away the taste, then put down his cup that clattered with porcelain fragility against the saucer in his trembling hands.

"Thank you . . . Father," Claere Liguon said. "For . . . coming here to see me."

"My dear child," he replied in a rusty voice, breaking into a cough. "What is it, what did you want to see me about? Are . . . you—that is, are you feeling—I mean, there is no . . . *discomfort?*"

She stood in silhouette against the pale winter light of the window. For a moment, she said nothing. And then, "My Father, I must leave you and Mother now. I must go and offer myself to Death who waits in the Northern Forest."

"But," the Emperor said, knowing that his words were in so many ways ridiculous. "But . . . really, you cannot mean it? I didn't think you meant it, my dearest, what you said about going, that is. Must you go . . . so soon?"

"If I am Death's destined Bride, then there is no time to lose. The world waits."

The headache receded and sobering cold rushed to the forefront again in his mind—cold, fearful, wrenching anguish.

"You would really do this?" he whispered, leaning forward, lifting his silk stocking-clad feet off the footstool so that they could be better anchored on the floor—anything to ground him.

"Yes. . . ."

"But—how?"

And the dead one approached him, and then reached out with one winter-cold hand and laid it on his cheek.

The Emperor felt an icy shock.

"Father," she said, leaning over him, while the faceted jewels in the Crown that still rested on top of her grand wig caught the faint light from the window and suddenly sparkled above her like a halo. "I require nothing but a fast carriage. And . . . I want Fiomarre—the man who struck me—to be in that carriage as I travel to my final place. He is bound to me somehow—it is his own making—and I have no way to explain, except that I know he must be with me now."

"What?" the Emperor exclaimed, falling backwards once more against the pillows. "Oh, no, no . . . God, no," he muttered, closing his eyes and wrinkling his brow, while rubbing the bridge of his nose as though to eradicate all pain, all thought.

"Please . . . my Father. You *must* allow me this!" Her wooden voice rose in volume and strength as she made the visible effort to inhale air deeper into her lungs. "If you will deny me this, I will walk out of this chamber and this Palace and make my way on foot. . . ."

"But oh, not Fiomarre! He is a traitor and the son of a . . . traitor—"

The Infanta was watching him sharply. "Tell me more of him, Father," she suddenly said. "This betrayal, all of it. What have the Fiomarre done that you hound and persecute their family thus? For I have heard a tale of impossible, unspeakable woe from his lips. And his tale explains to me what motives led him to hurt me so—what horrible, mad hatred in response to an equally horrible, mad tragedy. For, this Fiomarre is a madman and yet, I believe he was driven to it. He has . . . just cause to be."

"How can you say this, child, now after what he's done to you?" the Emperor said, so as not to answer her question directly. To admit to the whole Fiomarre situation—even now, after all that had happened—was unthinkable. No, he could not divulge any of it, could not compromise the precarious advantage he had with his planted spies in the Sapphire Court. Not even to give a certain peace of mind to his poor daughter. . . .

And so instead he said in his most casual statesman-diplomat tone, with only a slight pause in a certain place: "The Fiomarre, Claere, are a despicable lot. As . . . was the father, so are his two sons—three I should say. Though the youngest is still a boy, I hear, these days. . . . In any case, do not concern yourself with the details of their betrayal—they are ugly and not for your sweet, innocent ears, my dear girl. Certain matters of the world are not fit for young ladies of Royalty who will one day rule—"

"I am *dead*, father!" she interrupted, her voice also rising but in a manner of labored breathing, barely creating a semblance of living emotion. "For Heaven's sake, 'sweet and innocent' is never again to be said of me! Once, maybe—I was innocent, yes . . . frail and sickly in life, withdrawn and repressed, each living breath taken as though such an act required permission, and all the while waiting for the moment of my death without even knowing it. . . . And now I am *strong!* Dead and strong and *unreal*—an impossibility! And do you honestly think I will, one day, rule anything? Unless—maybe I will rule at Death's side as his Cobweb Bride."

The Emperor exhaled loudly, a sigh of resignation and despair. Looking up into her terrible pale face, the things he saw reflected there made him unable to dissemble any further, merely deny.

"I will not speak of Fiomarre any longer, Claere. Enough, do not ask me things I cannot answer. And—do not ask me why. Simply take my word as your Father and your Emperor."

"In that case, my Father and my Emperor, I must beg leave to depart the Silver Court. And if there is no blessing, I will proceed without it."

Josephuste Liguon II had no heart to deny her, especially not now. After a long pause, "Very well . . ." he said. "A carriage will be made ready for you, and you can leave on the morrow—"

"No! I must leave *now*, Father. There is no time, no time to waste, not a moment. . . ."

He nodded again. And then in a dead voice called the servants to arrange his daughter's final departure.

As he did this deed of love for her, the Infanta raised her hands slowly and touched the platinum and diamond Crown that she wore.

She paused briefly, as though considering her next movement, or memorizing the moment. And then her cold, numb fingers gripped the precious metal. She removed the glittering Crown and placed it carefully on the nearest pillow. And then she removed her wig, pulling at it without mercy and knowing no pain, until a cascade of pins that held it in place scattered on the floor. Underneath, her thin pale hair, ashes-and-wheat, was revealed, gathered into a small twist in the back and pulled so tightly that it was flattened against her scalp. Traces of white powder remained, dusting the rim of her hairline.

The elaborate, coiffed wig fell to the floor, ignored.

The Crown sat twinkling with lights on the pillow, and she paused another instant to observe it.

Then, she turned her back on it in silence.

Tussecan was not all that different from Oarclaven, maybe just a tad larger and more crowded, Percy thought, as their cart clattered into town along the wide, cobblestone-paved and treacherously icy thoroughfare which the road had become. The blanket of show had melted into brown sludge on the edges near the storefront walks alongside the buildings that lined main street. And the sludge got iced over into two deep perpetual ruts on both sides of the street from all the traffic of carts and carriages and sleds that wore it down into slippery smoothness.

It was late afternoon and urchins bundled in woolens took running leaps and then slid on their feet along the icy grooves, flailing with their arms to maintain balance and then barely getting out of the way of oncoming equipage traffic. There were cries and hoots and laughter in the air together with the pungent scent of wood-smoke from the many piping chimneys. Percy took it all in as she sat hunched over in the cart, her thickly bundled feet dangling next to Jenna's.

"Goodness, what a messy little town," said Lizabette from the back, rubbing the side of her sharp, cold-reddened nose with her mittens. Lizabette, who it turned out was the daughter of a school headmaster in another town just south of Letheburg, was a fount of running commentary on everything from the density of snow at this time of the season, to the correct pronunciation of words, to the so-called gauche tactics of the mercantile class—as she referred to the street vendors who plied their trade in small carts and earned her annoyance. The more Lizabette shared her knowledge and lofty opinions, the more Emilie rolled her eyes behind Lizabette's back and then made nose-thumbing gestures.

Gloria, the Oarclaven blacksmith's shy daughter, remained perfectly quiet and distracted for the entirety of the journey as she sat next to Percy. Then, at one point during their "rotation" switch, she got out of the cart to walk, still without speaking a word.

The other young women—Flor, the sisters Catrine and Niosta, and the Letheburg girls, Regata and Sibyl—giggled and talked on and off among themselves, occasionally including Percy in their conversation. Jenna just sat humming loudly, and at one point broke out into a flat rendition of "Cobweb Bride, Cobweb Bride, come and lie by my side," until Emilie reached over and pulled her kerchief around her face and shoved it into her mouth—at which point Jenna sputtered with indignation while Percy hid a smile.

"And what exactly makes you call this town messy, Lizabette?" Grial said, as she skillfully maneuvered Betsy's reins while the stately mare plodded along, pulling them with no visible effort. "Looks to be rather a neat and orderly place to me—pretty buildings with new roofs, and those newfangled glass windows everywhere, freshly painted red panes, doors with shiny brass handles—why, I'd say it's a very presentable place, this Tussecan! Even the smell is right—right about now, smells like hot cinnamon buns and pumpkin soup!"

"No offense, Grial," said Lizabette, and everyone stared at her, waiting for the proverbial offense to drop, "but compared to Letheburg or even my own distinguished home town, Duarden, this is a provincial outpost. I mean, just look at those shabby carriages, not one sporting a noble crest, and the jostling crowds of townsfolk all dressed in Lord knows what. . . ."

And then Lizabette went silent, since pretty much everyone else in the cart surrounding her was dressed in Lord knows what. Percy and Jenna wore poor woolen hand-me-downs (even if one accounted for Percy's mother's so-called "heirloom" shawl), Emilie bundled in a greasy old quilted coat, while the two sisters from farthest down south wore near-beggar clothing. The two well-dressed girls, Sybil and Regata, chose wisely to keep quiet. And so Lizabette pulled her own stylish coat with shiny brass buttons closer together and decided for once to keep her opinions to herself.

"Aha!" Grial exclaimed suddenly, "I smell it! Yes, on the wind, there's warm stew in somebody's pot! Or, at least a fine leather shoe, eh? Or is it hickory? Or just freshly baked bread? In any case, who's hungry?"

"Who's not?" Regata said with a groan, while all around came the chorus of "Me, me!"

"What should we do, ladies?" Grial continued. "We have a long road ahead of us, no doubt, once we pass the town, since it's the last outpost between here and the Northern Forest. But it is getting late in the day, and the cold's going to bite our noses off and leave us with little red stumps, unless we warm up. We'll rest up tonight in Tussecan, I say. Who's with me?"

"Me! Me!"

"Ma'am . . . Grial," said Niosta who had just climbed into the back of the cart, trading places with Emilie. "What are we gonna do for money? We don't 'ave nuthin' to pay for any lodging or food. Really, we weren't plannin' on it. Just find a spot in somebody's barn's all we need."

"Aha!" Grial said again. "But 'nuthin' is what's indeed required for us to get food and lodging here in Tussecan. In fact, not only nothing, but probably less than that. About half of nothing will do. And certainly, since we're talking about nothing, not even money is required, if you get my drift."

"Not really," Emilie said from the side of the cart where she now walked.

"Huh? I'm confused! That is, Ma'am, I'm confused—sorry," Jenna said.

Grial gave a sudden bark of laughter. As always, it sounded a bit crazy, but also harmless.

"Here's the deal, my pretties. It may be our impossible Cobweb Bridal luck, or just—well, who knows what really, probably nothing—but I have a cousin here in Tussecan, and her name's Ronna Liet. And Ronna's an excellent woman for oh-so-many reasons, the most important, as far as we're concerned, being that she owns and runs an inn. Not just an inn, but a fine and generous inn with two stories and at least a dozen grand and yet delightfully cozy rooms, if I remember correctly—it's been ages, I say, since I've been here last—and it's called Ronna's Imperial Crown and Dream. Or, maybe Ronna's Regal Lethe Palatial Arms? In any case, here it is, ladies, right there, see this house coming up ahead? That's it! There's our free food and lodging!"

And with another bark, Grial pulled up Betsy's reins while the cart rambled to a slow stop in front of a pleasant looking storefront with a brass-decorated shingle hanging on clean new chains and fresh red and green lettering that said "Ronna's Inn." Just below, in smaller white letters it said "Welcome, Dear Travelers!"

Sibyl, whose father was a Letheburg tailor, attempted to read the lettering on the sign and moved her lips silently, while Lizabette proudly read the sign out-loud in a school-marmish tone of voice.

Percy, who could read because her mother had made sure of it, said nothing. She and her sisters had been fortunate to have been taught letters by Niobea with her "city learning," and spent many winter nights before a flickering candle, turning precious parchment pages—one of the three books that were in their house, each one treasured and re-read a hundred times, and stored in her mother's ancient dowry trunk. But just because she could read did not mean she wanted others to know about it, especially now, as they were deciphering the lettering on the sign above the inn, and Lizabette was showing off.

"Yes, yes, well," Grial said, as she started to maneuver the cart into the inn's small alley on the side of the building. "And so it is, as you can see, exactly as I described."

Just as they almost had Betsy turned around and into the alley, a very fast-moving vehicle driven by four very fine horses—followed by a groom and four spares, and flanked by an escort of another four riders—sped by the street, sending up icy sludge in every direction and scattering urchins.

The girls walking next to the cart jumped back to get out of the way while those in the cart had their necks craned to look. And then Lizabette gasped and her mouth fell open. "Did you see that carriage?" she cried, raising mittens to her cheeks. "It bore the Imperial Crest! And those horses? All purebred Arabians, no less, with braided tails and curled manes! And those Imperial uniformed knights! Good heavens, who could that be, here in this provincial outpost of a town?"

"And you said Tussecan has no crests," muttered Regata.

In moments they were in the back of the inn, and everyone got off the cart, grabbed their belongings, and helped Grial unhitch Betsy. At the same time a matronly woman dressed in warm red woolens with an apron came out from the back door and, seeing Grial, beckoned with a smile and a nod.

"Hello there, Mrs. Beck!" Grial cried in her loud sonorous

voice, turning to wave, and finishing up with the cart. "I've brought visitors for you and the Mistress—all Cobweb Brides, to boot! Have you got room in the barn for my Betsy here? Oh, and a room or two for the girls and me would be nice too!" And then she added, "Now, go on in, ladies, don't just stand here in the cold! We've got plenty of work to do tonight!"

Everyone hastened inside. Percy was one of the last ones, because she and Jenna helped Grial take Betsy into the barn and got her settled in a clean and warm stall between two other horses. Then Percy pushed Jenna forward and into the back entry of Ronna's Inn.

What Grial said about work was not a joke. They ended up waiting tables, scrubbing dishes, and helping Mrs. Beck and her women with the meal to pay for their supper and beds, which was more than fine with Ronna Liet, the innkeeper and Grial's relation, a slightly plump and short woman in a full brown skirt topped by a starched white apron, a clean cotton blouse, and an easy smile on her face. Her expression was lively, with more than a bit of an attitude, and she had greying hair sticking in messy frizzy tendrils from underneath her bonnet.

That frizzy hair was obviously a family trait. When they unbundled inside, Grial turned out to have an unruly mop of witchy-wild hair with enough kink in it to make you dizzy if you stared at her head too long. But she was also revealed to be a younger woman then Percy had expected, middle-aged to be precise, and with a rather shapely figure that was not done justice by her messy multi-colored dress.

"Cobweb Brides, you say?" Ronna began, following Grial around, as soon as the girls were shown to their various tasks. "Well, indeed. They're all over town, like vermin. First, a day ago when the Decree was read, there were mass hysterics and families weeping, as you can imagine. Then the town practically emptied. Our own girls have all gone on ahead—including half of my serving staff, which is why we're so shorthanded now—

while these newcomers from all parts are passing through. What a mess!

"We have at least three of them staying in the inn tonight, and I think two more came in just earlier and are eating right now. Very subdued and haggard-looking, the poor things—quite unlike your own lively lot in that sense. But as long as they don't bother the other guests and do their part in paying, I don't mind, I suppose. Though, if you ask me, this whole thing is crazy and sad." And Ronna shook her head, then rested hands on her ample hips.

"Tragic it is, but what can we do? Death's demand it is, and we mortal fools must comply if we want to go on with the mortal part." Grial spoke this while putting on a rather sooty and grease-stained apron that she removed from her own bag of belongings; she was getting ready to help in the kitchen. And then she added, "So, dumpling, tell me how you've been. What's the talk these days? Any juicy gossip for me? Letheburg's all gone dry, what with the Cobweb Bride business. They've even forgotten the Ducal warring in these here parts."

"Over there, child." Ronna pointed to a place on the hallway table for Jenna who'd just come in from the kitchen, to deposit a laden tray of freshly baked dinner rolls. And then she replied, "Yes, the Red and Blue Duke's armies had a meet over Lake Merlait—the same night that Death stopped, they say. Horrific stuff happened, and apparently they carried half the men home in pieces—living pieces!" Ronna shuddered.

"You don't say!" Grial rubbed her nose with the back of her hand and smeared a spot of greasy soot into a large streak. Percy, who stood nearby arranging clean dishes on another hall side table, reached over and handed her a wet dishcloth.

"Thank you, pumpkin," Grial said, cleaning her face.

"Oh, oh! And worst of all," Ronna said, "Duke Hoarfrost himself is one of those . . . you know, *undead*. He's been struck a mortal blow, fell through to the bottom of the lake and came right back out as you please, an iced-over madman—so aptly named, wouldn't you say. Who knew that he'd become the very thing that he was named? So anyway, he and Goraque declared a truce and he just marched back home to his godforsaken Keep. And now Hoarfrost's terrorizing the locals—not just on his side of the lake but here too, in Goraque territory!"

"How so?"

"Supposedly—" and Ronna leaned in closer to Grial as though not wanting any of the girls to hear—"he's patrolling the land with his armies and hunting all of you Cobweb Brides. Rumor has it he wants to stay among the living forever and so, none can get through and into the Northern Forest, which is just rotten awful, if you ask me."

Grial exhaled loudly. "Oh, my . . . yes."

"And," Ronna continued, "there's supposedly this—this— well, a particularly terrifying knight. Some say it's his own son—who's dressed in midnight-black armor and slays anyone who tries to fight through! Ugh!" She shuddered again. "I certainly do not envy any of your pretties."

"To be slain by a mysterious knight in black armor when one is on one's way to meet Death—yes, that indeed is a hoary fate," Grial said. "Though, sweetie, how does the slaying part work these days? I thought that was the whole point, no one *can* get slain?"

"Ah, Grial, you're right! What am I blathering?" exclaimed Ronna, slapping herself on the hip. "My sources are daft to be spreading such tales at a time like this. There's probably no black knight, and this is all a whole crock of—"

"Well now, I wouldn't go so far as to say there's no black knight. He may very well exist, and I thank you kindly for warning me and the girls ahead, as to his possibility, especially if he is liable to hack us to pieces. Now, if you'd have told me there were a dozen black knights, or a bushel and a peck, or a whole platoon of them, I would find that a bit hard to believe. But one frightening fellow? Certainly within the realm of the reasonable."

Flor and Regata came into the hallway from the kitchen, carrying the supper main course in a large covered kettle destined for the dining guests of the inn. While Ronna pointed to the side table, they deposited the heavy kettle upon an iron pot rest. And at that point, Flor, who had the most experience in the kitchen, being a baker's child, cleared her throat and said to Ronna: "Begging pardon, Ma'am, but Mrs. Beck sends the pot roast, and here it is. But—" And here Flor paused, with an almost fearful expression surfacing—"but I'm not sure the dish came out quite . . . right."

Ronna frowned. "What do you mean? Mrs. Beck is the finest cook in town! What are you saying, girl?"

Flor turned extremely pale and then flushed pink and clutched her hands together until her knuckles turned white. "I— that is, Mrs. Beck is no doubt a wonder, and it's not that the roast is burnt or anything, but—it has the wrong *smell*."

"What?" Ronna exclaimed. "Does it smell *bad?*"

"Oh, no, no! That is," Flor continued bravely, "what I'm trying to say, Ma'am, is that the nice cut of meat does not *have* any meaty smell at all—you know, the roasted sweet aroma that comes when it's all done and cooked up juicy an' ready to be served. Well, this piece—a very nice rump slice, to be sure—it just doesn't smell *cooked*, although I've been supervising it over the fire for the last hour at least, upon Mrs. Beck's instruction, Neither does it smell wrong, it just, well, it looks a little odd, is all, and that there's no smell at all—"

"Did you tell Mrs. Beck?"

Flor again paled. "Well . . . No, Ma'am. I know how much pride a fine cook such as Mrs. Beck takes in their work, so it's not my place to criticize. When my Pa makes bread in our bakery he tells us never to say anything because it's his job to know how to bake things just right and only the paying customers can tell him their opinion, while it's our job to make sure we don't make mistakes when we do the baking—"

"All right, let me see this thing," Ronna muttered. She lifted the lid off the hot kettle and leaned forward to sniff the vapor that started to rise immediately.

She took several deep breaths while Grial and the others watched in silence. And then Ronna frowned deeply and put the lid back down.

"You're right," she said. "It smells like . . . *nothing*. In fact, less than nothing. Wood shavings would have more smell. Didn't Mrs. Beck add several cloves of garlic in there? What in the world?"

"She did, in fact, and I helped her. We also put in dill and potatoes and carrots and two large onions finely cut up. It's all in there, if you look. But none of it smells like *food*."

"Funny you bring this up now," Grial said. "But over the last day or so I've noticed that most food has been a little odd, to say the least. Even back in Letheburg. Tastes like hay or sawdust, and feels like lumps of clay going down."

"Hmm. . . ." Ronna's fluid eyebrows moved in and out of a frown, and she appeared to be deep in thought. While the girls stared at her, she approached the tray of baked rolls and stared critically at then.

And then she leaned forward and sniffed.

"Hah!" said Ronna in triumph. "Now these smell perfectly fine! Come, all of you, tell me I am not soft in the head, take a whiff."

One by one, Grial, Jenna, Flor, Regata, and even Percy came to smell the rolls.

When her turn came, Percy inhaled a sweet floury smell of freshly baked breadstuff that made her mouth water, and there was an almost painful rumble in her stomach. None of them had eaten yet, what with getting the supper ready for the guests. . . .

"The rolls smell scrumptious, baked to perfection," Grial said. "My compliments to Mrs. Beck and all of you lades who helped. Now, the mystery of the pot roast remains, however."

Ronna went back to the kettle and lifted up the lid. Everyone gathered around it, staring at the dish inside, the chunk of meat surrounded by diced vegetables and steaming sauce broth. In fact, everything looked very much uncooked. As though the items were just placed into the pot over a minute ago.

Percy saw the meat and for a moment—maybe it was a trick of the eye, but it looked pink and raw and absolutely uncooked to her. In fact, if she hadn't been sure she was looking at a separated chunk of some poor animal, she could almost say the flesh was moving, quivering, was somehow *alive*.

Percy stepped back, because all of a sudden everything flooded her, the awareness, all of it, and she started to gag.

And she was not the only one. Regata, already on the pale side, went livid and swallowed, then staggered back and rested against the hallway wall.

And then Jenna began to scream. "Oh God! Oh dear God, it's just like the one my Pa couldn't kill! Oh, dear God!"

"Hush, child, hush. . . . Oh, you poor dear, what is it?" Grial said, and took Jenna in a hug.

"Her Pa butchers livestock," Percy said quietly. "The other day, there was . . . a problem. There was a pig in their shed and. . . ."

"*No!*" Jenna shrieked and struggled to escape Grial's hold, and put hands over her ears while squeezing her eyes shut.

"Oh, goodness!" Ronna said, "Hush, girl, what will the guests think?"

"I'd better not speak any more, Ma'am," Percy said. "It was rather horrible, and Jenna was the one assisting her Pa that night, so—"

"All right, that's enough then," Grial said, stroking the wheat-colored top of Jenna's tightly braided head in soothing motions. It seemed to work immediately, as though Jenna was a puppy and Grial had a magic touch.

In that moment a side-door opened and Lizabette, wearing a

starched apron, peeked in from the large dining room where she had been setting out the flatware and dishes, and asked: "Pardon, Ma'am, but your guests are waiting for the meal. When are we serving?"

And then Lizabette noticed everyone's long faces, not to mention Jenna, barely composed and huddling against Grial.

"Oh . . . my," Ronna said, paying no attention to the new arrival and staring off into space. "Something just occurred to me. This cut of meat is *fresh*. It has just come in from the butcher's earlier this morning. All the meat we've been using to make meals before that has been frozen and sitting in the inn's pantry in the cellar. And—"

"And it has all been butchered either last week or at some point before Death stopped," Grial finished for her.

"Yes!"

"Oh, my."

So what does that mean, exactly?" Flor said. "What's wrong with it?"

"It means, girlie," Grial said, running her tongue against her mouth then pursing her lips, "that all the meat and other foodstuff that's been killed or plucked or fished or harvested, or otherwise had its life or existence cut short *after* Death's stopping, is in the same suspended state—let's call it *undeath*, shall we—and cannot be used."

"What? But we'll starve!" Regata exclaimed. "That is, pardon me, Ma'am and you Grial, Ma'am. And also, that doesn't explain the rolls! They seem to be fine! Why aren't they also undead?"

"Undead rolls? Goodness, how gruesome. But—aha!" Grial exclaimed in turn, and quickly leaned forward and grabbed a puffy still-warm roll off the tray, then bit into it. "Mmm, delicious indeed. So then, who thinks they can explain this miracle?"

"Bread flour comes from grain that was harvested months ago in the fall," mumbled Percy softly, not looking at anyone and sort of examining the dishtowel in her hands.

Grial whirled around with excited wide eyes and a sudden crazed look on her face and pulled Jenna by the shoulder turning her along with herself with one hand, then pointed with her other hand at Percy.

"That's exactly right, duck! You have it!"

Percy stared at Grial's extended finger, while everyone else stared back at her.

Then Lizabette spoke again, addressing Ronna. "Ma'am? So then, what should we do about the hungry guests?"

Ronna put hands on her hips, took in a deep breath, and turning to Flor, said: "So, you're a baker's daughter, is that right?"

Flor nodded.

"Excellent! I think for starters you're going to march right back into the kitchen and tell Mrs. Beck to fire up that oven. . . . A couple of the rest of you will come along with me and we'll take a look in the pantry to see what other grains and dry goods we have. I'll pay all of you girls extra, on top of your free night's lodging of course, but since we *are* short-staffed—"

Everyone groaned. It was turning into a horribly long evening and an even longer night.

Chapter 8

Claere Liguon, the Infanta and Grand Princess of the Realm, was impervious to the rolling movement of the splendid Imperial carriage. Despite its handsome padding and brocade pillows and other interior comforts, the carriage had been jostling along the icy roads for over two hours, moving at a speed entirely too wild for two of the other three passengers occupying the seats.

The first was a man seated directly across from her. Vlau Fiomarre had stilled in a state of apathy, his once-handsome bruised face turned to stare impassively through the slit in the window curtains at the rushing whiteness of the winter countryside. He wore a plain borrowed jacket and winter coat that had been given to him in the Palace guest quarters—not shabby but obviously the hand-me-downs of a ranking servant. As such, it was still a resounding insult.

The other two passengers of the carriage were a different matter. In the seat of rather dubious honor next to the Infanta sat Lady Milagra Rinon, First Lady-in-Attendance, clutching a handkerchief to her lips, bundled in an ermine cape-coat with a voluminous hood, both the coat and its wearer as pale as the snowscape outside. And across from her, next to the motionless Fiomarre, was Lady Selene Jenevais, also in Attendance upon

Her Imperial Highness, equally pale and shaky from the road sickness, wearing a fox-fur coat.

Or maybe it was not merely the road sickness. The two Ladies had to attend an Imperial animated corpse and spend several hours confined in *her* presence and that of her murderer; queasiness and terror came with their duty.

The Emperor had insisted upon this escort. The Infanta wanted nothing and no one to slow down her journey, but in this the Emperor would not budge. In addition to the two Ladies of her Court, and a spare team of four horses that was driven by a second groom following immediately behind, there were four distinguished and valiant knights assigned to guard the carriage. Initially the Emperor had wanted to send along a whole cadre of soldiers, but relented, and the four knights were a compromise.

The Infanta herself wore unusually plain travel clothes for someone of her rank—a basic coat of deep sienna red wool, untrimmed, and hooded—and underneath she had changed out of her bloodied court dress into a plain grey gown which resembled a convent habit in severity and probably belonged to a maid. She looked nothing more than a mousy servant herself, and her Ladies-in-Attendance would have thrown shocked looks at her attire had they not studiously avoided looking at all in her direction, if possible.

On the third hour of such breakneck speed, just past noon, they had arrived in Letheburg. The Infanta herself required no stop, but the driver had paused in order to exchange the teams of horses and give the rest of the passengers a brief respite. While the horses were tended to, the two Ladies-in-Attendance stretched their stiff limbs outside and used the facilities of the best inn, all the while being watched carefully by the four knights who also availed themselves of the break, one at a time.

Fiomarre was escorted under guard by two of the knights to relieve himself if necessary, and then he was back, silent and unprotesting, in the seat across from the Infanta.

For a few minutes they were alone in the carriage, just the two of them. Claere did not blink, looking at the now familiar man before her who had struck her a mortal blow only two days earlier. He in turn avoided her infernally unfaltering gaze—the gaze of a dead wild creature, a bird with glass eyes—and observed his hands, at present free of shackles. He had spent the night before in a guest apartment in the Palace, and had kept his word to remain and attend her.

And now, here he was, and here she was, and it seemed at rather odd moments that the carriage was closing in on him, on her, and they were sharply aware of one another again, reliving that moment of greatest closeness and intensity, the stroke of death, the drawing of life that bound them together.

"What do you think about?" Claere said, breaking the stifling silence. Her breath came laboring to form the words, precise like the strokes of a clock.

He looked up with a barely contained jerk, and for the first time in hours his eyes focused on her face.

"I—" he said.

"What are your thoughts now, Fiomarre?" she repeated. "You must be in a very dark place. I am . . . sorry. For everything that happened to you—including myself."

His brows moved and he exhaled loudly then looked away, down, to the side—anywhere away from her. And then he barely spoke, in a faint whisper: "It is too late . . . for sorrow."

"No," she said, in a strong voice, unlike his own. "It is never too late. I should know. I am on borrowed time. While you have all the time in the world. Or—well, maybe not all, maybe not quite. . . ."

"What do you want of me, Liguon?" he exclaimed suddenly. He was looking directly at her, and his face had turned several shades deeper red with emotion. "You want me to beg your forgiveness for cutting your life short? Well, is that what this is about, this mockery of a pleasure trip in the country? Why am I here, with you, and not chained in the dungeon of your accursed father—where I, a damned man, properly belong? Why? Can you tell me that much, or are your plans for my torment so subtle that I cannot even begin to guess—"

"It is not my intention to torment or punish you. I already told you this much when I said you were a free man. Free to go or stay. You can rise and leave, right now, if it is your choice. No one will stop you, if I order it—and I will. My only stipulation was for you to honor my investigation of your family's fate. For, I must understand what has come to pass, the full course of events that have resulted in this misfortune for you and me, for so many. . . ."

"There is nothing to understand . . ." he said. "I see now that you may very well be a fool innocent among vipers, that you were indeed unaware of your Imperial Family's underhanded cruelty—but it will not diminish my hatred for you and yours. No matter how prettily you speak or how honorably you appear to act."

"I do not appear. I *am* exactly as you see."

"Very well! Then why do you take me with you on this one-way trip? What kind of investigating of my so-called fate can you accomplish in the forests, in the middle of nowhere, while headed to meet Death in order to present yourself as his Bride?"

And he glared at her with a triumphant smile, as though having caught her red-handed in an act of dissembling—tangible proof of Liguon dishonor.

But the Infanta returned his look with her own birdlike stare, and she said, "My understanding of your family will be based on my understanding of you. You are one and the same."

"What?" he said.

In that moment the carriage door opened and Lady Milagra, followed by Lady Selene, were helped to ascend the stair and then they seated themselves, and the door was closed by a bowing footman.

Fiomarre went silent and dead, turning away once more. The newcomers gave him frightened brief looks.

"Begging Your Pardon for the delay, Your Imperial Highness," began Milagra, sitting as far away on the bench seat as possible from the Infanta.

"Driver, proceed!" the Infanta said loudly on a harsh breath, ignoring the Lady. And then she stopped breathing again, and stared out the window as the carriage commenced moving.

"If it's permitted to speak—I believe, Your Imperial Highness," Lady Selene said in a soft careful voice, "the driver tells us we will be at the last town bordering the Northern Forest before nightfall. It's a tiny fringe town at the very edge of the Dukedom of Goraque, called Tussecan, I think. Right after it, begins the wilderness."

The Silver Court was in turmoil after the assassination of the Infanta. But because of the odd coupling of this event with Death's stopping and everything that it entailed, the turmoil was low-key and subdued. Everyone spoke in whispers, courtiers of all ranks hurried in the halls, not stopping for longer than a moment to exchange information, and a lull of winter silence seemed to have descended upon the Palace.

On the second day after the Event—a word with capital letter emphasis, as everyone in the upper crust was beginning to refer to it, echoed readily by the upper servants—the food they were eating stopped being suitable for consumption.

They hardly noticed it at first, thinking the fault to lie with themselves, a lack of appetite, a malady that temporarily blocked the senses of taste and smell.

But toward suppertime on the end of the second day, it could not be denied—possibly it was at about this time that they had run out of older foodstuffs *harvested* before the Event, depleting supplies of freshly consumed edibles. The most grisly discovery was that newly butchered meat was *alive*—if butchering was the right word to refer to the unspeakable atrocity. The produce too, anything that was freshly cut from the hothouses, was suspended in that same *undead* state. Cooking things did not seem to have any effect. Fire did not consume them, hot water did not scald or in any way tenderize.

Priests were brought in, and Masses went on, full-time now, in various chambers of the Palace and its surrounding lands. In other, more clandestine chambers, other more occult rituals took place, such that went without a blessing from the church.

The sudden urgency to meet Death's demand for his Cobweb Bride finally became more than clear to everyone—either the world complied, or they would all painfully starve . . . unto eternity. For not even death would come as a blessed relief.

And seeing how dire things had become—beyond obeying an Imperial Decree, beyond familial honor—this was now a common struggle for all to *exist* without pain.

Merely living was no longer an issue.

It was at that critical point that all women—from the highest-ranking noble to the nameless low-born—suddenly found themselves to be prospective Cobweb Brides.

The Duke Claude Rovait stood in the partial shadow of a long sparsely-used Imperial Palace hallway, staring through the window outside at the convoluted walls and the balcony overhang of another Palace structure, directly opposite, and no more than fifty feet away. Here the walls of the Palace angled and curved onto themselves, so that standing at the window and looking out one could observe the rest of the hallway beyond the bend, but from the outside looking in, as seen by looking into the opposite window near the balcony.

It was a very useful vantage point, unknown to many, but used regularly by the Imperial spy network of those who worked on behalf of the Realm under the leadership of the Duke of Rovait and the Duke of Plaimes. Here they could discreetly observe the Court in a far busier portion of the corridor that was centrally located. And here, to this locus of movement, it seemed, they've finally pinpointed a pattern of unusual activity.

Activity that could be pinned down upon enemy agents working on behalf of the Sapphire Court of the distant southern Domain.

Claude Rovait had his strong suspicions for many months that they had been infiltrated, but had come upon the pattern only a month ago—very subtle initially—and his other observers were positioned here and at other vantage points around the clock, until they could be sure.

Soon, they were. They observed questionable contacts between unlikely individuals, overly casual and quick exchanges, and most of all, they observed messenger birds being received and dispatched from this exact balcony near the window, around the bend of the hall.

And now, Rovait patiently watched a small dark speck of a pigeon hopping along the railing of the balcony, waiting. The pigeon was here earlier that morning, and possibly as a precaution on their part no one came for it. But this time, it was back, and he knew he was about to see positive results.

In about fifteen minutes, his wait was justified. The window near the balcony opened slightly, and what looked to be a woman's hand—he could tell astutely from the delicate shape and the sleeve—reached out, and the bird immediately alighted. The hand withdrew together with the bird. Then moments later, the bird, with obvious remnants of dry feed scattering from its beak, and surely a concealed message somewhere around its feathered torso and feet, took off again, rising up, soaring in a black speck against the white winter sky.

The balcony window shut once more. All that remained was for the Duke to see who would come walking around the corner, either in his direction, or the opposite—where another one of his men stood ready to take note—and he will have his hostile operative in the bag, so to speak.

In his mind he counted, and just before he reached twelve, a laughing threesome strode boisterously toward him in the hallway. He knew them immediately. The Duke proceeded to lean down to adjust the buckle of his shoe, fumbling and making noises of frustration, then rising just in time to see Lady Amaryllis Roulle, Lady Ignacia Chitain, and Lord Nathan Woult, the three charming and trend-setting troublemakers known in Court as the League of Folly, saunter by, making their typical flighty and condescending commentary—at the same high volume level as though the disturbing current events of the last few days did not concern them.

Without bestowing any overt attention upon them he observed the women's sleeves and recognized the fabric on one of them.

As he looked, he also noted the raven-haired beauty Lady Amaryllis throwing him a darting glance.

"So my dears, when will you be off to play Cobweb Brides?" said Lord Nathan Woult mockingly as soon as they were past the stretch of hallway where the unfashionably-dressed Duke of Rovait busied himself with his footwear.

"Why, as soon as possible—anything to accommodate your desire for that fresh rare steak. Isn't that so, my dear Nathan?" Lady Amaryllis retorted.

Lady Ignacia made a sound halfway between a snort and a giggle, tossing her bright auburn hair. "Honestly, now, I wouldn't mind a bit of steak myself," she added. "Only, this is all very dire and misfortunate, and I am not sure I am up to such an . . . uhm . . . adventure."

"None of us are, sweet," Lady Amaryllis replied sharply. "And yet, we must. There is not a moment to waste, for oh-so many reasons, the least of which is steak. So off we go, right now."

"What? *Now?*" Lady Ignacia's pretty rosebud mouth fell open.

"But—aren't you forgetting something, sweetlings?" said Woult. "Such as—the plumbing of your wardrobes for suitable attire would take at least all the rest of the afternoon and most of this evening? Anything less would be an outrage to fashion."

"I say, indeed, Amaryllis, how will we manage to get ready to leave today? This is a bit overly hasty, isn't it? Sort of daft, really."

The Lady thus addressed whirled around and stopped in the hallway, overtly pouting, looking from one of her friends to the other.

"If you are not up to it," she said, "then I am off on my own. My sweet Papa's not going to miss me or the Curricle of Doom."

"Oh heavens, not the Curricle of Doom!" Ignacia gave a small scream. "You cannot think to drive that thing in such weather?"

"What weather?" Lady Amaryllis snorted. "Look outside, my dear, it is still and dead, a Winter calm. The snowflakes are hardly coming down, and the Curricle has taken me on far rougher trips than this. The one immense advantage is that it will be the fastest thing on the road, and we can run over a whole battalion's worth of other Cobweb Brides on their way to the same place we'll be heading. Less competition, you know."

"Hah! Now you're jesting completely," Nathan exclaimed. "You can't mean to say you actually *want* less competition in this endeavor? Would you really have Death pick *you* as his very own, one and only? I thought the point was just to have a thimble of fun, and to let the other damsels and ladies stampede the Grim Fellow?"

"Nathan, I hate to say this," Ignacia mumbled. "But I do believe this has all crossed the line beyond fun and into duty a long time ago. And you know what happens to Amaryllis when she perceives a challenge. We are in for it now. Adventure is unavoidable."

In the deepening evening twilight the forest was a crystalline thing of blue pallor and barren black tree branches. It had began to snow again, softly, and the snow dusted the world, deepening all layers and filling the still air with sparkle in the light of the rising moon.

Beltain stood shifting in place, feeling his body freeze slowly, and moved his fingers and toes in reflex, bundled as they were in layers of wool inside the boots and gloves and underneath the deadly cold of the metal mail. Only motion could keep one from freezing now, during night patrol. His warhorse stood nearby and he would periodically pull its lead to make it take a step or two to stay alert.

As near as a few feet away, and ranging onwards, scattered about the forest were his men. A small discreet fire burned on the ground in a very deep, semi-concealed pit that had been dug out with great difficulty with ice picks, and they took turns warming their fingers over the embers. Occasionally a black form would move past, to report to his ranking officer who would in turn report directly to Beltain.

Somewhere deeper in the forest, at least three miles away, was his father. Duke Hoarfrost was patrolling a stretch of icy wilderness where a living man would have greater difficulty, but a dead man might as well make himself useful. Several other undead Chidair soldiers were with Hoarfrost, and the living men who reported back and forth between them, were suitably wary of the task.

Over the course of the afternoon and evening they had intercepted at least several dozen potential Cobweb Brides. The women had been found making their way through the forest and along paths, and many had come along the major road leading north-west from Tussecan. They were young and not-so-young, most sorry and haggard, walking alone and in groups of two or three, some carrying bundles, others empty-handed and resigned to not having to come back. There had been at least ten noblewomen complete with servants and carriages to accompany them. The carriages had been stopped easily, any guards surrendered or beaten off, and the women were all herded together and then taken in small groups back to the ducal Keep and settlement that was situated deeper in Chidair lands, to be placed in custody and held indefinitely.

Several times the women themselves or their guards resisted, or fought back, or ran. The Chidair patrols had to give chase, and at times there had been brief skirmishes. Beltain had given his men a direct order to avoid bloodshed as much as possible, and if a fight was inevitable, to seek to overpower instead of strike killing blows.

"No maiming," he had also told them. "Do not take limbs." Doing so was the cruelest thing possible under the circumstances, since death could not relieve anyone, but limbs lost were gone forever and mortal pain had no relief.

Beltain thought of pain, the dull ache in his own battle-weary body, the bruises slowly healing underneath the wool and mail and the everpresent cold. He thought of what it all meant, what they were doing, what *he* was doing. And yet he did not allow himself to think too far, for that would invoke questions, and he could not bear to question things, not now. . . .

"My Lord," said one of his men, Riquar, bearded and bearish, emerging from the shadows up ahead in the direction where the road lay, and beyond it, Lake Merlait. "There is a quickly moving carriage of sorts, coming this way. Looks to be well-guarded too, and extra horses. How should we proceed?"

Beltain exhaled deeply, watching his breath curl in pale vapor. He then moved toward his horse. "Proceed as before," he replied, gripping the saddle, mounting with some difficulty, but unassisted by a squire—a testament to his determination and sheer strength. "Set up the ambush teams on both sides of the road, then bring out the roadblock. But make sure the cut tree is visible from a distance, giving them advance notice. I want no overturned carriages and unnecessary damage, nor hurt innocents."

"Yes, sir."

The man disappeared ahead, and Beltain whistled, giving the signal for patrol on alert. He leaned forward in the saddle and urged his horse forward, while all around the forest came alive with dark moving figures of his men, converging rapidly upon the road south of their location.

Beltain rode carefully, avoiding clumps of unpassable brush and snow, while branches struck him occasionally on the helmet and shoulders and chest plate, sending blasts of icy fresh powder over the minimal exposed area of his already numb face. His powerful horse knew the forest well, and he relied upon the beast's ability to avoid pratfalls and find its own way.

Soon, he and his men were at the edge of a clearing. The roadway spread on both sides of them, one end leading southeast to Tussecan, the other disappearing further north until the road itself became a forest path, then dissolved into hoary impassable woodland in Chidair territory and beyond. Here was no-man's land, the boundary between Chidair and Goraque, spanning all of the thoroughfare and the northern lakeshore, technically lands belonging only to the King of Lethe and ultimately to the Emperor of the Realm.

Which meant that he and his Chidair soldiers had as much right to be here as that carriage.

The clamor of its approach and the galloping horses announced its coming half a mile ahead, as might the best of court chamberlains. Beltain wondered who would have such urgent business at this hour, and here, on the outskirts of civilized territories. He had little doubt this was all somehow related to the Cobweb Bride situation.

Three Chidair soldiers plunged forward and down the snowy embankment dragging a felled pine tree, cumbersome with evergreen branches, many of which were still loaded with packed snow. They arranged it across the roadway, then retreated to both sides and hid along the snowdrifts and shrubbery flanking the road.

Everyone waited for Beltain's signal in silence.

One more bend of the road, and the galloping carriage came into view, a dark expensive thing carried by fine horses, with two wrought-iron lanterns hung in the front to illuminate their way with a golden radiance against the blue night. Their illumination extended just far enough to reveal the sudden obstacle lying before them.

The driver reacted swiftly and pulled up the team just short of the fallen trunk and branches, with a yell and clatter and angry protesting neighing of the horses. Coming immediately after, a groom barely reined in the four spare horses, and four mail-clad knights burst forward, passing the carriage and flanking it on all sides, their mounts pulled up and rearing in frustration. The knights were armed—for Beltain could see the sudden glint of bared steel in the moonlight—and they sat atop great horses, true pedigree beasts bred for heavy combat.

The same moonlight also revealed Imperial insignias and coat-of-arms on the clothing of the knights and decorating the sides of the carriage.

Very interesting. . . . But damn, thought Beltain, this was not going to be easy. And unfortunately this exchange was very likely going to be deadly.

He gritted his teeth. His right hand encased in the gauntlet went for the great sword at his side. And his mind filled with steel and winter.

Raising his left hand in a sharp motion Beltain gave the command to attack. At the same time he drove his warhorse forward and emerged crashing through the shrubbery of the raised embankment and down onto the road, readying his sword-hand for a deadly blow.

His men burst forward with cries but he paid them no more heed, for he had entered the battle mindset and was oblivious to everything but the enemy.

The closest of the knights came at him with a yell, but Beltain advanced like a battering ram and his blow brought the man down from his horse so that he was dragged several feet in the saddle. Beltain had already turned away and was engaging the second knight while his men swarmed the fallen knight and immobilized him with nets and ropes.

"If you can help it, do not strike to kill!" Beltain exclaimed, and then regretfully had to act against his own orders and hacked the knight's right arm off after plunging the sword deep into his chest in a purely defensive strike. The mortally hurt man screamed and continued screaming while blood poured out of him, black in the moonlight, and sluggishly froze in the snow. "Forgive me . . ." Beltain whispered as he severed another limb so that the knight could not resume his attack as an undead, and instead slumped forward then fell from his horse.

"Surrender!" Beltain yelled hoarsely to the third knight who was approaching from the other side of the carriage. "Surrender now and state your business and I swear upon the name of Chidair you will not be harmed!"

"No, it is you who will surrender, villain! You will lay down your arms before your betters. We are Peers of the Realm, on Imperial business," replied the third knight, keeping a shrewd distance, having seen how two of his comrades have fared against this one knight. His face was uncovered halfway and his helm's partial visor remained up so that Beltain could see two dark intense eyes underneath heavy brows. At his side, the fourth knight approached and the two of them maneuvered their horses so that they had their backs turned to the carriage protectively and their swords drawn.

"Will you attack both of us at once, Sir Knight—if that is what you truly are? Or will you send your rabble to take us on?" spoke the fourth knight, his low belly-rumble voice echoing through the forest. He cut a great figure, a huge hulking shape, helm covering his face—truly, a giant not unlike Beltain's own

father, the Duke Hoarfrost. Indeed, he seemed familiar and
Beltain thought he might have seen this one in the ranks before,
might have even fought him in courtly competition, but could
recall no name to match the figure.

"I and my men have no wish to attack either of you,"
replied Beltain in a cool steady voice. "But if it comes to a fight,
I promise your honor will not be besmirched. I am Lord Beltain
Chidair, son of the Duke Ian Chidair, Lord of the lands which
you are about to enter. Who are you? What is your business
here? Who sits inside the carriage that you guard?"

"Since when has it become necessary to explain one's
presence on a public road?" said the smaller knight with the
heavy brows. "I am Baron Carlo Irnolas, Peer of the Imperial
Silver Court, at my side is Lord Givard Mariseli, and we are on
the business of the Emperor."

"What of the carriage?" said Beltain, motioning with his
blood-stained swordblade. "Who is inside?"

The two knights glanced from one to the other. Finally the
baron spoke, after a pause just significant enough that Beltain
suspected he was not about to impart the whole truth: "Within
are . . . two noble ladies of the Silver Court. You must swear not
to harm them. You must let us be on our way!"

Beltain sighed. This was truly not to his liking but he had to
proceed. "These two noble ladies—are they by any chance on
their way to present themselves to Death as Cobweb Brides?"

Another long pause. Then Lord Mariseli, the larger of the
two men, exhaled loudly, and said, before the baron could
interject, "Why, yes, they are."

"In that case," Beltain said, "I may not allow you to
proceed. I am under orders not to allow any potential Cobweb
Brides to pass through this forest and the lands, by order of the
Duke Hoarfrost, my father. Set down your weapons and
surrender and I swear neither the ladies nor yourselves will be in
any danger. I must simply take you to the Chidair Keep where
you will be accommodated according to your noble rank. If you

resist, I will be forced to injure you with mortal wounds. And yes, I will remove your limbs so that although at present you cannot die, you will be crippled—just as your unfortunate comrade-at-arms over there." And he pointed to the fallen undead knight who sprawled in a barely moving mess with only one leg and one arm still attached to his torso, his body twitching and emptying of the last of his blood. . . .

"This is an outrage!" Baron Irnolas exclaimed. "We are knights under Imperial Orders, and we are sworn to lay down our lives for—" And then he grew silent. Instead, with a quick desperate movement his sword arm lashed out and he struck Beltain on the left side, blade slamming against his shoulder.

Beltain reacted swiftly, turning his torso to lessen the impact of the blow, yet could not avoid the strike completely. The blade did not pass the chainmail or the plate, and yet the impact of it was powerful enough that his left arm went numb momentarily and he knew that serious damage was done. But he ignored both the pain and the numbness and instead struck out with the blunt flat side of his own blade and delivered a resounding slam-blow against the top of the baron's head near the ear. The blow was designed to disorient or even knock him out, and apparently it succeeded. Dazed, the baron teetered in his saddle. Beltain used that instant to push the knight backward, so that he toppled over. Beltain cried out to his men, "Net him! Quick!"

Meanwhile Lord Mariseli roared his anger and attacked Beltain who somehow parried him with his sword. Beltain's powerful right arm received the bone-jarring impact and held—just barely. And the next instant they grappled, still in their saddles.

Fighting Mariseli was like being mauled by a bear, and it did not help his concentration at all that in that instant Beltain heard one of his men shout, "Hey, you, stop! My Lord, there are women escaping from the carriage!"

With a desperate gasp for air—for his chest was being
squeezed by the giant knight—Beltain used a single burst of
violent strength to free himself. He then twisted sharply,
ignoring the agony in his wounded shoulder, and slammed his
other shoulder and elbow like a battering ram into his opponent,
shoving him backward and out of his saddle before this bear of a
man could resume the grapple-attack. It was one of his
trademark unbeatable moves. And this time again his men were
there, with nets, and they confined the raging knight, so that he
flopped like a bound whale on the snow and roared his fury on
top of his voice.

Panting loudly, Beltain did not waste a moment, and rode
around the carriage in pursuit of what looked like two desperate
female figures bundled in expensive winter fur capes, running
back along the road the way they originally came from. Several
of his men had a head-start and were rapidly gaining on the
escapees.

One of the ladies screamed, a shrill terrified voice, and then
began to thrash in the arms of one of his men who was the first
to catch up with her. In an instant she was joined by her
companion, and the two screamed, so piercingly and incessantly,
it seemed, that some of the men who had surrounded them held
their ears while others cursed and spat in the snow.

Beltain's mount carried him up to the group and he
commanded in a tired and angry voice, for silence.

The ladies must have sensed his authority immediately,
because they complied. Beltain squinted, seeing in the moonlight
two pretty faces, frightened and yet proud in that indelible
manner of the noble aristocracy. They were both shaking and
breathless from all the screaming, but their expressions were
unusually resolute, so that once again Beltain felt a twinge of
regret at what he had to do, how he had to act.

"I am Lord Beltain Chidair," he said. "You will not be
harmed." Unfortunately, his stern irritated voice did not soften
the meaning of his words.

"Then have your men unhand me this instant!" exclaimed one of the women, dark-haired and more classically beautiful of the two. "I am Lady Milagra Rinon and my companion is the Lady Selene Jenevais, under the protection of the Emperor. You have neither the right nor the authority to prevent our free movement in these lands."

Beltain watched the lovely shape of her face, the dark full lips, the moonlight-glittering eyes widened with outrage, and he thought, *In the name of God, please do not cry, oh do not start to cry. . . .*

But this one was a hard beauty, and there were to be no tears. Her steady gaze upon him did not falter. And her companion was apparently following her lead in all things, for she too held steady and her rounded childish face remained remarkably brave.

"Ah, Madam, my pardon," he replied, his tone softening with weariness. "However, I regret that in this forest it is my authority and that of the Duke my father that stands. So, without much more unpleasantry and distress, for your sake I insist you comply. It's getting late and rather cold. I ask you to come with me, and you will be treated respectfully, upon my word as a Knight of the Realm."

"Hah!" the lady replied. "You, a Knight? That status will not be for long. Wait 'til the Emperor hears of this—this—"

But he ignored her sputtering and turned to his men.

"Check the carriage to see if anyone else is within. Then, assist these two Ladies of the Court back inside. The knights are to be kept bound upon their horses. We head back to the Keep."

He turned his horse around and followed two of his men to the carriage, without looking back to see if his command was being carried out. He heard only small initial exclamations of protest this time, then silence. Indeed, thank God for small blessings—such as no female shrieking.

The carriage, a fine regal vehicle indeed, stood gaping

open, and no one else was within. Satisfied with the cursory examination of its interior, Beltain turned away, intent on the moonlight and snow and allowed his men to handle the rest. The horses were rounded up, the now-perfectly-docile ladies escorted back inside as politely as possible.

Remarkable, really, it occurred to him suddenly, how docile indeed, how quiet they had become.

As though they had achieved their end.

When the carriage rolled away surrounded by the escort of Chidair soldiers and their knight, when there was nothing else but snowfall and crackling of branches on both sides of the road, Vlau Fiomarre dared raise his head from the snowdrift in which he hid.

Next to him was *she*, the one he'd made into an animated corpse. She lay flat against the ground, just as he had thrown her, and he had piled fresh handfuls of snow upon her, burying her in the whiteness. Next, he had hidden himself practically on top, also digging into the snowdrift next to the roadside shrubbery, having covered their tracks the best he could while the commotion took place. While the two Ladies-in-Attendance had run, as instructed, in the opposite direction, screaming on top of their lungs to create the necessary distraction, he'd helped the Infanta from the carriage, then half-carried her stiff cold body up the small slope, praying in his mind they not be seen—while another detached part of his mind seemed to be looking down at himself with astonishment at the madness of such actions.

"They are gone . . ." he whispered eventually.

No response. Underneath the snow, she did not stir.

He rose and stood up, brushing the snow from himself, watching the spot where she was concealed.

It occurred to him that maybe, just maybe, he really buried her this time, and maybe she will now rest in true eternal peace, silent at last. . . .

At this thought something in his chest painfully twisted, a

spasm of pain, followed by a corresponding tug at the back of his throat, forming immediately into a lump.

No, he thought, swallowing the lump, the pain, *no, I will not sense, will not feel*—

In that instant the snow shifted and slowly she sat up, moving with peculiar effort and stiffness, then took in a deep shuddering breath which she used to speak. "My flesh . . . seems to resist movement. . . . It is the cold. . . . I . . . require . . . a moment."

And he gave her the moment, watching her in cold horrible silence, as she sat, moving her hands and elbows stiffly. He did not offer assistance and she did not ask, as she then raised herself from the ground with supreme effort, then shook the snow from inside the folds of her simple coat. She adjusted it and her head covering, finally raising up the hood—not because she needed it, but to keep up appearances of someone living. Her hands moved oddly, like angular limbs of a doll.

"Thank you for your help," she said unexpectedly. "You— you are—free to go now. I can no longer insist on keeping you at my side, because now everything has changed. Go!"

He stood for a moment speechless. In the moonlight he could see her pale skin and the great stilled eyes, unmoving, glittering with ice, for they had frozen in their sockets.

A terrible chill crept up his spine, separate from the chill of winter, for he realized that he was living the ultimate nightmare—he was alone in the moonlit night in the wilderness, with the shade of the one he'd killed, standing directly across from him. But for some reason all he could think of was the pitiful pallor of her skin and sunken cheeks, her small upright figure, and those great peculiar unblinking eyes, dark and fathomless and tragic in the glamour of the night.

"I will go with you," he said. "You—will need protection in these parts, apparently. You will need someone to help you reach Death's Keep."

"No. I cannot have this," she replied. "You and I are reconciled in my mind. It is over, truly. From now on you are to be free of any regret or guilt for your actions toward me. I have no control over your hatred of my family, but at least you will have no guilt on my behalf. And I bear you no ill will any longer, not even curiosity as to your motives. So, please . . . go."

But he said, "No! I may be a dead man in the law, a dead man, but I am a man of my word. I've given you my promise not to escape."

"This is not an escape. This is but the end of our reckoning."

"Oh, but it is not!" he exclaimed then, taking a step closer toward her, staring directly into her eyes, so that if she had not been dead and stiff with cold she might have taken a step back. His dark eyes were fierce with intensity. "You have no control over hate, my hate, indeed," he said, "and thus you have no control over me. I *choose* to stay. With you. Do you understand, daughter of Liguon?"

"No guilt . . ." she said. "I want no guilt."

"No guilt!" he exclaimed. "No guilt, no guilt, no guilt! Only fury and hatred and retribution! You cannot get rid of me so easily as all that, not unto death even, for you are not the one to forgive me—only the Almighty can do that, and such a thing is not to be. Thus, a damned man, I follow you."

This time she said nothing in reply. She merely turned away from him, and began walking slowly, her feet sinking in the snow, moving away from the road and deeper into the forest.

Panting hard with emotion, the vapor of his breath swirling white against the ice air, he followed her.

Chapter 9

"Percy! Percy! Peeeer-cy! Wake up!"

Jenna was shaking Percy who surfaced out of a dreamless deep sleep to a groggy state of confusion.

"Huh? What?" For a moment Percy did not know where she was, and thought she was in her own bed and it was her younger sister Patty calling her. "Go away, Pat . . ." she muttered, starting to turn over onto her other side, only to bump into a lump that was another warm body. . . .

Everything rushed back, and Percy came awake with a sickening sense of immediate reality, and lifted her head, squinting. They had been lying four to a bed in a small room in Ronna's Inn, and the warm lump was none other than Emilie, still asleep and snoring softly into the pillow. On the other side of Emilie was another one of the girls, but Percy couldn't tell who it was, since she was covered completely with the blanket.

Jenna had slept on Percy's other side at the edge of the bed, but now she had crept out of bed and was whispering loudly, "It's not Pat, it's me, Jenna! You know, Jenna Doneil! Time to get up, an' we oughta get going!"

"Oh, Lord . . ." Percy muttered, sitting up with a groan and rubbing her face. "It is even dawn yet?"

The shutters on the one small window of the room had been

drawn and it was impossible to tell whether there was any light outside.

"Dunno," said Jenna, "but we oughta get going! I just feel it, we need to hurry, hurry!"

"And that would be why?" said Percy in sleep-deprived irritation. She sat up completely and lowered her bare feet to the wooden floorboards. Ouch, the floor was freezing cold.

The night before had been an insane flurry of rushing about back and forth from the pantry to the kitchen and trying to cook breads and porridges for an inn full of hungry guests. They were all of them bone-weary when they finally managed to eat their own share, clean up the kitchen and drag themselves to beds.

While Percy and Jenna set about using the chamberpot, washing up, then putting on their clothes, layers upon layers, the other girls were stirring too. Emilie got up with a huge yawn, clutching her old tattered nightshirt tighter about her against the chill air of the room. The unidentified person on the farthest edge of the bed hidden underneath the blanket turned out to be Gloria Libbin, the Oarclaven blacksmith's daughter, and she nearly fell out of bed, also seeming to forget where she was, initially.

Out in the hall, the inn was coming awake, and they could hear footsteps and voices. They came downstairs one by one and Percy and Jenna were the first of their group.

Ronna the innkeeper was already out of bed and Mrs. Beck got the lounge fireplace going and retreated into the kitchen to begin the day. "Morning, girls. Be sure to have a bite to eat before you head out," said Ronna kindly, glancing at the two. "That goes for all of you."

Jenna tugged Percy's sleeve. "Are we going to be ridin' in Grial's cart again?" she whispered loudly.

"I don't know, that would be up to Grial," Percy replied. "She may not be going on past Tussecan. Remember, she only did us a kindness yesterday. It's not like it's our cart to do with as we please."

"Well, child, it certainly *could* be your cart, if you ask me nicely." The overly bright voice belonged to the familiar frizzy-haired woman, and Percy nearly jumped, turning around at the ringing sound of it.

"Good morning, pretties!" Grial said, pushing her way past them into the doorway of the kitchen, then dragging them by the hands inside. "First, a bite to eat, as Ronna says, or two bites. Maybe even three . . . or four. . . ." And then she broke into a cheerful cackle.

"Grial, what do you mean?" said Percy, taking a roll from a huge tray left over from last night, and sat down on the end of a bench at the cook's table.

"Well, here is the deal, duckie. You go on and take my cart with the rest of the girls, while I stay here in town and visit a bit longer with Ronna, my blood relation. I entrust my darling Betsy and the cart to you, because I know you will take excellent care of her—the cart and Betsy, that is, both of them are a she, and both require excellent care. When you finish up that Cobweb Bride business, you come back here to Tussecan, to this inn, and just drop them off."

Grial was smiling as she finished.

As she listened, Percy's mouth slowly came open. "But—" she said eventually, "but I can't do that! How can you say that, Ma'am? I mean, I am not sure I can . . . well, drive the cart into the forest, and what will we do when the road runs out and we have to go on by foot? And what do I do about Betsy's feed? And what about rubbing her down in the cold and—and—"

"Oh, phooey! You'll do just fine!" Grial exclaimed, taking a large mug of hot tea that Mrs. Beck came to pour for her. She then drew closer to stare at Percy across the table while Jenna watched them with excitement.

"Thing is," Grial said in a conspiratorial voice, "let me tell you a little secret, girlie. That road—those roads, all roads and paths in fact—*they never end.* You might think they do. You might think they just narrow and fade and disappear in the hoary depths of the forest? Not so, not at all! They merely *go into hiding*, and you just have to search a bit harder to see them. Now, Betsy can always see them. Why? Well because she has a knack for it, and because she's Betsy. So, if you have Betsy along with you, there will always be a road, and where there's a road, there's a cart—if you follow my drift. Just trust your instinct, and when you can no longer do so, allow Betsy to take the lead."

Percy and Jenna were staring at Grial, mesmerized by her words. . . . Until Grial broke the spell by hitting the table surface with the palm of her other hand. She set down her mug, then got up to fetch some butter for the rolls from the pantry.

Percy opened then closed her mouth again, while a grin broke through. She glanced over at Jenna, saying, "Goodness, I guess then we have a cart!"

Jenna let out a happy squeal, followed by a series of squeaks.

"What's all the shrieking?" Lizabette came into the kitchen, followed by Regata and the rest of the girls.

"We have a cart! We have a cart!" Jenna intoned with a huge grin.

"We do?" Catrine said. "Well, gracious us, that's just grandiose, as me Ma would say—may the good Lord rest her! I never expected no cart for so long as we got it!"

"Me neither," said her sister Niosta. "And the good eatin' too." And she grabbed two rolls from the tray.

"Grial's just too kind, that she is coming along with us to the forest." Lizabette took a hot mug of tea for herself and a plate of oatmeal and settled at the table.

Percy swallowed a chunk of her roll and looked up. "She's not—not coming, that is. Grial said I can drive the cart and bring it back when we're done with it."

"You?" Lizabette set down her mug and stared at Percy over her sharp nose. "Why, that is just . . . odd."

"Why?" said Percy. "I can handle the cart just fine. My Pa has one very similar, and a horse too."

"But you're—you're—"

"I'm from a small village. A place where people drive carts. While someone like you is from a large town, and I'm sure you have better things to do with your hands than rub down a horse or pull the reins. Isn't that right?"

Lizabette opened her mouth then thought better of it and went quiet. However she still had a displeased expression on her pinched face.

"Percy driving is fine with me," Sybil said good-naturedly.

"Me too," said Flor, who had just heard the news and came over to the table with her own bit of breakfast.

"Me three!" Emilie said, slurping her tea.

Gloria, coming to sit at the farthest edge of the table next to Emilie, just smiled.

They set out on the road in the bluish dawn. Grial and Ronna stood at the doors of the inn and waved them goodbye as Percy climbed up on the tall driver's perch and took the reins while the rest of the girls settled in the cart with their things and this time three of them remained to walk alongside it.

"Get along now! Whoa, Betsy!" Grial cried, and hearing her mistress's voice Betsy reacted by starting to walk in her sedate powerful manner before Percy had a chance to gently adjust the reins. Soon they were moving down the street along the same main thoroughfare in the direction that led out of town, northward.

The streets were mostly empty at this hour, though there were occasional pedestrians and carts, and yes, several young women walking, who looked suspiciously like they could have been Cobweb Brides.

"Isn't it exciting?" said Jenna, as she skipped and hopped every other step. "We are all going to be Cobweb Brides!"

"We can't all of us be Cobweb Brides, Jen," said Flor in mild amusement, walking alongside her.

Lizabette, riding in the cart, gave a snort.

Within a half hour they were close to the northern outskirts of town, since Tussecan was not a large place, no matter how it might have seemed the night before when it was bustling with supper-hour traffic and townsfolk. This early in the morning the air seemed crisp and actually bluish with haze, if you squinted to look.

Can air be blue? Percy thought, as she watched the road and the surrounding red-shingled rooftops from her tall driver's perch. It certainly seemed colored, or at least tangible somehow, as it swept the chimney smoke to rippling puffs, here and there, as she glanced around.

At last they passed the farthest outlying buildings, and the thoroughfare continued onward past empty fields on both sides, and occasional shrubbery. The sun rose, pale and veiled against the winter white sky, and just ahead of them was the dark shape of the looming Northern Forest. From the distance it looked like a streak of unresolved shadow against the northern horizon, but soon enough, they knew, it would become great trees, predominantly evergreen pine and fir. And then it would surround them.

Occasional young women were seen walking along the road. Some passed them, others—after asking where the cart was headed—dropped to an even walk alongside it.

"It's safer in a big crowd," said Percy to one or two of the stranger girls. "If you're all heading to be Cobweb Brides, you might consider walking with us."

"Do you know where to go?" asked one young skinny girl-child with a heavy accent, who trudged along the side of the road and stuck to their group.

"Not really," said Percy calmly. "But we all know it's somewhere North, inside that forest, and for now there's this big comfortable road. So, one step at a time."

"Sounds good to me!" replied the girl, with an olive-dark face and very black doe-eyes, speaking somewhat awkwardly. "I'm Marie, and I'm a'gonna walk with you, if you don't mind."

"We don't mind!" Jenna put in, clapping her mittens together cheerfully.

Marie started at the sound, and Percy immediately felt sympathy for her, frightened and tiny and mousy-dark, in her much-darned poor excuse of a coat.

"Where are you from, Marie?" she asked, to put her at ease.

But the girl seemed to become even more flustered at the question.

"Are you from Letheburg?" Regata asked kindly. "Because that's where Sibyl and I are from."

"No . . ." Marie replied after a pause, blinking her eyes nervously. "We—my family lives in Fioren now, but before that, we came from . . . far away."

"Farther than Duarden? I am from Duarden." Lizabette said smartly. "It is quite centrally located, you know, in a small but prime area. Because if you keep going you will hit the Silver Court directly, and I doubt, from the looks or sounds of you—no offense—that you are from the Imperial neighborhood."

"I—I am not from your . . . Realm."

Most everyone turned to stare at Marie at that point.

"Please . . ." she said, "I hope you don't mind, I have been living here in Lethe almost two years now—"

"Good heavens!" Lizabette said. "Are you from *Balmue?* Because your speech, that accent, why—"

"I—we came by way of Balmue," spoke Marie, her voice almost breaking into a whisper at that point, "but that was in the end. First, we came down a big river, I don't know what you would call it, but we call it *Eridanos—*"

"Gracious, that is in the Kingdom of Serenoa, is it not? One of the four kingdoms of the Domain, the other being Balmue our southern neighbor, and then even more south, and to the east, the

Kingdom of Tanathe, and finally on the other side, south-west, the Kingdom of Solemnis."

"Yes, *Serenoa*," said Marie, and she pronounced it differently, more liltingly, and again everyone stared.

"Is that where you're from?" Jenna said in wonder. "What's it like?"

Marie's alarm lessened somewhat and a wistful expression replaced her fear. "Beautiful! Yes, Serenoa is beautiful and green, and a little cold on the top, like your Lethe here, but very warm down below. It is the most northern part of the Domain, and the two share a border across the mountains. On the west, Lethe, on the east, Serenoa. But we had to go around, because no one can go over the mountains, so we went down and sailed the river Eridanos, and then crossed into Balmue, then we came back up north."

"But why?" blurted Jenna. "Why did you leave?"

Marie thought, and a worrisome expression returned. "I don't know," she said. "But I think my parents just wanted a new life."

"Exactly," said Percy. 'Why else does anyone move from one place to another?"

But some of the girls continued to stare somewhat.

"You're not spies, are you?" Lizabette said. "But then, if you were, you wouldn't admit it, would you?"

Marie opened her mouth and looked like she wanted nothing more than to disappear on the spot. "Oh, no, no!" she hurried to say. "No, please, of course not spies! My father carves wood for furniture! We live in Fioren and my parents sell the chests and boxes! Oh, no, no!"

"I think we've scared Marie enough," Sybil spoke up loudly. "The poor girl is in the Realm now, and she's going to be walking with us, so enough nonsense!"

"Spy my arse!" Niosta added, and winked at Marie, then at her own sister Catrine. And they both stuck their tongues out at Lizabette when she was not looking.

Marie exhaled in relief, and mostly avoided eye contact with anyone, but she now resolutely trudged along with the cart.

They moved for a few minutes in blessed silence, with only the creaking cart and the crunching snow.

Jenna began to hum:

"Cobweb Bride, Cobweb Bride,
Come and lie by my side. . . ."

and again,

"Cobweb Bride, Cobweb Bride,
Come and lie by my side. . . ."

Lizabette wrinkled her forehead and said, "Will you not do that please, child? I have the beginnings of a headache and it's hardly past dawn. Not good to be having one this early."

"Oh, sorry!" said Jenna, and went marginally quiet. Her cheeks and nose were pink from the cold air, but you could tell she was just bursting with energy, as her steps came with a bounce. So, instead of humming she started running in zigzags in front of Betsy, with her arms stretched out to the sides like wings.

"Look at her, the big goose," said Regata, walking next to Flor. But she was grinning as she said it.

The forest drew closer, and soon the first tall sparse trees began showing up on both sides of the road. All sound seemed to disappear, except for the occasional crunch of snow underfoot and the clumps falling from branches, and the fast sudden beating of bird's wings.

The cart rolled slowly, and had to veer off to the side a bit several times in order to allow faster vehicles to pass. Because, there had been occasional carriages and curricles along this empty stretch, and you could hear them coming from miles away in the forest silence. There had been one in particular, a curricle traveling at breakneck speed, crammed with three passengers. In the blink of an eye that they could tell, they were two fine ladies and a lord, with one lady in the driver's seat. They were all wearing fancy winter hats with plumes, and it was a wonder the hats did not come flying off.

"Did you see that? Fancy aristocrats!" Sybil said matter-of-factly—her thick reddish brows rising in amusement—as she leaned to stare in their wake, from her seat in the cart next to Lizabette.

"Indeed, and those tri-color plumes are the height of fashion at the Silver Court this season!" replied Lizabette, patting her own somewhat stylish hat.

"Do noble aristos really go to be Cobweb Brides?" Emilie folded her shawl closer around her reddened snub nose.

"I think," Percy said, "it doesn't matter if you are noble or a nobody, when it comes to being a Cobweb Bride."

Jenna immediately picked up the humming.

"Cobweb Bride, Cobweb Bride,
Come and lie by my side. . . ."

Suddenly, Gloria, the quietest person Percy knew, began to recite in a loud melodious voice:

"Cobweb Bride, Cobweb Bride,
Come and lie by my side.

Here, the cool touch of stone
And the feel of my throne
Will not make you recoil.
Here the worm-ridden soil
Covers ancient white bones."

Everyone stared at her, including Marie, and even Jenna

went absolutely quiet and nearly ran into Betsy, as they listened. Gloria continued to recite, as though she had memorized the words a long time ago and they were merely coming out now, like easy breaths:

"Time suppresses the groans
Of your own mortal kind;
Soothing dark fills the mind.

Here with me you will reign,
If true love you don't feign
With a smile on your face.

Dressed in pale spider lace
You will come unto me,
Make your choice clear and free.

With the breath from my chest,
Lips of stone on your breast,
You will know Death's cold kiss. . . .

Do not find me remiss.
First your heartbeat grows still;
Dissolution of will.
Then you sink with me, deep,
Into dark, final sleep.

No regrets must there be,
Promise me."

The words ended. There was absolute silence, except for the creaking of the cart.

"Goodness!" said Lizabette. "What . . . was that?"

"Did you just make that up, just now?" Emilie said.

Gloria nodded.

"That was actually somewhat poetic . . ." Lizabette said. "I wasn't even aware you could read, much less compose."

"How did you do that?" Jenna exclaimed. "How, how? Gloria, how did you do that?"

Gloria shrugged, then said quietly, "I am not sure . . . I make up rhymes in my head. Sometimes."

"Rhymes! Sometimes!" Jenna squealed in exuberance. "That rhymes! Just now, you did it again!"

"Headache?" Lizabette reminded, holding on to her forehead.

But Jenna was not to be denied this time. "How does it go, Gloria, the whole thing, please? 'Cobweb Bride, Cobweb Bride . . .'" She began to sing in her ringing but somewhat flat tone, just slightly off key, just enough to be endearingly annoying.

Percy bit her lip in suppressed laughter.

Tired, cold, and in pain from his compounded injuries, Beltain stood at attention in the icy-cold chamber of his father, the room with the broken window and the snow drifts piled on the windowpane among the shards of broken glass. Together with the cold, milky dawn light seeped inside, illuminating the bulky shape of Hoarfrost.

The Duke sat in the chair with his back to his son, before a single flickering candle lowered inside a tall glass to keep it from being extinguished by the gusts of wind that freely travelled the room. He was reading something—a roll of parchment, thought Beltain—that looked as if it had been delivered by a messenger, for Beltain could see the red silk ties and the crumbling remnants of a broken seal littering the mahogany surface of the large table.

The seal seemed familiar, but he was not quite sure, not from the distance at which he stood. Besides, he was in that state of exhaustion where he almost ceased caring. His vision was swimming from lack of sleep, and his newly damaged shoulder was in agony. It seemed that all of his recent injuries were hardly healing, and now, this. Damn that knight who bear-wrestled him. . . .

"My Lord . . ." Beltain began. "Father, I've delivered another group of prisoners. Among them are Imperial knights and two ladies—"

"Quiet!" Hoarfrost's bark-like exhalation of breath interrupted the younger man. He continued to pore over the writing, and Beltain was about to offer to read it for him when his father turned around, crumpling the sheet in his beefy hands and then held the parchment over the candle.

The thin material caught on fire soon enough and Hoarfrost tossed the flaming ball into the cold, unlit hearth of the fireplace nearby where it was consumed and fell apart in tiny reddish sparks. His fingers had seemed to hold the flames momentarily also, but the dead flesh could not have known it, the burning pain. . . . The dead man slowly and methodically extinguished his fingertips by rubbing them against the icy front of his surcoat tunic.

"Now then," said Hoarfrost, turning to his son like a creaking tree-trunk and actively shaping his mouth into a rictus that was intended as a smile. "How was your night of hunting, boy?"

"Well enough, father," replied Beltain. "There were many women—poor girls mostly, bedraggled creatures—that we've caught all over the forest and the vicinity. And, as I mentioned, I've detained an interesting group of noble prisoners, including Imperial knights and two gentlewomen."

"Imperial knights, eh?" said Hoarfrost.

"Yes, sir . . ." Beltain found it uncanny to stare too long at the motionless eyeballs, frozen in their sockets.

"Where are they, these Imperial visitors?"

"Here, in the Keep, my Lord. They have been given food

and a space to rest, some spare quarters—"

"You are far too charitable to your prisoners, boy!"

"I—was not sure what you intended to do with them."

Hoarfrost sat back in the chair with a creak. "True enough, I have not decided yet. It might be easiest to kill them and have them join my ranks here in Chidair."

Beltain felt cold rising inside him.

"Kill . . . the women?" he said softly. "How will that help you . . . or your ranks?"

"It will certainly get them out of the way and out of the Cobweb Bride running. Plus, with the dead, less mouths to feed in town. More resources for the Keep. Plenty of solid reasons I should have them killed. They can do the laundry and they wouldn't even need to stop for sleep."

And Duke Ian Chidair laughed with the rhythmic sound of bellows.

Beltain felt a sudden spasm of dizziness in his head, while the room seemed to shift momentarily. He grasped his hands before him until the fingers lost all feeling and took a staggering side-step in order to remain standing.

Hoarfrost noticed his condition. "What's the matter with you?" he said. "Shaking, boy? You are almost as white as I am."

"It's been a long day and even longer night . . ." Beltain continued to grasp his hands before him. "And, I've not yet recovered from my previous wounds. . . . Earlier, one of the Imperial knights mauled me rather badly. I—would appreciate a bit of . . . sleep, my lord."

"I see, whelp," Hoarfrost said. "Maybe I should have you killed after all, so you won't ever have to worry about these mortal concerns again, eh? I could grant you the deathly stroke myself, what do you say, boy? Clean and fast. No? Well then, take an hour and lie down for a nap, then a bite to eat. Then, back out you go, we have more Cobweb Brides to catch. And— you'll see—things are just beginning to get exciting. . . ."

Speaking thus, Hoarfrost glanced behind him at the once-again cold hearth of the fireplace.

"May I . . . take my leave?" Beltain said softly, feeling the muscle strength in his legs dissolving. Another minute of this and he knew he would not be able to keep himself from collapsing.

"Yes, get your sorry carcass out of here, before I make you a carcass indeed," Hoarfrost replied. "I'll be taking my personal patrol out into the woods and expect to see you back out there shortly. Dismissed!"

Harsh wheezing barks of laughter followed Beltain as he headed out the door. And then, silence, and the whistle of the ice-wind through the broken window. The cold seemed to come with him as he walked to his own quarters in the Keep. Cold, permanently lodged in his mind.

The threesome that comprised the League of Folly had travelled all night. Though no one would admit such a frivolous sentiment, this was an improvement over having to attend another excruciating midnight ball and pretend to eat entirely raw *living* flesh at the buffet. Lady Amaryllis Roulle, wearing a smart burgundy-red riding habit—even though she was not going to be riding any beasts, merely controlling them via harness while perched on a high seat—drove the Curricle and the two fabulous black thoroughbreds like a madwoman, while Lord Nathan Woult and the Lady Ignacia Chitain held on to their seats for dear life.

They flew past towns and villages, took a brief stop to dine at Letheburg around midnight (waking up an understandably crabby innkeeper and his staff to serve them something either raw or like tasteless sawdust, then pack a picnic basket of the same for a later "snack" on the go), then back on the road they went. It was crisp and clear indeed, without snowfall or the least bit of inclement winter weather. And except for the wind chill in their faces, luck was with them as far north as Tussecan, after which, smack dab in the middle of the road, it ran out.

The Curricle's right wheel came off the axle. Goodness knows how or why it happened, in the faint bluish light of dawn, but, as a result, the Curricle teetered, and while Amaryllis hastily attempted to pull up the horses, stopping them sharply and pulling with all her strength, the thoroughbreds reared.

Next thing everyone knew, they were all on their sides, and the Curricle of Doom had capsized ignobly, sliding several feet with the momentum, the sole remaining wheel spinning in the air, then stopping to rest with the wheel lodged deep against a snowdrift-covered roadside hedge. One of the horses was pulled along, and tripped, then rose up again, miraculously unharmed but screaming in equine fury. The other remained upright, and pulled at the Curricle, dragging it even further along and lodging the solitary attached wheel deeper into the show.

To add insult to injury, the small travel lantern hanging from the front was snuffed out in a blink, and with it went all their light.

Lady Ignacia screamed and Lord Nathan screamed, then uttered curses that were beyond his vocabulary under normal circumstances. Lady Amaryllis, her hands entangled in the reins, was alarmingly silent, having ended up pulled halfway out of the curricle and onto the iced-over road and just barely away from underneath the feet of the thoroughbreds. She lay, panting, then moaned, while Lady Ignacia attempted to crawl out of her seat in the back next to Woult.

"Damnation and bloody hell!" cried the young man over and over, as he assisted Lady Ignacia from their sideways position. Finally they freed themselves from the overturned vehicle and were upright, standing on the road.

"Amaryllis, dear, are you alive?" Ignacia said in a horrible soft voice, picking up her capsized plumed hat, then straightening with gloved fingers her emerald-green cape over a sage travel dress—all without attempting to approach her fallen friend. And then she began to shriek again, and in-between shrieks managed to say, "Woult, do go get her out, go see if she lives! Oh, God in Heaven!"

"Amaryllis?" Nathan tried, lowering himself in a crouch before the motionless female, while stretching out one splayed hand to keep the rearing horses away—as though a mere hand could.

"Yes . . . help me up," said Amaryllis at last. She moved her head then slowly raised herself up on one elbow, then fell back again with a sharp exclamation of pain. "Hurts like something horrendous . . ." she managed to say.

"What hurts, my dear?" Lord Woult drew himself closer, knelt, avoiding the horses, then took a careful hold of her.

"Ah! It's my side! Nothing broken, I venture, but I'm afraid a bruise is imminent. My wrists are all entangled and my knee is scraped, and oh, my ankle—damn it all! And look, the Curricle is a godless mess!"

Amaryllis bit her lip but did not cry as Woult managed to free her gloved hands and got her upright so she could stand, leaning on him heavily.

"What a filthy idiot mess, what indignity!" Amaryllis muttered.

"Be glad you're safe, and Curricle be damned," Nathan replied soothingly in her ear.

"Yes," said Ignacia, "for it could have been infernally worse! We are all safe! But—What happened, exactly?"

"Here, you help her stand while I deal with recapturing the beasts," said Nathan, handing Amaryllis over to lean on Ignacia's shoulder.

"Recapturing? The beasts are hardly 'loose' that they need be recaptured, silly boy," retorted Amaryllis smartly, proving that she was indeed sufficiently well. "Just grab the reins and tie them down for now, while we deal with the Curricle."

"Whatever happened?" Ignacia repeated.

"I haven't the faintest idea in all of the blessed Realm."

Amaryllis tried stomping her feet and found that one of her ankles was indeed in poor shape and practically burned with agony when she put her weight on it. "All I know is," she continued, "we were flying along just fine, and suddenly the accursed wheel went—just like that, in the blink of an eye. I tried to slow us down but . . . well, as you see."

"Did the grooms fail to have this vehicle checked properly?" Nathan said, panting with anger and exertion. He had captured the reins of one of the thoroughbreds and was now wrestling with the other as it reared and stomped around, jerking at the fallen Curricle with every move it made. "Whoa, whoa, down, girl—or boy—or whatever you are, you violent brute—"

"Now really, Nathan," Amaryllis protested. "You know your horseflesh; these are fine boys, do not insult them. They are perfectly innocent and had nothing to do with any of this, the poor dears. Thank all the stars in Heaven they are not injured!"

Minutes later the horses were secured, and Amaryllis limping but able to stand on her own.

"So what are we to do now?" Ignacia said unhappily.

"Well, I suppose I could walk on back over to that town we passed just recently and see if we can get help."

"No! You aren't just going to leave us here unprotected, Nathan!" Ignacia's blue eyes grew round with imagined terrors.

"She's right." Grimacing in severe discomfort, Amaryllis rubbed her side with one hand. "We're in a nasty wilderness, and this is dangerous enough as it is, with highwaymen and cutpurses lurking lord knows where, and now, with all the Cobweb Bride stragglers that will be making their way here past us. None of them can help us properly, and I am sure more than one of them would be only too happy to rob us down to our petticoats."

"Besides, there's that black knight . . ." said Ignacia.

"What black knight?"

"Not sure, m'dear, but at the roadhouse, when we stopped for a breather in the last town, someone mentioned him—a terrifying merciless creature of a man. Supposedly, he is a mercenary, or maybe an executioner, possibly in the employ of the local Duke. Dressed in all black mail, astride a black beast, with horrid minions, he—they haunt these forests, hunting all who pass here, and Cobweb Brides in particular."

"Who told you that? What poppycock!" Nathan said.

"Well, I wouldn't call it poppycock." Ignacia smoothed down her hat plumes and adjusted the contraption on her head. "Particularly when it could very well be true. These local nobles are as good as savages. You've heard of the interminable rivalry between Chidair and Goraque, the so-called Red and Blue Dukes? They fight a war every season like clockwork, and it's in their blood. So, why not black robber knights lurking in the woods?"

Amaryllis stood deep in thought, with hands on hips, and her normally perfectly coiffed black hair flowing in semi-disarray. She was looking at the fallen equipage. "We could try to lift this thing back upright."

Ignacia turned to her with an angry bobbing of hat plumes. "What? Just the three of us, and you lame as a partridge? Amaryllis, my dear, I wouldn't be surprised if you've struck your head when you fell. This is beyond impossible."

"Well, it could be worth a try," said Nathan. "Amaryllis, sweetling, do limp on over to my right and you'll lift from that end. Ignacia, you and I, as the only two able-bodied creatures, will push with all our might from this angle. . . ."

With much grunting and long minutes of misplaced effort, they managed to shove and drag the Curricle out of its place in the snow bushes, then grunted and groaned twice as long to get it precariously upright.

The Curricle of Doom, aptly named, wobbled on its one remaining wheel and leaned heavily to the right against the axle pole, at an alarming angle. Nathan went down the road to look for the other wheel, the culprit that had caused all this mess. The thoroughbreds, now docile and tired after that long fast drive, obediently stood nearby.

Ignacia wiped her brow with the back of her glove and sat down on a fallen travel chest that had been in the small back seat with her and now reposed in the road. "Now what?" she said tiredly. "So he retrieves the jolly wheel. How will we re-attach it?" And then she wailed. "I am freezing, tired, hungry! I just want to be in bed with a hot cup of tea right now, Amaryllis! This is no longer fun! I demand a relief to this—this *horror!*"

"Oh come now, Ignacia, don't blow this out of proportion, we've just capsized. It's a minor thing, all things considered." Amaryllis watched Nathan approach, rolling the large wheel before him.

"How in blazes do you plan to re-attach that thing?" said Ignacia with irritation. "Have you any blacksmithing skills? Proper tools? And where are the lugs that you need to fasten it? Probably rolled away halfway down the road, lord knows where. . . ."

"Lugs?" muttered Nathan. "And what do you know of curricle wheel lugs, m'dear?" And he threw Ignacia a very peculiar glance.

"Nothing! I know nothing of *lugs* except that *at present* we don't have them. You might think otherwise, Lord Nathan Woult, but I am not the ninny you might think I am! Yes, I've heard the grooms talking, using that 'lugs' term when they were adjusting the wheels."

While Ignacia chattered, Amaryllis glanced up and down the road. Surprisingly there had been no passerby in the long minutes that they'd been downed. The portion of the road behind them, winding south-east, had filled with pallor along the horizon over the treetops where the sun was due to rise shortly.

"Look, it's dawn," Amaryllis said. "How pretty and crisp it looks here on the outskirts of the Realm."

"Well I think it's perfectly horrid," Ignatia said. "We ought to be moving forward or heading back, doing something or . . .

or getting assistance from *someone!* In the very least, someone ought to be down this infernal road who can help us! Where is everyone? Not even one puny vagabond Cobweb Bride!"

Just as the last petulant word echoed into silence, from far behind them down the southeasterly road came the faint sound of voices, approaching.

Female voices. Girl voices.

And amazingly, in this dawn-lit no-man's land, there was laughter and singing.

Chapter 10

From the driver's seat, Percy could barely feel the cart swaying underneath her as it rolled along the northern road. She held on to the reins with stiff, mitten-covered fingers as Betsy plodded with confidence, hooves crunching on the fresh show that dusted the beaten-down thoroughfare. Occasional fat snowflakes came fluttering down like sudden bits of dislocated cloud in the blue dawn. They landed on tops of shawls and hats, sprinkled all the exposed surfaces like "heaven's sugar and flour."

God is cooking, Percy's Gran used to say. *When it's winter and bitter cold, He sends down heaven's sugar and flour, so that we can make sweet bread and stay warm.*

Sugar and flour? Brr, it was cold!

The girls were singing all around her. Every one of them—except for Lizabette who protested that it was far too cold to speak, much less sing, and that they will all lose their voices and go hoarse permanently, and no one, much less Death, would want to marry them and become attached to a "husky virago."

At which point Niosta and Catrine stopped singing and held their faces to suppress coarse laughter.

"A less than dulcet voice never stopped a man before from marrying," Sybil remarked with a twinkle in her eyes. And then she picked up the song again in full voice.

Emilie started to cough.

"You see!" Lizabette exclaimed. "She is losing her voice already!"

But even Percy herself could not hold back, and hummed the chorus—so quietly that probably only she alone could hear herself—while vapor curled from her lips.

For the last few miles they had all picked up and memorized Gloria's far-too complicated grim verses of the Cobweb Bride "song," and, led by Jenna's earnest voice, had somehow put it all to music, to the tune of "My Shepherd's Pot Is Boiling," or maybe it was the "Little Red Apples" nursery song.

The cheerful discrepancy was obvious (while the air was still indeed frigid from the night). And yet it felt good somehow to belt out at the top of one's lungs such happy tunes coupled with such gruesome lyrics as "worm-ridden soil" and "Death's cold kiss" and especially "diiiiissoluuuuuuuution of will"— "Whatever that means," sang Emilie, as she added her own bit of harmony.

"'Dissolution of will' indeed! Where in the world did you come up with that one? What notions, what long words, Gloria!" Lizabette commented occasionally.

Gloria simply shrugged and continued walking with two other girls who were taking their turn not riding the cart.

In the distance, up ahead, there was something on the road.

Percy felt an instant pang of worry for their safety. She squinted into the bluish dusk, pulling on the reins to slow down their movement.

"Oh look, what's that?" Sybil said in that same moment, seated on Percy's right and sharing her vantage point. Her feet dangling from the cart stopped moving.

"Everybody, quiet!" Percy's voice rang out, and all the girls went silent immediately. It suddenly got so very quiet they could almost hear the dawning forest breathing in blue and silver dusk.

"Oh no . . . looks like a carriage wreck," Niosta said, from Percy's other side.

Marie, the so-called "foreign girl" from Serenoa—their

newest and very young looking straggler, who had joined them only a few miles earlier—shivered. Covering herself in her threadbare shawl, she inched nearer to the protection of the cart.

"Or, it could be, someone's up to no good," whispered Flor. "What if it's an ambush of some kind? What if it's the black knight?"

Percy felt a cold lump of fear forming in the depth of her belly. And by the looks of the others, she was not the only one. But she could not show it, could not let them know she was afraid, because Grial had given *her* this cart to drive.

"Be on your guard, and get ready to run, if needed," she said firmly.

And so, they slowly and quietly advanced forward. Betsy the draft horse took soft, cautious steps in the crunching snow, and the cart wheels barely creaked.

But they had nothing to worry about.

"Oh, gracious, I recognize that tri-colored plume hat!" said Lizabette, as they approached.

And indeed, in a few more feet they could distinguish a familiar curricle standing semi-upright at an odd angle in the middle of the thoroughfare—the same one that had passed them a few hours ago—and its three aristocratic occupants. One lady was seated on top of a fallen travel trunk. The other stood nearby, awkwardly keeping one foot from resting flat on the ground, milling from one foot to the other, and holding on to two very handsome thoroughbred horses. Meanwhile, a gentleman was busy fiddling with a possibly broken wheel.

"Hello there!" exclaimed the seated lady, and quickly stood up, waving her arms, her hat with its plumes bobbing, her expensive emerald-green cape catching underfoot, so that she nearly tripped in the snow.

The gentleman let go of the wheel and turned likewise, waving at the approaching cart.

"Greetings to you! We mean no harm and require assistance!" said the gentleman in a ringing baritone accustomed to haughty command. In the blue light of dawn, he was handsome and elegant in his winter greatcoat, with a fur hat rakishly slanted over his dark hair.

"Good morning to you," Percy said, pulling up the cart, and stopping Betsy just far enough away so as not to spook the other horses, and also just to be cautious.

Meanwhile Lizabette responded at the same time, interrupting her. "M'Lord! M'Ladies!" exclaimed Lizabette ingratiatingly, "is anyone hurt?"

"No," said the lady in deep burgundy red, holding the horses.

"Yes!" exclaimed the other two.

"The Lady Amaryllis here has a sprained ankle, and she does require assistance back to town," said the lady in green.

"Yes," echoed the gentleman, shaking snow off his gloves and dark coat. "As you can see we've run into trouble. Take us back along this same road, and you will be well compensated."

The walking girls gathered closer around the cart, and everyone was staring at the aristocrats, and then back at Percy.

"Well," said Percy thoughtfully. "I'm sorry, but I'm afraid we can't go back. We are all Cobweb Brides on our way to find Death's Keep."

"You did not hear me, I presume?" said the gentleman, with a sharp edge entering in his voice. "I mentioned that you will be *paid*—very well, I add."

"Yes, I heard, M'Lord," Percy replied, "but it is not the point. We cannot turn back now. I am truly sorry, but I've been entrusted to take this cart and this horse and all these girls, as far as possible *forward*. I cannot make detours."

"And why not? Why is that, exactly?" said the lady in green. Her previous nonchalant tone was now different.

"Because," said Percy, feeling herself going numb and yet more resolved with every word, "going forward *once* is dangerous enough. I cannot risk extending this trip for any of us."

"Will a few hours make any difference to any of you?" the lady continued, coldly and bluntly. "You are all going to your *deaths*, you do know that?"

"Yes," said Percy. "But only *one* of us will find it—if *I* can help it."

Everyone looked at her in silence. The girls had gone very still; the nobles likewise, taken aback at the audacity and force of her words.

And then she added, more mildly, "If you like, however, I will make room for you in our cart. We all take turns walking. If the lady who is hurt needs to sit down for the whole duration, it is understandable. But that's the best I can offer."

"Why, this is an outrage!" exclaimed the lady in green, stomping one fine booted foot against the packed snow. "Do you know who we *are?* We hail directly from the Silver Court! The Right Honorable Lord Nathan Woult is before you, and this here is the Lady Amaryllis Roulle, and I myself am the Lady Ignacia Chitain! Have you any notion of what and whom you refuse?"

Percy was sorely tempted to say something she would truly regret, but held herself back.

"We are so sorry, Your Ladyship, My Lord!" muttered Lizabette. "Perchance you can have my seat here, I would be happy to oblige, really, all of us would be!"

"What's wrong with your cart?" said Gloria suddenly.

"This is not a cart," said the lady in red, limping a few steps forward. 'It is a *curricle*, and it has lost a wheel. Have you any notion of how to fix something like this? Any of you?"

"Why, what an excellent idea, Amaryllis!" said Lord Woult. And to the girls he said, "If you can fix this wheel, you will be paid very, very well!"

Niosta and Catrine looked at each other, clever dark eyes glittering in the dawning light. "Well," said Catrine, "I think me an' sis here can take a look. My Pa and uncle taught us, they know all about carts and carriages."

"Oh, good!" Lady Ignacia said. "So your father fixes carriages?"

"Well, not 'xactly, M'Lady," said Niosta, with another glance at her sister. "He do know how to rob 'em however. But he sure know how to fix broken wheels on the robbed carriages!"

Lord Woult's face was impossible to describe.

Percy said quickly, "There will be no robbing here, of anyone. Now, can the two of you girls please look at that wheel?"

With a few more exchanged glances and fleeting wicked smiles turning into disguised hard giggles, the two sisters hopped down from the cart, and went closer to look. The rest of the girls got down also, to stretch their legs and stomp for warmth. A few approached the curricle, and milled around, while the ladies gave them wary, cool glances.

Percy sat in the driver's seat feeling like a lump, afraid to let go of Betsy's reins, and torn between giving in entirely and helping these fancy people with whatever they asked, or holding her own and ignoring them.

Fortunately, it took only a few minutes of poking and prodding, and Niosta announced, "We can fix it, just need lugs, there's two missing, is all. Found one down in the snow, so just need one more, and it'll be all right and hold up."

With an exhalation of relief, Percy nodded, then tied up the reins, and leaned under the seat for the toolbox. Grial kept one well stocked, fortunately, and there were lugs and nails and twine aplenty, together with hair pins and incomprehensible bits and pieces of heaven knows what.

In moments, the wheel was lifted up by several girls, and reattached properly to the axle pole. Catrine forcefully turned the lug nuts with her surprisingly strong and grimy little fingers (frequently blowing on them for warmth when they turned numb with cold), with Niosta hammering the lugs for good measure, calling them "rotted bastards" and periodically spitting in the snow. Then the whole lot of them tested the curricle by rocking it side to side, then shoving it a few steps forward and seeing it roll nicely.

They were done, and Lady Amaryllis, the one with the limp, immediately nodded her curt gratitude, and moved up with the two fancy horses, which the gentleman helped her hitch properly to the curricle.

"Remarkable! Excellent! Well done, and our thanks!" said he, a light-hearted and frivolous expression returning to his handsome face. He drew out a handful of gold coins and passed them out to the girls nearest, then turned his back on the whole lot of them, as if they ceased to exist. The two ladies occupied themselves with dusting off their capes, re-loading their trunk, and then the one in a burgundy outfit was assisted back into the driver's seat.

"Are you certain you can handle the driving, my dear?"

"Of course! Honestly, Nathan, you must know I am not driving with my feet!" she protested, and then they were talking and laughing in artful courtier tones once again.

Percy stopped listening, and while the girls giggled and counted coins, and took their time getting back in the cart, she adjusted the reins and said firmly, "Whoa, Betsy!"

But before they moved even a few steps, the black thoroughbreds and curricle and nobles all clattered forward and past them, flying north along the road.

"Well! That was rather interesting!" said Lizabette.

"Huh . . . I thought they'd turn back," Percy said softly. "There are no more towns ahead of us, and that lady is more hurt than she realizes."

"Stupid fancy lords'n ladies," Regata said. "Where do they think they're going anyway? The Northern Forest? Wouldn't be surprised if they're not right in their heads, after that wreck!"

"And then the black knight gets 'em!" Emilie giggled.

"First they need to make it that far. I say they break down

again in a few miles." Catrine swiped her nose with the back of her mitten. "And that'll mean more coins for us!"

This is not a game, not for anyone, Percy thought. But she said nothing. The morning had grown brighter, as the sun rose and shimmered faintly like a pearl through the milky overcast of winter clouds.

"I'm hungry!" said Jenna. And she dug into a basket for leftover rolls. "Who wants some?"

We're going to run out very soon. . . . Out of rolls, out of time, out of warmth, out of everything.

"I—this body—cannot walk—any farther," whispered Claere Liguon.

They were drowning in snowdrifts waist deep. The Northern Forest was a sea of whiteness and bare tree trunks, with nothing but vaporous haze on every horizon, so that the sky and land blended into a uniform pallor. The only frame of reference was the rare fogged-over glimmer of the risen sun. Its disk appeared to be sliding through the cloud-mass overhead, fractured into angular shards of light against the dark silhouettes of infinite branches.

Vlau Fiomarre knew they were lost, had known it for some time now. And yet he followed the small pitiful shape of the dead Infanta as she stiffly and relentlessly moved forward for the last few hours of the night.

He had lost all sensation in his appendages. At first his feet and hands and face burned with the cold fire. Then all went numb, limbs moving through conscious will alone, as though not his own—*someone else* was making him put one foot ahead of the other. *He* was going to die very soon now; there was not the faintest doubt. . . . And yet, just as *she* remained undead, *he* was going to also become neither one thing nor the other, suspended in that hollow place between life and death.

Death is the loss of sensation . . . he pondered, taking

shallow and ragged breaths of freezing air, each breath scalding his lungs.

And then the Infanta stopped. And she admitted she could go on no longer. "My body is—a corpse," she uttered, each word issuing with a grating hiss of forced breath. "It has no warmth of its own—and has become too stiff—too frozen to allow movement in the joints by my will alone. Soon, I will be unable to talk. Once that happens, simply leave me be. Go back, find a road . . . and save yourself."

"We are lost, and there is no road," he panted. "Even if it were right behind us, I would not leave you now. We perish together—"

In response, came a faint terrible *creak* of laughter.

She stood, like a pillar of salt, faintly shaking in place in an effort to maintain vertical balance. "Perish?" she gasped. "There is no such relief in store for us! Unfortunately we will *not* perish, but we *will* freeze, and then malinger, yes! Covered by endless snow, unable to move, going softly mad, eternally, in the prisons of our bodies . . . until the spring thaw. And then, we will regain the use of our carcasses, and, as it warms up even more, we will perhaps start to rot, and worms will come to eat tunnels through this flesh and crawl throughout, and birds will come to peck—"

"Then I will *not* perish!" he snarled. "And it looks like your mouth is not frozen enough, and you can still talk quite well!"

Fury at *himself*—at *her*—it was the thing driving him onward, he recognized suddenly. *Fury* was all that remained.

And just as he was certain that all he could do was be consumed with it, alone within his own hell, there was something else. . . .

From a distance came the sound of wolves—nay, it was the baying of hounds in the forest, and then a distant noise of men perpetrating damage, comprised of breaking branches, crackling snow, and footsteps crunching, voices low and subdued.

All together—after the infinite white silence—they seemed like thunder, as they awkwardly *broke* the forest.

"No . . ." whispered the Infanta. "Oh, no . . . Please, you must cover me with snow, then run!"

"No!" he replied harshly, and suddenly lurched forward with all his remaining strength, narrowing the space between them. And he put his arms around her (around the lump of cold, the pillar of salt, the lifeless burden), and he lifted her up—and she was a dead weight, yet she was weightless in his hands and in his mind, like a dry withered stick—and he carried her, crashing forward, gasping for air, lungs convulsing with impossible effort. . . .

Snow was all around, coming to swallow him in its wintry quicksand; sharp branches struck his face, drawing thin ghoulish scratches upon his nunb, battered skin. And the sound soared on the wind, still carried in the distance, and drew closer . . . as yet he moved forward, wallowing, running . . . wallowing again.

He carried her thus, deeper into the Northern Forest.

Only an hour before noon, just as the girls approached the outskirts of the Northern Forest, and drew close enough to see the frozen white shores of Lake Merlait through the sparse trees in that direction, Betsy stopped in the middle of the road and refused to move any further.

Behind her, the cart rolled to a standstill.

"Whoa, Betsy!" said Percy, clucking and gently snapping the reins, to no avail.

Lizabette, taking her turn walking next to the cart, meaningfully stomped her feet in place to stay warm, while Sybil and Regata, walking next to her, decided to take the opportunity to use the nearby shrubbery to answer nature's call.

"What's the matter with her?" said Emilie, whose nose, red from the frost, was running. She had been sniffling and wiping it with the back of her mitten all morning.

"I don't know." Percy tied up the reins, removed her own mittens, and then slid down from the cart. Pulling her shawl back, she leaned down to examine each one of Betsy's legs, then the hooves and shoes. Nothing seemed to be amiss.

She then checked the harness, the bit, and made sure the blanket was not chafing any of the spots where the leathers were tight.

Betsy's nose was normal and lukewarm to the touch, vapor curling from her great nostrils. She moved her dark gentle eyes wherever Percy moved, and was as calm and healthy as anything.

"What in heaven's name is wrong with her? We should be moving!"

"I really don't know," replied Percy, continuing her examination, walking around the large horse.

"Maybe she's hungry too?" Jenna piped up from the back of the cart. "Should I could give her a roll?"

"No!" said Lizabette, Percy, and half the girls simultaneously.

"She has her grain in the bag, plenty of it. If we feed her rolls, we're not going to have enough food for us, Jen," explained Percy kindly.

"Want to try leading her, maybe? Pull her forward?" said Emilie, sniffling, and wiping herself with her dirty yellow coat sleeve.

Percy nodded, then took the bridle lead in the front of Betsy and attempted to pull the large draft horse behind her.

Nothing. Betsy made several unhappy snorts, and merely braced her legs against the beaten ground of the thoroughfare.

While they were occupied thus for several long minutes, several other strangers, mostly girls, passed them on the road.

Finally Percy climbed back into the driver's seat in frustration, and took the reins, pulling and releasing them repeatedly, while making more clucking noises. She then wiped her forehead and pulled her shawl closer about her. The lump of cold fear in her stomach was back.

"Betsy," she said at last, gently, relaxing the reins. "Where would you *like* to go?"

And suddenly, like a miracle, the draft horse moved. She took a few steps forward, but then started to lean them to the right side of the road—the side away from the lake and closer to the forest. Finally Betsy approached the shoulder of the thoroughfare, and continued walking, directly into the shrubbery at the side of the road.

"Whoa!" exclaimed Percy, pulling the reins hard, thinking they were about to plunge directly into a snowdrift. But as they neared the very edge, the bushes parted around them. Percy realized that Betsy had found and followed a small but solid path off the main road. It meandered around tall drifts and trees, but it definitely led north and into the forest. And the amazing thing was, it was entirely *invisible* from the main thoroughfare, unless you *knew* to look for it.

"Smart girl, Betsy!" said Percy, with a grin of relief. "So this is why you stopped! You knew about this path, didn't you?"

"But why would we want to use this tiny path leading Lord knows where, instead of the nice big road?" grumbled Lizabette. "It is unsafe!"

"Not so," responded Percy. "Just think about it, everyone can see you on the big road. Anyone can ambush you. But here, we are on our own secret little walkway. Besides, I think Betsy knows exactly where she's headed. Grial was right, Betsy *would* know the right direction!"

"That's ridiculous," Lizabette said. "How would a horse know the way to Death's Keep? Is the way, perchance, lined with hay and carrots?"

"And how would *we?*" retorted Percy. "I think the horse has as good a chance as any of us, and likely better. If you don't like it, you are welcome to continue on your own along the big road—the one that's lined with broken carriages instead of carrots."

"Right!" Lizabette snorted. But she grew silent and

continued walking with the cart.

They proceeded moving along the path for a quarter of an hour, frequently making sharp turns as it meandered around trees (which appeared denser and denser) and shrubs and tall snowdrifts that had risen into winter hills.

Jenna and Sybil periodically whistled—Sybil raising her ruddy brows up and down in time to the tune, so that her pale freckled face was in constant fluid motion—while Emilie wiped her nose and broke into more and more frequent fits of coughing.

"Emilie, you need to cover up with that blanket, keep it over your face, and stay in the cart for the rest of the day," said Percy, pointing to a bundle of their spare belongings in the back.

Emilie nodded with visible relief, breathing hoarsely, and climbed deeper in the back of the cart, then curled up under some burlap.

As the bleak sun rose higher, stopping to cast its fog-diffused glow from directly overhead, indicating noon, they noticed a change in the general silence.

It came from within the forest. Far away, echoed the sounds that only men make, when men are soldiers on a hunt.

"Oh, this is just perfect!" Lizabette hissed. "Look where this accursed path is taking us! Directly into danger! If only we had stayed on the big road!"

"Hush!" Percy hissed, right back at her. "No one has seen us yet, and no one says they must—if we stay quiet and take care! We have to go forward *into* the deep forest at some point or another, you knew that very well all along, didn't you? It's the one thing we must do eventually, is go into the forest!"

"So then we'll just get caught, sooner than later!"

In that moment, as the two of them were facing off, just up ahead, and from very *nearby*, came the soft sound of shifting snow. Then, a single branch cracked . . . but it was enough. It had originated directly off the path, a couple of feet away from Betsy.

Everyone, in the cart and walking beside it, froze.

Percy grabbed the reins to pull up Betsy, and held them tight. So tight, she could barely feel her fingers. . . .

The snowdrift fell apart to reveal two possibly human shapes—and maybe the shadow of a *third*, but no, there was no one else, Percy blinked—that had been completely buried in the white powder. A man wearing shabby inadequate clothing, with dark hair and skin that was wan from the cold, held close to him another tightly bundled shape, vaguely female. She was covered in a faded and worn red cloak over grey spun wool, and appeared motionless.

"Please . . ." said the man in a croaking voice, then was interrupted by a fit of coughing. "Please do not be afraid, I am unarmed! Please . . . help us! My—*sister* here is very ill, and I beg a stranger's kindness only—"

He took a few steps forward, and Percy watched him hold on to the bundled girl—if that is what it was—with extreme care.

For one tense moment, everyone in the cart and around it stared.

"Are you Jack Frost?" said Jenna suddenly. "'Cause if you are, and you look all blue, I am not scared of you."

"Stop! You say you are unarmed," Percy said, ignoring the youngster. "Put your 'sister' down and show your hands."

Another long pause.

Then the man very gently lowered the precious bundle he was holding, so that she lay on the path at his feet in the snow. One death-white hand could be seen, as it slipped from under her covering. He straightened, putting both his arms out slowly so they could see.

"His hands are blue too!" Jenna was fascinated, forgetting all fear. "And look, *her* hand is pure white, like clean snow! She must be the Snow Maiden! I knew it, Jack, admit it, you are Frost himself!"

"Oh, hush already, Jenna!" Flor spoke up, though not unkindly. "Lord, but you have a mouth on you, child!"

But Percy continued looking at him, closely . . . because the stranger before her was full of inexplicable dissonance. And it seemed there was a *shadow* standing just behind him . . . or maybe kneeling . . . or lying on the ground. But then it was gone, when again she blinked.

He was handsome, in that strange fierce way that some men with really dark hair could be, and his features were fine, exquisite even. And yet, they appeared damaged somehow, swollen, as if they bore the aftermath of heavy bruises.

Niosta seemed to have read Percy's mind, because she blurted from the back of the cart, "Looks like he took a beating. . . ."

"I am unarmed . . ." repeated the man softly, continuing to stand with his arms opened wide.

From the distance the sound of men and hounds came brazen and resonant, and possibly closer. . . .

"Who are you?" Percy said, in a voice betraying nothing.

"I am *nobody*. And my poor sister here is even less . . . I beg you show us kindness."

"Are they after you?" Regata, standing nearest Betsy, observed the stranger warily. For the first time her friendly, calm demeanor became opaque, and her gloved fingers tugged nervously at the fine forest green wool of her well-tailored Letheburg coat. "Because this is Chidair land, and the black knight must be out hunting right now, I expect—"

"No!" he hastened to reassure. "They are hunting, yes, but not *us*—no one knows about us, and we pose no danger to you, on that I swear—"

"Is your sister very sick?" Lizabette interrupted. "Why is she not moving? What is wrong with her? Is she contagious?"

Percy thought she saw an unusual intensity in his expression, almost the hauteur of a nobleman. But it was fleeting, and then he shook his head wearily. "No, not contagious. . . . But she is very ill—from the *cold*. Please, if I might ask you to allow us to travel with you? I will walk, and she needs but a small place in the cart, to rest—"

"How many more people are we going to fit in this cart?" said Lizabette. "What are we, a traveling tinker circus?"

"You did not seem to mind when those three aristos wanted to take up seats here. Besides, we are on walking rotation," Percy reminded. "There is room."

"Yes, well, but at this rate, for how long? Emilie is already out of rotation with a chill, there's all our bundled stuff, and now this sick girl too! Meanwhile, you're sitting pretty all the way, and giving everyone orders—"

"I am *driving* this damn cart!" said Percy.

"Aw, c'mon, there is plenty of room still," muttered Catrine, while Niosta and Flor nodded.

"She can have my place!" said Jenna, hopping out of the cart.

That decided it.

"All right, get her up here," said Percy to the man, maintaining a gruff, stern voice. "But don't try anything, because if you do, we *will* take you down like a steer, and truss you up, and leave you to freeze."

"Yeah, and we'll take your pants too! And your shirt and cloak!" said Niosta, while Catrine chortled. "My Pa robs carriages for a living an'e show us how to deal with fools like you!"

"Thank you," the dark-haired stranger said, in a serious tone, ignoring the jesting. He carefully picked up the bundle that was his sister. As Percy watched, it seemed for a moment that another shadow-form lay in the snow right next to the bundled girl. But again, merely a strange trick of the hazy light. . . .

"Are you sure she ain't dead?" Niosta muttered, watching the stiff shape being placed in the cart, cloak arranged over her, face still in shadow, mostly covered, and only two very limp white hands now showing.

But then, like clockwork, one hand moved—almost like a doll, it might have seemed—and she clutched the wool, drawing it to her. A rasping female voice sounded.

"Where—are we?"

"Oh good, you're still with us," Sibyl said with an effort at cheer.

"So now, who are you two? And what are your names?"

"You . . . may . . . call me . . . Claere. . . ." The new girl in the cart spoke with difficulty. She had a peculiar way of breathing before uttering each word, and Percy assumed it was due to a raging chest cold from which she must have been suffering. Her hood slipped aside to reveal a girl with very sickly white skin, and with great haunting eyes, appearing overlarge in her pinched, oval face.

"Oooh! We *may* call you? Well, your high and mighty Majesty, so glad you oblige us with your dee-light'ul name!" Catrine teased, not unkindly.

The man gave her a hard, almost stunned look, while Percy said, "That's enough now, leave her be."

She then gently moved the reins and directed Betsy forward. The cart began to roll, with more girls walking, and the man walking also, right alongside his resting sister.

"And what should we call *you?*" Percy directed her question at him.

"Jack Frost!" exclaimed Jenna.

"Vlau," he responded. "But you can call me anything you like."

"I expect, I shall be calling you and everyone 'run!' very soon, if the hunters come upon us. By the way, I'm Percy Ayren, from Oarclaven, and we're all Cobweb Brides. Some of us have been walking from as far back as south of Letheburg. Our journey lies into the forest, to Death's Keep."

"Good," he said. "Because our journey lies in the same direction."

Chapter 11

Lady Amaryllis drove the Curricle of Doom bravely forward despite a lingering ache in her ankle. Seated at her side, Lord Nathan gave her frequent close glances throughout their lighthearted banter. Behind them, in the smaller back seat, next to the travel chest, Lady Ignacia made herself comfortable against a pillow and pretended to doze, with her fur-trimmed hood raised against the wind, concealing both her plumed hat and her chilled face.

"Are you holding up well, Ignacia, darling?" said Amaryllis flippantly, as they made their way in the full but hazy daylight, with sparse trees and Lake Merlait on the left side, and thick forest on the right.

"Goodness, *you're* the one with the sprained ankle, m'dear! Heaven only knows why you must insist we continue this silly excursion! As for me, I am utterly bored and exhausted," retorted Ignacia in a similar tone. "Was just making a brave attempt at sleep, in order to dream of *food*—you know, succulent filet of smoked salmon drowning in white sauce, and roast duck in cream and mushroom puff pastry with dill and chives—"

"Stop that immediately! Ah, but you are far more evil than Amaryllis!" Nathan exclaimed. "And speaking of pastry, what have we that's even remotely edible in that trunk next to you? If

I recall, only the bread and croissants seem to have any flavor to them. . . ."

While they chattered, there was a sudden explosion of sound in the forest, just a few feet off the right side of the thoroughfare.

A horn blared deafeningly. . . .

And then dark figures mounted on horses, and even more men on foot, burst out everywhere around them. . . . Snowdrifts stirred, and more figures rose up, moving like elemental creatures of winter, white and slate and grizzled silver all in motion. Were they even human?

Amaryllis could barely keep hold of the reins as her black thoroughbreds reared up, for the second time in one day, neighing in terrified fury, as they were immediately grabbed from all directions by dark soldiers. There were vague flashes of ice-blue surcoats emblazoned with insignias, and then the curricle was jerked and held, by a least half a dozen mail-clad men-at-arms.

Amaryllis cried out, and Nathan and Ignacia's voices sounded next to her and behind—

"Halt, upon pain of death! Stay where you are! Do not move!" The command was issued by several of the mounted helmed men, in peculiar strained or stilted voices, while another announced: "You are trespassing on Chidair land! What is your excuse?"

After the first shock, Amaryllis had regained her tongue. "Chidair land? Since when is a major thoroughfare considered Chidair land? We are noble travelers of consequence, on a free road, and this is an outrage! How dare you accost us or hold us? And as for 'pain of death,' gracious, where have *you* been?"

In reply the speaker laughed harshly. "Where have *I* been? If you must know, M'Lady, I've been in battle, and I've been *slaughtered*, and yet, here I sit!" Speaking thus, he removed his dirt-stained, dented helmet and revealed a grey bloodless face, frozen-motionless eyes, and what appeared to be a major gaping wound to his skull.

Amaryllis gave a scream and shrank back, dropping the reins in reflex. Nathan gasped.

"Yes, you see, pretty Lady, I'm a dead man. And so are most of the rest of us. Now, answer the question, what are you doing here? Or else you'll learn the meaning of 'pain of death' without actually dying!"

"We are traveling from the Silver Court," said Lord Woult with grim determination. "And as such, you have no claim on us, not even if this *were* Chidair territory instead of a free road."

"Any Cobweb Brides here?" said a soldier leaning in from behind the curricle, drawing close and grinning wide with his own dead face—pale and bared of helm, and sporting even more gruesome mortal wounds across the neck and jaw, a hollowed eye socket, severed ligaments and sinew and raw bluish-violet flesh. Ignacia made a small stifled sound, then drew away as far as possible from him, leaning forward.

"Maybe . . ." said Amaryllis.

"In that case, you are to surrender now, upon the orders of Duke Ian Chidair—and lo, here is Hoarfrost Himself, arrived to deal with you!"

And as the denizens of the curricle looked on, the soldiers on all sides moved aside as from the right of the road, on the forest side, out of the snowdrifts and the overgrown hedge, emerged a tall warhorse. Mounted on it, sat a huge giant of a man. His barrel chest was clad in a damaged and tattered blue surcoat with Chidair crest and colors, covered with multiple faded bloodstains, poorly fitting loose mail plate over a damaged hauberk, and neither helm nor gauntlets. His wild tangled hair stood up like an unruly briar covered in frozen bits of lake bracken, leaves, twigs and other indescribable dirt. He was thus stained from head to toe, soaked and marinated in the lake, and then frozen . . . and lastly, dusted with snow.

However, the most disturbing part of him was his eyes—

eyeballs opened wide and frozen in place, motionless and unblinking.

"Welcome to my lands, three pretty ladies! Or is there a lad amongst you? Aha, yes! A pretty lordling, I see!" Hoarfrost's voice was a deep bellowing roar, and each word punctuated with hissing breaths driven by a mechanism of solid gears.

"I am Lord Nathan Woult, and your so-called welcome leaves much to be desired, Duke," said the young man bravely, attempting to rise from his seat in the curricle. But he was immediately pushed back down by two thick mail-clad arms, as burly soldiers held him motionless.

"Stay, boy, stay!" roared Hoarfrost. "Are you a Cobweb Bride too? Or is it just these two lovelies?"

"How dare you!" Amaryllis could hold back no longer. "Have you no fear of the Emperor? Or is your honor besmirched entirely? Now that you are neither dead nor alive—yes, I can see quite well by your utterly *filthy* appearance—do you answer to Death alone, or perchance to no one at all?"

Hoarfrost bellowed with laughter. "You have said it, by my arse! Exactly so, girlie! I now answer to *no one*, and least of all to Death, the cold bastard! Now shut your pretty mouth, and sit tight, as I take you all to be my honored guests! That's right, you are all *guests* of the Duke Chidair now, and as such, you will sit pretty in my Keep! And if you please me well, I will let you stay among the living a wee bit longer!"

"Provincial savage!" said Amaryllis, while Nathan squeezed her arm meaningfully, so that she remain quiet.

But Hoarforst ignored her completely now. He continued shaking with laughter, as he sputtered to his men: "Take them away and put them with the others. And take care with the excellent horses and that fancy bit'o carriage—"

But as he started to turn away, Ignacia's voice sounded, ringing loud and unusually forceful, from the back seat of the curricle.

"Wait, Duke Hoarfrost, Ian Chidair! You might want to

listen to what I have to say to you!"

"Oh, Ignacia, hush!"

Duke Hoarfrost paused and then slowly turned around, his barrel chest, perforated with holes, hissing loudly in the general silence. "And what have you to say, little bird?"

"Only this—you have been told to expect *me*."

Hoarfrost stilled entirely. No hiss of breath; only macabre frozen eyeballs regarded her.

"I am the one," continued Ignacia, a fierce new energy coming to her usually complacent and vacuous pretty face. "The one sent to parlay with you on behalf of Her Brilliance, Rumanar Avalais, the Sovereign of the Domain, and soon to be the sole ruler of all the surrounding territories."

And as Lady Amaryllys and Lord Nathan stared at their dearest "friend" in shock, observing her in an entirely new light, all manner of details suddenly clicking into place, she continued:

"I am the Right Honorable Lady Ignacia Chitain of Balmue, and my true allegiance lies with the Sapphire Court and its Sovereign, and none other. For several years now I have been placed within the Silver Court to infiltrate and report to my real liege, and I am now at liberty to disclose my true role to you, because of the present circumstances."

"Ignacia . . ." whispered Amaryllis, while blood drained from her cheeks, and cramps of ice seized her innards. "Is this a—joke?"

But her friend did not even deign to glance at her. "No joke at all, Lady Amaryllis. My apologies to you—and to Lord Woult—for the continued deception. It was nothing personal."

The Duke's hissing bellows came to life again. "How do I know that you do not lie now, and this is not an elaborate bit of nonsense to escape my hold?" Hoarfrost uttered, measuring every word.

Ignacia had a quick answer. "The missive you have received contained an invitation from the Sovereign to form an

alliance against the King of Lethe and the Emperor of the
Realm. In exchange for your cooperation, you were offered
neither Life, nor Death, but the guarantee of perfect Eternity."

About an hour after noon, Percy asked everyone if they
wanted to take a small break. The forest remained noisy
with men, distant echoes and footfalls and voices coming from
all directions, but so far they had been amazingly fortunate, and
the little path had kept them safely meandering deeper into the
woodland.

Next to a comfortably large snow-hillock and several thick
bushes, Percy pulled up Betsy, and the cart stopped.

"Quiet, quiet, now! For the love of God, keep quiet!"
Lizabette repeated, as the girls scattered behind bushes to take
care of bodily needs.

Percy got out Betsy's grain bag and hung it around the
horse's neck for her to feed. There was no time to unhitch Betsy
and get comfortable; this was going to be a short rest stop. She
then stomped around to wake up her numb feet in their thick
woolen wrappings. A few steps away, the man called Vlau stood
hunched over and motionless, near the equally motionless,
pitiful Claere, where she lay in the cart right next to sniffling
Emilie and a few small sacks of their belongings. What a sorry
sight they all made. . . .

"You hungry?" said Percy, looking at him. "We have a roll
or two to spare, for you and your sister." She then took out the
basket with the bread and pulled out two flour-dusted rolls, now
day-old, but perfectly edible and tasty.

He looked up with weary apathy, and started to refuse.

"Eat! It'll warm you up."

"My sister—she is too sick to eat."

"Well, then *you* eat, and we'll see to her later."

He paused, parting his lips, about to speak, considering . . .
when Percy reached out and put a roll in his hands.

"Take it. I'll be back in a moment. Meanwhile, don't try

anything, all right?" Not waiting for him to respond, Percy then turned away, bit off a big chunk of the other roll, and while still chewing, went into the shrubbery to take care of her own natural business.

When she returned, most of the girls were back, and Flor, the baker's daughter, was busy making a small fire in a hastily dug pit. "Bring me twigs, dry sticks, pine needles, pine cones, tree bark—anything you see! I can use it all to stoke the fire. Anything you bring, just watch, I can use to make a fire," she whispered bossily, tucking long wisps of flax-blond hair out of her face and deeper under her kerchief shawl, and several girls immediately started looking.

While they were milling about, it started to snow.

"Oh, just what we need," Lizabette grumbled, shivering, as large fluttering snowflakes landed on her lashes and cheeks. She pulled her coat collar up, and her hat lower down over her ears. Her long nose was red, and for that matter, so was everyone else's.

"What if someone sees the smoke from the fire?" Sibyl asked.

"They won't," retorted Flor. "Not with *my* fire and my snow pit they won't."

And interestingly, she was right—she had arranged the walls of the snow pit just so and perforated them with several horizontal outlet tunnel holes, so that the smoke was oddly diffused and never rose more than a foot off the ground before dispersing.

When the little fire was burning steadily, fed by endless twigs and other kindling, Regata brought out a small iron kettle, and packed it full of clean snow for boiling water.

"What are we going to do for tea?" said Jenna, as the girls all gathered around the fire pit, and took off their mittens to warm reddened fingers against the rising steam. "Should I gather bark?"

"Bark tea? What an abomination. . . ." Lizabette vigorously rubbed her frost-bitten fingers, then held them splayed over the warm vapors escaping the boiling water. "Might as well brew dirt."

"Check the basket." Percy pointed to the bundle with the rolls and other supplies. "I think Ronna, bless her, gave us a small bag of *real* tea leaves."

The tea was immediately located and a generous pinch went into the boiling water. Then Jenna and Regata uncovered two drinking mugs of fired clay, and they were filled with tea and passed around, warming many small frozen hands and fingers, not to mention their insides.

Percy sipped the heavenly warmth when it was her turn, then took her mug to the cart, and offered it to Emilie who pulled off the blanket from her miserable face just so that she could drink.

"How are you, child?" Percy held the back of her hand to the other's burning forehead.

Emilie muttered something incoherent, then wrapped herself back in the blanket.

Percy returned to the fire to refill the mug, and this time she approached Vlau and his sister.

He took the mug without protest. "Thank you . . . I—I will give it to her myself."

Percy watched as he drank a few eager gulps, then leaned forward, barely pulled back Claere's hood, and made a show of trying to pour the hot tea past the sick girl's lips.

For some reason, Percy's gaze lingered on the two of them, lingered closely. And she noted the way most of the liquid seemed to miss the mouth and dribble on her chin. . . . And how the color of the girl's face was so ashen white, so incredibly unreal, and the lips were bluish, with not a hint of blood underneath the skin. . . .

And then Percy blinked, and she saw it, a shadow lying alongside the sick girl in the cart. The shadow was like smoke and dark soot, and it looked exactly like the smoky shape at her grandmother's bedside back at home in Oarclaven.

Percy recognized it, and she suddenly *knew*.

"Vlau," she said in a soft voice. "You don't need to give her any more tea. You know *what* she is, don't you? If you do not— I am very sorry to have to tell you this, but—your sister is no longer alive. She—she is not going to need tea or rolls ever again. . . ."

He looked up at her, with his dark intense, stricken gaze.

"How did you know?"

Percy shrugged, then sighed. "I just know. I can *see* . . . some things, I suppose."

"What things?"

"There's a *shadow*," said Percy, speaking very quietly, so that the girls giggling around the fire and sharing chunks of bread would have no chance of hearing. "The shadow is next to her. I think—it is her *true death*. But because all death has stopped, the shadow has nowhere to go, nothing to do. So it just waits there, at her side. At each person's side. I know, because I have seen it before."

"Please . . ." he said, "I beg—I ask you not to tell anyone."

"I won't."

He nodded, with some relief.

In that moment, the hood over Claere's face moved back, swept by a thin, show-white hand, delicate as a swan's neck.

Clare's great hollowed eyes, frozen into eternal stillness in their sockets, were watching Percy.

It seemed, all her soul was contained in that silent gaze.

And then the dead lips parted, and there was an inhalation of breath. "Thank . . . you . . ." whispered the dead girl, as her breath gently faded. And then she was again silent, disappearing into herself.

Percy gave a small nod, then left them be, and returned to the warmth of the fire.

In a quarter of an hour they were done with eating and tea and restoring some warmth into their bodies. Flor put out the fire with the same care she used to create it, and she sprinkled delicate handfuls of snow gradually on the dying embers, so that the resulting smoke was absorbed and dispersed low on the earth. In the end, they piled more snow to create a drift in place where the fire pit had been, so that no one would know. And then Catrine and Niosta used branches to dust and smooth the snow all around their campsite.

"They will still see our footprints, will they not?" asked Jenna.

"They might. But then, they'll also see Betsy's hoof prints and the wheel tracks. Nothing can be done about it. Let's go!"

"Let me just sweep this bit, just a little more—"

"No, Jen! No need, the best we can do now is be on our way. Now, climb in the cart! Hurry!" Percy spoke firmly, and Jenna scurried to obey her.

"Percy, you know how, back home, the older women all get together and talk?" Flor suddenly said in a low voice, while getting in the cart and settling down directly behind Percy.

"Yeah, I know." Percy wondered what this was leading up to.

"Well," said Flor. "Supposedly your Ma always complains that you are slow-witted and can't do anything right. But what *I* think, is—you're just pretending. You pretend you cannot do anything when in fact you can do all kinds of things . . . really *well*. Like what you're doing now."

Percy said nothing.

"I mean," Flor continued, "it's not just you. My Ma talks about me, too. She says these things about me, calls me an idiot and a slowpoke, when all I do is work and work around the oven, and she just complains and gives me more and more to do—"

Percy still said nothing, and picked up the reins.

"—so what I'm trying to say is, Percy—you don't need to

pretend any more. Not with me, or any of us. And—" here, Flor finished in a whisper—"thank you for taking care of us so well."

I've stopped pretending a while ago. . . . Ever since I walked out of my father's house, knowing it will be for the last time.

Percy silently drove the cart.

Claere Liguon, daughter of the Emperor, lay huddled against coarse wooden planks, on a thin layer of hay covering the floor of the jostling peasant cart.

She had never been near hay in her life—nor would she ever be, now—but in death, she now experienced its simple brittle softness.

Hay and snow. . . .

On one side of her corpse, right underneath her stiff ivory elbow, were baskets and satchels of unknown stuff underneath canvas and burlap. A large lumpy sack butted up against her waist from the back, and she—her cold lifeless body—felt the strange sensory distance of its touch, as though perceiving the world through thick molasses. And on the other side of Claere was a very sick peasant girl, cuddled in a thin blanket, coughing and sneezing every few moments, and blissfully unaware of who or what reposed right next to her.

There were more female shapes and voices all around, some girls seated in the cart, others walking right next to it.

All sound was surreal—slightly distorted, elongated, as if coming from a distance of thick atmospheric layers, or as though heard through water.

She listened to the strangeness, or listened *despite it*—to the soft whisper-level litany of their conversation, occasional gentle banter, bursts of giggles, and then long bouts of weary silence . . . at which point the resounding silence of the forest was revealed, woods oppressed by the weight of snow, and the crackle of timber, the slithering of the ice wind. . . .

A large pale draft-horse pulled their cart. And the driver was another peasant girl, her solid back covered with a length of woolen shawl, which was all that Claere could see directly from her vantage point. That girl, Percy, was far quieter than the others, introspective. And this one *knew* somehow, had known Claere's true condition with an uncanny sixth sense.

Claere recalled a sympathetic steady gaze of intelligent eyes of an indeterminate swamp color, somewhere between blue and grey and green, and more like slate ashes. The girl's round peasant face with its cold-reddened features was bland, but the strange depth of the expression gave her away somehow as something more complex. . . .

She sees me, sees my death. Who is she? And why can she see this when no one else can?

Claere's stray random thoughts were like winged things beating against the shutters of her body, her broken human shell. She lay back and watched the grey pallor of the winter sky through glass eyes, while the cloak hood had shifted from her face, giving her a wide panoramic view. Clouds of varied whiteness and vapor and darkness sailed across the sphere of heaven, streaking past each other in infinite layers of cotton and torn smoke. The depth of heaven overhead was infinite.

Clare—the *conscious thing* that was Clare—felt a pull, a reeling vertigo, until she imagined herself lifting like a bird and then falling inversely into the distance of sky, a soul taken at last. . . . If she could breathe, she would be breathless with the infinity, if she could cry, there would be a river pouring out of her. . . .

But she had been drained of all her waters already, days ago. And her river that had run red and abundant like wine was now all gone—for what is blood but the wine of life?—while she, what remained of herself, was but a flopping, convulsing fish in its final gritty dregs.

And he—the man who had done this to her, the murderer and the victim in one—now walked at her side. There he paced, with only wooden planks of the side-rail wall of the cart between them. And she *felt* his overwhelming presence somehow, felt *him* with more clarity than anything else in her world.

Marquis Vlau Fiomarre.

She had taken to repeating his name in her mind upon occasion, she noticed this recently. And she was doing it now, again, repeating the name like a litany, a strange prayer. It had started when she first learned it, the name of her murderer. And at first she savored its knife-edge sound in order to fathom him, his motives. But in the forest, earlier today, when they had been on the run, she realized that she had been repeating his name as an anchor, holding on to the shape of it in her mind as he carried her through the forest, as she felt the wall of his body around her, through the veils of thickness—of her death—felt him lifting her, bearing her aloft. . . .

Vlau Fiomarre.

She sensed him now, walking at her side, for he was ever nearby. He had remained with her strangely, maybe out of guilt, or maybe driven by remnants of the need for vengeance. A wave of cold distant fear inundated her, as she imagined for a moment what kind of new exquisite revenge he could possibly have in mind, what other thing of occult dread and evil he might attempt to do to her, the "accursed Liguon."

But then just as easily the fear and suspicion drained from her. And she knew with a sudden surety that it was no longer what bound them.

She remembered his face, every moment of him seared into her mind, from that first fateful instant he stood before her in the Silver Hall, to the moments of his dark raging passion as he stood in chains and told his mad story of injustice.

And now, all she had from him was a dark fathomless intensity. It encompassed him, this intensity, this darkness, this infinite focused presence.

She was drowning in it, in its abysmal virile strength. And

somehow, just at the edges, there was a new thing. . . .

A craving was born.

Vlau Fiomarre.

She could never admit it, nor would she divulge it, not even to herself much less to him—the murderer, madman, her anchor, and her destruction.

In truth, she did not even have the words for it, for this desire—whether for constancy, for unwavering strength, or merely for a fixed point in her storm. He was her death—and yet, her blade of life, of clarity, to cut through the thick roiling swamp of personal darkness.

She needed him.

Vlau.

Another half hour, and the snow started to really come down, while the shadow of the weakling sun disappeared completely through the thick afternoon clouds. The wind increased—enough to cause small spinning flurries, and to make it feel bitterly cold—as Betsy, the cart, and its occupants slowly advanced along the path.

Despite the frequent meandering, they and the path were moving directly north.

And now, their entire world had become a lace veil of falling whiteness.

Betsy plodded forward through the snow, her hooves leaving deeper prints in the fresh power with every minute, as the newly fallen flakes accumulated.

The girls whose turn it was to walk next to the cart had their meager cloaks and shawls and winter coverings pulled tightly over their faces, so that in most cases only the eyes were showing. They walked, leaning into the wind, taking each step forward with effort.

Those in the cart huddled together and used whatever spare blankets they had to cover themselves.

Vlau, the only man among them, paced onward relentlessly,

holding on to the cart next to where lay Claere. The dead girl moved her lily-white hands occasionally to pull the cloak over her face whenever the wind revealed too much of it.

Percy drew her nice wool shawl as much over her nose as possible and periodically tucked each mittened hand under the shawl for extra warmth, holding the reins with the other. She wrapped her skirts as closely as she could over her knees and legs. Still, whenever the wind gusts blew hard in her direction, she could feel the cold's fiery bite through the insufficient fabric and along her upper thighs. Underneath, her old, well-worn cotton stockings were inadequate for such long winter exposure. At least her wrapped feet were still dry. . . .

We are going to die, all of us, tonight.

And then, as soon as she thought it, reality immediately intruded, cheerfully reminding her that there was no longer the option to die—not for any of them, no matter what. Death had ceased, and they were all being given a bizarre reprieve.

Well then, we are simply going to freeze to the point *of death, but continue to move onward like toy soldiers, our bodies shutting down, burning with cold fire then growing numb, yet still imprisoning us. Not a bad prospect!*

Lord help her, Percy was growing more amused with every mad thought. Indeed, this was insanity—and, at the same time, it was more cheerful and yet more depressing to contemplate than ordinary death that would have been so *final*. . . .

To stop herself from such morbid amusement, Percy glanced behind her and, in a low voice, asked how everyone was doing.

Several voices mumbled that they were all right, or tired, or simply cold.

Seated next to Percy this time, Lizabette wondered out loud if they were ever going to stop for the night—that is, when the night actually arrived.

"When it starts getting dark," Percy said. "We still have at least three hours of daylight. See, the snow is starting to let up a bit."

"Lordy, but how quiet it is!" Jenna suddenly said from the back of the cart.

And it was true. Everyone noticed that there were no more distant voices, no more baying of hounds echoing through the forest. Even the snowfall had slowed somewhat, and with it they had a return of slightly better visibility. Only the wind gusts continued their ragged whistle-song among the tree branches.

"The patrols must have gone home." Regata was hunched over and holding the fur-trimmed edges of her hoodlet closely over her face.

"Or maybe they've stopped for a bite to eat."

"Or maybe," Percy said thoughtfully, "a changing of the guard."

"They're on rotation too!" Jenna giggled through her shawl, keeping her face from the most direct wind gusts.

"Hush!" Lizabette turned around and shoved the younger girl on the arm. Jenna quieted and put her mitten to her mouth.

But it was too late. . . .

In that instant, a terrible noise sounded from directly up ahead. It signified their greatest fear—a heavy weight of pounding iron hooves, ringing mail plate, the wild crackle of striking branches, and the angry neighing of more than one great war beast forced to plunge forward in an attack. . . .

"*Run!*" exclaimed Percy. "Everybody, run!"

The cart exploded with motion. The girls sprang up and scattered, many helping each other, some grabbing their small sacks of belongings. Semi-conscious Emilie was dragged down, together with her blanket, and carried bodily by Regata and Sibyl into the nearest shrubbery.

Vlau, his eyes flaring with life, momentarily froze with inaction. It seemed he was actually considering whether to stay and fight, because his hands reached for a non-existent sword at his side.

Good grief, is he a nobleman, or at least someone in the service of the upper crust? Well, that explains some things. . . .

He threw one maddened glance at Percy. But seeing her motioning him away wildly, he turned to his sole responsibility, his lifeless sister, and he picked her up and carried her in his arms, running into the forest.

Percy alone remained. Why? She was unsure. But Grial had asked her to do this, and Flor had thanked her, and she couldn't exactly leave Betsy. . . .

Seated in the driver's seat, latched onto Betsy's reins with an iron grip, she held her breath. Her mind was reeling, and a brick of cold terror settled in her gut.

They were upon her in three heartbeats.

First, several running foot soldiers came crashing on both sides of the path, moving in parallel with it. In their wake, two mounted figures moved suddenly to cross it, and then—as though noticing the trail's existence for the first time— immediately returned and entered the path directly. The first, on a bay horse, was a light rider in leathers, with a pale blue surcoat with Chidair crest and colors, over a chain hauberk, and bearing a lance.

Behind him, on a pure black charger, came *he*, fully plated, and helmed, dull ebony metal covering every inch of him, and nothing showing, not even eyes, under the lowered faceplate.

The black knight.

As the others came thundering past, the lance bearer paused, seeing Percy, but the black knight motioned with his hand, and the rider moved onward, riding off the path and into the forest to hunt the others. The rest of them passed by like a thundering wave, and were gone.

It was thus that the black knight alone came to a stop before Percy and Betsy and the cart.

In that moment, a hard gust of wind whistled directly at her, and Percy shivered. . . .

The black war stallion, controlled by *his* great gauntleted hand, slowed to a measured walk, a monster becoming docile. It took three more paces, and then stilled, just a hand-span away from Betsy. It was a testament to how truly enormous the stallion was, that next to him, the thick-limbed draft horse appeared a tiny filly.

In the new silence Betsy snorted.

Percy stared directly ahead, and up at *him*.

And the black knight regarded her.

"Who are you, girl?" he asked, in a surprisingly soft and weary baritone. "Are you, too, a Cobweb Bride?"

Whatever it was about his voice, *something*, maybe the mortal weariness—Percy could not be sure—but it emboldened her, just so that she recollected herself enough to breathe.

"And what if I am?" she said in an unusually insolent voice, meanwhile amazed at herself, at her own, previously unheard-of intonation.

"Then regretfully I must take you with me."

Percy felt a sort of breathless madness come to her, fill her head to bursting. . . . She tied off the reins, got down from the cart, and then walked forward to stand directly before him.

"And what if I refuse to go? What will you do, slay me on the spot, Sir Knight? Oh, wait, that does not work anymore."

Gusts of wind blew in the pause of silence.

"You are trespassing," he then said quietly. "What do you think should be done with you? Oh, wait, hacking your limbs off will still work."

"Do you really need another disembodied arm or leg? Why not simply let me go? I'll be on my way and out of your lands before you know it. My business, Sir Knight, is not with you but with Death and his Keep."

Did she imagine it, or did the knight sigh?

"It is precisely for that reason why I may not allow you to go on. But—enough dawdling. Here, take my hand and come with me willingly, or be lifted up by the scruff of that shawl of yours. . . ." And speaking thus, he pressed his war stallion forward and bent down from the saddle to reach for her.

Percy reacted to the great black gauntlet moving in her face, and she sprang back with agility, and ended up behind Betsy, and then on the other side of the cart. While the immense weight of the metal plates of the knight made them clang together like wicked bells tolling, he and his war beast maneuvered around Betsy. As though they were a single giant entity, they went after her, deceptively slow and measured.

In wild desperation, Percy rummaged over the side of the cart, grabbing for anything she could think might serve as a weapon. Her hands fell upon a large cast-iron saucepan—another blessed gift from Ronna—and she took it by the handle.

In that instant, the black knight was upon her, and his giant gauntlets were clasping her shoulders and waist, lifting her as though she were a feather; and she felt herself tossed up to the front of his saddle.

And then, before she even knew what she was doing, Percy reacted. She swung the saucepan in a wild arc, barely missing her own head, and crashed it with all her strength against the black knight's helmet—inches away from her face.

Holy Mother of God, but what did just happen?

The ice wind whistled, and there came a pause—as the knight went still suddenly, and in his embrace she could feel his body losing its iron cast, its solidity and resistance, and all his strength dissolved around her—in one impossible instant of awareness.

And then the black knight *fell*.

And she, still in his embrace, fell also, somehow still trapped by his weakened hold. . . . They crashed from the saddle onto the snow, he landing on the ground first, and she fortunately landing on top of him, instead of being crushed by what looked to be an anvil of black iron plate. . . .

Holy Mother of God.

Percy lay where she had fallen, still holding on to the skillet. She was stunned, but only for the duration of one breath, and then, disentangling herself from *his* cold metal arms, she crawled. The black warhorse had screamed then shied away, and was now prancing ten feet from Betsy, who continued standing calmly through the entirety of this incident.

The black knight lay on his back in the snow.

Panting hard, vapor curling from her lips, Percy stood up, ignoring a painful bruise on her knee, adjusting her fallen shawl, shaking snow powder from her dark tangled hair, all the while watching *his* great motionless shape, the limp gauntlets. . . .

She then dropped the saucepan and put her hands to her mouth.

"Did you kill him?"

An amazed whisper sounded behind her. And there was Gloria, followed by Niosta and Marie, covered in white powder and emerging from a snowdrift thicket.

"Percy! Holy Lord! Is he . . . dead? You *killed* the black knight! How? What did you *do?*"

"I don't—I don't know!" she was saying. And then, again reality hit hard.

"He is not dead, remember!" she exclaimed. "*Remember?* No one is dead!"

"So then—"

"He's out cold, is what he is!" Percy picked up the heavy iron skillet and pointed at him with it. "I used this, got him on the head, somehow. So now he is going to wake up eventually, and 'kill' *us!*"

"Oh no . . ." Marie whimpered.

"But before he does," Percy continued, "we're going to make sure he cannot hurt us or do anything to us."

She approached the knight again, crouched beside him to check for signs of animation. "We need to tie him up, and quickly. . . . But first, let's get him into the cart. . . . Help me, everyone!"

But it was easier said than done. The black knight weighed far more than an ordinary man, covered head to toe in metal plate as he was.

"Let's strip him!" Flor emerged from hiding, coming from the other side of the path. "And hurry! The other hunters are still out there, and they already grabbed Catrine, Regata, and Sybil, and I think I saw them going after Lizabette—"

Niosta swore in foul gutter language. "My poor sis!"

But Percy and Gloria were already busy removing whatever portions of plate mail they could from the knight.

The first to come off was the helm. Percy raised his visor, bracing herself for the sight of a burly monster, and instead saw a pale bloodied face of a young man, surprisingly fine in appearance, with regular features, sculpted cheekbones and chestnut-brown wavy hair. Removing the helm altogether, she ascertained that not too much damage had been done by her blow with the saucepan. He had a minor bruise on his forehead, and a swollen lump on the right side of his head, above the back of the ear. Surely these wounds must have come about earlier, perpetrated by someone else. . . .

Altogether, he was still breathing.

As enough other pieces came off, they were able to lift him bodily at last, and the five of them together managed to drag him onto the cart, deep in the back.

"Get as much of this plate off him as possible," said Percy, getting back into the driver's seat. "And then tie his hands and feet, leave his woolens on, and put a blanket over him. Cover the armor too! Don't leave any of it lying around, just in case his men come looking."

"What of his fearsome horse? Should we shoo it away?"

Percy snorted. "You think you can? Anyone want to get up close to it? No?"

"Not me . . ." grumbled Niosta, using many loops of thick twine to bind the fallen knight's wrists and ankles. "It can run back to hell if it wants to."

At Percy's careful urging, Betsy started walking forward again, directly at the war stallion. And her surprising determination made the much larger beast move backward, and then turn and gallop out of their way into the thicket, where they heard him neighing in fury and crashing through brush for several minutes—as though he were loath to abandon his fallen master.

"Lordy, Lord, what are we gonna do with him? I mean, it's the *black knight!*" whispered Marie, in her teeny little voice with its funny accent, as they sat swaying in the cart. She had picked up the phrase "Lordy, Lord" from the others, and was now using it at every opportunity.

"Wait—where's Jenna?" Percy suddenly felt a pang of fear. It was as if she'd left her mind back there in the snow . . . how could she have forgotten?

But in a few minutes—speaking of the devil—Jenna herself came running from up ahead. And she took them further up the path to where Vlau, Claere, and Emilie were concealed in a hedge. The two girls were lying motionless—*one very sick and one very dead*, thought Percy—and Vlau stared at Percy and the others with amazement.

"How did you manage to escape?" he asked.

Percy only snorted.

But Gloria lifted up the blanket in the back proudly, revealing an unconscious young man partially clad in black armor, and thoroughly trussed up, and she pointed at Percy, and then at a cast-iron skillet sitting on top of an ebony chest plate.

The look on Vlau's face was priceless.

"Enough foolery, put the two girls back in the cart, and let's get going before the patrol returns—and at which point we may not be so lucky." Percy watched them all settle in. She then took the reins with newfound confidence, hid a smile, and said, "Whoa, Betsy."

For some reason, despite the stunning events and the

relentless cold and the wind and *everything*, she felt herself buoyant as a snowflake, light as a feather. . . .

She felt herself flying.

Beltain awoke in blue twilight. He inhaled deeply, with a shudder, and the freezing evening air entered his lungs.

His face, everything, was numb. Also, for some reason he could not move, and he was still in the forest. There were soft female voices all around him, lilting, rising in girlish chatter, and the deep natural silence was punctuated by the crackling sounds of a nearby fire.

He opened his eyes wide, and there was the golden glow on the ground, diffusing the bluish shadows of the tree trunks with warmth, in a small diameter of about fifteen feet.

He was lying under a burlap blanket, in the cart—the *cart!*

Everything came rushing back.

With a visceral jolt of awareness, he struggled to rise, realizing immediately that he was bound.

God in Heaven! The last thing he remembered was reaching down for that peasant girl to pull her up to his saddle. . . . She had been a strange brazen thing, and they had exchanged some pointed words—something about chopping off arms and legs and the philosophical impotence of Death. . . .

He recalled lifting her up, and then she did something—*she hit him!*

Beltain felt a cold fury mixed with chagrin, as he realized in those brief seconds that, not only had she hit him, but she had *knocked him out.*

A thickset peasant girl in a woolen shawl had accomplished what no tourney knight, no battle opponent had ever managed to do to the undefeated champion Lord Beltain Chidair since he was a small boy, fencing with wooden swords—

His *sword!* And for that matter, his horse! And where the hell were his men-at-arms?

With a parched groan, he turned his head, seeing a face immediately loom over him, while the other girlish voices around the fire quieted down.

The girl looking down at him, illuminated by the warm gold glow and bluish shadows, was likely no older than sixteen, and had a plain oval face, with no particular or distinguishing features—so nondescript indeed, that the only way he recognized her was by her woolen shawl, of an unmistakable older style, but vintage quality. The shawl was pulled back somewhat, revealing a few wisps of dark ash-brown hair over a pale forehead.

And then she said, "Good evening, Sir Knight." And her voice—its strange, compelling combination of mockery and command, coupled with a semblance of indifference—her voice quickened him and invoked a dull rage. . . .

"Where am I?" he managed to croak through his parched lips. "What happened? How did you—"

"To be honest, I am not entirely sure what happened," she said, continuing to lean over him, and he watched her reddened nose and her frost-chapped lips moving, and the escaping vaporous tendrils of her breath. "Now, try not to struggle too much, or the ropes might give you a burn eventually. For now, you're not going anywhere. It seems, you're somewhat beat up, but it's none of our doing. I venture, the reason you passed out was because you were already hurt pretty badly, even before I— hit you. For which I apologize, but I'm *not* at all sorry."

"Have you any idea who I am? Or what you've done?" he said.

"Let me get you some tea first, then you can berate me properly." And then she was gone, and he heard the girls whispering, a few stifled giggles, and moments later she was back with a mug of hot brew.

She placed her hands underneath his head, and her touch was firm but more gentle than he expected, as she lifted him enough to put the mug to his lips. Warm tea water hit him like heavenly balm, and he swallowed in reflex, gulping at least six times before coming up for air.

Oh, how cold he had been—only now was he able to sense the true extent of it. . . . And now, oh, how he ached all over, stewing in a dull general agony of many days' worth of battle bruises, since earlier that morning when he had collapsed for a single hour of sleep that his father had deigned to allow him, before having to return to his duties. How he had slept in that hour like a dead man! And yet the sleep had done him so little good, after the wrestling bear-hug with the Imperial knight, an embrace that had nearly crushed his ribs, the night before. . . .

"They will come looking for me," he mused, moving his lips wearily, and at the same time imperceptibly tensing the ropes on his feet and his wrists, bound together mercifully before him (as opposed to being bound behind his back, which would have forced him to lie contorted on his side). He tested the bonds and they were too well tied, unfortunately. He could do nothing to escape them, not in his present condition.

"I've no doubt they will," the girl said, putting the mug back to his lips. And again he drank. And then, things slipped away. . . .

The next moment he remembered coming to again, it was dark. Blue early evening had turned to deep indigo night.

The little fire still burned, but the voices had quieted, and there were a few soft snores coming from all around him, and in the cart.

Beltain made no sound, did not remember moaning, but again, the girl was back, looking into the cart and leaning over him. She must have been on lookout duty, or tending the fire while others slept, because she was so quick to appear nearby— quick to rise, quick on her feet, like a wild forest animal. . . .

They were all Cobweb Brides, he remembered then. This was still the forest. . . .

"My men . . ." he said. "I would not have allowed any harm

done—to you. We simply take you back home with us. My
father—his instructions are not to allow any of you to pass—"

"And why is that?" she whispered, arranging the cheap
burlap blanket over him, tucking it around his head and under
his chin, fingers grazing his jaw where there was a growing dark
stubble. "Why not let Cobweb Brides pass? Are you as wicked
as they say you are, O black knight and your black father?"

"His name is Hoarfrost—he is the Duke, Ian Chidair, and
they call him Duke Hoarfrost—"

"And what do they call you, son of Duke Hoarfrost?"

"Beltain."

"Bel-*tain*," she repeated. "Not at all as frightening as *the
black knight*."

"And your name? You are?"

"I am," said perversely. And then she turned away and left
his side.

Beltain closed his eyes and slept.

He awoke again, still in pitch darkness, this time because of
snow. Silence and cold snowflakes covered his cheeks, and he
felt utterly numb, as though the whole world itself was trying to
bury him in winter. There was no wind, but enough powder had
come down to put out the tiny fire, and sprinkle the blanket.

He should have felt more cold, but instead there was a solid
weight of a body pressed against him, warm wool on all
sides. . . . And he craned his neck just barely, enough to realize
she was sleeping at his side, wedged in a half-seated position
between him and the wall of the cart. Her voluminous shawl was
pulled over them both, and the snow piled harmlessly on the
outside.

Somewhere on the other side of him, from deep in the cart,
someone coughed—a phlegmy rasping sound of profound
sickness that did not bode well.

And for some reason, hearing it, he coughed also.

The girl next to him woke up. He sensed her tensing,
shifting her weight. Then her dark silhouette rose up somewhat,

so she was now in a seated position, and the shawl covering momentarily left him—replaced by an in-pouring of cold—as she seemed to look out over their campsite, in the darkness.

She lay back down eventually, and the shawl was also back in place, covering him.

And then a warm hand reached out, and he felt its feather-light touch on his forehead, as she swept snow from his brow, then lingered, warming his forehead with her palm.

And in that strange warmth, he submerged immediately, into a morass of dreams.

Vlau Fiomarre huddled in the snow, at the foot of the cart, in the darkness. They had given him what looked to be an empty potato sack to lie on, and another rag of a blanket to cover with.

The notion of "warmth" had become a distant thing of the past. He was numb, and he hardly cared.

The Infanta lay just above, in the cart. He was *aware* of her utter silence, her non-being—just as he had been aware of her, every waking moment, ever since this morning when they had emerged from hiding in the snow.

Indeed, knowing where she *was* had become an obsession.

His entire existence, all the unrelenting hell of it, had been reduced to this one focus, one single-minded duty. He had to take her there, they had to find Death's Keep, at which point—at which point he knew not what, but it had to be achieved, this one remaining purpose . . . for her sake.

Earlier, when the cart had come upon them, he was oddly relieved, because now their world had expanded to include others—he could observe her lying there, and walk beside her, knowing that she was in the relative safety of a minor crowd, and the reduced functionality of her frozen limbs could be preserved a few hours longer. . . . And this safety in numbers was also a comfortable illusion that allowed him to pretend she was *not* what he had made her into—since the girls had assumed she was merely sick and not *dead*.

All except one. The one called Percy, who was in charge of the group, silently and firmly.

She had known somehow, known *what* Claere Liguon was without knowing *who* she really was. How did she know?

And then Vlau thought of the most recent moments of terror, when the black knight and his men had come upon them. His first instinct had been to flare into action—for in a fight he could be deadly lightning—but he knew he had no means to fight properly on their behalf now, no weapons. And his body had been ravaged by the punishment of the Imperial guards, and then the prison, and lately, the relentless hours of trudging through the cold. . . .

In such a state of weakness he could not risk *her*.

Those other poor girls running in all directions, deeper into the forest—it was probably what had saved them both, as they hid, just off the path, after first running forward alongside it, directly *through* the thick hedge growth, for endless insane moments—and all the while he was carrying her. . . . What had also saved them was the girls' obvious footprints left in the snow, pointing elsewhere, leading the hunters away.

The two of them, in the hedge, had left fewer traces that could be observed among the twisting roots. In addition, Vlau had swept away his own footprints, covered the Infanta with snow, packing it tightly around her, then covered himself, and tried not breathing, while the forest crashed all around them with the violence. . . .

And then, their impossible luck had held, and the black knight was no longer a threat. How and why had it come to pass? Was he indeed defeated and captured miraculously by that peasant girl? No, it did not make any sense, none of it. But then, none of it mattered. . . .

Why was he doing this now? Why follow the dead one? What release could be had at Death's Keep, if any, for either one of them? What new illusion?

He had no answers, only an endless burning rage that had no quenching. He hated her and himself, and he did not know how to be rid of her, how to wipe her from his mind—so he had to stay at her side, follow her, and *know*. . . .

He lay thus, burning in a fever, in the icy cold of the night.

At some point, sleep took him in its soft delirium, and he dreamt of snowdrifts rising all about him, and softly falling flakes of pearl whiteness, and her pitiful shape swaddled in a cape, and underneath it a plain servant's grey gown covering her fragile limbs. In his dream he lay against her cold body, full length, covering her with his own, while the snow piled up around them and the silence grew, rich with lavender twilight. . . .

And as the cocoon built, they were encased completely, and strangely, he could yet breathe, for the snow was now like soft cotton, porous and neutral to the touch, and there was now an odd impossible disembodied glow about them in the violet dusk, a faerie light. . . . And then, he thought, in that odd preternatural silence and illumination, he could suddenly hear a rhythmic sound, gentle and delicate, like the fluttering of a butterfly. . . . It was her heart!

She was *alive*, was breathing! She had been brought to life somehow, magically restored, and her body was no longer marble, but warming with the impossible coursing of blood in her veins, blood that she had regained somehow. Warm and pliant she had become, lying pressed against him. . . .

And in wonder he reached out, parting her cloak, and then pulling at the laces of her gown, to reveal her pale, soft shoulder, and the delicate column of her neck, whiter than snow in the strange ethereal luminescence around them. She did not struggle, only shifted against him slightly, opening her great smoke-colored eyes wide, letting her slim arms fall to each side pliantly, letting him untie the laces at her throat, then pull the fabric apart, as he searched lower—yes, there, underneath her tiny perfect bud of a breast with its rose tip—searched for any signs of the wound he had inflicted upon her with the long sharp blade of his familial dagger, plunged directly into her heart.

He stared, mesmerized, in an unspeakable effusion of joy and relief, and there was nothing there—not a scratch, no traces of the wound, her skin unbroken, without a single blemish.

He trembled then. . . . And at last, in the warm intimate lavender glow, the last remaining pressure of darkness and agony inside him burst, and he wept with exultation, pressing his face against her warm perfect skin, wallowing against her breast, his lips melded to her flesh, burning, burning, while she put her soft gentle arms around his neck, caressing him, whispering his name over and over, like a prayer, a litany. . . .

Vlau.

Percy came awake like a startled bird, in the pre-dawn twilight. Light was barely seeping from the east, or rather its precursor was changing the nature of the darkness.

The snow had stopped falling at some point in the night. At least an inch of it had compounded to line the sides and edges of the cart and the bundled bodies of the sleepers so that they all looked like uniform white bumps in the morass of a great white sea. . . .

Percy blinked, seeing the campsite entirely still and everyone asleep, most of them piled in the cart. Only the peculiar young man called Vlau, Claere's so-called brother, lay in a bundle on the ground.

Next to Percy—she remembered with a sudden jolt of visceral terror—lay the other young man.

The black knight was lying at her side.

Heaven help them all, this was insane!

She glanced down and saw the shadowed planes of his half-covered face in the twilight, the powdering of snow on his cheeks, the closed eyes and long dark lashes on which more white powder had accumulated.

Beltain.

He barely breathed, seeming frozen and rather near death himself.

Percy stilled her own breath, watching him so closely, so tensely, for any signs of the *shadow*, for a gathering of soot in the air nearby to indicate he was no longer one of the living. . . .

But no, there was no unnatural shadow coagulating around him, and thus he was not dead—at least not yet. . . .

She had been focusing so hard on him, on seeing the pending death, that it seemed for a moment she had experienced a sudden vertigo instant of tunnel vision.

Percy blinked again and again, trying to clear her sight, and looked up and away from him, this time seeing with the periphery of her eyes the definite *shadow* next to the nearby silent shape of the girl Claere.

It was unmistakable. Which meant, she was seeing true, and *he* was indeed not in any immediate danger for his life.

And as Percy looked up and down, from him to Claere, as though adjusting her eyes, by comparison, to differing levels and degrees of "sight" through a pair of imaginary spectacles, her gaze happened to glance higher—past their campsite, and beyond the path, toward the denser growth of trees and directly north.

And it was then that she saw the *shadow keep.*

There, in the hazy distance, the translucent shapes of night darkness had coalesced into a distinct faraway structure that had the form of a fortress or a castle, with shadow turrets and towers, and shadow walls rising with sharp fine crenellation into the paling sky . . . then fading into it, translucent, like bits of storm cloud.

Death's Keep loomed over the horizon of forest, and its highest central tower pointed due north.

Percy's breath caught and she forgot everything else.

"Oh . . . God," she whispered. "It is here!"

"What is here?" The black knight, Beltain, woke up. His eyes glittered liquid in the pre-dawn dusk, as he watched her, from inches away.

"Death's Keep!" whispered Percy loudly, forgetting caution, and continuing to stare at the horizon. "I can see it! There, in the distance, it stands! It has to be it, and none other!"

"What?" He attempted to rise and look, but failed due to multiple reasons (he was tied up; he was as infirm as an old man), managing instead to move only his head and neck weakly. However, others were waking up around them, and there were a few snorts and soft neighs of the newly-wakened horse, as it stomped in place.

"What is it?" Niosta's worried sleepy voice sounded.

"Look straight north, there, near the line of trees, what do you see?"

"Huh?" said Jenna, waking up, and then sat up in the cart, and craned her neck to stare as directed. "Where? I don't see nuthin'!"

"It's a great big fortress!" Percy continued, feeling herself shaking with emotion she had no words for. "It's right over *there*, and there are towers, many towers, and battlements—"

But just as she spoke, dawn intensified.

Twilight was fleeing, together with the last shadows of night.

And with it, the shadow structure in the distance *faded* also.

Even as Percy was looking at it, she saw it dissolve into the rapidly paling greyness of the sky of morning. First the edges of the towers went, then the walls, as though wiped from the horizon with a stroke of an invisible giant hand.

How it could be gone? It made no sense!

And yet, it occurred to Percy, it did make sense. Death's Keep was but another one of his shadows. And all shadows fled with the coming of the light.

Percy exhaled the breath she had been holding. "It is gone," she said. "But—I know now where it is—where it *will be*—and how to look for it."

"What do you mean?" Gloria came to and was listening in to all of this. "What do you mean, Percy? What did you see?"

"I mean, I am almost certain, but if we travel fast enough tonight, by evening we shall reach the spot past the trees where I had seen it . . . and when the dusk comes, it will *appear*."

Chapter 12

It was time to hurry and start the fire, and boil the morning water.

"Cold, cold! So cold!" Jenna sang, as she jumped up and down in place to warm her young limbs, after being the first to visit the bushes to take care of nature's business.

The other girls were also gone to their makeshift latrines, but not too far from their tiny campsite just off the path.

Percy hurried to take care of her own nature's call, then returned back in haste to see how Emilie was doing. The sick girl was the only one who had not moved or reacted to anything this morning, and by an odd coincidence she lay next to Claere and her ever-present shadow.

Percy huddled over her and felt her forehead, which was burning up. In answer to her touch, Emilie barely moaned.

A sorrowful terrible feeling came to Percy. She could do nothing for this poor girl—nothing but offer her plain hot tea and half a roll to eat. None of them could do anything. What Emilie really needed was to be indoors in a warm bed, and someone who knew medicinal herbs to feed her a tonic and watch over her. . . .

At least, as Percy examined her with the special *sight*, Emilie was not yet so far gone, and there was no shadow around her either. . . . But she was not out of danger, not at this rate. . . .

"How . . . is she?"

Percy almost started when the dead girl, Claere, spoke up.

Looking at Claere, Percy bit her lip, then gently replied: "Not too well, but she still has the fight in her. . . ." And then she added softly, "And how are *you?* Is there anything I can do to help—to *ease* you?"

Claere, pale and delicate, with her great, beautiful, dark eyes in their sunken, smoke-fringed sockets, looked at her serenely. "You can take me all the way to Death's Keep. . . . Please . . . Get me to his doorstep, and I will be grateful beyond all things. . . ."

Percy nodded again. "I promise . . . I will do all I can."

And seeing Vlau watching their exchange with his strange fevered intensity, she addressed him also. "Don't worry, I mean it. And don't lose hope, for your sister or yourself. Whatever happens, our journey may yet give us all some kind of respite."

Saying that, Percy stepped away and went to take care of Betsy who was calling attention to herself by various hungry horse noises. Meanwhile Flor had started to make a fire for the tea. Niosta and Jenna gathered kindling, and then they passed around the few remaining portions of bread rolls and leftover common foodstuff.

Throughout their hurried movements, the black knight was observing them all from his spot in the cart. And Percy, in turn, watched him with discreet sideways glances. Finally he said, "I need to relieve myself. Will you untie me at least so that I can take care of it?"

Everyone immediately went silent. Percy, who was rubbing down Betsy's legs and adjusting her blanket, did not answer immediately.

"If I untie you, will you promise upon your honor as knight not to try to escape?"

"Upon my honor, I will not."

He was glaring at her with his steel eyes. Last night his eyes had seemed colorless, indistinguishable in the firelight and in the early dawn light when she had been up-close to him. But now, she could see the storm pallor in the blue.

Percy stopped what she was doing. She wiped her forehead with the back of her hand and straightened.

"Then, Sir Knight, you will just have to piss in your woolens."

And Percy returned to working on Betsy.

Jenna giggled, and Gloria hid her face.

He did not skip a beat. "I *could* do that," he said. "But how many of you will then have to sit in my piss, here in this cart?"

Jenna and Gloria and Niosta all chortled, this time.

"I will take him and watch him," Vlau said suddenly. "You can loosen his feet, and he will manage—"

"Are you sure?" Percy said, maintaining a very straight face. "Can you hold him? He is a fearsome knight. And you are?"

"I am a man who has held a sword before," the dark-haired brother of Claere replied, without a trace of levity.

"Percy, you could lend 'im the saucepan!" Jenna exclaimed.

In the cart, the black knight's expression was darker than night.

"All right." Percy nodded to Vlau, and then she approached Beltain and started untying his feet. "If you so much as kick me," she said, leaning over him, "I will wad up your mouth, and not only will you have to wet yourself and stay that way, but you'll ride till evening with an old sock in your mouth. Understood?"

"Under other circumstances, I would promise you an intricate and drawn out death, for all of this," he replied, craning his neck to within inches of her face. "But now I'll just have to settle for promising to thrash you—"

She ignored him entirely. Once his feet had been freed, she and Vlau raised him up in an upright position, helping him out of the cart and then to stand up.

Beltain took a moment to steady himself and regain the use of his nearly atrophied limbs. Grasping the side rail of the cart with both his tied hands, he took a few steps in the snow. Even though he was mostly undressed down to his undergarments, with only a few pieces of armor remaining, he was so tall and formidable that Percy had to raise her chin to look up at his face.

She stood back and let him walk on his own. He made it as far as behind the nearest shrubbery, with Vlau following closely. Vlau was not a short man, but he was dwarfed by the black knight's stature.

When the two men returned some time later, Flor had the fire going, and the tea was ready. Percy sat in the cart with a mug, pouring tea into Emilie's mouth while holding her head up. Emilie swallowed with difficulty, and she was very weak with a fever.

"All done? Get him back in here," said Percy, without looking in the knight's direction.

Beltain had been swaying on his feet, and had sat down on the edge of the cart with some difficulty and, no doubt, secret relief. No, he was not going anywhere on his own, thought Percy. Gloria and Vlau helped pull him deeper inside, and the black knight collapsed, closing his eyes. He was unconscious.

"When he wakes, give him some tea," Percy said to Gloria. She then took a small bit of bread for herself and chewed it without tasting, gulping it down with hot tea.

In the meantime, Vlau returned to stand at Claere's side like a strange sentinel.

Just as they were done eating their poor breakfast, and it was almost full light, Lizabette arrived.

She was staggering through the snow along the path, back from where they had come from, haggard like a shade and covered with snow.

It was a miracle she was alive, and not the frozen walking dead. . . .

Jenna noticed her first. "Lizabette! You're back! You got away from the hunters!"

Everyone turned to stare, and Niosta ran up to her, asking about Catrine.

"Oh L-l-lord . . ." Lizabette whispered in a rasping voice, "g-g-give me s-s-something warm to d-d-drink, please!"

Someone immediately passed her a hot mug, and she drank it down wordlessly, hands shaking, standing where she was, and then walked the last few paces to the cart and collapsed.

The girls gathered around her. Her hands and face were dangerously white and cold to the touch, and she appeared to have some degree of frostbite. They started to gently pat down and squeeze her fingers and arms, and her feet, trying to get the blood moving. Gloria pulled a blanket over her, and Jenna blew warm breath at her face and cheeks, then placed her palms to them.

"What happened, Lizabette?" Percy asked when the other girl was back to some semblance of normalcy, sitting upright and shivering in the blanket.

"I ran, and then they g-g-got me!" she began. "Oh Lord in Heaven, there is so m-m-much to tell! I've been walking all night!"

"Probably why you're still alive and not completely frozen . . ." Percy said.

"How'd you get away? Where is Catrine?" persisted Niosta.

And Lizabette told them. She told them how, when the patrol had arrived, she had run into the forest, but in moments was grabbed by at least two men-at-arms. "I don't know what happened, but when I looked back, it was as if I was lost completely . . . there was no trace of the path, or the cart, and I could only see Regata in her nice coat on the other side, being taken also, and hoisted up by a filthy mounted man, who then rode off with her somewhere. . . ."

"Did you see Catrine?"

"No!" Lizabette said, her usual, somewhat snotty intonation returning, which was surely a good sign. "But I did notice one strangest thing. . . . As those ruffians dragged me behind them, we doubled back to where I had been at first, and when I looked behind me from *that* place, I could suddenly *see* the path again, and the cart and Betsy, in the distance! And you were there, Percy—but you were, all of you, somehow *transparent!* You were *fading!* You, and the horse, and the cart! And as we moved further away from the path, you disappeared altogether—not out of sight, like around a tree or something, but it was as if by magic, you dissolved into the air!"

"All right, I don't really understand what you mean, but do go on," Gloria said.

"Afterwards, they continued dragging me some distance, and then there were others, equally gruesome and filthy, and they kept running up to my captors, or riding by, and they were all supposedly looking for their captain—who it turns out, is none other than the terrifying *black knight* himself—"

Jenna and Niosta and Marie exchanged looks.

"—and so then they sighted a great monstrous warhorse running loose, that must have been *his.* But the knight himself was not on it—was apparently missing. No one could catch him—I refer to the horse, not the knight. . . . And so they stopped and made camp, and there was a great big fire, then at least a dozen more of them arrived there, all talking—"

Lizabette paused with a shudder, and asked for more tea.

"What were they talking about?" Jenna asked. "Are they looking for us?"

"Yes!" Lizabette drank thirstily from the mug, holding it tight with her reddened fingers, for warmth. "They are looking for us, naturally. But even more so, they are looking for *someone else.* . . . I could hardly believe it, but supposedly, the Emperor's own daughter, the *Infanta* herself, is somewhere in this forest—

right this very minute!—also on her way to become a Cobweb
Bride! Can you imagine that? They say she has gone mad, or
maybe she is dead—but in either case, the Duke Chidair himself
is on the lookout for her—you know, the one they call Duke
Hoarfrost—"

As Lizabette chattered, taking momentary breaks to gulp
down the tea, Percy grew more thoughtful.

"As for me," Lizabette continued, "I must tell you how I
got away, because it is very *important*. . . . Listen—at some
point those two cretins watching me, had taken a few steps
aside—to gab with their superiors, I suppose, or whoever else is
in those patrols—and I simply started running. It was as if some
kind of crazy terror came upon me, I just ran, and in seconds I
had gotten away. . . . I could hear them follow me. But then, all
of a sudden, there was that path—I recognized one spot on it,
early on, back where we had just gotten on it. . . . So I turned
onto our path, just because it was easier to run on it than to crash
through godforsaken bushes. . . . I knew they were going to be
upon me in a heartbeat—"

"Oh, go on!" said Jenna, very attentive.

"Well, I ran for about twenty feet along the path, and then I
looked behind me, and I saw them, at least three hunters in
pursuit of me. They ran this and that way, and *they did not see
me*. I was right there, in front of them—I even stopped running,
and just stood there, in the middle of the path. But it was as if I'd
gone invisible! And for that matter, it was as if they could not
see the *path* was there, either!"

"So what you're saying—" Percy began.

"I'm saying there's something unnatural going on! Magic!"

Everyone stared at her.

"No, I have *not* gone daft!" exclaimed Lizabette, "I tell you,
this path we're on, it's very special! I wager, it's all Grial's
doing, somehow! She must've spelled it for us, to keep us safe,
or—"

"I actually believe you," said Percy. "Because there is no

other explanation as to why we have been so impossibly *lucky* all these few days. I mean, the forest is full of the patrols, and they've been so close—"

"Yes, and they are looking for *everyone!* And now, oh, I wonder," Lizabette interrupted, "where the Infanta is! Just to think, that the Grand Princess, Claere Liguon herself is somewhere, maybe on our path—"

"She's in the *cart!*" Jenna said suddenly. "*Claere!* Oh, Lordy, Lord!"

There was absolute silence. They paused, every face turning to the back, where the unobtrusive sick girl had been lying next to Emilie. . . .

"Noooo . . ." said Gloria.

In that moment, the hood covering her face moved, and for the first time Claere spoke loudly, in a peculiar mechanical voice, and they all heard her.

"I am indeed she. . . . I have left behind all things— including my *life*, and my father's court—to travel to Death's Keep. And this man—" her pale slim hand pointed at Vlau—"is not my brother, but he is here to accompany me."

Vlau spoke not a word, and appeared as still and intense, and somehow as lifeless as ever—or possibly even more so. Only his gaze burned.

"*What?* Your Imperial Highness! Oh, I cannot believe it, a thousand pardons if we have offended! Your clothes—your disguise, surely—they are so *common*—that is, begging pardon of Your Imperial Highness—" Lizabette was babbling. She immediately sat up, and attempted to bow clumsily. Several of the other girls also curtsied awkwardly, and Jenna was staring in amazement.

Lizabette continued speaking rapidly, in a high voice, forgetting how cold and uncomfortable she had been only moments ago. "Dear Lord in Heaven, this is just impossible, an honor beyond imagining! Oh dear, oh dear!"

She then put the back of her hand to her mouth, and giggled almost hysterically, and shook her head, and held her face in both hands, unable to stop talking. "Of all things! Well, imagine that! The blessed Infanta of the Realm, here in this cart! All we need now is the black knight to keep us—"

"He's in the cart," said Percy.

Lizabette stared at her, shook her head in bemusement.

"No, really, he's in the goddamn cart," Percy said again. And Marie and Gloria simply pointed.

In that moment, Beltain stirred, coming awake underneath the burlap blanket. Next to him were a few removed pieces of black armor.

Lizabette glared in his direction, her jaw dropping.

They set out along the path, moving quietly and in haste, while the winter sun remained hidden by the heavy morning overcast. Lizabette had insisted that as long as they did not abandon the safety of the path, they would be practically invisible to any patrols or hunters in the Northern Forest.

Huddled for warmth, Lizabette continued to cast stunned glances at the two high-ranking occupants of the cart, on either side of her, while Percy drove them forward. The walking girls moved carefully near Betsy, afraid to step even an inch off the road, so as not to be seen. . . .

"Are you really, really, *really* sure we're safe here?" Jenna kept asking.

"As certain as I can be," Lizabette replied, meanwhile glancing discreetly at the Infanta in her threadbare burgundy cloak.

"One thing I cannot understand," Percy mused out loud, "is why *he*—the black knight there—was able to find the path and see me on it. . . ."

She turned around to stare at the young man in question, who semi-reclined, head resting against a sack of someone's belongings, and watched her drowsily with narrowing eyes.

"Why and how did you ever manage to notice me and Betsy, Sir Knight?"

"I don't know. . . ." His answer was barely audible. "Who is Betsy?"

"Our horse!" Jenna exclaimed.

"Our horse indeed! In Heaven's name, Jenna, how should *he* know a silly thing like that?" Lizabette said, giving the knight a wary and ingratiating look.

"He's been in this cart long enough; he should know our saint names by now . . ." muttered Percy.

"I know yours," he said, all of a sudden. "You are *Persephone*. Your saint was the one who's been to Hell and back. Or to be exact—an ancient pagan goddess who was beloved by the god of the Underworld himself, and who was doomed to spend half her lifetime there, and the other half, in the mortal world of men—"

"And who do you think was this god of the Underworld?" Percy said.

"Death . . ." came the serene voice of Claere Liguon, the Infanta. At the sound of it, Vlau, walking alongside her place, visibly started.

"Death, and none other, indeed," replied the black knight. "So then, Persephone, what does it make *you?*"

"It makes me the Cobweb Bride."

"If only it were that easy," the knight said.

"Oh, but it *is* that easy." Percy clenched the reins tighter with her mitten-covered hand. "Death either takes me, or he does not. And tonight we find out."

"How?" Lizabette—who had missed the early pre-dawn sighting of the shadow structure—was now confused.

"I have seen this place where we are going," explained Percy. "Death's Keep shows itself only during the in-between times of twilight—dawn or dusk."

"*You* . . . are not the Cobweb Bride," the Infanta said. "*I* am. For, as you know, I am dead. And thus, I am his already."

"She's *dead . . . ?*" Marie whispered. And the other girls stared in horror. Those riding in the cart, moved away from the Grand Princess . . . then, realizing that they were instead drawing closer to the *black knight*, decided to stay in place, and froze like trapped deer.

"How? How can she be dead?" Gloria babbled. "She is talking!"

"My father is dead also, and yet he talks and rides and commands," Beltain said softly. And then he added: "And he, the Duke Chidair, is apparently hunting for Your Imperial Highness. I must therefore deliver you to him."

"No! The evil Duke Hoarfrost cannot have her!" Jenna said. "She is the Snow Maiden, and Vlau is Jack Frost, and—"

"What are you raving about, Jenna?" Gloria, still shaken up, was now trying to keep the cold wind away by adjusting her wool scarf over half her face.

"No one is letting Hoarfrost have any of us." Percy said firmly, blinking and facing straight ahead, into the wind. "Sir Knight, even if you were not incapacitated, and you somehow *could* take us now by force—if you had any honor, you would now concede that the right thing to do is to allow us to complete our journey."

"And why is that, *Percy?*" his baritone sounded from behind her.

"Because the world must be set aright."

There was a moment of silence.

"That may be so," said Beltain. "But I still serve my father. And as such, I must obey his orders."

"Even if the orders are wicked, and will result in bitter evil for so many? Nay, for *all* of us?"

"I obey my father!"

"You obey his shadow! Your real father is *gone*. And he cannot command you ever again." Percy knew she spoke mercilessly, and yet somehow it felt good to wound him thus, in such a small way. . . . It was petty of her, yes; and furthermore, she regretted it immediately. But still, say it she must. . . .

"Oh, but the rules have changed." The black knight's manner remained impervious and hard as steel. "The dead and the living are now in an equal position here in the mortal plane. I cannot be sure if it is my father or not. And thus, in a true *agnostic* position, until proven otherwise, I choose to obey."

"Lord Beltain Chidair . . . you are a philosopher," Claere Liguon mused.

"I am a man who would perform his duty."

"And is your greater duty to your Lord father, or to your Emperor? Who is your true liege?" continued the Infanta.

Moments passed, and he did not reply.

"For a long time, the answer was easy: 'they are one and the same.'" The black knight spoke softly, as though recounting an old story to himself. "My father was my liege lord, and he served the Royal House of Lethe, and they in turn bowed to the Silver Court and hence your illustrious father, the Emperor. Thus, my ultimate liege lord was the Liguon Emperor. But now—"

"But now, what?" the Infanta said, and her voice had taken on a commanding strength, as she drew more air into the cold bellows of her lungs for each utterance. "What is different now, in your allegiance? Think, Lord Beltain! There is but one broken link in this chain of ancient vassalage, and it is not you, but *your father*. He has apparently betrayed his loyalties to the Imperial line, and if you follow him in the downfall, you suffer the dishonor also. So tell me again, and think well on what you say—*who is your true liege?*"

"I don't yet know . . ." replied the black knight.

"*I* do . . ." said the man they knew only as Vlau.

Claere grew still, and did not make any effort to turn in his direction. But she was listening intently.

"What can *you*, of all men, have to say on this matter,

Marquis Vlau Fiomarre?"

"Wait . . . he's a *marquis* . . . ?" Lizabette whispered, while Gloria and Flor and Niosta and Marie and Jenna just stared at each other with rounded eyes, and remained very, very still.

"For myself, I can have nothing," replied Vlau Fiomarre, as he strode relentlessly alongside the cart. "But for him, there is now one true solution. The Liguon he may choose to serve now would not be the father, but the *daughter*. Thus, in his own father's eyes, he may be differently forsworn."

The cart rolled along in absolute silence.

"Furthermore," continued Fiomarre after a few heartbeats, "If I were in Lord Beltain's place, I know what decision I would take. I would choose to serve *this* Liguon."

And then the Marquis did not speak again.

"Why? Why are we not dead?" Flor was wondering out loud, a few hours after, while noon had passed, and the relentless cold stood all around them in the forest. "I mean, we should all be dead by now, our fingers and toes and noses falling off, in this freezing outdoors, with only tea to keep our insides warm!"

"Maybe we *are* dead," Niosta said sullenly, through the thick scarf over her nose.

"You are not dead," said Percy. "Trust me on this."

"What I think," Lizabette said, "is that it's all this magical path's doing. And the cart too—it is no doubt enchanted to keep us safe. In fact, I am absolutely certain of it."

"Maybe you're right." Flor shivered, with her nose in her red shawl. "Because nothing else makes sense!"

"Remember, the whole *world* does not make sense," Percy said softly. "And neither does this whole Cobweb Bride business. And yet, it is the only thing we can do—to try and do something, the best we can, with what we know."

"But we don't know anything," said Jenna, walking behind the cart and swatting the back rail occasionally with a dry twig she had picked up somewhere.

"We know where we're going."

"Only *you* do, Percy!"

"And how exactly is it that she knows?" Lizabette said. "Who died and made her all-knowing queen?" And then she hushed, realizing the irony of her words.

"Yeah, no one died, and that's the problem, Lizabette," said Gloria.

And then for a few hours more they all were mostly silent, while the path meandered deeper into the forest, and the wind gusts tore at them.

There were a few times when the sound of patrols out on a hunt came in the distance, and the black knight became alert. But no one approached even close enough to call out.

Percy turned around to look at him, saying, "I beg you not to try and make any noise, Sir Knight, or you shall be gagged. . . ."

At which he merely looked at her, unblinking, with his steel-colored eyes.

In the late afternoon they stopped for a short break, and huddled around a very small fire, passing around the two clay mugs with hot tea. There were no more bread rolls left, and hunger was now a dull gnawing beast in their insides.

Emilie's condition remained mostly unchanged, as she lay under a blanket in the cart, breathing laboriously, wedged somewhere between the Infanta and the black knight.

As evening approached, Percy stared closely at all the landmarks, trying to recall the exact location of the fortress made of shadows. There was a clearing up ahead, at the foot of some hills covered with a mixture of bare trees and evergreens.

"I am almost sure this is the right place," said Percy, as Betsy pulled the cart up, and stopped with a snort, because now the path before them seemed to have dissolved into the ground cover of show.

"So what do we do now?" a few of the girls asked.

"We wait for twilight."

And wait they did. Percy rubbed down the horse, and fed it some grain, while they made another fire, at the edge of the clearing, watching the rolling snow hillocks and the border of trees. Everyone took turns to deal with nature's business around the edges of the shrubbery lining the path behind them. And then they returned for the boiling tea.

Just before dusk came, there was a precursor of it in the air, a sensation of repose, a solemnity, as the sky went from pale grey to slate, and then to a flowering of darkness.

The pale vista of snow and spare clumps of brush before them began to *transform*.

First, there was a thickening of the air. The shadows seemed to rush toward it, plucked from the fabric of the sky and the forest like wisps of smoke.

The ice mirage rippled, and the walls took shape, growing heavenward before them, swept upright like grand sentinels to blend with the sky.

And in a few heartbeats, the walls were *solid*, obscuring the forest behind them.

Tangible, massive slabs of granite formed the structure of the Keep. It rose hundreds of feet up, with distant towers and battlements, as grand as the Imperial Palace of the Emperor himself.

"Lordy, Lord!" Marie and Jenna and a few of the other girls exclaimed, the ones who had never seen a large city structure before. . . .

And then, as true twilight came down, turning the world deep blue, there appeared a shape of a grand gate in the walls, like a maw of pure darkness.

Percy watched it all, and not until that last instant did it sink in—*this was it.*

Time to face Death.

She took a few shallow breaths, forgetting the outer cold

and the frigid air, because of the block of ice that was now formed in her gut.

Fear is a cold bastard. The only way to overcome it is to act—to take the first step and just move forward.

And the only way to overcome cold was to burn.

Percy thought of things that were warm, hot, scalding— hearth fires, piles of blankets, boiling water, the sun in midsummer. But the cold inside her was insidious permafrost, and she was still trembling. . . .

And then she thought of things that would turn *her* to fire— injustice, her Gran lying on her deathbed back home, taking each agonizing last breath unto eternity, her mother's weary accusing, judging, condemning eyes, and her father's gentle pity. And she thought of her two sisters, of all of them, running out of bread at last and contorting in hunger, and she thought of the animals being slaughtered and not dying—

And Percy *burned.*

There was no cold frigid enough now to keep her afraid and hesitant.

"I am going in," she said simply, while everyone else around her paused in indecision, seeing the dark wonder take shape before their eyes.

"We are all going in . . ." said the Infanta. And with the help of Vlau Fiomarre, she got up from her place in the cart, and she took a few steps in the virgin snow, like a clockwork doll.

With a grunt of pain, the black knight was up on his feet also, without anyone's help, and with his hands still tied.

Percy threw him a glance of momentary concern, but he shook his head at her, and said, "I am coming with you."

"Those of us who go inside may all be dead shortly."

He smirked, and for the first time Percy saw his face in a halfway smile. "I highly doubt I am a Cobweb Bride," he retorted. "And as for dying shortly or lately—we will all meet that fate eventually, if the world is set aright."

Percy took a few steps toward him, and she reached for the rope on his wrists. "I trust you then, Sir Knight." And his bonds were cut with a single flick of her small sharp knife.

Percy walked then, before all of them, her feet crunching in the snow, to approach the dark looming gate of Death's Keep.

But behind her she heard the frightened young voice that tore at her heart. . . .

"Percy . . . Percy!" Jenna started to sniffle. "I am afraid, Percy! Oh, I don't want to go in there!"

"Then don't, child," said Flor kindly. "You know you can just stay out here and watch Emilie and Betsy? No one says you have to go in there! Stay. . . ."

But for the first time in days, it seemed, Emilie spoke up, barely breathing, through a fit of coughing. "I am . . . coming too . . . please—" Her voice sounded feeble from the cart.

And then Jenna wept outright. "But I'm afraid to stay out here alone!"

Percy turned and then came back around and took her hand. "You're not alone. Come, Jen, we'll go in together, all of us, even Emilie, even great knights and ladies!"

And holding the small mitten-wrapped hand in her own broad one, Percy and Jenna walked forward into the darkness.

Chapter 13

U p close, the gate of black smoke was not solid, but a curtain of vapor, or fine mist. Perfectly opaque, the mist stood before them like a waking dream.

Percy reached out with her fingers and she touched it, and it came apart at her touch, with a buttery softness of flannel and cotton, a welcoming sensation.

Enter me, the mist seemed to say.

Percy closed her eyes, and still holding Jenna, they plunged forward into the mist.

There was a strange peculiar tingle along each point of her skin that lasted a heartbeat, and then Percy sensed they were on the *other side*, and she opened her eyes.

Jenna gasped.

They were indoors. Around them, loomed a great hall of perfectly dull grey stone. Tall gothic arches and columns punctuated its length unto the horizon on both sides, and the niches held fading, dissolving darkness.

There was no visible end to this hall.

If you looked farther out, in search of a wall, the darkness seemed to rush in, and created a fadeout at the horizon.

And if you looked up, there was only night, and then, a strange illusion of starry sky. Except, this sky was so unreal, that it recalled to Percy the sensation of closing one's eyes and pressing on the eyelids to "see stars."

Meanwhile, the rest of their group passed through the veil of mist and appeared one by one in the hall behind them. Since there was no real frame of reference, nothing resembling a gate of any sort here, it looked as if they were simply materializing out of the air.

"Percy . . ." whispered Jenna. "Oh! Where's the gate? I don't see how we came in! How do we get back?"

"Hush, Jen . . ." Percy squeezed her hand.

"I don't think we're getting back . . ." whispered Flor, looking around them in resigned caution.

"*One* of us is not getting back," Lizabette said sharply, while shivering in her coat. "For my own part, I certainly hope it is not me, and thus expect to be out of this dismal hell at some point, having done my part for this whole Cobweb Bride business."

The knight stood looking around, meanwhile, and there was an interesting expression on his face that Percy had not seen before—a kind of soft curiosity and wonder.

Vlau Fiomarre was helping the Infanta remain upright, and here in this otherworldly *indoors*, she had thrown back the hood of her burgundy cloak, and her soft, ashen, colorless hair came undone and swept around her shoulders in delicate wisps.

Gloria and Marie, both helping Emilie stand, were all shivering together silently.

"What next?" said one of them.

Percy toed the floor, seeing only ordinary slabs of granite stone underneath. Except for the stone floor, the hall was bare otherwise. It was also lacking snow or dust, or even air drafts of any kind. There was no living movement, only a kind of lukewarm serenity. . . .

"Is anyone cold?" Percy asked. "Because I no longer feel it. It is not winter here—wherever *here* is."

Several people shrugged negatively.

"Should we start walking?"

"Where to?"

"Anywhere," said the Infanta. And then she started moving forward.

Percy watched her *shadow* follow—and Vlau also, her second loyal shadow.

They all advanced a few steps, and it seemed the few columns they kept their eyes on as markers, *moved* along with them, so that despite "walking," they had not in fact moved at all.

Percy, who had been instead watching the slabs of granite beneath their feet, noticed that the slabs were identical, down to the imperfections and cracks in the granite. . . . Every step she took, brought her to the next slab in an optical treadmill, without actually moving her anywhere.

"Stop!" said Percy.

And everyone came to a nervous halt.

"We are not moving anywhere," she observed.

"Indeed, I noticed." The black knight glanced at her scornfully. "But this is curiously refreshing exercise, if you've been lying around all day in a *cart*."

"What this is, is an unholy nightmare," muttered Lizabette.

"The kind one has after eating too much lard an' spiced beans—" Niosta added, with a nervous giggle.

It occurred to Percy that this hall had not heard the sound of an ordinary human giggle in, possibly, an eternity. . . .

"What if one of us walks in one direction, and another walks in the opposite?"

"A clever idea, Gloria." Percy let go of Jenna's hand and pointed Gloria in the other direction, and the two of them started to pace apart.

That seemed to work, and they had moved away from each other by at least fifty feet along the hall, at which point Jenna exclaimed, "Oh no, you are both fading! Stop! Come back, please!"

Percy looked behind her, and their figures all seemed to be *semi-translucent*. But as she and Gloria returned to their original spot, they again became fully corporeal from the perspective of the others.

"What do we do now?"

"Time to end this exercise in futility," the Infanta said. And then she drew in breath and called out in her ringing mechanical voice: "Death! I am here, and I am yours if you will have me! Show yourself!"

Her voice echoed, then faded in the silence.

And then, from a great distance of miles—or possibly, years—came a reply.

"Come to me . . ." said a masculine, cold, human voice.

And in the next instant, a wind came rushing through the hall.

They followed the sound of the voice, and moved in the wind's wake, seeing funnels of dust rising along the dull slabs of granite . . . dust that had not been there an instant before. . . .

And this time, as they walked, their movement was real along the length of the hall of dreams, and they could measure progress and see the changing of shadows in each niche. . . . Along the lower arches there were now low-hanging cobwebs, their strange silvery white lace decorating the curves of ancient ashen stone.

The cobwebs grew thicker, like garlands, and the stone itself took on a brighter hue. . . . Everywhere, Percy noticed, it was now rich with a new pallor, and what had once seemed granite now better resembled bone. . . .

A hall of bones and cobwebs.

There was no longer mistaking it; they were not in a dream place but inside a monumental *tomb*.

Death's sepulcher was the grandest, most magnificent

grave, with columns of bone rising to fade into a ceiling of pale white cobwebs, an upside-down sea. . . .

"Ugh! There had better not be spiders!" Flor shivered.

"Where do you think cobwebs come from, fool?" hissed Lizabette. "Of course there are spiders—probably thousands and thousands of them! Probably hiding all over that nasty ceiling, ready to drop on our heads!"

Flor squealed in terror—possibly with more terror than at the prospect of meeting Death.

"Hush!" Gloria said. "I hate spiders too, but I kind of don't think there are any *here*. . . . I think, here the spiders are all long dead. . . ."

"Well then, a small blessing," Flor said sharply. But she still cringed and tried not to look up.

Percy meanwhile, was walking closely near the Infanta, and she noticed how her death-shadow seemed to solidify with each step, while the hall gradually transformed all around them into what it was now, a graveyard of cobwebs and bones.

Up ahead, the general whiteness seemed to congeal, and it was now taking on a particular physical shape.

Between two grand columns of bone, twice as thick as the rest, upraised on a dais, stood a pale grandiose throne.

It was ivory; softly matte and exquisite, carved with intricate designs. And it bore two sharp spires rising from the high back, while the seat was smooth and flat, unadorned with any carving.

"Lordy, Lord!" whispered Marie, clutching her trembling hands together. "What manner of enormous giant king must sit here. . . ."

They approached, and now they could see cobwebs spun all about the skeletal throne like fine lace, with strings of infinite symmetry, casting concentric garlands between the spires of the back, and then rising up into the ceiling. . . .

The throne was empty.

They stopped before it, just when the cobwebs had become too thick, and to approach any closer would have meant touching them, sweeping apart their dream lace. . . .

"Where are you, O Death?" Claere Liguon said.

Percy watched her shadow.

And then, she blinked, and glanced at the throne, and it was now *occupied*.

Or had it always been thus? Was it merely a matter of clearing one's eyes to see Death on his Throne?

Death was a man in black, clad in a doublet and hose, with a starched wide collar of lace. He reposed on the throne, leaning to one side in a weary manner, one petrified arm lying on the armrest of curving bone, the other propped underneath a gaunt bearded chin trimmed in the pointed manner of a grim Spaniard. His black hair was short-trimmed, and over the left shoulder, pinned with a dull brooch of faded silver, poured a black ermine cape.

Death's face was indescribable.

It was simply *not there*—a blank spot, a shadow within shadows. . . .

Percy stared at him, stunned, a cold sensation returning to fill her gut with an endless dark weight of visceral fear.

"Where are you, O Death?" repeated the Infanta.

And it was then that Percy realized that no one else but herself could see him.

"He is here . . ." she said, softly.

Everyone looked at her. Even Death on his throne, seemed to move a finger—or maybe a single inhuman breath moved the hairs of his beard.

"What do you mean?" Flor and Gloria were staring at her.

"What do you see?" the Infanta asked, turning to Percy.

"I see him," Percy said, taking a few steps and drawing nearer the throne. "He sits there. . . ."

"Oh! Is he . . . a grinning skull?" Flor asked.

"No, a man."

"And why is it that *you* can see him and none of us can?"

"That, I do not know."

"It does not matter," the Infanta said, turning upon her the gaze of her great, smoke-shadowed, *desperate* eyes. "Ask him, on our behalf. Speak to him! *Please!*"

"I am certain he can hear us just fine," Percy said softly. "If Your Imperial Highness would speak, and if *he* would answer, I will relay his words. . . . So far, however, he is silent."

"Ask him," said the black knight suddenly, "if a dead man has the right to command the living."

In that moment, Death's hand, white and gaunt like ivory, moved on the armrest. And with one finger he *beckoned* Percy to him.

Oh dear God in Heaven, no. . . .

Percy took one step forward, and now she was faced with breaching the web barrier, thin threads of silver, spun in delicate garlands, cast before her like fine cobweb rain. . . .

She moved a breath forward, and *they*, the infinite cobwebs, were upon her, as she felt their stifling deathly silk upon her face. Every hair along her skin stood up in strange soft revulsion, a serene wordless horror.

With an involuntary shudder, she stepped yet again, feeling them brush against her skin and hair and lips. . . .

And again. . . .

And then she was moving them apart with her fingers, and she was before the dais of the throne.

Death sat before her.

Even this close, his face was still a hollow shadow, while the other details of his human shape were visible with intricate clarity. She could see the fancy stitches of the black velvet fabric of his doublet, the exquisite pattern of the collar lace, the lines of his hands, and the polished sharp claws of his fingernails.

"Take my hand," Death said.

And she reached forward and touched her hand to the ivory

shape with finger claws. . . .

In the moment of contact, she felt a cessation of breath, and a bolt of darkness suppressed her vision.

And then everything returned, and she could see and hear, and breathe.

And she still held Death's cool hand. Rather, it was perfectly neutral against her palm, neither cold nor warm, so that it seemed to exist in a shadow-place that had no concept of temperature.

There were several gasps behind her.

They could all see *him* now.

She was holding Death's hand, and thus, they could see him.

"Your Cobweb Bride is before you," said the Infanta, Claere Liguon. "Surely, she is present—if not myself, than one of the others."

"Come! Approach! You are the first to have come through my Gate and into my Hall, and I will see you," Death said, and this time his voice was audible to all, to match his physical aspect. With a flick of the wrist, he released Percy from her hold of him.

And still they could see him.

"Come!"

The voice broke the somnolence of the hall with a jolt of dark fire. It seemed to run along their nerve endings and cut them with a dull ache that was at the same time infinitely sharp, as though an ice blade had scraped along their skin and left behind a razor burn of winter. . . .

The girls, compelled in every manner possible, moved forward, some holding each other, and others stepping forth alone.

They walked through the thick curtains of cobweb silk, and they stepped up to the dais of Death's throne.

"I am here . . ." each one whispered, "take me."

. . . here. . . . here . . . me . . . take me . . . I . . . here . . .

am . . . me . . . take me . . . I am . . . here . . .

Their voices blended in the strangest dream sequence.

. . . take . . . me . . . here . . . here . . . here . . . I . . . I . . . I . . . am . . . am . . . am . . .

Percy watched and listened in amazement. She was not speaking, she felt no need to answer, but everyone else in the hall was responding, mesmerized and softened in a strange apathy of receptiveness.

Even the men had stepped forward. Beltain and Vlau were glassy-eyed, as they stood before Death, whispering silken words. . . .

The Infanta—a statue of dun stone, a column, a pillar of salt—stood before Death, her eyes closed, her hands opened at her sides, softly reaching out, offering herself. The personal death-shadow at her side appeared ready to spring, poised just on the brink of an ultimate resolution.

Dissolution of will. . . .

And Death was watching them all, observing closely, attending to each word of intimacy, each unique offering of the self.

It seemed to Percy that an eternity had passed. She was a silent, fully-conscious witness to a nightmare dreamscape where there were only suspended beings and snaking *words, words, words*, coming forth to slither into ragged smoke and shadows.

She wanted to cry out their names, to reach out and start shaking each and every one present. But what held her back was a sense of obligation, of something still unresolved.

Because it occurred to her that in this hollow, colorless, shadowed manner, Death was making his choice.

And then the suspended shadow-state came to an ending, as suddenly as it has begun. Death's voice broke the creeping, overflowing, humming non-silence.

"No. . . . *She* is not here!"

Everyone came awake, some blinking, others shuddering.

The black knight glanced around him, and Vlau Fiomarre immediately approached the Infanta, reaching out with one hand in reflex to support her upright.

"Mourn . . ." Death said. "None of you are the one I seek. There is no Cobweb Bride in my Hall. Not even *you*—" and he pointed to Claere, the dead maiden among them—"nor *you*—" and he pointed to the very sick Emilie, who truly appeared to be near the brink, between life and death—"nor *you*—" and he pointed to Percy.

They stood in stunned dullness before this pronouncement.

Heartbeats passed.

Death settled deeper on his throne. And then, like smoke dispersing, he resumed his previous state of non-being. Before their eyes, he stilled, froze, congealed, petrified, solidified, slowing down in every physical way like a wound-down clock, and—if such a thing were possible—becoming even more motionless.

And he started to *fade*.

"Wait! Wait, O *lord of nothing!*" the Infanta cried out. "Do not leave us to this unresolved existence! As the daughter of an Emperor, I invoke the ancient privilege of kings! Tell us what we must do to serve you! *Anything!* Only do not abandon us to this impossible fate! I am beyond fate already, I am yours, yes! But these poor people, they will starve and linger in eternal agony! Please, I beg you, take me unto you, for their sake!"

"You offer me nothing. . . . I require my Cobweb Bride . . ." Death's voice sounded, from a tunnel of psychic distance.

It was then that the hall of white cobwebs and grey smoke and ivory bone seemed to narrow around them with an overbearing sense of oppression, a crushing weight of stones settling on their chests.

The grave was settling, shriveling *inward* upon its bones, and the entire illusory world contained within its scope was contracting. . . .

Dissolution of will. . . .

Percy saw the terrified confusion, the utter despair on the faces she had grown to know so well these past few days.

And Percy rushed forward and reached for the fading hand of ivory with its long polished claws. She felt Death's touch once more, the shock of nothingness and the blackout of all her senses.

This time, she held on, and she *faded* together with him, passing gently into the *other place* that was even deeper than his grey hall, more remote than the deepest grave.

She entered *serenity*.

Percy held Death tightly, clutching his still hand, the atrophied fingers worthy of a skeleton, and yet covered with supple, ethereal skin.

Her eyes were open wide, pupils dilated to the intimate grey pallor that was now the whole world, containing her like a mother's womb. And she either stood or floated, dizzy with vertigo caused by the lack of any physical frame of reference.

Except for *him*.

Death was before her, at her side, and he was no longer clad in black garments of human mourning.

Instead, he was pure white. His doublet, hose, lace, his hair, skin, all was incandescent pallor of sparkling sun upon snow, shining with a radiance that yet did not blind.

And this time—here, now, in this impossible, unreal *interior* of the mind—she could at last see his face.

Death was an elegant young man, and his features were exquisite. His eyes were smoky and glorious, and he smiled at her with gently curving lips worthy of a god of love.

"Oh! But you are neither ancient nor withered!" Percy could not hold back. "You are as beautiful as—as—"

He looked at her with a soft expression of bittersweet profundity.

And she recognized at last the nature of his sorrow and his

secret.

Death was a Bridegroom.

He was dressed in splendid white, for his Wedding Feast.

But there was no Bride.

"Yes," he spoke, perceiving her ultimate moment of comprehension. "Now that you have followed me here, *inside*, you can see why I wear dark mourning in my Hall, while here I am revealed in my true *eternal aspect* that cannot change, not even to match the temporal circumstances of my grief."

"Your grief? But why?" Percy asked. "What has happened to you? And to *her?* Where is she, this Cobweb Bride? *Who* is she?"

"All these things you ask, I do not know, and I cannot remember."

"But—" Percy's facial features were fluid in confusion. "How is that possible?"

Death, the exquisite young man, sighed. "If I knew, I would have no need to ask the *world itself* to help me. For that is what I have done."

"What you have done is stopped life itself! Don't you know that the world cries out for you, plunged into unrelieved agony? While you were never properly welcomed, you were a dependable relief for us all, in the end, at the proper time for each one of us . . ." whispered Percy. "If you arrived too soon, we cursed you. Indeed, we dreamed that you would not arrive at all, not ever. . . . But now that our fool dream has come to pass, we admit our desperate need of you!"

"You need me . . ." he echoed.

"*Yes!* But you have abandoned us, and we don't know what to do with ourselves after we are *broken.*"

Death sighed, and it seemed that the radiance around him dimmed somewhat, in sympathetic sorrow.

"Since the dawn of existence, you mortals have feared dying, feared the unknown and the *pain* of it, and yet, pain is a part of *life*, not death. And I—I am the first moment *after* pain ceases," he pronounced. "It is life that fights and struggles and rages; life, that tears at you in its last agonizing throes to hold on, even if but for one futile instant longer. . . . Whereas I, I come softly when it is all done. Pain and death are an ordered sequence, not a parallel pair. So easy to confuse the correlations, not realizing that one does not bring the other."

"But we are mortal idiots, and we only care about pain, not causality," retorted Percy, rather proud of having used the word "causality" in a formal conversation outside of a book (specifically, it had been within a tattered volume of sacred hymns, indeed, a monk's reading primer, which together with two other books, she had secretly borrowed from her mother's small trunk of personal treasures—why in Heaven's name was she now thinking of that book? For that matter, why was she talking so much? She never talked like that in the real world, only thought such things in her mind . . . all these wild and twisted and strange and arcane things she would never verbalize).

Death softly smiled, as though he knew the exact course of her thoughts—which, surely he did. "Is your mortal pain not a good thing, then?" he asked her. "For it means you are alive."

"Oh, but you misunderstand us! Yes, we welcome the pain that comes with living, but we fully expect it to end at some point—and to vary in intensity. And, did I mention, to *end?*"

"Then know this, mortal maiden—I too know pain without end, as a result of what has come to pass. I feel pain for not being able to continue doing what I do, what must be done. . . . For I am not merely an immortal aspect of being, I am its function. And as such, I suffer far worse, for being unable to perform my part, than the world can imagine."

"Then how do we find this Cobweb Bride for you? If she is indeed what you require—"

"Again, I do not know—"

"But, if you know nothing, how will you know her? Have

you ever seen her before? Do you know what she looks like?"

"I will *know* her."

"How?" Percy asked again, getting oddly frustrated.

"I will . . . recognize in her a part of myself."

"Do you mean a physical resemblance? Or, is it a spiritual affinity? Maybe a beauty spot? Eye color? The shape of her teeth? Freckles? The amount of dusty cobwebs in her hair? Because really, since she is a *Cobweb* Bride—"

"Stop . . . " whispered Death.

And then a strange light came to his wondrous smoke-colored eyes. He turned away, looking into the uniform greyness around them, and looking somehow *beyond. . . .* And he uttered, as though remembering, in an ancient language that Percy had never heard but somehow understood:

"She is covered in white . . . white cobwebs of a thousand snow spiders . . . she lies in the darkness. . . . Her skin—it is cold as snow. . . . Her eyes, frozen in their sockets. . . . Her gaze, it *lives*. It is fiercely *alive. . . ."*

Percy heard a distant wind rising, and it lifted each hair along her skin. . . .

"What do you see, mortal maiden?" Death asked, his beautiful face still turned away. "What do you see when I speak these words? Tell me what you see, for I am *so close now*, so close to knowing!"

Percy shivered. "I am sorry, but, if you insist, I only see a whole lot of grey nothing . . . and now, to be honest, I see the back of your head."

Indeed, looking at his profile, turned more than halfway from her, she pronounced this nonsense—because she was abysmally exhausted—and because fear had returned, tugging at her, and the only way she knew how to counteract fear was to either be ridiculous, or somewhat rude. "What I see . . . it is all rather pleasing, indeed, no unsightly skull visible, and I am happy to inform you that you do not have a bald spot, unlike my Pa, who actually has a small one on the very top—"

She knew she was babbling. After all, she was *inside* Death's head, the deepest place. None of this was *real*, and talking about the external appearance of that "head" seemed like a very natural thing to do in this perfectly insane and ludicrous moment. . . .

"I am sorry," she finished. "I'm sure this is not quite the thing you were asking. But since I am *inside you*, within a mad dream, I might as well amuse myself. Indeed, do you happen to have a mirror? Because then I can *show you* exactly what I *see*— and if you might perchance want to know what your face, or the back of your head looks like—the back of Death's head, hah!—I can oblige—"

And the moment she spoke, the mirror was before them. Full length rectangle, silvery perfection of glass, without a frame, and only cast in contrast by the grey universe of mist all around them—a dislocated chunk of perfectly carved ice, a winter crystal, a northern fjord. . . .

"It is as I had hoped. You have been my mirror so far," Death said, and his words were rather cryptic. "And now, what else do you see?"

"I really am not sure—" Percy protested.

"Help me!" Death whispered. "Look!"

Percy glanced only once, seeing a full-length reflection of herself: tired, ordinary, dull, ungainly—the usual unpleasant sight she encountered every time she looked inside a tub of water or the little old hand mirror that belonged to Gran. . . .

But when she glanced from the corner of her eye, expecting to see the reflection of the handsome man in white standing next to her, all she saw was . . . *cobwebs.*

"Hmm, I think *you* should look now," she told Death.

But he regarded her sadly, and he confessed another secret.

"Death cannot look at itself," he said. "When I look in the mirror, I see nothing at all—as ever I must. Only others can look at me, and I, in turn, can look at the entire world."

"So, what exactly does this have to do with your Cobweb Bride?" Percy felt her mind reeling in another fine layer of confusion.

"You, who can *see* death—in a way that no one else can," he whispered, "you can see *me* in places that I myself may not look. She, who is my Cobweb Bride, bears a part of me, and thus, she has been eternally hidden from my searching gaze. A torn piece of my very *self* rests with her and upon her—an ember of me—and it covers her like a cloak of invisibility, shielding her from my own sight."

"That is the most insane thing I have ever heard," said Percy. "How on earth—or in Heaven—does something like that even happen?"

"At the moment of proper death, every mortal whose turn it is to come to me, receives a piece of me unto them, and becomes my betrothed. It is a favor, a token of our union."

Percy stared, with a glimmering of comprehension.

And then Death added: "Yes, you understand at last—you are *all* my betrothed at the time of your passing. When you receive my token, you are irrevocably marked as mine. And being mine, you come unto me, as naturally as rushing water into an empty vessel—indeed, you are then made into a *liquid fire*, flowing smoothly into the *receptacle* that is myself—together with *that* which is already mine. . . ."

"And this is what happens to all who die?"

"Indeed, it is your mortal destiny. Except, it did not happen this one time. My Bride received my favor, but *did not come to me*—does not come even now, to this day! And because she has my favor, I can give it to none other, and no one else can die in their proper turn."

"So, a single token, a favor . . ." Percy mused. "Wait! How exactly does that work when so many people die at the same moment? Do you give out several favors at once, like bunches of daisies? Do you even *have* that many favors? What do they look like? Am I babbling again?"

Death's lips curved into a smile.

"How does water pour through many holes at once? It is a paradox of simultaneous being. My one favor is granted to my one betrothed—an infinite number of times over. And yet, even if one drop remains behind—one drop of my *will*—and does not return to me, I am *diminished*. And I no longer can dissolve you unto eternity."

"But water does not diminish in its *nature* if it loses a few drops! And neither does fire cease being fire if it sheds tiny embers!"

"And yet, though I burn, and though I flow, I am neither fire nor water. I am Death complete, and none other. And I require the fullness of my eternal being in order to perform my function. Once I mark a mortal, that mark—and that mortal— must return to me, else I remain suspended in my own unrealized purpose."

Percy rubbed her forehead in a fine example of mortal pain and frustration. The long mirror still floated before them, suspended in grey nothingness. And she glanced at it again and again, seeing her abysmally mundane reflection, and seeing *nothing* where his masculine shape should have been reflected— rather, the silken pallor of the spider webs, stretching unto infinity.

"So. . . . All you see when you look for her are *cobwebs*. . . ."

"No," he replied. "It is what *you* see—when you look in the mirror at my reflection. I meanwhile see nothing; only my token shadow calls out to me from an infinite distance, informing me about cobwebs all around, about the whiteness of snow, and her open eyes. . . . And that is all. Indeed, I cannot see any of it, I am only *told* it is thus. But if *you* observe closer, you might be able to see more—not only her, but along with her, my token self. Look for it, and tell me *where* my Cobweb Bride and I are hidden!"

Percy exhaled.

She had a dizzy moment of existential vertigo—what in all God's Creation was *she*, of all people, doing *here* and *now*, inside Death's oh-so-cavernous cranium, when she could instead be at home back at Oarclaven, eating buckwheat porridge by the fire?

. . . by the fire, listening to Gran's unending death rattle . . .

. . . eating buckwheat porridge, but only tasting ashes . . .

No!

The world was all wrong, and it needed to be set aright.

Percy inhaled.

And she looked back into that blasted mirror, at the sea of white cobwebs, swaying. . . .

She blinked and cleared her vision, and she looked for a shadow, any familiar shadow, that she knew to recognize as a shadow of death.

Look closer . . . Impossibly, the shadow itself seemed to be calling her.

"What do you see?" Death's eager whisper sounded in her ear. But this time she did not take her gaze off the mirror and the cobweb ocean, an animate morass, wallowing, moving, like reeds in the wind.

Look closer—through the cobweb filaments of her hair and along each strand shine stars. . . .

Percy looked so close that she now saw each silken cobweb strand at the finest microscopic level; saw past each one, and beheld an entire forest of strands. The cobwebs were now motionless, for as she focused on them, examining each one with utter precision of *thought*, they were held and suspended by the touch of her mind, lifted and then swept aside, as she advanced deeper into their ocean.

She was looking for Death's shadow avatar, a token given to his betrothed. She could sense it, just out of reach, and she could almost touch it.

And then she saw them—she saw the *stars*.

Tiny distant pinpoints of light, lavender and ruby and gold and cerulean and white.... So many other colors of the rainbow!

The points of light winked in and out of existence, while the cobwebs moved before them, swaying like aerial seaweed. And yet, it was an optical illusion, for the stars did not shine along each strand—rather, they were plural reflections upon round liquid surfaces. . . .

Liquid surfaces of human eyes.

Her eyes.

They were wide-open, framed by pale frozen eyelids, and they remained perfectly motionless, in stasis. A world of despair and agony and longing was reflected in them, along with the pinpoint lights and, yes, death's unmistakable lurking shadow. . . .

Where did those reflected lights come from? Percy tried to visualize their sources, only inverted, as in a mirror. The pinpoint lights looked to be "gathered" in a cluster, or aligned in a geometric pattern. What was this pattern?

For it was reflected in the *living* eyes of the Cobweb Bride.

And this same *pattern of light* was the only evidence, the one single clue, to her clandestine location.

"I see her," Percy said. "She is looking at . . . strange light. It is distant, but there are so many colors! Where could it be?"

"Ah!" Death sighed. "You are so close!"

"What?" Percy said. "All right, you did mention snow spiders earlier. Could this 'starlight' be the reflection of some truly monstrous spider's eyes? I mean, this great big ugly thing with eight hairy legs, the size of a barn, could be watching and guarding her right now, having first covered her in horrible sticky cobwebs—ugh!"

"Snow spiders of winter have spun the webs in my hall once. But it was all such a long time ago. In your mortal reckoning, many ages past . . ." Death remembered. "I have not seen them since they first decorated my hall with their lace. It may be that I have taken them all unto me. . . ."

"Is it possible you missed just *one?*" said Percy smartly. "Might *it* be out there now, having grown big and fat, and stolen away your Bride?"

"The world is infinite, and anything is possible," Death said, his handsome face growing again melancholy.

"Since here I am, at present stuck in your head, and making up ghastly monstrous spiders," said Percy, "why not help me truly look for her, your Cobweb Bride? But—not in here, where I might conjure even more nonsense. Instead, help me *out there*, in the real *world*. Out there, I have nothing better to do than freeze in that forest, along with the other poor girls. And simply going back home would be of no use to anyone. So what do you say, Your Majesty, Death?"

"If anyone can find her, mortal maiden, it is you."

Percy would have hid her smile, if not for the fact that she was presently inside Death's mind where everything was already out in the open and on display, including true inner states and involuntary human reactions.

And thus, she joyfully smiled at the compliment—one of the few she had ever received in all her sixteen years.

And then, just as suddenly, she experienced a shock. . . . Because Death, the beautiful young man dressed in white, with radiant smoke-colored eyes, suddenly took her by the shoulders and kissed her on the lips. . . .

The world exploded.

His lips were like a breath of summer. Where they touched her, she felt filaments of lightning coursing through her, echoing along each nerve ending with dark fire, until she could feel the extent and reach of *all* the shadows in the universe. . . .

They were all extensions of him.

And then he released her, but drew back just a space, remaining so very close, their faces barely apart. . . .

Percy was lightheaded. She felt her cheeks burn, and her

lips had no sensation at all—it was as if they had been branded, and the branding took away all living energy, transforming it into an eternal conflagration that radiated in an aural nimbus around her, bathing the surface of her skin. . . .

She had never been kissed before.

And now, her mouth had been *consumed.*

Percy looked up at him, up-close, seeing his perfect lips and sacred features, as he too observed her with his haunting eyes. And now there was a new gentleness in his gaze that she had not seen before—a shadow of infinite kindness.

Do not fear me, but do not long for me. . . .

"My Cobweb Bride has my favor," Death whispered. "But you—now *you* have a fragment of my heart."

And as she stared, wondering, he told her: "It is a part of me that I have never given before. . . . Use it well."

"What does that mean?"

But Death smiled, and he drew so near that she could see the smoke quartz shadow-pupils of his immortal eyes.

This time there was no kiss, but she drowned, just the same.

Chapter 14

The hall of shadows was dissolving. The whole world was like the surface of a deflating bellows, and everything seemed to be *converging*—the distant columns, the bone arches strung in spider silk, the unseen darkened walls, the swaying cobweb ceiling. . . .

When the floor of granite started to *soften* underfoot, Beltain was absolutely sure the grey hall of bones was coming undone around them.

And then he saw the girl named Percy reach out to grab Death's hand. . . . In those moments, Death was fading, becoming translucent, and as she touched him, Beltain could have sworn there was a peculiar flash, as if dark lightning had struck her fingers. . . .

And then Death, the *man*, had disappeared, and Percy collapsed in a faint at the dais of the empty throne.

Meanwhile, she who had turned out to be the Emperor's dead daughter, the Grand Princess they called "The Infanta," stood upright like a pillar of tragedy, stunned by Death's rejection. She had been so certain she would be chosen as the Cobweb Bride, Beltain realized, that now she had lost all remaining purpose. And the courtier at her side, the strangely intense marquis, seemed just as confounded by the circumstances.

What had come to pass between those two, Beltain did not even venture to guess. He and his ducal father, in their remote Chidair territories on the northernmost edges of the Kingdom of Lethe, kept themselves habitually and generally uninformed of the latest goings-on at the distant southern Silver Court. Thus, any news of the Infanta's untimely "death" and its gruesome details had not even reached them. Even had the news been circulated, Duke Ian Chidair and his son cared very little about court intrigue and politics. At the Silver Court, the Chidair were considered "wild" and "uncouth savages," good only for "warring and jousting," and their extremely rare appearances had done them little to no credit in the eyes of *le belle monde*. . . .

But none of it mattered in the here and now.

Beltain saw Death disappear and Percy fall in a faint.

The other girls were screaming in terror. And she just lay there, motionless, one hand thrust out, and her ash-brown hair tangled up in her woolen shawl. From where he stood, Beltain could not even see her face.

"What's happening, oh dear Lord, what's happening!" a thin, tall, spindly blond girl bewailed. He recalled her name was Flor, or maybe it was Niosta.

"Someone, assist her . . ." uttered the Infanta, pointing at the fallen girl.

He was not sure why, but he took a step, and then another, feeling himself initially reeling from his weakened state. In those excruciating moments he was aware of deep soreness down to the bones. He was now suffering the full extent of his malady, muscles aching all over his body. But the next few steps were easier. . . . And then somehow he had moved past the morass of cobwebs near the throne, and he bent down to where she lay.

Up close, in the pale, constant, disembodied illumination of the hall, she was such a plain thing, with rounded features in an ordinary peasant face. Her cheeks were more plump and ruddy than was even remotely allowed by courtly beauty standards.

Her equally reddened nose was somewhat blunt and wide, and her lips chronically chapped from the cold.

For a span of three heartbeats he observed her closed eyelids, thick eyelashes, and the well-defined straight dark eyebrows—probably the only pleasing aspect of her appearance, giving her forehead and brow line a determined intensity.

And the next instant her eyelids fluttered. She opened her eyes with a shuddering inhalation of breath, and saw *him* hovering above *her*.

He stared down at her, saw the dull indeterminate color of her eyes, and also their cool, rational, indeed, *hard* expression. It immediately jolted him into the moment, reminding him of how abrasive she was, and also, that the world was coming down around them. Thus, he took hold of her, and raised her up with sure ease, even though he was not at his full strength.

"Let me go! What is happening? How long was I gone?" she muttered.

"Hmmm . . ." he said, while checking the side and back of her temples and behind her ears, as he held her up in a seated position, then pulled up her woolen shawl back over the soft, listless hair. "Nothing seems to be damaged."

Then he added: "How long have you been gone, you say? Long enough for us to see you fall, and for me to walk five paces."

"Percy! Oh, Percy!" exclaimed Jenna, coming in that moment to crouch at her side. "Oh, what did Death do to you when you grabbed him?"

"He didn't do anything, Jen. We had a long talk, looked into a big mirror. . . . Oh, and now I know the Meaning of Life— or rather, a few insane things about the nature of existence that I didn't know before," Percy said flippantly, putting one hand down on the floor to prop herself up, and attempting to stand, while pushing back against Beltain's chest with the other, without directly looking at him.

But he anticipated her, and had his hand around her back

and arms, and lifted her to her feet.

"Thank you. . . . I see you are in better health, Sir Knight," she told him with a guarded glance at his large hands. No, she definitely did not trust him.

"I appear to be, indeed." And he released her absently. "Though I am still far from my usual, at least now I can stand and walk on my own—precisely like a healthy three-year-old. The extended rest in the cart did me some good, and I owe you thanks for that, at least. The irony is intolerable."

He spoke thus, looking at her, and seeing from the corner of his eyes a strange monochrome chaos taking hold around them.

"Why didn't he choose one of us for a Cobweb Bride? Is he punishing us now?" Another nondescript girl, the one called Gloria, spoke up, woefully glancing around them, while barely holding up and embracing the very ill girl—what was her name, Emilie?

Beltain assumed that by "he" she meant Death.

And as he pondered this, more and more distant lines of perspective skewed, and the shadows moved in closer. The throne of bone now seemed to be the only structure of solid matter standing in a fluid, rapidly dissolving universe.

"What should we do?" some other girl cried.

"Oh Lord, I think I know what is happening!" said the shrill one called Lizabette. "This strange hall, this *everything*—we are inside Death's Keep, yes? Well, the entirety of Death's Keep is *fading*, in the same manner as Death himself has just disappeared."

"Yes. . . . Since this is a place wrought of shadows, it only makes sense that it would," the Infanta spoke.

"Then we need to leave . . ." Vlau Fiomarre said suddenly. He held Claere's elbow, and attempted to pull her after him, in a direction *away* from Death's throne. "Quickly! We must return back the way we came from."

"Agreed," said Beltain. "And not a moment too soon. . . ."

But Percy remained standing calmly, and she took the youngster Jenna by the hand.

"Yes, Death's Keep is fading," she said, "but there is nothing to fear. We cannot outrun it, nor should we try. . . . The shadows of death cannot take us with them. Indeed, they cannot hold us back or even *touch* us—neither the living nor the dead— because the *connection* between Life and Death has been *broken*. Don't ask me how I know this—too long to explain now. Just believe me that if we merely *stand in place*, remain here, right where we are, it will all soon disappear altogether."

"But—" Jenna clutched Percy's hand, and the child was shaking.

The others also had paused, and everyone was looking at Percy, at this inexplicable strange girl, giving her the burden of their hope and their expectation.

"What if you're wrong? What if it swallows us along with it?" Beltain said.

The world was so close now, silver chaos and cobwebs. . . . And the ivory of the throne was turning to translucent smoke. . . .

In that moment Percy looked up at him and met his eyes.

"It's almost done . . ." she said. And although she spoke to everyone, it seemed in that heartbeat that she was speaking directly to *him*. "Close your eyes now. It will be easier thus. Close your eyes, Jen, Marie, all of you. . . ."

And compelled strangely by the quiet steadiness of her voice, Beltain lowered his eyelids, thus shutting out the shadows rushing at him, shutting out the feel of the unearthly wind against his skin, the universal silver. . . .

And the next time he opened his eyes, it was to snow. And then, cold blasted his senses.

A wintry scene of indigo night was all around—the familiar clearing surrounded by forest—and moonlight painted the world with immortal glamour.

Percy helplessly shut her own eyes in that last instant of vertigo, as the shadows flooded in, and she was drowning. . . . For a moment she doubted her own claim that Death's Keep would simply fade and return them to mortal reality.

But suddenly there was a blast of cold air. And then Betsy's wonderful familiar neigh came from nearby.

They were back in the *world!*

Percy felt unimaginable relief. She and the others were standing not too far from the edge of the clearing, in the pristine snow, with no footprints to mark their passage to this spot, and thus no explanation other than a supernatural one.

She inhaled the icy cold, and could not help grinning, because they were all "safe," at least for the time being—back in the here and now, and no one was dead, or better to say, no one had to die for real, and no one was chosen for a Cobweb Bride. . . .

But oh God, no! There was still all that had to be done, so much! She had promised Death to find his Cobweb Bride. . . .

The shadows were so prominent now, so tangible. . . . Everything was different now, after Death's kiss. . . .

And then she felt Jenna's cold little hand still desperately clutching her own.

"Oh, thank the Lord!" exclaimed Flor and Gloria, shivering a few feet away.

Percy blinked, and she hugged Jenna, saying, "See, Jen, all is well! We're back!"

Behind her, the tall black knight stood regarding her, with an unreadable gaze of his shadowed eyes.

"Blessedly, you were right. What now?" he said.

"I don't know . . . I cannot think!" she replied honestly. "First, we must all have fire and hot tea! And Emilie needs to go back in the cart and lie down—"

Percy turned her back on him and left to check on Betsy,

while Emilie was helped by three girls to gently crawl back into the chilly snow-sprinkled interior of the cart, and shiver under her usual blanket.

"We might as well camp for the night right here," said Flor to Gloria and Niosta, pointing them to brush and twigs for kindling. Thank goodness for moonlight, else they would have been stumbling along in the darkness.

While everyone rushed about, getting the fire going in the same spot they had the afternoon before twilight came, the Infanta stood motionless. They walked around her with frightened courtesy, and she was a column of futility.

Vlau Fiomarre was a similar dejected sight, standing next to her like a loyal sentinel. At some point, when others had moved away, she whispered, drawing in enough breath so that only *he* would hear. "Leave me."

The dark haired man glanced at her, and said, "No."

"Why not? It is all done. I am of no use to anyone, not even Death. *Leave me!*"

But he remained, silent and steady, frozen in his place.

"Why?" she said. "What more despair must I have, to have my murderer at my side, always?"

"I cannot . . . leave you."

"Oh, Heaven and Hell!" she uttered, then sat down in the snow.

Drawing his poor cloak closer around himself, he sat down beside her.

Meanwhile the fire was a healthy small blaze in the pit, tended by Flor, who pored over it, sprinkling twigs, and finally allowed Marie and Jenna to suspend the snow-packed kettle over it with a thick branch, balanced on top of two pails—a newest contraption she came up with to keep the kettle hanging just right.

But no one was giggling, and there was little talk.

"What will happen now? What about all that Cobweb Bride unfinished business? Should we go home?" someone spoke up, now and then, but no one had an answer, and occasionally they all glanced at Percy, who did not speak much either, but busied herself with passing around mugs.

They had no food left.

"I am hungry . . ." whispered Jenna, but was hushed. And then she received a full mug of hot brew to mollify her.

"Drink, child," said Lizabette.

A few minutes later, Lizabette approached the Infanta, and with an awkward curtsey offered a hot mug to the Marquis Fiomarre.

The black knight sat near the fire, wrapped in his borrowed blanket. Even in the warm golden light of the flames, his skin seemed ashen white, and he looked again near-death. The bruises around his face and forehead were more swollen and blue than before, but some appeared to be healing.

Percy handed him a full mug of tea, and he took it wordlessly, and drank. She watched the muscles of his exposed throat moving with each swallow, and the woolen gambeson, without the external layer of armor, covering his wide shoulders.

"When you're done, get in the cart," she said curtly, and then moved away.

"As my lady wishes . . ." he said with a twinge of mockery, in her wake.

They all huddled together for warmth that night, lying in the cart. Even Vlau Fiomarre had crawled in, because at this rate he knew he was freezing far beyond repair—and yes, he still expected he would need the use of his limbs, even if death would not take his frozen mortal flesh. And indeed, the Infanta insisted he stay alive, by giving up her own usual spot there, saying that she no longer mattered, and even if her body froze to rigor, it was not anyone's concern. She also insisted that her dark burgundy wool cloak was given to Emilie for additional warmth.

The dead girl thus sat down on the ground near the wheels

of the cart, directly in the snow, and closed her eyes. It did not matter if more fresh powder came down in the depth of night, she did not even bother to cover herself against the elements.

Percy glanced at the eternal shadow sentinel standing in silence next to the seated Infanta. And it seemed to her that the *shadow* had gained in strength somehow, was more tangible. . . . Or maybe it was but a trick of the darkness.

Some time after midnight, Percy woke up, lying between Gloria and Jenna on one side, and the black knight on the other. He had taken the same spot in the cart as when he had been tied up and restrained, but this time his arms were lying free. And he had moved in closer and placed one arm in the groove of her neck and his elbow was pressing at the back of her shoulder. It was the touch and the pressure that had woken her. . . .

Percy had the strangest sensation of being strangled by him. One move, and his heavy arm would curve inward and crush her windpipe, and she felt an instant of panic.

She took in several deep breaths, then put her hand tentatively on his arm and slowly pushed it away.

He woke up with a shuddering breath, then pressed himself even closer against her, the entire length of her back, and his arm returned, this time to lie against her waist. His face was now directly in her neck, sinking into her woolen shawl and the few wisps of her hair. Thus, breathing against her throat, he slept.

Percy lay for a long time, afraid to move a muscle, with eyes wide open to the blue night. But eventually the great expansive warmth of him was so comforting that she let go and slept also.

When the light snow fell toward morning, she was so warm otherwise that she did not even feel its light touch against her exposed skin.

Dawn came spilling its pallor unto the blue of the forest. And in those ephemeral moments between light and darkness, the snow-filled clearing engendered massive walls of granite that obscured the forest. Above them, like surreal stalks growing toward the light, arose towers and turrets, painted in exquisite gradations of dun heather and graphite smoke against the lightening sky. . . .

Death's Keep was back.

The last shadows of the night converged to shape its unearthly mirage and overlay its temporary translucence upon the winter world.

But it lasted for a few moments only, growing solid enough to reveal the dark gate of perfect onyx black, which again beckoned mortals to enter. . . .

They would have slept through it all, except for Jenna turning over and pulling her bit of blanket away from Percy, and elbowing her in the gut for good measure.

Percy's eyes flew open, and she sat up, brushing off snow, shivering, pushing herself away from Beltain's warmth on one side, and squirming Jenna on the other.

And she glanced at the clearing, where now only a ghost of the keep remained, and she saw its last vestiges dissolve into the light of morning.

Before it was all gone, the Infanta's upright death shadow had turned toward it slightly, as if in acknowledgement of its master's stronghold.

And then the shadow turned back to its grim post at the dead girl's side. But Percy had the sensation that it had looked at *her* also, acknowledging her too—but how? She was unsure. . . .

The black knight awoke. Percy felt his gaze upon her, and then he was up, his large limbs extending around her, stretching, and she involuntarily moved away, and then slipped out of the cart, landing on her feet. . . .

"Good morning," she muttered, to no one in particular, stamping her feet to get the blood circulating in her numb toes.

And then Percy saw the frozen, vaguely human shape that had been the Infanta, sitting like a sack forgotten in the snow.

The dead girl was covered, overnight, by a thin layer of white powder that reposed evenly on her head, cheeks, nose, lashes, brows, sculpting her shape into crystalline delicacy, so that here was indeed a life-size doll—made of candied ice, folded into a seated position, with her hair like spun sugar, and her brows like caramel dusted with confectionary powder. . . .

"Oh, Lordy, Lord! The Princess is the Snow Maiden!" Jenna's loud whisper came in awe, from behind Percy's back.

"Your—Your Majesty—Highness," Percy whispered, steadfastly ignoring Jenna, and crouching down before the Infanta. "Are you—can you hear me?"

The frozen sugar doll slowly opened her eyes. The movement of her eyelids caused snow powder to rain down from her lashes, and her revealed eyes were motionless cabochon jewels.

And then there was a sound of softly crackling ice as her lungs inflated, and she parted her bluish lips and spoke, one word at a time riding upon the escaping breath.

"Please leave me be. I am dead, and I am useless."

And the Grand Princess went silent. Only her death shadow regarded Percy.

Percy had the strangest desire to grab the shadow by the hand, and feel its tangibility, test its solid nature in her own living grasp.

Instead, she refrained and spoke again. "Forgive me for speaking out of place, Your Imperial Highness, but you are neither useless nor truly dead. For as long as you are here, upon this mortal earth, moving and speaking and thinking, I say you have some use left in you. Whatever it might be, I don't know. But you might have to think on it, in order to find it."

"Thank you . . . for your kindness."

"Nothing particularly kind in pointing out the way things are," said Percy. "I've seen how some truths can hurt, worse than being beaten. But not this one, Highness. If anything, I know what it's like to be useless. And you're far from it. You're the daughter of the Emperor! And your *will* can command and accomplish more things than I, or any of the girls here, can even dream of. . . ."

"But none of you are dead. . . ."

"We might as well be! If you recall, Death still does not have his Cobweb Bride, and nothing has changed. The world is still broken. When all food runs out, we'll starve, and eventually our bodies too will be like yours, and yet we will all remain, neither dead nor alive, with no relief in sight for anyone, great or low, unless—"

"Now is a good time for you to tell us what really happened," the black knight interrupted, coming up to stand behind Percy, "last night, between you and Death."

Others in the cart had woken up, and Percy realized that they were all listening.

"What happened is, I am going to *find* her," she said suddenly, rising from her squat, and wiping snow from her knees.

"What?" Beltain said.

But Percy was staring at him hard. And then she looked around at the others, Gloria and Marie clambering down from the cart, Vlau and Flor and Niosta standing behind her, Emilie squirming under her blanket, Lizabette paused in rummaging through their supplies.

"I spent . . . what felt like hours inside Death's mind," Percy said. "And now I am going to find that Cobweb Bride, whoever and wherever she is, because . . . because I *can*."

"But how?"

Percy closed her eyes. She took a deep breath and then visualized, in her mind's eye, a very specific *shadow*. And she reached for it, in all directions, with her thoughts.

In a mere span of a few heartbeats, she felt its distant pull. She opened her eyes, and then pointed in the direction of the pull. It was as simple as taking a breath. . . .

"There," she said. "It is south, I believe. I feel it calling to me."

"What is it? *What* is calling to you?" The black knight observed her with a complex expression of doubt and scrutiny and wonder.

"The Cobweb Bride's true death. It waits, alongside her. They are both in one place, but they are separate . . . and an unknown abyss lies between them."

As Percy spoke thus, Jenna was staring at her. And there was, for the first time, uncertainty and fear in her childish eyes. Jenna was afraid of *her*.

"Percy? What are you going to do?" whispered Jenna.

"First, we're all heading back, some of us to Oarlcaven and the rest of you onward to your own homes." Percy replied. "You go home and stay there, Jen. And the rest of you girls, too. If someone asks, we tell 'em the truth, we've been to Death's Keep, and *he* did not want any of us. There's no shame in that."

"But what if they don't believe us?" Lizabette said.

Percy shrugged. "What can they do? Send us back out? Worry about what the neighbors say? Phooey!"

"My Ma is going to be really mad . . ." whispered Flor. "She was hoping, if I were to be chosen by Death, our family would get that promised gift of the King."

"Mine too," said Gloria. "My Pa says, at last he might get some use out of me, instead of 'highfalutin rhymes and foolery.' And now he's counting the imaginary coins and thinking he'd build on to the barn with it, enlarge the smithy, and get a second cow. . . ."

"That's just too darn bad," Percy drew the back of her hand across her reddened nose. "But you can blame it all on me, if you like."

"My parents will be sad too . . ." Marie whispered. "I have three sisters, and I am the oldest, and we don't have much. Father is getting old, and no sons to help with the woodworking. They said I—I may not come back. . . ."

"Marie, I am sorry. . . ." Percy stared at the tiny dark youngster.

But Marie already shrank away, huddling in her darned coat, staring at the ground.

And so Percy returned her attention back to the Infanta, and lowered herself again before her. She gently touched the Infanta's exposed hand—it felt like a block of marble, cold and unyielding.

"Can you feel this, Highness? Begging pardon, but I am touching you."

"Yes . . . but, it is distant, as if through many layers of clothing, past my skin. But oh! And now—now it feels more solid somehow. Indeed, I can feel *you* more than anything else I touch. . . ."

Percy decided to ignore the implication of the dead one's words.

She can feel me, because I can feel death. . . .

"Then you are alive enough to care about what happens. I suggest you go home, Highness, back to your faraway palace and your Emperor father, and your mother. I venture they'll be happy to see you!"

"The Silver Court has no place for me. They know not what to do, how to behave around me. My Ladies-in-Attendance cringe and shrink away from me. I do not blame them."

"But you're the Princess!" Jenna suddenly exclaimed. "You can do what you like! You can tell 'em all to pack up and leave, if they don't like you being dead an' all!"

For a long pause, Claere Liguon did not answer. Gears were turning, deep in the clockwork of her mind, choices, despair, all mingling.

And then she spoke: "Maybe. . . . Maybe I will return. To stand again before my Father and Mother. To look at them, one last time. . . ."

"A fair choice, Your Imperial Highness," the black knight

said. He then bent before her, and offered her his hand. "Allow me to assist you."

At his words, Marquis Vlau Fiomarre visibly started. And momentarily it seemed to Percy that he would step forward and dispute the knight's right to serve the Infanta. He was staring so; the fierceness of his gaze was palpable. It was unclear what manner of bond there was between this courtier and the Grand Princess, but this was clearly a loyalty bordering on jealousy. . . .

But the Infanta saw none of it. Turning her head slowly and with difficulty to look up at the great towering figure of the knight, she put her ice-marble hand into his, in a gesture of courtly trust. And he lifted her easily but with great care, so that she straightened by degrees and at last stood upright on her stiff legs.

"I thank you, Lord Beltain," she said with a regained measure of grace.

And, amazingly, the knight bowed before her.

"I have seen many things of mystery and wonder, since I have been in your presence," he said, while his quick all-encompassing gaze touched upon others present, not merely the Infanta. "And I see there is much honor and worth in this Emperor's daughter. Therefore, it would be a true dishonor on *my* part not to serve her—Your Imperial Highness."

"And what of your father, the Duke?" Claere Liguon asked.

Beltain's expression became cold and resolute. "I am hereby forsworn," he stated suddenly. "My father would have it so that Death does not resume his function. He would fight *for himself*, to remain as he is, neither dead nor alive, and everything else be damned. And I have at last decided that such a course of action is wrong."

"Will you then swear to serve me?" The Infanta's smoke-eyed gaze upon him was profound.

"Yes."

"I have no sword to dub thee as mine," she whispered, recollecting herself suddenly, as though remembering protocol and courtly manners. "Thus, I will place my hand upon your shoulder, instead of a blade."

He nodded, and lowered himself, kneeling with some residual difficulty from his weakened state.

And Claere Liguon reached out with her thin hand to acknowledge him. Placing it on his right shoulder then his left, she dubbed her first knight-at-arms.

The water boiled in the kettle, and they had a quick drink of tea, before dousing the fire and proceeding back along the path. Percy picked up Betsy's reins and looked back at the girls in the cart and at the empty clearing behind them.

They were leaving it, to return south through the forest.

The black knight was walking alongside the cart, on the other side of the marquis, and it was the stoic Vlau Fiomarre who now appeared to be the one struggling, at times laboring to take each step.

Beltain claimed he was sufficiently hale enough to be included in the walking rotation, even though there was more room in the cart now, since three of the girls were no longer with them, having been captured by the patrols two days ago. Thus, he moved at a steady pace, with his heavy leather boots, and his composed face did not register any discomfort or pain that he might have been feeling. His heavy black armor plates and helm lay in his place in the cart, together with his blue surcoat in Chidair colors, and he remained unburdened, using the blanket as a cloak over his woolen gambeson.

Percy occasionally glanced back to see if he was shaking from the cold, but he remained stubbornly unaffected by the occasional gusts of wind. Yes, he was definitely on the mend. . . .

The other patient in their cart, Emilie, was also doing surprisingly better. Her fever must have broken overnight, because she was coherent, and had drunk the morning tea with a steady hand, despite her running nose and sunken cheeks.

On the other hand, by this point in the journey, all their noses were running to some extent. Everyone sniffled occasionally, and wiped their faces with the backs of their mittens, and tried to breathe through scarves and other bits of clothing.

The sky remained steadily overcast, but no new snow fell, all through the morning. The path along which they retraced their steps—Betsy's 'magical' path—took them steadily south, through the Chidair land.

At some point they heard the sounds of distant riders, as the Duke's patrols continued their duties. The forest echoed them, and the tree branches cracked occasionally, but no one approached.

"Do not fear. If my men encounter us, I will keep them from taking any of you," said the black knight at some point. "Indeed, I would like the chance to talk to them and see if any will come with me, now."

"You mean, if they would choose to abandon the Duke's command?" Percy asked.

"Yes."

"And would they do such a thing on your behalf, Lord Beltain?" asked the Infanta from the back of the cart, where she sat motionless, with neatly folded limbs, next to Emilie.

"I believe," said Beltain, "a number of them would. The men are all loyal to Chidair—that is never under question. But not all of them see my father as their proper Lord now; I could see it shaping already. The unity in the ranks has been compromised. Instead, there's uncertainty in their eyes, and hesitation, such as when we were told to bring in the innocents, the poor girls on their way to be Death's Cobweb Brides—all of *you*. The divide had grown, so that already the dead ride with the dead and the living with the living, on patrol. They separate naturally, without needing to be told."

"The *dead* ride?" whispered Jenna in horror.

"Some of the dead are with us now, Jen, remember your manners . . ." Percy said gently.

"Yes," Beltain continued, "the dead fill half the Chidair ranks now. During the battle with your Duke Goraque, is when it all happened. . . . But, enough."

"Is that when your father was . . . slain?"

"I said, enough. . . ." The black knight grew silent, withdrawing into himself.

Percy looked away from the steel expression in his eyes, and instead watched Betsy walking forward in the deep snow.

It was around noon, when the ebony war stallion belonging to the black knight thundered onto the path, crashing through the hedge.

He still had his saddle attached, but his blanket was skewed and he was covered with two days' worth of snow, and he was neighing furiously. But the great horse had apparently seen or heard—or otherwise *sensed* his master's approach.

"Jack!" the black knight exclaimed. "Am I glad to see you, boy! Come to me, Jack!"

And the stallion immediately approached, quieting, and snorting a few times in relief. When he was just a few paces away from Betsy, Beltain advanced toward him, and took him by the bridle, capturing him easily.

The stallion snorted again, and then reached out to nuzzle his master, who patted him down in turn with a previously undemonstrated affection, and thoroughly examined him with care.

"Good boy!" said Beltain, brushing off the flanks with his strong bare hands, and then checked the feet. At last, he cleared off the white powder from the saddle, and then said with much satisfaction, "Ah! My sword is intact! You did not lose it, Jack!"

And all the girls stared in curious awe as the knight unbuckled a long velvet-trimmed iron scabbard, semi-concealed

by the blanket, and partially drew a long blade by the wide
pommel, checking it for possible damage. Satisfied, he re-
sheathed the sword.

"And now," said the knight, "I can ride."

And he easily raised one booted foot in the stirrup, and
mounted without assistance. "When next we stop," he added, "I
will don the armor."

It was late afternoon, and the weakling sun shone through the
overcast, showing itself in spots. They were halfway through
the forest, and almost out of the Dukedom of Chidair, when a
patrol drew close enough to cross the path, and thus break
whatever enchantment there was that had kept them invisible all
this time.

"Halt!" cried their leader, a mounted man-at-arms. And
then he saw the black knight, once more fully armed and
helmed, riding ahead of Betsy and the cart, and he motioned to
his half a dozen men to stand down. "Lord Beltain! It is you! By
God, what happened? We'd thought you fallen somehow, and
your horse was—"

"Riquar! It's good to see your blasted beard!" Beltain's
baritone sounded in some relief, Percy noted. "As you can see, I
am blessedly unharmed. But tell me, how is my father?"

"The Duke is furious, as you can imagine. He's looking for
you, day and night. He—pardon me, my Lord, but he raves so
frightfully that some of us are uncertain as to how to handle him.
He's been riding on patrol himself—*every patrol*—without
taking any break, with his—his *other* men, the ones who are like
him . . . the *slain*. And as for their horses, I fear, the beasts
cannot take this kind of pressure without rest, they need to be
changed and fed, and some stable time—"

"I understand. And what of the innocents, the strangers
taken?"

"We have our orders," Riquar said. "But it's a shame,
because we bring them in, the sorry things, and then they are

locked up in the Keep with the others. Rumor has it, they may end up . . . well, in a not too good a way, if you understand my meaning, my Lord."

Beltain watched him with a grave demeanor, seemingly evaluating him.

"Riquar, I am glad I have come upon you, of all my father's men. Because of what I am about to tell you now—it is something that you might find hard to fathom, or maybe not so hard."

"What is it, my Lord?"

"I have broken with my father, the Duke Chidair. And I now serve the Imperial Line of Liguon directly—Wait! Before you speak or act in a manner you might regret, consider this—as you say, my father *raves*. He is no longer the same man he was before his life was taken from him. And under God, there is no law that says you, or any of us, must obey the questionable orders of a dead man. . . ."

There was a long pause. And then the man-at-arms called Riquar nodded. "I am . . . relieved, my Lord. And yes, I still willingly call you thus—*my Lord*—for you are now the one I would serve."

Riquar turned around, glancing at his men, some mounted, and a few on foot. They were milling around in some uncertainty. But it was short lived.

"And what of the rest of you? Are any of you still doubtful, or unwilling to be forsworn?" the black knight asked them in a loud commanding voice. "If so, if you have families in the Keep, or fear reprisal, leave now and rejoin my father's forces. I will not begrudge you that. Otherwise, state your allegiance to me, now."

There was another pause, a few mutterings about "serving insane dead men," and then, one by one, they spoke up. "Aye, I pledge myself to you, Lord Beltain Chidair."

"It is well, then!" the black knight spoke. "I take you as

mine. Now, these people behind me are under my protection. Treat them fairly, and we will escort them out of Chidair lands. And then, any of you who are willing, will ride along with me, onward and south."

The men nodded variously. And then they dispersed on both sides of the path, running or riding discreetly to accompany them through the forest.

Percy felt strangely comforted by the sight of the knight on his great charger, and next to him his new loyal man, riding in the front, conversing in soft voices. At some point they glanced back specifically at the small hooded form of the Infanta, and then resumed talking in circumspect voices. Percy wondered how much truth about the Grand Princess the black knight had imparted to his second-in-command, and whether he intended to keep her royal presence among them mostly a secret, as far as the rest of the men were concerned.

The girls in the cart had grown particularly quiet, and now and then they exchanged whispers and wary glances at their new escort on all sides.

"What if the Duke Hoarfrost himself shows up?" Gloria suddenly whispered. "Will there be a battle?"

"We can only pray, not!" Lizabette retorted, shuddering.

And then they all remained quiet for a very long time, listening to the snow-laden branches crackling in the forest and the occasional birds fluttering in the bare trees.

They reached the place where their narrow secret path joined the large thoroughfare, just as the world dissolved in blue twilight.

"Do not stop here," said Riquar. "For I know the Duke will be here at some point in the night, with his infernal patrol. Indeed, just a few turns up ahead on the big road is where we make ambush, if you recall, my Lord."

"Yes, I know." Beltain pointed with his gauntlet-clad hand further south. "We go at least another league in the direction of

Tussecan, past the lake. It should be relatively safe once we are beyond this side of Merlait and in Goraque lands. The truce between Goraque and Chidair holds steady."

And thus they drove on, now in full dark, without torches, and with the moon barely visible through the overcast. Percy felt her eyelids heavy with drowsiness, her throat parched, and she was numb with the unending cold, barely feeling Betsy's reins through her mittens.

Just as she was nodding off completely, and jerking awake every few moments, the knight and his men came to a stop ahead. Percy's heart gave a jolt, which woke her enough to pull up Betsy's reins without going into a ditch. The other girls in the cart were mostly sleeping, and there were murmurs and yawns.

For once, someone other than Flor started the fire. It was a large roaring fire, and not half as neat or carefully hidden as she would have made it, but then, they—these men—were also more confident and less afraid of every shadow. . . .

The horses were tended to and then the men sat down around the flames, and the girls warily joined them, one by one. Then, the kettle was brought out, and water set to boiling for tea.

Best of all, Riquar and his men had some food with them.

Oh, the happiness that a few chunks of bread and ripe old cheese brought to the girls! All of it was completely edible, for the grain was reaped and ground to a flour and the cheese was aged well before Death's cessation.

Percy was so hungry she had forgotten the last time she had eaten at all. One of the men-at-arms, a man with an older weathered face and kind watery eyes, brought several thick crusty baguettes of bread over to them, passing them out generously. Percy looked into his eyes, seeing a flicker of the golden flames and indigo night mingling.

"Thank you," she said to the soldier, while tearing off a large chunk.

Across the fire, she saw the black knight, his helm

removed, leaning forward to take up a drinking cup, the flames highlighting with gold and violet his dark brown hair, slightly curling. His face, with its fine chiseled lines, was austere, strong, and his bruises were fading. Without the swellings and bruises, she realized, he was more comely than anyone. Indeed, he was handsome to an exquisite degree of pain (for it hurt her strangely now, to look at him directly for more than a few instants)—and less beautiful than only *one* man she had ever seen—and *he* had been no man at all, but Death.

In that moment, Beltain glanced her way, and she saw the grey-blue depth of his gaze, stilling momentarily upon her. It was physically *tangible*—sharp somehow, and intimate.

And then he looked away.

That night, Percy slept alone in the cart with the girls and the marquis, guarding his lady, the Infanta.

The black knight slept alongside his men, in a half-seated position, with his back to a tree, his head and torso covered with a better blanket than the girls could provide.

As the fire gradually burned lower in the night, the shadows around them stood thick and undulating, with the forest at their backs, and the thoroughfare not too far away.

In the distance, the sound of timber cracking under the weight of snow, of wilderness and Duke Hoarfrost's remote patrols, was an echo of living night.

They reached Tussecan the next day, by late mid-morning. The drive was uneventful along the major road, with a few travelers and potential Cobweb Brides passing them in the opposite direction, heading north where they came from, and giving a wide berth to the knight and his men. Percy had an urge to tell them all to just turn around and go back home, because *none* of them were Death's Cobweb Bride.

But she kept quiet, so as not to draw attention to herself or any of her fellow travelers. Nether did she want to explain to anyone else how or why she knew it.

Tussecan seemed at first to be as usual—dirty sleet-filled streets and deep ruts made by cart traffic bisecting all roadways; smoke from many chimneys rising up into the overcast sky in stacks of hazy slate.

But the knight and his small convoy, followed by the rolling cart, were met with wary stares. And the girls all noticed how few people were out on the streets, compared to the last time they were here, just three days ago.

And then the difference came to them. There was no pervasive smell of food that gave the town its warm welcoming atmosphere—no roasting meat, no wafting aroma of fresh baking bread, no pungent mulled cinnamon, cloves, and apple cider. . . .

They stopped at Ronna's Inn, upon everyone's insistence, and because Percy reminded them she was supposed to return the cart and Betsy here, as Grial had originally told her.

"What a shame, we'll have to walk the rest of the way," whispered Flor and Gloria and the other girls.

"Fancy livin', one does gets used to it!" muttered Emilie through her stuffed nose, apparently feeling well enough to comment.

Mrs. Beck, who happened to open the door, exclaimed in amazement at the imposing sight of the mounted knight on his great war stallion, and the men-at-arms. She immediately sent a maid rushing off to get the mistress of the establishment.

"Don't worry, he's not going to hurt you!" said Jenna very loudly, so that the other girls held back giggles, and a few of the solders looked away with grins.

And Mrs. Beck, recollecting herself, replied with dignity. "Well! I should certainly hope not! For then, who'll be cooking for him and his fine men?" And she bustled off too, after the maid.

Ronna Liet came out moments later, plump and warm-faced, and she curtsied deeply before the knight. "Oh, I do bid you welcome, my Lord!"

"Thank you for the hospitality, but we will not be staying," he replied, with a polite nod.

"Is Grial here?" Percy said. "I've brought Betsy back, and here's the cart, all safe and sound."

"You have!" Ronna smiled, looking at Percy, and seeing all of them. "Oh, so good to see you again, girls! None of you'd fallen to the cutpurses or villains on the road, or turned out to be Cobweb Brides? Oh, bless you—don't tell me any of it, I would much rather not know anything about this horrible business. . . . But, I am sorry to say, Grial is not here! She has gone back to Letheburg—why, it was on the very same day you all left—and she told me that, if you would be so kind as to drive the cart and Betsy all the way there and hand it to her at home, she'd be ever so grateful!"

"Oh!" said Percy.

"I hope that's not too much of an inconvenience, dear?"

"Good gracious, no! That's just—it couldn't be *better!*" Percy grinned in wonder, her wool shawl falling back as she rubbed her temples enthusiastically with the back of her mitten.

It was exactly then that the sun shone past the clouds. . . . And in the sudden brightness everyone was looking at her—at her puffy reddened cheeks and nose, the wisps of her ashen hair sticking to her forehead, the bright living energy of joy in her eyes. Even the black knight's silver-blue gaze rested on her, she noted with a sudden jolt.

"Lordy, Lord! Does that mean we get to ride in the cart all the way home?" Jenna cried suddenly.

"Yes, you goose!" Flor smiled, her thin face lighting up.

Good thing the black knight's men-at-arms had sufficient coins with them. Because not only did they end up stopping for a meal at the inn, after all, but Ronna refilled the same large food basket that the girls had brought back with them, and then the Chidair soldiers bought additional foodstuff and supplies for the ride ahead.

The only thing they had been told was, they were going to be traveling considerably far south, and the knight had likely divulged the details only to Riquar.

His plan was, as far as Percy could tell, to accompany the Infanta back to the Silver Court, and in the meantime the girls could hitch a ride in the cart as they drove past their various homes along the way.

Since Percy had decided on her own that she was making the same distant journey, it was understood that the men could certainly use the cart and her driving as a discreet means of conveyance of the *undead* Royal in their care.

Thus, they set out again shortly, some time past noon, with Percy driving Betsy with a much steadier hand now that she had had a chance to sit indoors and warm up with a hot meal of fresh baked goods and porridge. Everyone else had perked up too, at least somewhat, and Emilie had an extra warm blanket around her.

Vlau, the strange, dark haired marquis, now rode in the cart, at the Infanta's side. As they made their way through streets and the outskirts of town, he had acquired a habit of blocking anyone's view of her rather pitiful body by leaning frequently between her and any onlookers, as though he were a living shield.

"What's with him?" some of the Chidair men discussed among themselves, Percy could hear. But she did not have a chance to hear their suppositions, because such talk was hushed.

Soon they were outside of Tussecan, on a far more familiar road west toward Oarclaven. The overcast afternoon continued, growing late, and at some point small flurries came down, snow sprinkling their cloaks and making the horses sneeze, and the wind started up again. The thoroughfare wound with austere shrubbery on both sides, past snow-covered fields, with bushes in sharp slate-grey and black contrast against snow, and very few travelers heading in either direction.

Percy drove steadily, watching the tall riders ahead of her and Betsy, watching the black knight's straight, powerful back, with its somewhat stained blue Chidair surcoat over ebony armor. He did not look back even once for many miles, although his men periodically moved up to glance curiously at the occupants of the cart, the girls with their multicolored kerchiefs, hats, and shawls—at which point Vlau Fiomarre would again lean in with an intense dark look, blocking their sight of the Infanta.

In another hour, they were entering the familiar village of Oarclaven.

A lann Ayren was lying abed as usual, in his slow apathy, when they heard noise outside, and a solid knock on the door.

Niobea barely lifted her drawn face, without moving from her kneeling position in the corner, before the holy icon. She had been spending most of her days there, between chores, and sleeping. Praying, praying, lips moving silently, eyes shut tight, fingers on the rosary. . . .

But no matter how much she prayed, how loudly the sacred words flowed and resounded in her mind, she could not escape the death rattle *sound* coming eternally from the narrow bed on the other side of the room. . . .

"Patty, get the door."

"Who could it be, at this late dinner hour?"

Their youngest daughter, pale and weary, and no longer as fresh-looking as it seemed she had been only a week ago, rose up from her almost invisible place at table, letting go of a bowl with a clumsy sudden clatter.

She opened the door, letting in blue afternoon twilight, and a gust of bitter cold.

"*Percy!* Oh My Lord, Percy, you're back!"

Niobea stopped praying, as though the holy book slammed

shut in her mind.

Their bed creaked, and Alann was sitting up just as suddenly. . . .

Percy Ayren stood at the door of her father's house. She had stepped up onto the porch and took several deep breaths before knocking.

Behind her on the street, the black knight and his men-at-arms had come to a stop. They surrounded the cart, which was now empty of several of the girls—Gloria Libbin had been dropped off in front of her father's smithy, and Flor Murel left them at the bakery. Lastly, Jenna Doneil crawled out of the cart, and gave a great big hug to Percy, hanging on her neck for several long seconds, and sniffling into her shawl, before running out to her own home, just a few houses over.

And now here they were, at *her home*.

Percy knocked, hearing her heart hammering in her temples, hearing the soft clanging of metal armor of the men behind her on the street, Betsy's snorts, the sound of neighbors across the road opening shutters to stare. And a few moments later, her younger sister Patty opened the door.

"Percy!" she had cried, and then she was pulling her inside, saying something, that Percy could barely hear. . . .

Because there was the *sound*—her grandmother's death rattle, filling the house with its dark rhythmic agony, just as it had, days ago.

Inside it was warm, in contrast with the chill outdoors, and darker than usual, with no light but the rust-orange glow of the hearth. Her mother was up, and almost staggering upright, with a lost expression on her face, a mixture of shock, disbelief. She had been praying, Percy realized, seeing her mother in a new light, and experiencing sudden pity. How dark it was in their house, all brown and soot-covered filthy wooden planks. . . .

And then several heartbeats later, her father was at her side, and he took her in a bone-cracking embrace, hugging her and pressing his lips to her forehead while muttering her name. "My daughter, Persephone! I didn't think I'd see you ever again, oh my child! *My child!*"

And then Patty, who had looked out on the porch, was back, saying there were all these strange, armed men out there, and horses, and a great big knight, no less. . . . Then, Belle came rushing in through the front door, behind Patty—she'd been out in the back doing something near the barn—her beautiful face also thinner and older than Percy remembered it to be.

"Percy! You are back, daughter!" Niobea finally found her tongue. She approached her slowly, then put her hands around her shoulders, pressing them on both sides, and then drew her fingers along the woolen shawl—the precious one she'd given to Percy. She felt its prickling texture, running her fingers lightly on the wool, back and forth, then adjusting a few wisps of hair on Percy's forehead.

"Pa . . . Ma . . . I'm back, yes," Percy spoke breathlessly. "I am so glad to see you! And—and I am well, and *alive!* You know, I've been all the way to the Northern Forest, and Death refused to take me . . . so here I am again."

"You're back home. . . . Good!" said Alann. "I am glad that foolery is over; it is all no good, just as I thought. You are safe, child!"

Percy listened to the rattle sound of her grandmother's unending breath. "How . . . how is Gran?" she finally managed to say, even though, without needing to look or be told, she knew it already.

"The same . . ." Niobea signed with a shudder. "Your grandmother remains the same."

Percy took off her shawl, and shook it out, then handed it gently to her mother, handing back the precious heirloom. She then took off her soggy dirt-soaked mittens, and put them down on the table.

Next came her coat, which she hung on a peg at the door, in

the usual place.

Finally, off came her wet snowshoes. Her mother had not yet reproached her about bringing in the wet snow on her feet past the doorway and leaving melting dirt on the beaten floor, but the lessons stuck with Percy. She unwrapped her feet, and took off her under-socks, and put her numb feet into her old pair of wooden clogs.

Then she straightened, shook the folds of her skirt with its dirtied bottom edges, and smoothed it around her, and patted the top of her dress down neatly.

Last of all, she smoothed her hair with her fingers still raw from the cold, and wiped her brows with her fingertips.

With a shuddering breath, she took the few steps to cross the room, while the sound of the death-rattle was growing louder as she neared it.

And Percy stood by her grandmother's deathbed.

Bethesia lay, as she had lain so many days ago, breathing with the rusty gears of a clockwork mechanism running down and yet never ending. . . . Her skin was the color of greyish silver, and the sweat at her brow glistened in the red firelight, emphasizing her hollowed cheeks and the skeletal structure underneath.

When Percy leaned over her, the old woman opened her film-covered eyes and they moved slightly, watching her in impotence.

Help me, the eyes seemed to beg.

And then Bethesia moved the gnarled fingers of one quivering hand to point to the shadow, her loyal sentinel in the corner.

Percy glanced, and she saw the rich pocket of darkness, the familiar shape of smoke and soot.

She was so jaded now, having seen Death's shadows in so many varied forms. . . . What was *this* one but another shadow?

Percy put her hand on her Gran's ice-cold fingers, and she

squeezed them tight, feeling a twinge of response, the lightest pressure. The old woman knew her and responded, and there was a world of love in that tiny contact.

"I am so sorry, Gran . . ." she whispered, leaning closer and putting her lips on her grandmother's forehead.

Bethesia's feathered lips quivered into a smile.

"L-love . . ." the old woman exhaled the word. The eyes were looking up at Percy, warm and dark, nothing but filmed over memories of once-burning youth and grace.

The shadow at the foot of the bed regarded them.

And then Percy reached out, and she put her hand forward, into the darkness, into the *depth* of the shadow, the turbulent spot where it was thickest.

And there, she rummaged around in the morass, and she took hold of *something*.

Her other hand still held her grandmother's.

In one hand was the dying old woman.

In the other hand—her death.

Percy reached deep into herself, reaching *inward* for a fragment that was once given her as a Gift by a glorious white Bridegroom—a fragment of *his* heart. The moment she found it, the triangle of connection was complete.

Death, dying, dead.

With one thought, clean and sharp like a blade of smoke and dreams, Percy *pulled*, and drew the three together.

With a hard snap, the shadow-form at the foot of the bed was jerked toward her, swallowed like a flapping serpent tail of vapor, and was somehow diminished into nothing, drawn in . . . and the old woman on the bed suddenly started, her shallow chest rising upward, taking in one powerful final rattle-breath, her eyes opening wide, then closing in ultimate gratitude.

And then, with that breath, she expired.

Percy stood, sharp and resonant, feeling the opulence of silver and steel and fertile darkness in her mind—inside, everything was overflowing with rich inner sound, and ringing like bells at Mass, and now there was a strange small wound also, a hurting spot in her chest in the vicinity of her own heart. She stood thus, *tolling on the inside*, while holding her dead grandmother's hand.

And outside—outside her mind, in the room—there was, for the first time, perfect *silence*.

The shadow in the corner was gone.

Her father and mother and her two sisters stood frozen, stunned by the serenity.

"What—what have you done, child?" Alann exclaimed, coming alive at last, rushing to his mother's side.

But Bethesia was gone.

"What? What has come to pass?" Niobea was speaking, hearing her words as they hung in the air, tangible, solid, silver-hued. "Persephone, daughter! What have you done?"

"She is at peace now. . . ."

"But *how?* Percy! What has happened? Who—how is this possible now, when no one can die? You *killed* her!"

And then her mother stared at her, and she made a holy sign of God, and she whispered, beginning softly, and then screaming: "You are *her*, aren't you? You had gone and come back and you are different, because you are his *Cobweb Bride!*"

Percy gently released her Gran's cold lifeless hand, and she turned to look at Niobea directly. For the first time in her life she was meeting her mother's despair-soaked accusing gaze without fear, guilt, or weakness—or even any emotion at all.

"No," she said. "No, mother. I am *not* Death's Cobweb Bride. I am his Champion."

The End of Cobweb Bride, Book One

The story continues in . . .
Cobweb Empire, Book Two
Coming Soon!

Author's Note:
Imaginary History and Geography

If you've made it this far, you are probably wondering about some of the liberties taken with history, in particular the fantasy version of the Renaissance, and the unusual European geography and topology in this alternate universe.

Cobweb Bride takes place in an imaginary "pocket" of Europe sometime in an alternate version of the 17th century Renaissance. I've modified the continent of Europe by inserting a significant wedge of land between France and Italy, dissolving Austria and Hungary into Germany and pushing the whole thing up north, shifting Spain halfway to the east and lowering the northern shores of the Mediterranean by pushing the southern portion of the continental landmass further down south so that the French Riviera is now where the sea is in our own reality.

Imagine a cross, with Germany up north, Spain to the south, France to the west, and Italy to the East. In the heart of the cross lies the imaginary land that comprises the Realm and the Domain.

Other minor liberties taken include the referral to some physical parcels of land as "Dukedom" as opposed to the correct term "Duchy." Royal and noble titles, ranks, and their terminology are similar, but not the exact equivalents of our own historical reality.

The culture of the Realm and the Domain is an uneven mixture of French, Italian, Spanish, and German influences of the late Middle Ages and early Renaissance. The language spoken is Latin-based "Romance," and the linguistics are also a mixture of the same.

And now, please turn the page to see a list of all the character names with a pronunciation key.

List of Characters

(Dramatis Personae)

With Pronunciation Key

Death, Lord of the Keep of the Northern Forest

Village of Oarclaven (Lethe) (Oh-ahr-CLAY-ven)
Persephone (Per-SEH-phonee) or **Percy** (PUR-see) **Ayren** (EYE-Ren), middle daughter
Parabelle (Pah-rah-BELL) or **Belle** (Bell) **Ayren**, eldest daughter
Patriciana (Pah-tree-see-AHNA) or **Patty** (PEH-dee) **Ayren**, youngest daughter
Niobea (Nee-oh-BEH-ah) **Ayren**, their mother
Alann (Ah-LAHN) **Ayren**, their father
Bethesia (Beth-EH-zee-ah) **Ayren**, their grandmother
Johuan (Joh-HWAN) **Ayren**, their grandfather
Guel (Goo-EHL) **Ayren**, their uncle from Fioren (south of Letheburg)
Jack Rosten (ROS-ten), villager
Jules (JOOL-z), Jack's second son, promised to Jenna Doneil
Father **Dibue** (Dee-B'YOU), village priest
Nicholas (NIH-koh-luss) **Doneil** (Doh-NEYL), village butcher
Marie (Muh-REE) **Doneil**, his wife
Faith Groaden (GROW-den), village girl
Mister **Jaquard** (Zhah-KARD), villager
Uncle **Roald** (ROH-uld), villager, the Ayrens' neighbor across the street.
Bettie (BEH-tee), village girl

Kingdom of Lethe (LEH-thee) *(Realm)*
The Prince Heir **Roland** (Roh-LUND) **Osenni** (Oh-SYEN-nee) of Lethe
The Princess **Lucia** (Liu-SEE-ah) **Osenni** of Lethe
Queen Mother **Andrelise** (Un-dreh-LEEZ) **Osenni**
Prince **John-Meryl** (JON MEH-reel) **Osenni**, son and heir of the Prince.

Dukedom of Chidair (Chee-DEHR) *(Lethe)*
Duke **Hoarfrost, Ian Chidair** of Lethe
Lord **Beltain** (Bell-TEYN) **Chidair** of Lethe, his son, the black knight
Rivour (Ree-VOOR), Beltain's old valet
Father **Orweil** (Or-WAIL), Chidair family chapel priest
Riquar (Reek-WAHR), Beltain's man-a-arms
Annie, girl in the forest

Dukedom of Goraque (Gor-AH-k) ***(Lethe)***
Duke **Vitalio** (Vee-TAH-lee-oh) **Goraque** of Lethe

The Silver Court (Realm)
The Emperor **Josephuste** (Jo-zeh-FOOS-teh) **Liguon** (Lee-G'WON) **II** of the Realm
The Empress **Justinia** (Joo-STEE-nee-ah) **Liguon**
The Infanta **Claere** (KLEH-r) **Liguon,** the Grand Princess
Lady **Milagra** (Mee-LAH-grah) **Rinon** (Ree-NOHN), the Infanta's First Lady-in-Attendance
Marquis **Rinon** of Morphaea, her father
Lady **Selene** (Seh-LEHN) **Jenevais** (Zheh-neh-VAH-is), Lady-in-Attendance, of Lethe
Lady **Floricca** (FLOH-ree-kah) **Grati** (GRAH-tee), Lady-in-Attendance, of Styx
Lady **Liana** (Lee-AH-nah) **Crusait** (Kroo-SAH-eet), Lady-in-Attendance, of Morphaea
Lady **Alis** (Ah-LEE-s) **Denear** (Deh-ne-AHR), Lady-in-Attendance, of Lethe
Baron **Carlo** (KAR-loh) **Irnolas** (Eer-noh-LAH-s), Imperial knight
Lord **Givard** (Ghee-VAHR-d) Mariseli (Mah-ree-SEH-lee), Imperial Knight
Doctor **Belquar** (Behl-KWAH-r), head Imperial physician
Doctor **Hartel** (Hahr-TEH-l), Imperial physician

Kingdom of Styx (STEEK-s) ***(Realm)***
King **Augustus** (Uh-GUS-tus) **Ixion** (EEK-see-ohn) of Styx
King **Claudeis** (Kloh-DEH-ees) **Ixion** of Styx, deceased
Queen **Rea** (REH-ah) **Ixion** of Styx, deceased
Marquis **Vlau** (V'LAH-oo) **Fiomarre** (F'yoh-MAH-r) of Styx
Micul (Mee-KOOL) **Fiomarre** of Styx, Vlau's father
Ebrai (Eh-BRAH-ee) Fiomarre, Vlau's older brother
Celen (Seh-LEH-n) **Fiomarre**, Vlau's younger brother
Marquise **Eloise** (Eh-loh-EEZ) **Fiomarre**, Vlau's mother, deceased
Oleandre (Oh-leh-AHN-dr) **Fiomarre**, Vlau's younger sister
Lady **Ignacia** (Eeg-NAY-shuh) **Chitain** (Chee-TAY-n), of Styx/Balmue

Kingdom of Morphaea (Mohr-FEH-ah) ***(Realm)***
King **Orphe** (Or-FEH) **Geroard** (Geh-roh-AHR-d) of Morphea
Duke **Claude** (KLOH-d) **Rovait** (Roh-VEY-t) of Morphaea
Andre (Ahn-DREH) **Eldon** (Ehl-DOH-n), the Duke of **Plaimes** (PLEY-m's), of Morphaea
Duchess **Christiana** (Khree-stee-AH-nah) **Rovait** of Morphaea
Countess **Jain** (JEY-n) **Lirabeau** (Lee-rah-BOH) of Morphaea
Lady **Amaryllis** (Ah-mah-REE-liss) **Roulle** (ROOL), of Morphaea
Lord **Nathan** (NEY-th'n) **Woult** (WOOL-t), of Morphaea

The Road

Grial (Gree-AHL), witch woman from **Letheburg** (LEH-thee-b'rg)

Ronna (ROHN-nuh) **Liet** (LEE-eh-t), Innkeeper at **Tussecan** (TUSS-see-kahn), Grial's cousin

Mrs. **Beck** (BEH-k), cook at Ronna's Inn

Jenna (JEH-nuh) **Doneil** (Doh-NEY-l), butcher's daughter from Oarclaven

Flor (FLOH-r) **Murel** (M'you-REH-l), baker's daughter from Oarclaven

Gloria (GLOH-ree-ah) **Libbin** (LEE-bin), blacksmith's daughter from Oarclaven

Emilie (Eh-mee-LEE) **Bordon** (Bohr-DOHN), swineherd's daughter from south of Oarclaven

Sibyl (SEE-beel), tailor's daughter from Letheburg

Regata (Reh-GAH-tah), merchant's daughter from Letheburg

Lizabette (Lee-zah-BET) **Crowlé** (Krow-LEH), teacher's daughter from Duarden (Doo-AHR-dehn)

Catrine (Kaht-REEN), sister of Niosta, from south of Letheburg

Niosta (Nee-OHS-tuh), sister of Catrine, from south of Letheburg

Marie (Mah-REE), girl from **Fioren** (F'YOH-rehn), originally from the Kingdom of **Serenoa** (Seh-REH-noh-ah) (Domain)

The Sapphire Court (Domain)

The Sovereign, **Rumanar** (Roo-mah-NAH-r) **Avalais** (Ah-vah-LAH-ees) of the Domain

Kingdom of Balmue (Bahl-MOO) *(Domain)*

King **Clavian** (Klah-vee-AHN) **Sestial** (Ses-tee-AH-l) of Balmue

Marquis **Nuor** (Noo-OHR) **Alfre** (Ahl-FREH), ambassador of Balmue, Peer of the Domain

Viscount **Halronne** (Hal-RONN) **Deupris** (Deh-oo-PREE), Peer of the Domain

About the Author

Vera Nazarian immigrated to the USA from the former USSR as a kid, sold her first story at the age of 17, and since then has published numerous works in anthologies and magazines, and has seen her fiction translated into eight languages.

She made her novelist debut with the critically acclaimed arabesque "collage" novel *Dreams of the Compass Rose*, followed by epic fantasy about a world without color, *Lords of Rainbow*. Her novella *The Clock King and the Queen of the Hourglass* from PS Publishing (UK) with an introduction by **Charles de Lint** made the *Locus* Recommended Reading List for 2005. Her debut short fiction collection *Salt of the Air*, with an introduction by **Gene Wolfe**, contains the 2007 Nebula Award-nominated "The Story of Love." Other work includes the 2008 Nebula Award-nominated, self-illustrated baroque fantasy novella *The Duke in His Castle*, science fiction collection *After the Sundial* (2010), self-illustrated Supernatural **Jane Austen** Series parodies *Mansfield Park and Mummies* (2009), *Northanger Abbey and Angels and Dragons* (2010), *Pride and Platypus: Mr. Darcy's Dreadful Secret* (2012), *The Perpetual Calendar of Inspiration* (2010), and a parody of paranormal love and relationships advice *Vampires are from Venus, Werewolves are from Mars* (2012).

Vera recently relocated from Los Angeles to the East Coast. She lives in a small town in Vermont, and uses her Armenian sense of humor and her Russian sense of suffering to bake conflicted pirozhki and make art.

In addition to being a writer and award-winning artist, she is also the publisher of Norilana Books.

Official website:
www.veranazarian.com

CPSIA information can be obtained at www.ICGtesting.com
Printed in the USA
BVOW031135150713

325976BV00002B/39/P

9 781607 621133